To fly high enough and head west as the setting sun
silhouettes the curvature of this planet, is privilege enough.
But do that whilst gazing down upon the plain of Giza,
the olden shadow of Khufu illuminated by its geometry,
then a conspiracy against convention is unavoidable.

THE
BASTION
PROSECUTOR

EPISODE 1

AJ Marshall

MPress books

The Bastion Prosecutor
Episode 1

First published in the United Kingdom in 2008 by MPress Books

MPress Books Limited Reg. No 6379441 is a company registered in Great Britain
www.mpressbooks.co.uk

British Library Cataloguing in Publication Data
A catalogue record for this book is available from the British Library.

Where possible, papers used by MPress Books are natural, recyclable products
made from wood grown in sustainable forests. The manufacturing processes
conform to the environmental regulations of the country of origin.

ISBN
0-9551886-1-X
978-0-9551886-1-9

Typeset in Minion
Origination by Core Creative, Yeovil 01935 477453
Printed and bound in England by J.H. Haynes & Co. Ltd, Sparkford.

AUTHOR'S COMMENT

Essentially, this book is a 'stand-alone' work of fiction. Significantly, however, it is also the second instalment of a trilogy, through which the threads of high adventure, intrigue and drama continue to weave. As in many adventures, love has a part, as does deceit and greed. In this book, we see their true colours.

To précis the storyline of the first book, with its six hundred pages, is difficult. After all, space, the Moon, Mars and the ancient civilisations of planet earth, blessed as they were with extraordinary knowledge, are overwhelming props. However, the following pages do paint an adequate picture, albeit monochrome.

So, should you find yourself marooned on a remote desert island, completely unable to source *The Osiris Revelations*, then please be sure to read this introduction, perhaps even a few times, as the backdrop will become more vivid.

Thereafter, should you choose to do so, and I hope you do; step in.

Be prosperous and of long life.

INTRODUCTION

The story so far . . .

Lieutenant Commander Richard James Reece is the survey leader for Osiris Base, a permanent encampment on Mars. The year is 2049. There is also a longer established and larger base on the Moon, called Andromeda. Richard Reece is a former military and space shuttle pilot, having previously served on Andromeda Wing; he is British. Appointed to Mars for three years, he envisaged a quiet, uncluttered time. Two things happened however, that would subsequently change his life forever: meeting Doctor Rachel Turner, Osiris Base Principal Medical Officer, and finding, in the wreckage of a remote, long abandoned alien spaceship, a flight log. The writings in the log bear an uncanny resemblance to those of earth's ancient civilisations. Richard Reece studies the text and succeeds in deciphering it.

Close to the wreckage, Reece also finds a number of strange, fractured, crystals. They contain latent energy of enormous potential. Knowledge of the discovery, and its implications, soon reach earth and not only the government agencies for which it was intended, but also unscrupulous, corrupt, multinational conglomerates. Their aim: to gain possession of the crystals, harness their electricity-generating potential and hold the world to ransom. The race is on.

Earth's natural resources are almost exhausted. Anxious governments press into service an experimental spaceship before it is ready. Capable of incredible speeds, *Enigma* reduces a Mars retrieval flight to mere weeks. However, its highly sophisticated systems computer has another agenda. Tom Race, an American astronaut and the ship's former commander becomes embroiled in a prophetic struggle against synthetic intelligence.

Misplaced trust and eventual betrayal, allow the International Space and Science Federation to secure the first valuable consignments, but impatience and political conceit degrade their potential. Now, the remaining crystals must be retrieved from Mars. The race sees new participants, but there can only be one winner.

DEDICATED TO

Those who enjoyed the first book and let me know
Those who provided priceless reviews and criticisms
Those who have pressed me for the sequel

Encouragement indeed

Perhaps most of all

A FUTURE HISTORY

ACKNOWLEDGEMENTS

Penning the manuscript to this novel was the fun part. Bringing, subsequently, the two books that comprise this work to fruition, involved the efforts of other people. To mention their names and offer my sincere thanks is both a pleasure and a privilege. I take this opportunity to do so. Firstly though, to my family: Sandra, Laura and Aron, for their unconditional encouragement, and again Laura, for turning the first page. Also, to my mother Beryl, for being at the centre of things.

Brenda Quick
For an indispensable pre-edit critique, uncompromising advice and a crucial continuity appraisal, which has made this novel much better than it was.

Core Creative: the team
Awesome design, despite my determined interference.

Sarah Flight of Sutton Publishing
For careful editing and valued opinions.

Andy Hayward and colleagues at Haynes
Essential for the essentials.

David Marr
For an honest critique that only a good friend can give.

International friends and colleagues
For linguistic translations.

Tim Leonhart of BookMasters
Our man in America.

Temporary Temples
Images of our changing oasis.

Carol Waters
The final eye.

FACT

Throughout the second half of the twentieth century and particularly during the cold war, secret government agencies funded by their proponents pursued programmes of research and application using techniques of extrasensory perception. One such technique, known as *Remote Viewing*, entailed the use of trained psychics or 'RVers' to 'travel' using only their minds: distant and often inaccessible locations being 'surveyed' with startling accuracy. Research information, results and their consequence, remain veiled in secrecy.

Lying under a Cairo suburb, Heliopolis was once the supreme religious centre of ancient Egypt. Believed to have been established long before its first mention in historical records, Heliopolis was a wonder of the ancient world. It was also the principal religious centre of the Pyramid Age, and its theology inspired and motivated the construction of the great monuments on the Plateau of Giza. The mysteries of the all-encompassing, omniscient Egyptian gods were celebrated by generations of initiate priests at Heliopolis as they serviced temples to the Great Ennead. This enduring priesthood was famed for its learning and wisdom throughout the ancient world: so many of their secrets still lie undisturbed.

The earliest detailed images taken of the Martian surface by an orbiting satellite identified two areas where clearly defined structures appeared 'artificial'. Within a region known as the Elysium Quadrangle appeared pyramidal features - two large and two small. Subsequent images have shown the same detail. In the region known as Cydonia Mensae, another series of structures have seemingly significant features, one of which appears to be a five-sided pyramid.

Recorded over several centuries and throughout the world, complex and beautiful markings continue to appear. Not just in arable grasslands, but also in reed beds, forest tops and even sand, many of these 'crop circles' have distinct and striking features. Tending to manifest on or near ancient, sacred sites, acknowledged in the past as places of power, many of these formations have blatant mathematical connotations and symbolic implications. Each year more arise, particularly in southern England. As increasing quality, intricacy and size continue to astound, deciphering their apparent encoded meaning is recognised by some as a prophetic necessity.

The ancient Maya stand alone as the celebrated civilisation of Mesoamerica. Although isolated from continental Europe and certainly the eastern Mediterranean - human contact is thought to have been almost impossible - the Mayan culture displayed astounding similarities to those of Mesopotamia and ancient Egypt. Their pyramid building prowess, pictogram script and initiate priests serving all-powerful Gods in lavish temples lay testament to confusing commonalities. As did the Sumarians, the Indus Valley civilisations of India and the Egyptians, the Maya tracked celestial movements closely and created an accurate solar-year calendar based on their observations. They also made mystical connections between earth and sky, positioned and constructed their buildings using complex mathematics and became great farmers and traders. Even their legacy; ruined temples, astonishing artefacts and stone-carved graphic script, exemplify this stark reality.

Worshiped in the 'Mansion Of The Phoenix' in the ancient, religious city of On, the Benben stone is believed to have been of meteoric origin. Only much later, did the Greeks call On, 'Heliopolis', and their documentation sheds some light on this most sacred of Egyptian artefacts. The Benben stone's supposedly cosmic origin and most particularly its 'conical shape' has justified a great deal of conjecture that this stone was an 'oriented' iron-meteorite, and that its shape subsequently inspired the designers of the first, true pyramids. Factually, items of space debris that fall to earth, often with spectacular effect, and that are recoverable, are called meteorites. The sun-like display of such a happening would surely inspire stellar symbolism, and clear evidence of this is found throughout the religious beliefs of the Egyptians and many other ancient civilisations.

The history of ancient Africa features narratives of similar complexity and sophistication to any other ancient civilisation. Yet almost without exception, it is only Egypt that receives substantive consideration. Arguably, the pinnacle of African civilisation aside from the land of Egyptian pharaohs, the Kushite Empire occupied territories now known as the Sudan. More particularly, the city of Meroe was foremost in that empire as a commercial, cultural and religious centre that bridged Southern and Northern African trading routes. The Meroitic language, which used hieroglyphic script, remains undeciphered today. Extensive ruins now pay silent tribute to this once vibrant city-state and these include substantial stone-built pyramids. The unique and strikingly angular architecture of these mausoleums differ considerably from those built by the ancient Egyptians and cite similarities to structures recorded elsewhere in the solar system.

Ethiopia's claim to the lost Ark of the Covenant is contentious. However, it is to some extent documented. Many do believe that the sacred Old Testament treasure rests in the ancient capital of Axum, exactly where the Ethiopians say it is. Indeed, it seems likely that the Ark did arrive in Ethiopia in the late fifth century BC, about five hundred years after the time of Solomon and Sheba. There is some evidence to suggest that it was first installed on an island in Lake Tana, where it remained for eight hundred years before finally being moved to Axum around the time of Ethiopia's conversion to Christianity in the forth century AD. Also known as Aksum, Ethiopia's most ancient city has a history dating back more than three thousand years. Aksumite imperial power reached a peak some time after Meroitic Kush, which it finally conquered in the second century AD. Aksum, together with the strategic and fabulously wealthy Red Sea trading port of Adulis, became two of the most important cosmopolitan centres in the ancient world.

THE BASTION PROSECUTOR

EPISODE 1

EPISODE 1

CONTENTS

EPISODE 2

CONTENTS

EXTRACT FROM THE DIARY OF ADMIREL DIRKOT URKET - TAKEN FROM THE FLIGHT LOG OF 'THE STAR OF HOPE'

ⲟⲣⲙ 𓅃 ⲟ𓀭ⲙ ⲟⲟ𓀀 ⲗⲁⲥⲟⲣⲟ

On the eve of this final journey, I scribe these thoughts. Mostly for thyself, as I know many in kinship do likewise, but also for diarist, as destiny may this voyage foretell its course for my kind. This quest, at the least doomed, at most, the destiny of our souls, is as wanting as the light of a coming dawn. I am, I yearn, with the heaviness of heart that weighs with bidding forever farewell to my brethren, but blessed too with the smile of hope and gaiety of spirit that we may yet bring salvation to our creed. The history of my kind who abided on Homer, a fair body in the heavens of Zodiac, arises from the dusk of our mother place, the curtain of its lifelessness falling many myriad distant. Of all those that joyed on that most beau of celests only four vessels set forth. Two from the land of Sapia, five score and ten from the north, fair of skin and fair of pride yet fierce that none would cross. So too a dozen less a century from the south, white of hair and blue for seeing. From Meh Hecoe fortune bestowed a full century and four score, their kind dark of skin with hair black as night. Graced the last to account their lives from the consuming fire, but two score and a dozen less one from Mohenjo, thin of eye and yellow their look. These four chariots of kind sought the heavens, only these from so many, their beginnings consumed. Many suns passed and as many bodies. Monumental some, meagre others, until after a full celestial epoch the fairest place was behold and it was bequest them. In time, great places arose and prospered. The Sapiens of the north in Eridu, of the south in Atlantis. In Te Agi Wakhan the Mayans and in Mohenjo Daro the Harappas, all fairly multiplied. Ordained for two millennia all prospered, their numbers spreading the land until in much less time fortune changed. Great movements begot Eridu and later vast waters to eclipse Atlantis. Of Mohenjo Daro, a mountain of fire scorched so naught remained, but of Te Agi Wakhan the stone of light snuffed, its civil just to disperse. Of the stone that lit Eridu, two fragments were redeemed. One used thereafter to light Babylon, its great gardens a millennium to keep homage to those the lost. The other protected by a sacred casket, looked upon by angels until graced by understanding. Lo, over the annals of time the stone that gave Babylon life has too waned. So be it to those here gathered, entrusted by our brethren, the remaining to breathe life into this our last hope, The Star, should we be able to seek our kind and others for salvation. May Astrolias be with us, for in faith we will find the course.

PROLOGUE

14th May 2050

It was early when the hotel telephone rang. Richard was in a deep sleep. The intrusive, abrasive tone penetrated his dream, surreptitiously becoming part of it. It pulled at his subconscious, initially to no avail; Richard eventually responded with a jolt. A burst of adrenalin unsympathetically exiled him to reality. Sitting up, in opaque darkness, he fumbled unsuccessfully for the receiver; it fell silent. Groaning disapprovingly, Richard leant back against the padded bed-head. Then, after another equally frustrating search, he eventually found, by default, the switch to the bedside light; its dull, insufficient response struggling to illuminate the unfamiliar and unhomely room.

Richard had registered in the early hours, dropped his

case inside the door and immediately retired. Now, a few hours later, with a groggy disposition and tired, prickly eyes, he took a little time to orientate himself and gather his thoughts. He was still wearing his watch and pressed the face, illuminating the blue neon backlight. It lit his features with an expectant incandescent glow: the hour was disappointing.

'God, 03:30. That's all I need,' he complained quietly.

Then it began again.

A more unpleasant, penetrating tone would be hard to imagine, particularly at this goddamn time of the morning, he thought.

This time he picked up the receiver promptly, his own tone uncompromising, reflecting the humourless hour.

'Reece . . . UK Joint Forces,' he barked.

'Is that Lieutenant Commander Richard James Reece?' a well-spoken English voice enquired politely.

'Who wants to know?' pursued Richard aggressively.

A lengthy period of silence followed; both parties hesitated. Richard relented first, unable to maintain an unnatural obstinacy.

'Yes, speaking,' he ventured. 'One and the same.'

The caller's tone also offered some compromise.

'Apologies for the late hour, rather inconvenient I know. My name is Peter Rothschild, Central Bureau of Intelligence, MI9.'

'Now what does National Security want with me?' Richard interrupted suspiciously.

'We need to talk to you.'

'I'm listening.'

'Not on the telephone, Richard, we need you in London.'

To Richard, this man's easy use of his first name seemed patronising. He did not know him. Who the hell gave him permission? It made his hackles rise. The caller sensed this too.

'Lieutenant Commander Reece,' he offered more respectfully but still with determined emphasis. 'We *need* to speak to you, a matter of some gravity.'

'When?'

'Look out of your window, to the right, thirty metres; on the other side of the road. There is a car, a black Jaguar ZKZ.'

Richard sprang out of bed, stepped five or six paces to the window and shifted the edge of the curtain secretively. There it was, sidelights on, parked beneath a flickering streetlight, its driver engulfed in mysterious shadows. He walked back to the bedside table and picked up the receiver.

'I see it.'

'The car will wait for another ten minutes. Please do not miss it!'

With that, the caller hung up. Richard kept looking at the beige-coloured receiver, as if waiting for another equally sinister order to follow. After several seconds, and with the gentle purr of the dialling tone humming in his ear, he replaced it carefully into its receptacle.

He was in two minds: ignore the caller as some prankster who couldn't sleep, or go along with it. What about the car? That was no illusion. The fact is, he concluded thoughtfully, I don't have a choice; another clanger will surely terminate my illustrious career!

Relieved of his duties in the space programme pending court-martial for misappropriation of ISSF property, a charge he vehemently denied, Richard knew that calling their bluff was a luxury he could not afford. He had to comply with this enigmatic rendezvous; he had to cooperate.

Within minutes, he was dressed. Fawn chinos, a white t-shirt under a dark blue crew-neck woollen pullover and his favourite polished, brown brogues. He looked at his brief case, decided not to take it, and left the room pulling his navy-blue trench coat unceremoniously from a hanger in the wardrobe. On the rebound, the wire hanger caused several others to fall to the floor, their disproportionately loud clattering seemingly amplified by the silent stillness of the deserted hotel corridor. A reverberating thump as the room door closed, added to the inconsiderate finale.

Empty handed, save for his ID tag and telephonic pager, Richard walked quickly along several other narrow corridors following the signs for reception. Dimly lit, dismal, depressing, the ageing hotel's best days were clearly a distant memory. Eventually, as if emerging from a labyrinth, he arrived at the head of a curved stone staircase;

complimented surprisingly by an ornate Victorian cast-iron balustrade. Taking two steps at a time, he moved spryly down two flights, before the worn treads led to a sparsely furnished foyer; its deep red, wall-to-wall carpet displaying a floral design that appeared even more tired than he was.

He had thought on his arrival that this was an unlikely, even odd, venue for an interview; particularly with a reporter from the highly regarded periodical *London Review*. Nevertheless, he had requested a quiet, out of town backwater for the rendezvous and this place was as unobtrusive as it got. The 7 a.m. start? That too had seemed sensible at the time, helping maintain a low profile, even if it did mean him arriving the night before in order to avoid the commuter rush. He had done the commuter thing, several months of it . . . never again.

Richard nodded politely at the night porter who smirked back knowingly. Subsequently and with little respect, a heavy, wooden, rotating door ejected him onto the wintry street. Surprised at his reluctance to leave the dubious comforts of the Heathcliffe Hotel, he stepped out from under the twin-columned open porch and into the rain, only at this point realising that he had forgotten one essential item – his umbrella. This in itself was unusual, as few ventured outside, these days, without one.

A driving barrage of water soon had him cowering inside the large turned-up collar of his coat. Almost instinctively, he checked and rechecked the area, scanning the immediate nooks and crannies of this depressing milieu, something that had become a tiresome but necessary habit.

Neither surprised nor disappointed that the street appeared deserted, save of course for the mysterious driver who sat patiently in his impressive limousine some thirty metres away, Richard relaxed a little and walked towards the vehicle. The car's engine sprang to life, its sound muffled by the perpetual resonance of raindrops splashing onto the pavement and surrounding puddles; the ever-present gurgling sound of water washing down storm drains being so conditioned in his subconscious as to barely register.

Effortlessly, the car, with its long phallic bonnet, pulled up close to the curb, the nearside rear door conveniently in front of him. Richard hesitated, as if there was still a decision to be made, his soaking contributed positively to the process. The unusually heavy door took some effort to open. He climbed, slightly awkwardly, onto the back seat and barely had he time to swing the door closed, when the vehicle sped off into the night.

The limousine was spacious, at least in the back. A thick glass screen, behind two rear-facing seats, separated the extravagant passenger area from the driver's. The vehicle's engineering seemed impressive, as there was barely a sound. From the other side of the screen Richard could hear the driver's heavy, regular breathing. An intricate badge of office, in the form of a crown supporting a plume of three feathers, was etched centrally into the glass; it caught his eye for a few moments. He leaned forward to study it more closely. Each feather curled forwards towards the top and below the crown were two words written inside a heraldic scroll, *Ich Dien.*

'German, I think, maybe Latin?' Richard mumbled.

There was a strong, damp, leathery smell, it seemed to engulf him; Richard's own drenched woollen coat also contributed to the fusty environment.

Richard studied the driver, or what he could see of him, for several minutes. The man flagrantly ignored the auto-drive facility, the engagement of which was compulsory in urban areas. He also paid scant regard to local speed limits, a consequence of this offence being instant disqualification. Richard looked outside at the miserable conditions; intermittent streetlights offered little comfort. He focused on the numerous roadside cameras elevated on tall, skinny poles; he felt uneasy as they watched, rotating as they passed by like giant preying mantises. It won't be long before we hear a police siren, he thought. Richard also considered the route the driver was taking to the city, hardly the most direct.

A new experience, or perhaps a forgotten one, was soon to follow, however. The thick set, dark suited man responded to a message through his earpiece. He began to drive as if there was no tomorrow!

CHAPTER 1

ALLIANCE OF NECESSITY

Finally, an agreement had been reached: the photographs could be taken inside the cathedral, individuals by the High Altar, beneath the Golden Window, and group shots in the choir. Neither the Bishop nor the Dean had voiced disapproval at their last meeting, not since the order of service had been changed to accommodate a more prescribed format and consequently, guest numbers had been reduced. Considering the circumstances, a relaxation of the rules was appropriate. After all, Wells was one of the last dioceses in the country to see commonsense.

Rachel had hoped that the rain would abate, even temporarily, for her special day. After all, summer was fast approaching, but Richard had told her to stop dreaming and be sure to make all the necessary arrangements in good time. The service and reception would be between

2 p.m. and 6 p.m. – Somerset's allocation for electrical power in May. After a year of almost continuous rain she, and many others for that matter, had given up on seeing the sun again, at least from the ground.

A few months earlier, Richard had contacted an old friend in Mauritius. That island, along with Rodrigues, St. Brandon and Reunion was among the last remaining locations on earth where rain was intermittent and the sun's warmth still had an impact. At upwards of ten thousand dollars a night however, for even a modest hotel room, and no deals, Richard had long since given up on transporting friends and family to Le Morne for the ceremony. Anyway, François had informed him that the island was literally bursting at the seams with visitors, and that the government had capped the transient population in order to preserve law and order and maintain a basic level of services for its population.

The government's other highly controversial decision, which allowed nationals to sell their right of abode, had created a temporary haven for the rich and famous, but the revenues the authorities clawed back in 'residential tax' from this wholly inappropriate law was having little impact in sustaining the island's infrastructure.

No, Richard had given up the idea of going there, or anywhere else for that matter and was pleased to be tying the knot in his home county; Rachel was also content with the venue. Its rural location and waterlogged green however, would not stop the remnants of clamouring paparazzi that still pursued him, following the ISSF's disclosure of the Ark's flight manual earlier in the year. Despite his much-publicised interview on CNB News International, where he insisted that he was merely the discoverer, a delivery boy, and not a prosecutor of the divine ideal, many still believed that he was to blame for the gaping cracks now apparent in the religious bastion that was Christendom. His supporters, had he bothered to acknowledge them, a US based religious sect, continued to whip up the debate on the world stage, claiming that their beliefs were, after all, based on proven fact and not unsubstantiated historical texts.

The whole episode infuriated him and he had lost his job because of it.

Religion exists because people have, since time immemorial, believed in human values and spiritual necessity; not because of mythical figures, he had stated time and time again.

Nonetheless, the big day seemed to arrive astonishingly fast. Richard found himself standing with his back towards the famous green, looking up at the two inspiring towers, modelled in perpendicular style that flanked the glorious West Front of the Cathedral. How impressive they were; indeed the whole building was. He remembered absorbing and informative history lessons spent studying the inspiring structure during his school days, and in particular one pertinent description: 'there are few places in the whole of the British Isles more fascinating, both to the antiquary and to the ecclesiologist, than Wells, *City of Many Streams*'. How true, he thought, as he gazed in awe at the nine tiers of undamaged sculptures, most of heroic proportions.

'Secure in their niches for eternity,' he observed.

Richard glanced down at his shiny black shoes, smart creased trousers, black waistcoat and silvery-grey tie. A gold chain linked his left breast pocket to an adjacent buttonhole. He pulled the tail of his morning coat forward, more in surprise than to check its condition and lay. He looked up at the sky, sighting a rising, but ominous dark cloud above the pinnacle of the cathedral's central spire. It was then that the significance of the moment struck him; just as when the swinging steel ball of a demolition crane strikes a condemned building.

'My God!' he said aloud. 'It's stopped raining, it's actually stopped raining!'

At that moment, a condensed column of bright sunlight penetrated the base of the cloud he had focused on. The dark cloud lightened, its menace dissolving into an atmosphere that for so long had courted an alliance. With a whitish-yellow glow, the pole of light blasted a distant, unsuspecting hilltop, showering it with effervescing shards of brilliance that rejuvenated Richard's spirit and lifted his heart.

'Today of all days,' he gushed.

Unable to help himself, Richard held his arms up to

the sky, rejoicing at the sight of an expanding blue hole that repelled surrounding clouds like opening ripples on a pond. He looked around the ancient paved square, and to the west, across the green, its colour vivid and inviting; a gathering clan of familiar faces beamed back at him, happy and joyful. The women looked beautiful in large hats and summer dresses. There was his mother, a broad grin on her face. Then the group to his left parted, as if a vehicle was pushing through from behind. Richard looked through the gap; and to his surprise and delight, Rachel appeared. She looked absolutely stunning in a long, white, formal wedding dress with a flowing train that trailed majestically behind her as she walked slowly, almost regally towards him. Richard took her hand. He looked longingly at her face, which, partially covered by an elegant white veil, seemed somehow mystical. Those around them applauded.

'Shouldn't we meet first in the church, Rachel?' he asked, looking through the wispy veil and into her bewitching eyes.

Time seemed to stand still; her features, her expression, intoxicated him.

'Don't let it rain, Richard, not today, not on me,' Rachel implored. Richard looked up at the sky, blue like a tropical sea, the sun shone down on them.

'Not today, Rachel. Look,' he said, pointing upwards.

As she followed his gaze, a billowing, heavy cloud cast its shadow over them. It gathered and conspired, masking the sun; the sky grew dark, sullen. With nothing said and seemingly from nowhere, the people around them drew umbrellas. In a fluster, they tried to open them, all at once, squabbling for space and the opportunity to take cover. Then the unthinkable happened. It began to rain. Spitting at first, the drops making small circular marks on the pavements; within moments it grew heavy. Those around dispersed screaming; it was pouring down. Water rose around their feet and poor Rachel began to cry uncontrollably.

'You said it wouldn't rain, Richard, you promised.'

As she spoke icy water covered their ankles, it rose towards their knees. Rachel's dress began to fizz and bubble, she began to shrink, her body dissolving into the rising flood.

'Rachel! Rachel! Come back, I'm sorry, I'm sorry.'

Richard's head fell sharply forward as a result of sustained heavy braking. It woke him abruptly. The strong smell of mouldy leather and his cold, wet coat contributed to the discomfort he felt from a stiff neck and niggling headache. The uneasy sleep had done him no favours. He became aware of a face peering at him through the side window; its expression troubled and contorted against the driving rain. The man, wearing a dark green camouflaged anorak and a black sleeveless jacket, tapped on the glass with his knuckle. Silhouetted by several, bright, halogen spotlights positioned around the security checkpoint, Richard could see he was heavily armed. His standard Joint Forces 'Light Infantry Weapon' for one thing had an optional high velocity discharge sheath fitted, and a laser all-weather acquisition sight.

Richard fumbled for the switch. The soldier tapped again on the glass, this time with the barrel of his rifle, making Richard nervous. The driver operated Richard's electric window on his behalf and it slid open slowly, just a few inches.

'ID Sir,' demanded the guard bluntly, water dripping continuously from the rim of his protective helmet.

'Lieutenant Commander Reece, UK Joint Forces,' confirmed Richard, displaying his electronic tag.

The guard passed a small sensor over the tag without removing it from Richard's hand, almost instantly a tiny green light appeared on the instrument accompanied by a chirping sound.

'Thank you, Sir. You're clear,' confirmed the guard, who then looked up to acknowledge the driver with a nod, as if he knew him.

Immediately, the window began to close. Richard thanked the guard with an understanding glance, before the thick, well-fitting glass pane slipped tightly back into place, relegating the figure to his solitary, monotonous duties.

For no apparent reason the car suddenly accelerated; for an instant the screech of its tyres broke the frosty silence between the two men. His neck was forced back into the cold, clammy collar of his coat and Richard could no longer contain his discontent.

'Where the hell are we going, and what's the rush?' he enquired tersely into the microphone.

There was no answer.

'I *said*, where are we going?'

After a few seconds, the driver answered gruffly, his tone deep and gravelly. 'London.'

'Really? Can you be a little more specific?' Richard demanded.

Another period of silence followed. Reluctantly the driver responded. 'Admiralty Arch, near Trafalgar Square. That's all I am allowed to say.'

Richard could detect a Scottish accent in the man's voice, but one that had softened considerably; or perhaps one adequately disguised by his grumbling low tone.

'I know Admiralty Arch, I worked there for several months a few years ago,' continued Richard, disregarding the man's obvious preference for silence.

This time there was no response from the driver.

Conversation not one of your strong points then, thought Richard sarcastically, as he sat back in his seat again, feeling the effects of the early hour.

He considered the events of the previous months; his return to earth with an empty U-Semini case and the Ark's log being found in his cabin back on Mars. Why hadn't he hidden it somewhere more secure? He thought about the package that lay in his father's old workshop, placed, just a few weeks earlier in a deep, vehicle service pit by his mother and hidden by heavy wooden sleepers. Apart from her, that fact was an absolute secret. He felt sure that the contents of the package held the key to sustained human life on the surface of planet earth, and now, free of the constraints of ESSA or ISSF, he did not intend to divulge its location. The authorities inevitably would misappropriate the contents in any case, as they had done with the other Kalahari crystals.

He had made his decision; the package would remain where it was until the time was right. With four crystals that he knew about already depleted to worthless zirconium by inappropriate handling and insufficiently tested reactors, it would not be long before the remaining four went the same way. Indeed, the Long Island reactor had already received its second crystal.

What were they doing with this precious, unique, resource? They could be a gift from the gods, but here were the authorities squandering their remaining potential for short-term gains. How short-sighted they were, he mused. There *is* a better way to utilise the crystals, to prolong their life and extract their remaining energy. After all, the Babylonian stone had 'burned' for a thousand years; Admiral Urket's text in the Ark's log had stated that unequivocally.

It was political; the masses wanted their light, heat, hot water, to be able to cook; all the things that we once took for granted. Whichever party or government; whoever the leader; promising abundant energy, electricity; they would be elected.

Richard checked the time and refocused on the changing scenery outside the relative comfort of his limousine. They had been driving for almost forty minutes. He had unwittingly allowed himself to lose his bearings and the long, straight, signless, dual carriageway on which they were driving offered no clues.

Then he realised. There was no other road like it, not this close to London. They were driving along SPEED 1 - the Sovereign Procurement Expressway and Emergency Distributor.

The first of a number of protected and highly restricted highways, the SPEED linked major city centres directly with government defence establishments, the latter normally including barracks for contingents of the UK Rapid Reaction Defence Force. The UK Defence Force HQ was in Northwood and SPEED 1 linked it directly to Westminster. No messing, no hold ups and no congestion.

The construction of the expressway, taking almost three years, had been completed thirty years earlier, towards the end of the chapter of 'great civil unrest'. At the time it was highly controversial and understandably highly unpopular, requiring compulsory land purchase and property acquisitions by the state. Planning Permission had swept through Parliament on the back of the infamous 'Preservation of National Security' White Paper of 2012, which gave draconian powers to the police and security forces. The expressway was a means of deploying large numbers of troops from out-of-town barracks directly to the centre of the capital and the successful model had been repeated in the five major UK cities of Manchester, Birmingham, Edinburgh, Glasgow and Cardiff. It also allowed government ministers, high ranking officials and other VIPs to move quickly in and out of the major conurbations, particularly London's 'square mile'.

Richard's amazement grew as he considered the implications of using SPEED 1. The journey would have required approval from the very highest authority, perhaps even the Prime Minister's office.

With high mortar-proof partitions on either side, it was impossible to tell where on the expressway they were. Richard leaned forward and glanced at the vehicle's speedometer. Eighty miles an hour; it would not take long to reach Trafalgar Square. Then he looked up into the large rear-view mirror and at the driver's face; the man's peculiar, dark, sunken eyes and protruding forehead being clearly visible. There was enough light being reflected from the unusually complicated dashboard for Richard to notice heavy stress lines around his eyes, and a concerned, wrinkled brow. Richard continued to watch, absorbed, as the man's eyes glanced repeatedly in the mirror. He checked and rechecked the road behind; far too preoccupied to notice Richard staring at him.

After a while, the habit became such that it began to

unnerve Richard. Unable to help himself, he too began glancing over his shoulder, surreptitiously at first, but growing more obvious. The road behind remained a dark, dense blackness. Richard expected nothing less at this godforsaken hour. After several minutes, Richard felt the vehicle accelerate. He looked at the speedometer again. One hundred, one hundred and ten, one hundred and twenty.

'What's the rush?' Richard probed.

In the reflection, their eyes met; both focused on the mirror. For the briefest moment, their eyes connected. The driver remained silent, but gestured over his shoulder, before concentrating once again on the road ahead. Richard turned and looked back through the small, elliptical rear window into the distance. There, way back in the night, almost as far as he could see, was a pinprick of bright white light.

'Another car, just another car,' he ventured.

The driver's head shook gently from side to side.

'The road is closed, they have found us,' he uttered menacingly.

'Who has found us for god's sake?' demanded Richard, looking over his shoulder again.

The light grew brighter, closer. Richard became aware of the Jaguar's speed, its engine no longer purring, but whining, working, straining.

'This car's heavy. A ton twenty is the best I can do,' enlightened the driver, his eyes now barely leaving the mirror.

The remark passed over Richard's head as he contemplated, with mounting anxiety, the ever-nearing threat. White road markings flashed past. Within minutes, the growing dot of light split into two. Richard seemingly fixated, began to see the outline of a vehicle. It looked like a large sedan.

'Who the hell are they?' Richard asked.

The driver considered the question and shrugged. 'It will do no good to tell you,' he answered.

'Tell me damn you! . . . *Well*?'

'Spheron, it's Spheron, an assassination cell.'

'An assassination cell!' Richard repeated, sitting bolt upright.

Again, Richard looked over his shoulder. He stared into the blackness for several seconds before lolling back into his seat, his nonchalant body language thinly disguising a despairing rush of emotions. He began to accept the remark and the situation with an air of inevitability. Eventually, it was bound to happen, he thought. Something related to the crystals; everyone wanted the crystals, and if not the crystals, then some extreme religious faction.

Nervously both men monitored the ever-increasing intensity of the vehicle's headlights. As the seconds passed, the car grew nearer. To Richard, the dilemma seemed surreal; as if he were trapped within a suspended capsule, an inescapable bubble where time had no meaning. His irrationality was short-lived, however, as the vehicle closed aggressively to within a few metres. It sat on their tail, bumper to bumper, occasionally drawing back. When it did, trailing by no more than four or five metres, the driver flashed his headlights wildly. Glaring, blinding, perhaps to disorientate, perhaps to mask their intentions, but Richard could clearly see three men inside.

It was a large, bulky car; European, diplomatic, it looked sleek. The crest, a double eagle; it was German. It sat on their tail, drawing forward, then trailing away again by a few metres, occasionally swerving from side to side. Richard's driver watched their reflection intently. He remained steady, unflinching.

'They will try something soon,' he confided. There was no speculation in his tone. 'Just six miles to checkpoint Charlie . . . end of the road.'

Richard leaned forward in order to look as far ahead as possible. There were no restrictions, only the long, straight, funnelling road. The driver was right on both counts. In the far distance, Richard could see the glimmer of lights, undoubtedly the terminal checkpoint. Almost simultaneously, the intimidating sedan decelerated. It opened a gap of some twenty metres. Richard stared wide-eyed. Although impeded by the glare of powerful headlights, he watched, helpless, as the figure in the front passenger seat pushed something resembling a large tube out of his window. Within seconds, a blinding flash of white light illuminated the aggressors; it was like a bolt of lightning, momentarily turning night into day. Richard looked down instantly, his eyes smarting from an intense, unnatural brilliance.

'Keep your head down!' the driver ordered.

Richard ignored him and looked to see what was coming their way. 'It's a plasma grenade!' he screamed.

As if in slow motion, the burning football of high-energy plasma flew towards them. It spitted and sparked; a glowing whiteness with a fringe of neon blue.

'We're dead!' Richard exclaimed, ducking into the seat well.

Moments later the deadly incinerator struck them, sending an almighty shudder through the car. With the impact, the fiery ball burst into a multitude of sizzling, arcing, sparks, releasing a million volts of vaporising electrical potential in the process. Richard closed his eyes; there was nothing he could do. Not survivable, that's the end of it, he thought in that instant. The car buzzed and shorted.

'Keep down! The bastards! There's another wee surprise coming,' warned the driver again, his unguarded Scottish accent much thicker now.

Richard covered his head with his arms. This time the car swerved and vibrated violently as the plasma ball struck. The driver fought to maintain control. Richard could hear the tyres screeching as he was thrown from side to side. A strong burning smell permeated the car; pungent fumes leaking through ventilation ducts. Richard closed as many as he could find. Locked as he was inside this cocoon, nothing was worse than fire, he thought. The coat of arms etched onto the dividing screen inexplicably caught his eye again.

As the buzzing and shorting subsided, Richard climbed onto the seat to check behind. The sedan had closed again to within a few metres, its headlights illuminating the inside of the Jaguar, as if it was day. Richard turned to look again at his driver. He was gripping the steering wheel for all he was worth; white knuckles indicating the intensity of his focus and effort.

'How the hell did we survive that?' Richard ventured, more an exclamation than a question. 'We should be ashes blowing in the wind!'

The driver said nothing, his gaze shifting between the rear view mirror and the rapidly approaching checkpoint. Then Richard realised something. He focused again on the coat of arms. Three feathers in a plume through a crown, this was no ordinary car; it was special, customised; it was one from the Royal Family stable. *Ich Dien.* Yes, of course, he could be even more precise. There was no doubt in Richard's mind. Prince George, Prince of ...

'Here they come again,' interrupted the driver. 'They mean to stop us this time. Must get off this damned road ... not far to the checkpoint!'

Richard was only half listening. The penny had dropped. He knew his science. Only one system could insulate them from a plasma grenade: a dense magnetic field. That required a massive, heavy, copper wire coil, wound around a powerful electro-magnetic core. It struck him in an instant: the overly heavy door, a ZKZ that was only able to make a hundred and twenty miles per hour, thick hermetically sealed, copper tinted windows. This was no ordinary car all right and no ordinary driver to boot!

The rat-a-tat of machine gun fire on the side window brought Richard back to reality with a frenzied jolt. The sedan, with its superior speed, was almost alongside them. The first volley of sublets ricocheted harmlessly in all directions, the second similarly and the third. Clearly, the car was armour-plated as well!

'He's aiming at the tyres now!' Richard warned.

His driver swerved violently to the right, cutting off the advancing sedan and blocking its path. With an exaggerated motion, he swerved left and then right again, ramming the aggressor. The Jaguar's front wing heavily distorted the nearside doors of the sedan and the transferred momentum sent it crashing into the central barrier. Sparks flew; stones and debris flew; whipped up by the bouncing wheels on unprepared ground. The big German car veered violently left and right and then left again. It dropped back twenty or thirty metres, before coming at them again.

'Thirty seconds to the checkpoint,' shouted the driver, who by this time was also desperately flashing his headlights.

Another volley of sublets hit the Jaguar. This time, their rapidity, concentrated in one tiny area, drilled into the transparency of the rear windscreen. A blister appeared in the glass, then an almost concentric hole and then a jagged crack, with zigzagging branches suddenly radiating in all directions. Richard ducked instinctively. As if driving home their decisive attack, a heavy projectile burst through the breach. The explosive sound of fracturing glass reverberated in Richard's ears; he cowered. It was a mortar shell. With little momentum remaining, the shell bounced off the impregnated leather of the rear-facing seat and then again off the opposite seat incredibly close to where Richard cringed, head-in-arms. It came to rest, smouldering, in the wide, carpeted foot well. For the next few seconds there was an air of expectant carnage.

Nothing! The shell fizzled. It rolled against the rear seat.

There may have been some momentary confusion in Richard's mind as to what, precisely the failed device was, but not to his next response: he was having no more of the back seat and immediately actuated the dividing screen controller, lowering it as far as it would go. Was there time? The device continued to fizz and the column of black smoke that permeated its casing caused a nauseating, caustic smell. Using his body weight, Richard leaned on the screen, until the thick glass pane slipped the final few centimetres into its recess. Without hesitation, he scrambled head first over the top shouting, 'it's a magma eruptor!'

Using the seat's head restraint as a gymnastic horse,

Richard performed an acrobatic swivel, his feet swinging perilously close to the driver's perspiring face. The driver operated the dividing screen, master control switch. Barely had it embedded into its close-fitting housing, when the shell exploded. For a fraction of a second, the glass screen bowed under the tremendous pressure. Semi-liquified shrapnel and molten iron ore pellets peppered its inside face, but it held. The compartment bubbled with a yellow sulphuric gas which, ejected under pressure through the hole in the rear windscreen, trailed the Jaguar like the exhaust of a rocket motor. How lucky Richard was; how lucky they both were. The firing distance had been too short, with insufficient time to fuse the detonator for impact initiation; it had exploded using the secondary timing mechanism.

Richard landed with a thud, backside first in the seat. He looked up, gasped, and slid down into the footwell, recoiling again beneath his raised arms; the checkpoint barrier, although rising, was upon them. The thick metal pole struck the lip of the Jaguar's roof with a deafening smash as they passed beneath it. Using his legs, Richard pushed himself back into the seat. He looked into the passenger compartment; it was shot to pieces, full of smoke with flames flickering. He checked the door-mounted wing mirror; the dark sky behind them suddenly lit up with blazing white flashes as the checkpoint guards opened fire on the approaching sedan.

Unperturbed by the closing, electrified, steel barrier and

blatantly arrogant in the face of a wall of automatic fire, its driver careered through the narrowing gap. A soldier firing incessantly from the main position took the force of the recoiling barrier square in the chest, and it sent him tumbling backwards, propelling his rifle high into the air. The sedan bullied its way through and accelerated.

Richard glanced across towards his driver. 'I know this area. Follow my instructions,' he demanded.

The driver nodded, his attention fixed on the road ahead. Mostly pedestrian walkways, the City of London was no place for speeding cars, even at this time of the morning. Richard lowered his scorched side window wide enough to get his head out. In the distance, he could hear the wail of police sirens. He looked for road signs and landmarks, tracking several before he recognised a street name: Pimlico Road, at the junction with Buckingham Palace Road.

'Quick! Left here, Buckingham Palace Road. Take the first right, there is a bridge, Elizabeth something, then into Saint George's Drive!' Richard ordered.

The driver obeyed, sending the ZKZ screeching around the tight corners. The sedan was nowhere to be seen. Richard breathed easier. Moments later and as if on cue, the sedan appeared, rounding the same corner equally flamboyantly behind them. It leaned heavily and skidded sideways, covering the full width of the rain-soaked road.

'Next left . . . can't this thing go any faster?'

Amidst the confusion, the driver briefly glanced at

Richard. He was not amused.

'You want to drive?' he asked scornfully as he heaved the car into Warwick Way and put his foot down.

'No . . . thanks. Sorry, next right, Belgrade Road,' Richard stuttered apologetically. 'Four or five hundred metres straight, then third left.'

The two windscreen wipers scribed their broad arcs so fast as to almost become blurred, whilst the dull thud at the bottom of each cycle reverberated through the car like a bass drum. They skidded into Moreton Street with the sedan in hot pursuit. A clapping, echoing, burst of gunfire resonated from behind and another volley of sublets struck the back of the Jaguar. Richard could feel the car absorbing the attack. He glanced behind; every straight section of road saw them lose ground.

The big man handled his car like a racing veteran, pulling it left and right to avoid roadside obstacles and numerous pedestrian islands. On Richard's instructions, he violently swung the Jaguar, blocking any attempted overtaking, and then they surged straight ahead into Chapter Street. The engine roared, another breakneck acceleration.

'Left! Left!' Richard screeched. All the while sporadic volleys of automatic gunfire strafed the Jaguar. 'Four hundred metres to Horseferry . . . go for it!' Richard exclaimed. The engine roared again. They flew past the buildings and shops of Regency Street. 'Left coming up!' Richard pointed out. The big car veered into Horseferry Road slewing across the wet surface, followed, moments later, by the sedan.

Richard looked ahead; the few hundred metres to Strutton Ground took but seconds. 'Oh shit!' he screamed in exacerbation. 'Strutton . . . it's pedestrianised. Take a right, take a right!'

The driver slammed on his brakes and pulled the car right; too fast, he lost it. The Jaguar skidded, turning half-circle. The sedan, which was so close, veered to the left narrowly avoiding a debilitating head-on; it crashed over the kerbstones and into a row of green plastic refuse bins. The Jaguar roared off again, a gap opened, perhaps a hundred metres. Richard looked for a street sign, one bearing the name Great Peter Street flashed past.

The sedan quickly erased any advantage. Seventy miles an hour; eighty, eighty-five; soon it was on their tail again.

'End and left!' Richard advised watching the sedan's reflection draw menacingly close in his wing mirror. 'You can see it coming up! Then five or six hundred metres, next is Parliament Square. Be careful though, it's straight and wide. It is their last chance and they will know it!'

A sustained volley of accurate sublets shattered what remained of the rear windscreen; glass flew everywhere; several other deadly projectiles assaulted the dividing screen, pummelling the glass with a deafening, high frequency shrill. Richard's driver slammed on his brakes, sending the sedan crashing into the back of them. Another short opportunistic volley burst through the gaping hole and ricocheted wildly inside the passenger compartment. Richard felt several embed in the back of his seat, accompanied by muffled thuds; others bounced off the dividing screen. Richard ducked instinctively. The driver, amazingly, did not even flinch, but swerved his vehicle repeatedly left and right.

'I can't shake them off,' the driver complained. Sweat ran down his temples. 'They're caught-up, jammed!'

Again, he swerved left and right, trying to destabilise the unlikely coupling. As they passed St. Ann's Street, he wrenched the steering wheel with a massive effort, aggressively swerving right to pass on the wrong side and narrowly avoiding a pedestrian island. The sedan broke free, but too late to avoid the raised kerbstones. It crashed over them full on, shattering the illuminated plastic bollard into a thousand pieces; then it ricocheted uncontrollably off several parked cars.

Moments later, Richard and his driver found themselves turning onto Millbank. Richard craned his neck to look behind; the rear compartment had cleared of smoke: nothing, no sight of the other car. He scrutinized the reflected street scene in his wing mirror: still nothing. 'Can you see them?' he asked the driver, who glanced into the rear-view mirror momentarily before shaking his head. 'Then I think we have lost them,' Richard speculated. There was no reply from the driver. 'I think we can slow down,' Richard continued hesitantly. 'Straight ahead to Parliament Square, then Whitehall,' he advised finally.

The driver nodded but ignored Richard's appraisal and accelerated. Richard sat pensively watching his wing mirror. Perhaps it was wishful thinking, he brooded, now only half-believing his own comments. Through his partly opened window, the sound of police sirens seemed remarkably persistent. Undoubtedly they were growing nearer; soon they would see them. The road behind, dim and stark, remained devoid of any movement.

'We've done it!' Richard concluded. He closed his window to shut out the rain.

The driver was clearly not convinced and continued his acceleration. He nervously scanned the approaching abbey and to the right, Westminster Palace. Richard looked up at the illuminated clock face of Big Ben, still a symbol of national pride: it read 4:49.

Then, as they approached the junction with Great College Street, Richard caught sight of something; he looked again. 'Watch out!' he screamed. 'It's an ambush!'

Bearing down on them in the semi-darkness and at break-neck speed was the sedan. Richard's driver floored his accelerator pedal and took evasive action. The Jaguar picked-up speed and skewed right, but to no avail. The sedan launched itself at them. Like a missile, it shot out from the side street and across the main road. Richard shrank in his seat, bracing himself for the impending impact. With an almighty crash, the two cars collided. The momentum sent the Jaguar skidding sideways. It hit the high kerb on the opposite side of the road with a shuddering thud and flipped over onto its right side, careering down the road another fifty metres before being brought to an abrupt halt by a large concrete security post.

Some way back, the sedan under its own power, limped across the road until it too struck the kerbstones. Steam seeped from beneath its bonnet, before diffusing into the cold night air; an accompanying hissing sound bore testament to the damage. Inside the car, however, there was movement.

As the Jaguar's two crash pouches deflated, to hang like limp, punctured, party balloons, Richard shook his head; he took a few seconds to come to his senses. On this count, the driver appeared quicker off the mark. 'Get out, quickly!' he demanded. A smell of petrol permeated the air.

Within moments, pungent, acidic vapours caused Richard's eyes to smart and water. 'Petrol . . . fire!' he responded emphatically.

There was no time to heed Richard's warning. In fact, barely was there time to register its consequences when a muffled explosion fulfilled the prophesy: the rear of the Jaguar burst into flames. Acrid smoke soon seeped into the driver's compartment.

'Come on man, get out!' ordered the driver.

Richard was already on the case; repeatedly he tried the electric window, eventually banging the switch with his fist in desperation. He tried the door, wrenching its handle. Adrenalin improved their chances, but the heavy mechanism was distorted and completely jammed.

'No way, no way!' Richard blurted.

By this time, fire had taken hold behind the dividing screen. Bright orange flames ravaged what little remained of the expensive upholstery; licking the glass screen like a salivating cat waiting to kill. Soon the rear compartment glowed like a furnace. Richard followed the driver's gesture. He swung his feet around, half-supported by his seat and half by the driver's back. Both men pushed. Three, four, five times, Richard kicked the window; he used his heels and stabbed repeatedly. The glass was unbreakable. He barely made an impression.

The driver gave up on his support, he turned away to leave Richard hanging from the seat back and began fumbling below the dashboard in the area of the steering column. For several seconds he felt beneath the polished walnut fascia, running his fingers up and down. 'Where are you, wee lass?' he begged. The rear compartment was by now a raging inferno; radiated heat from the dividing screen turned their claustrophobic compartment into a stifling sauna. Richard levered himself away from the searing glass, half-looking for another escape route and half at the driver's seemingly futile attempt to find something.

'I have it,' called the driver. 'Turn away, shield your eyes,' he warned. With that, he flipped a switch or pressed a button, Richard could not really see, but instantly there was a muted explosion.

Richard uncovered his eyes to see the driver kick out

the windscreen almost in one complete piece.

'Go man, go!' the driver ordered.

Richard swung his legs awkwardly through the hole. Had he time to notice, he would have recognised the rectangular aperture as one made by an explosive ribbon embedded in the glass; similar to the systems employed on military aircraft canopies. With the car resting precariously on its side, Richard did well to avoid the fractured glass edges and the hot, distorted bodywork as he finally climbed clear of the wreckage. The Jaguar was by now almost completely engulfed in flames.

If that was not enough, a volley of machinegun fire peppered the burning hulk. Richard ducked as a neat run of circular perforations punctured the roof. He crouched as the driver's legs appeared through the windscreen, but the big man fell backwards unbalanced. Richard reached in, grabbed his belt and with one enormous effort pulled him clear. Another explosion ensued, glass flew in all directions; the dividing screen had finally shattered. The driver's face was bleeding and he winced in pain. There was no doubt in Richard's mind that he had taken some glass shards in the back, covering his own body in the process.

Startlingly close to where the two men stood and accompanied by a deafening thud, thud, thud, thud, another row of sublet holes instantaneously appeared in the cars roof. The driver pulled Richard down to his knees and shouted in his ear. 'Leg it man, leg it! Over there!

Towards the abbey, keep moving. Make it to Parliament Square!'

Richard nodded, but momentarily hesitated. The driver pushed him to get going.

'The police are coming, I'll be back for you,' he shouted again as Richard took off.

Richard sprinted across the open road looking north along Abingdon Street towards the Houses of Parliament; it was long, straight and exposed. Instead, he opted for the 'ambush street' and ran back towards it in the darkness. The word 'police' seemed strangely to concentrate his mind. He leapt a metal fence and cut the corner, but there, fifty metres ahead, was a solitary street light. He had no option but to run through its effect; he did so weaving left and right as fast as his legs would allow. A flurry of gunfire trailed him. He ran for his life. Two hundred metres seemed like two thousand. He darted right, a closing rat-a-tat chasing him around the corner. Sublets ricocheted off the ground and adjacent building. He disappeared into the darkness that was Deans Yard and all fell silent, even the whine of police sirens trailed away to nothing. A misty calmness pervaded the area. He slowed to a scurrying walk, all the while checking behind. He heard another car, but could not see it and then there was silence again, hollow, eerie.

Enveloped by the relative safety of this darkened hallow, Richard slowed further to an attentive lope, resisting the temptation to duck into every nook and cranny. He followed carefully the ornate metal railing that encircled the green and that ran behind the abbey. The rain had eased to a persistent, penetrating drizzle and the celebrated but ominous architecture of Westminster Abbey seemed to leak water from every orifice. Another illuminated street light ahead invaded the darkness; Richard quickened his pace. He listened intently as he skirted the southwest corner of the great building, but the gurgling of water from gutter pipes and the gargoyles faces seemed to roar loudly in his ears. There was a street sign: The Sanctuary.

As his progress left the abbey building behind, the intricacies of its early gothic structure crept into view; lying silhouetted against the low orange ambiance that was now London's electricity-deprived skyline. He crossed over the street, avoiding a number of puddles that filled depressions in the cobbled surface; one, which was closest to the house opposite, reflected the dull glow of an outside door light; a small, solitary bulb inside a large, Edwardian-type lantern. Two heavy stone columns supported a flat-roofed porch beneath which the lantern hung on a metal chain. The light caused the columns to cast broad shadows onto the wet, polished cobblestones. Inside the porch, a polished brass plaque mounted at head-height on the imposing wooden door drew Richard's attention. As he drew nearer, he could see that a crucifix had been deeply etched into its surface and below it lay a few lines of engraved text. For some inexplicable reason he wanted to read the engraving, as if the brief phrase held some directive for him. He checked the area: bleak, cheerless, but totally deserted and stepped briskly beneath the porch, focused on the broad, panelled door. For a few seconds he stared at the crucifix. It had a narrow peripheral band of inlaid black enamel that emphasised decorative contours giving clarity to its import. He was about to read the text when, from behind, from somewhere across the street, someone spoke. *'Pentiti odesso prima che sia troppo tardi. Presto sarai ne le porte dil cello!'*

The words were clear and penetrating, and what they meant Richard did not know, but they sent a haunting chill through his entire body. A shudder ran down his spine. Frozen to the spot, his heart missed a beat. For a few seconds he stood quite still, staring at the plaque, but not seeing the words. Slowly he spun on his heels. There, on the other side of the street, cloaked in shadow was a figure. Its head merged with its shoulders as if a large hood lay draped over both. There was no face, just blackness. Richard stood motionless below the lantern, gaping.

'Repent now, Signor Reece, before it is too late, for soon you will be at the gates of heaven,' the figure said again. The man's words: cold, deathly, resigned, cut deep into Richard's psyche.

From beneath an obscuring cape, the man slowly raised his left arm. He held what looked to be a pistol; it was bulky, with an overly long barrel. Unswervingly, he pointed it directly at Richard and took aim. Richard's eyes widened, he took a tentative step backwards and sideways, a thousand things rushed through his mind: Rachel, he would never see her again. The pistol barrel tracked him. For a few seconds they faced each other staring. Richard took another half-step sideways, trying to gain cover from the stone column, but to no avail, the man sharpened his aim and Richard stared down the barrel.

'Repent my son,' said the man finally and he squeezed the trigger.

The pistol seemed to explode, accompanied by a blinding flash. Instinctively Richard ducked. Something hit the stone façade immediately behind him with a loud thud. He fell to one knee, looking frantically for cover, somewhere to run. A large chunk of sandstone became dislodged and fell to the floor, dust rained on him. The figure raised his right arm; he clasped another pistol. This time there would be no mistake.

Richard was about to take his chance and run for it, but at that moment a pair of bright headlights illuminated the house. He dived to the ground as a police car, its wheels screeching, skidded around the corner at the top of the street. He pulled himself behind the column, chest on the ground. The car accelerated and bore down on them. Within seconds, it screeched to a halt between the two men, not three metres from where Richard cowered. A bright orange beacon rotated on the car's roof, casting orange streaks that swept quickly from corner to corner of the surrounding buildings. Richard's heart pounded, he climbed quickly to his feet and peered tentatively around the column looking for the figure. Knees half-bent, ready to run, he scoured every niche, but there was nothing, no one. The strange intruder had slipped back into the darkness as quietly as he had appeared.

The rear offside door of the police car sprang open. 'Quickly!' someone called from inside. Richard was familiar with the voice. As he moved he kicked something, he looked down at his feet. It was the broken piece of rock from the façade, a piece of trimmed cornerstone with two smooth, perpendicular faces and the other fractured and jagged. By the light of the lantern, Richard could clearly see something embedded in one of the smooth faces; he picked up the fist-sized rock and leapt into the car. Instantly, the driver screeched through an about-turn manoeuvre and roared back up the street, turning right onto Broad Sanctuary without bothering to look in either direction.

Within moments, they entered Parliament Square with a view to driving up Whitehall towards Admiralty Arch. The driver wasted no time in negotiating the square-shaped roundabout and screeched around a left-hand turn into Parliament Street. As he looked back through the rear windscreen, Richard saw the sedan also arrive at the square, but from St Margaret Street, adjacent to the Houses of Parliament. Evidently, having miraculously survived its crashing encounter, it continued in the wrong direction around the central square and then drove off quickly towards Westminster Bridge with a police car in hot pursuit. Several other sets of headlights appeared from different directions, some had flashing blue lights on their roofs and some orange. Richard sat back, only now appreciating his ample and very comfortable seat. He looked across at his driver raising a faint smile. A few seconds later, watching a gaggle of cars congregate and follow them up Whitehall, Richard shook his head disapprovingly.

'The cavalry . . . better late than never I suppose!'

The driver said nothing.

The police car passed beneath two reinforced barriers, before driving through a towering, ornate stone archway and into a large, open, cobbled square; impressively protected on all sides by historic, symmetrical buildings. There were several other cars parked in the square and several heavily armed military security guards watched them closely. A well-dressed man in a mid-length black coat and holding a large, black umbrella opened Richard's door as the car drew to a halt. As Richard climbed out he could see numerous dents in the car's bodywork and the nearside rear corner was stoved in, clearly the result of a collision. Richard looked back at the driver and then at the man, who seemed completely matter-of-fact about the whole thing.

'Lieutenant Commander Reece,' he said obligingly. 'A very good morning to you, Sir, we are expecting you.'

Richard gestured his pleasantries, before turning again

to his driver.

'Thank you. Nice driving,' he offered.

The driver acknowledged Richard's appreciation with a sharp nod, but unsurprisingly said nothing.

'Please follow me, Sir,' requested the man, offering a little space under the umbrella.

Richard tucked himself in beside the man and took what shelter he could. He pulled up his collar again against the cold and wet, pinching it closed with one hand. Well, I made it, he thought. Now . . . what next?

CHAPTER 2

DOUBLE JEOPARDY

Moon base Andromeda - same day
05:41 Lunar Corrected Time

'Commander Race, Sir, Colonel Roper has finished his meeting. He is on his way to the terminal. The commanding officer has asked me to give you the heads up. Your ship is being prepared.'

'Got it, on my way, oh and Saunders give comms a call, let London know, take off in fifteen minutes.'

'Aye aye, Sir.'

The spacecraft Tom Race had parked at Gamma 3 pier the previous day was one of two remaining S7 class vessels, this being the most recent craft to be named *Artemis*; so called after the renowned Constellation Lander of 2016 – the first manned vehicle to land back on the Moon's surface since the Apollo missions of the 1970s. The original *Artemis* had safely delivered and retrieved its five-man crew from the Sea of Serenity region no less than five times, manoeuvring faultlessly on all those occasions with its mother ship, the *Orion*. Those missions had successfully kick-started the whole lunar settlement programme. On 16th July 2019, fifty years to the day after the first manned landing on the surface of the Moon, *Artemis* on its final mission delivered the first of Andromeda's sectional accommodation modules. Now Moon Base Andromeda boasted almost two acres of pressurized real estate, some on two levels and a growing population of almost sixteen hundred permanent personnel.

The *Artemis* Tom flew, loaned from NASA, was a modified prototype model to the phenomenal Delta Class space fighter. Docked on Gamma pier, part of Andromeda's southern space terminal, this ship had had the majority of its flight test electronics removed in favour of a single passenger seat set in tandem to the forward pilot's seat.

Tom knew the S7 well; he had been a test pilot on the type back in the late thirties and had helped develop its successor. He was also more than happy at the controls of a Delta Class, although such opportunities were rare for him these days. With a good deal of the original payload removed, *Artemis* was a particularly agile craft. Half the weight of a configured Delta Class fighter and with a similar propulsion system, it had an incredible turn of speed and enviable manoeuvrability both inside and out of earth's atmosphere. Fortunately, the Moon's present position on its elliptical orbit gave its closest proximity to the earth, and if Tom utilised a sustained high power matter-stream coupling, he could make the transit to Europe in around three hours – substantially faster than any S2 shuttle could.

With Colonel Roper's meeting running late and a request for the next, in London, to commence at precisely 07:00 hours, Tom was already running late.

Tom had borrowed his old office for the day from his successor and quickly cleared the desk. He gently placed a few personal items in the left-hand drawer with a note, and passed his wristwatch over the sensor. The drawer locked and the sensor light turned red. He collected his best uniform jacket and cap from the stand and within minutes was on his way to the VIP terminal. At least *Artemis*'s speed would minimise the delay to London's Cityport, he thought. First, he would stop at operations.

Given permission to use *Artemis*'s matter-stream propulsion system below an eighty-five percent elliopherical orbit would also save a considerable amount of time for Tom, as the alternative was the retrorocket powered standard re-entry profile. Reactive propulsion to discharging a dense stream of nuclear electrons rearwards at atomic speeds could propel the S7 to almost two hundred and eighty lutens in space, equating to seventy three thousand miles an hour. Within the earth's atmosphere, however, materials technology was the limiting factor. Still, even now, almost a decade old, only a few unmanned projectiles could equal *Artemis*'s Mach 20. Nevertheless, if the matter-stream accidentally penetrated either of earth's two Van Allen belts then substantial damage would result, possibly allowing radiated particles from the sun's solar wind to seep into the atmosphere. This was the reason for limiting such propulsion systems to extremely high orbits. For Tom it represented a relaxing of very stringent rules and indicated the importance of the forthcoming meeting; he would have to be very careful.

The Moon base had started life as a series of inflated domes of various sizes, all linked by semi-circular walkways that rested directly onto the Moon's dusty surface. Andromeda 1, now the freight terminal, had formed the first collection of domes, but for several years had been superseded by the more conventionally built Andromeda 2 complex, known simply as Andromeda. Flexible structures held down by arrester cables attached to gas-fired subsurface pegs were obsolete and now all structures had to be resistant to meteoritic and space debris damage. To survive the penetration of an object up to one metre in diameter and still maintain internal atmospheric pressure: that was the requirement. Rigid titanium structures utilising advanced, self-sealing composite materials provided the answer, and with lunar-based fabrication now running at full capacity, Andromeda was growing at an impressive rate.

Unlike Antarctica, which had a similar sized settlement, there were no preservation treaties to protect the Moon. The 2012 Treaty of Antarctica prevented and controlled the exploitation of the continent as it thawed, but on the Moon, it was a free for all. Earth's principal industrial companies had amalgamated decades earlier to form mammoth conglomerates and they had provided the financial resources to fund early colonization whilst governments had watched apathetically. Now it was payback time. Mining, minerals and money, that was the reason man had come to the Moon.

As Tom neared the Operations centre, he stopped to look out through one of the large circular porthole-type windows, the far-reaching panorama, of which looked north towards *Lacus Mortis*, the Lake of Death. The grey-black landscape surrounding Andromeda was beginning to look like a scrapyard, strewn with obsolete machinery, equipment and vehicles: first generation water extraction plants and mining gantries being the most obtrusive. He knew that the cost of breaking and recycling these monoliths was expensive, but eventually something would have to be done, otherwise the Moon would become another waste disposal site: man's recurring legacy. Of considerable interest though, he mused, were the subtle changes he had noticed since his absence. Andromeda's real estate was increasing rapidly and yet industrial activity appeared constant; there were no new mines apparent and none had been reported on his flight brief.

He looked skywards. Colossus, the Chinese built mineral barge was clear to see, but she still only ran the round trip to earth every two weeks. He knew that from space control bulletins, and yet new accommodation was being added at an ever-increasing rate. Tom considered the conundrum for a short while. During his time as Executive Officer of the Shuttle Wing, a position he had only relinquished during the latter part of the previous year, Andromeda's population had increased at a controlled trickle, and that in line with increased industrial output. Why then the proliferation of unoccupied accommodation modules? Why make allowance for additional personnel who inevitably would not have a specific role to perform? Tom pressed his face against the glass and strained to see the Earth high off to his right. There it hung, veiled beneath a congealed blanket of thick swirling cloud; cold, and becoming more so, wet and becoming more so, inevitably hungry.

Again, he gazed across the Moon's landscape: undulating, vast, drab, but sun-drenched. Then he looked up into space, speckled as it was with countless stars and infinite potential. It was quite a sight, despite its familiarity. Perhaps an atmosphere, something humans had always regarded as an absolute necessity for life was becoming a liability. A necessity for evolution, yes, he considered, but surely not for expansion. Perhaps Earth's governments were beginning to look elsewhere for somewhere to call home. He checked his chronometer, it was time to change.

Tom almost filled the doorway in his bulky white spacesuit as the portal slid sideways with a quiet whoosh. He was familiar to most in the operations centre and caused little distraction to the twenty or so personnel who busied themselves at numerous computer terminals. Yules Bremner, the flight control coordinator looked up from his console and waved to Tom, beaming a broad smile, he was clearly pleased to see his former boss again.

'Hey Yules, how is it?' Tom asked, shaking his old friend's hand.

'Fine Sir, yeah, just fine, good to see you back on Andromeda. I hear you're gonna take over from the boss when he retires. I hear early in the New Year . . . Congratulations!'

'Well, it sure looks that way, what with the Enigma programme scuppered. Say, news travels fast around here,' Tom added with a knowing smile. 'Listen Yules, time's pressing. What's the score?'

'Flight plan's been accepted by Euro Control, Sir. Take off on the hour, six minutes from now. Window is plus or minus five minutes, due to the incoming shuttle.'

Tom nodded. 'I'm on it, and who is the duty shuttle driver anyway?'

'It's the rookie, Alec Waymann, and he's right on time, Sir.'

'Good. And the Colonel?'

'He's ahead of you, already on his way to Gamma pier.'

'Okay, better get going then. Apparently, this meeting in

London is going to take some time. God knows what it's about. On completion, I fly the Colonel back to the Cape. I will probably overnight, so don't expect me back for a day or two. Would you let Commander Moseley know, please?'

'Will do, Sir, oh and by the way, it's the Atlantic East-Sector 4 arrival procedure. High speed approved all the way into UK airspace. Use Alpha Alpha code 9191 for defence identification; they will be expecting your call at 08:53 corrected time. Don't forget to enter destination prefix EGVP into the nav-kit. It's the VIP Cityport you're heading for and not the new Orbitalport on the south side of the river. Cityport is in the heart of Westminster, closer to Whitehall, cut down the road time.'

Tom acknowledged the information with a sharp nod and slapped his old friend on the shoulder. 'Thanks Yules,' he replied. 'I'm on it and keep an eye on things for me.'

'Ha ha, yep, I'll do my best, Sir,' said the lanky American, turning back to his console.

Tom arrived at flight dispatch to find Colonel Roper having his suit zipped up and the life support terminals checked for integrity and correct functioning; the cockpit of the *Artemis* was only partially pressurised and so a full spacesuit and helmet was necessary.

'Suit check's okay, Sir,' said the operative. 'You're good to go!'

Colonel Roper acknowledged with a thumbs up and

turned to Tom. 'Damn meeting. Now they're calling themselves the Senate of Lunar Colonisation,' he barked, clearly frustrated. '*I* call it a lot of hot air. We need to make up time, Tom. Admiral Ghent is already in London. I've informed him that we are running late and he will record anything pertinent.'

The Colonel did not enlighten any further, but Tom knew there was trouble brewing. For one thing, the meeting's roll call read like a space administrator's who's who. Something was definitely going down, thought Tom. 'I understand the situation, Colonel,' he replied. 'If we leave right away, we should make London's Cityport by 09:00 hours Greenwich Mean Time.'

Roper took a deep breath. 'Better late than never,' he suggested.

'Guess so, Sir,' Tom responded, slightly perplexed by the remark.

As the three men walked purposefully along the transparent, semi-circular bridge towards the S7, Tom caught sight of Earth again. He stared; Colonel Roper followed his line of vision. Darkened and grey, even a little foreboding, it seemed like another planet when compared to the bright blue and white oasis, that had been impressed into both men's minds over the years.

Climbing the steel steps onto a small platform mounted at the same level as the craft's cockpit, Tom allowed the Colonel to enter and sit down first. The orderly passed two harness straps over his shoulders and the Colonel clipped the other three buckles into the five-point quick-release box. Tom checked them all for security before settling into his own seat. Within seconds, he was pressing buttons, closing the canopy and running the checklist. Knowing Tom of old, the orderly beat a hasty retreat and promptly closed the airlock portal behind him as Tom pushed the retrorocket thrust levers open.

'Andromeda control? This is VIP Access One, requesting take off clearance,' Tom called over the radio as his craft began to rise.

'Access One, you are clear for take off. Vector 315 degrees and clear the southern corridor before matter-stream initiation. Read back?' came the reply.

'Vector 315 degrees, southern corridor,' Tom repeated, scanning his instruments. Thrust control, oxygen, pressurisation and fuel all in the green he advanced the levers into the full power position.

Artemis rose vertically amid a cloud of recirculating Moon dust and then she pointed skywards and accelerated, it was 06:02 LCT.

CHAPTER 3

THE LAW AND THE LIGHT

After a short walk, Richard and the butler-like man, whose name Richard had learned was Grenville – just Grenville – entered a building on the west side of the quadrangle through a large, six-panelled wooden door. It was obviously original, but heavily modified internally by a similarly dark-green painted steel reinforcing frame.

Inside, Richard felt the comfort of the ante-room's warm, dry interior. The contrast could not have been more apparent and more welcome. Clearly, selected military establishments and government buildings were exempt from the current power rationing quotas and a building of this size would be very thirsty indeed, he thought. Richard sucked the sweet, clean, conditioned air into his lungs through his nose, almost grateful for the opportunity; there was no musty environmental backlash in this hallowed naval citadel. He unbuttoned the heavy collar of his overcoat and ventilated his neck by pulling the lapels open, while two armed security guards watched suspiciously. Dressed in black overalls, laced, black leather calf-boots and *Kevlar* flak-jackets, they loitered threateningly. Each wore a burgeoning multi-pouched canvas belt from which, in addition to other anti-personnel munitions, hung two Mk 19 stun-grenades. Richard offered a light-hearted, 'good morning'. Neither spoke. Bit of a habit around here, he reflected.

Richard followed Grenville into a small foyer. This was where the deep-blue, thick-piled carpet started. They took a sharp left turn into a long, wide corridor that seemed to go on forever. Richard looked behind, the carpet runner stretched out in both directions; like standing between two giant mirrors that created recurring reflections into infinity. He clumsily tripped on one of the intricately moulded, brass carpet-stays that protruded five centimetres or so across the lush velvety material.

'Mind your step, Sir,' advised the man unnecessarily.

They walked for another fifty metres, past ornate period furniture and grand wall-hung paintings; most housed within oversized gilt frames. The paintings depicted proud naval ships of bygone eras; others were of famous, historic sea battles. Richard recognised one, the famous scene from the battle of Trafalgar, painted by Nicholas Pocock. It was dated 1805. He was familiar with that scene: the closing stages of the great battle, being part of his education; a similar one hung on the quarterdeck at the Britannia Royal Naval College. This one must be the original, he thought, as he walked past, almost mesmerized.

By now, Richard knew that he had entered the architecturally significant Old Admiralty building, albeit by an insignificant rear entrance. Suddenly Grenville stopped; they were adjacent to a pair of tall, Edwardian, elegantly decorated, panelled doors. Immaculately finished in opaque white gloss and hand-painted matt gold paint, the doors were complemented by large, round, polished brass handles. Each handle distorted their reflection as they paused for a few moments outside.

'Wait here if you will, Sir,' requested Grenville.

He knocked twice and disappeared inside, closing the right-hand door behind him. Richard waited a little apprehensively. He felt scruffy, out of place. He rubbed his two-day-old stubble, wishing that he had at least shaved the previous day. Two or three minutes later, the same door partially opened.

'Please come in,' Grenville, said speaking from behind the door.

Richard almost had to squeeze in. He opened his coat and turned down his collar.

'Thank you,' he replied, with a courteous nod.

Inside, it was apparent that the impressive room, with its far wall an expanse of glass, had been orientated to capitalise on an early morning sunrise; much as the

Captain's quarters would, on a proud galleon sailing west towards the new world. With towering leaded panels and wide sash windows, it should have been flooded with light. Instead, a dreary, dismal outlook muted the room's ambiance. The lush blue carpet had stopped outside the large doors; exposing a wooden floor composed of small rectangular dark-oak blocks. The whole area displayed that deep, almost opaque lustre that only ten thousand polishes over some three hundred years can produce. In the centre of the room was a period boardroom table, no less than ten metres long and around which sat more than a dozen people. On the far side of the table, mid-way, a military officer stood up, his uniform that of a British Rear Admiral.

'Lieutenant Commander Reece,' he said in a refined English accent, 'my name is Admiral Hughes, assistant to the Chief of Staff. Please join us, you're very welcome and we much appreciate your time.'

Really, Richard thought, as if I had an option! Feeling a little awkward, Richard walked around the long table, removing his coat on the way. An orderly attentively relieved him of it; scurrying to hang it on a traditional wooden stand at the far end of the room. Richard was beckoned to sit down on a vacant chair next to the Admiral.

'You are very welcome, Sir,' Richard replied nonchalantly, trying not to grimace. 'I apologise for my attire, I wasn't briefed correctly.'

'We are all aware of the situation, Lieutenant

Commander Reece. A degree of secrecy was necessary considering the nature of our discussions this morning. We understand that you encountered a little trouble on the way?'

'You could say that, Sir,' Richard nodded.

'Not entirely unexpected, I have to say,' replied the Admiral with a concerned frown. 'Although we are a little surprised that it was so blatant. I trust our transport arrangements were comfortable.'

'Indeed, Sir, I felt like royalty,' replied Richard with a wry smile.

There was a murmur of stifled laughs around the table.

'Yes . . . quite.'

Richard glanced around the table, politely acknowledging the gathering that he had joined. All were impeccably dressed and Richard counted four other men wearing military uniforms; one, a completely grey, gaunt looking officer, wore that of an American Admiral. An impressive array of service ribbons adorned his jacket. Richard recognised many others, the role call read like a meeting of the cabinet. Interestingly there were only three women present; one, who sat opposite, caught his eye. Twenty something, she had shiny, shoulder length, auburn hair and a pretty face, complimented by a pale, porcelain-clear complexion. She typed furiously on the ceramic touch-pad of her laptop. From behind, there was no visible image on the thin, clear glass lid and through it

Richard could see the identity badge that was pinned to her lapel: Laura Bellingham CSHA. Civil Service, Home Affairs, he concluded.

To Richard's left, at the end of the table, sat an athletic looking man in his late forties. A little grey hair around his temples complemented his professional appearance and aura.

'Now that you are here in person, may I call you Richard?' this man enquired.

Richard recognised the voice immediately; it was Peter Rothschild.

'Delighted.'

'Good, then I'll begin by introducing my learned colleagues around the table. That will also give you an insight into the nature of our business today.'

Peter Rothschild gestured to his left. The first man wore a smart pinstriped blue suit, a white shirt and a navy blue tie. He was balding; the little hair he did have was grey and groomed backwards over his ears. Perhaps in his late fifties, Richard speculated.

'This is Doctor Raymond Martin. You will recognise him of course, as the Secretary for Home Affairs. Doctor Martin is also a member of the Prime Minister's Cabinet, as is Sir Gerald Seymour, Secretary of Defence and William Bryant, Energy Secretary.'

Richard acknowledged all three men with a polite nod.

'Next is Miss Bellingham, PA to the Home Affairs Secretary.'

Laura Bellingham looked up momentarily; she smiled faintly and then continued with her work.

'Then we have Professor Nieve,' continued Peter Rothschild. 'Eminent physicist and senior scientist for the Enigma project, I know that he has some specific questions for you a little later.'

Mildly amused by the Professor's unruly mop of white hair, the thin faced man looked out of place in his dark, old-fashioned suit, its style akin to the 1920s. His pale pink shirt was partnered with the hastily constructed 'double Windsor' knot of his dark blue neck tie, which was misaligned, as if he had left somewhere in a hurry. Richard could imagine him wearing a white coat and a monocle and carrying a precariously balanced pile of books in both hands.

'Morning, Sir,' he offered respectfully.

'Morning my boy. I am very pleased indeed to meet the man who defied not only my calculations, but also the laws of physics?'

'You mean the Enigma thing, Sir?' Richard enquired hesitantly.

'Indeed I do!'

'To the Professor's left is Major Theo Hurn, Operations Officer for space station Spartacus. I know that you two have already met.'

'Yes Sir,' concurred Richard. 'Morning Major, a long way from home?'

'Duty calls,' replied the Major, his American accent

having a southern drawl. 'But it is good to be back for a few days.'

'Good to see you,' agreed Richard, smiling.

'To Major Hurn's left is Captain Randle Myers of the United States Navy, he is personal assistant to Admiral Ghent and of course the Admiral himself. Admiral Ghent, as I am sure you are aware Richard, is the United States Secretary of State for Energy.'

There was no mistaking Admiral Ghent; next in line and sitting at the head of the table. The three men courteously acknowledged each other, Admiral Ghent's expression appearing less than friendly.

'The two empty chairs are for Colonel Roper, Operations Coordinating Officer for the Enigma project and Base Commander Cape Canaveral and Commander Tom Race, Enigma's Commanding Officer. They are flying in from Andromeda and will join us as soon as possible. To your right, Richard, is Abbey Hennessy, Senior Field Officer controller MI9.'

Richard looked at the woman; the gap between them was little more than a metre. She was in her mid-fifties. Her high cheekbones, porcelain skin and immaculate makeup made her appear a little intimidating and she was a definite power-dresser. Their eyes met for a few seconds, but she offered little emotion. Indeed, Richard sensed a controlled, contrived body language, making an accurate or reliable 'first impression' impossible. Richard sensed that his deduction was mutually felt.

'If you agree with our proposition Richard, Abbey will become your direct link, not only with MI9, but also the British government.'

On hearing that, Richard sat up in his seat. Pointlessly, and a little nervously, he adjusted the cuffs of his sweater. Abbey Hennessy had presence and, it appeared, a good deal of experience. Her expression was cold, almost clinical, but there *was* some warmth in her eyes, Richard thought. She was good looking in a way, with groomed, bleached fair hair, and as he had already noticed, she was immaculately made-up. Wearing a sharp, dark-blue, two-piece designer suit and a pristine, synthetically grown yellow carnation in her right buttonhole, Richard concluded that it would be risky to mess with her.

'Next to Admiral Hughes is the Right Reverend Charles Rawlinson, Doctor of Theology. He is an authority on religious history and the government's adviser on religious matters.'

Richard leaned forward to look past Admiral Hughes.

'A great pleasure, Sir,' he ventured.

'How do you do, Commander Reece?'

The Reverend Rawlinson wore a black suit and traditional white clerical collar, and was a little 'past it' for such a position, Richard thought, being in his late seventies if he was a day. With a full head of grey, neatly trimmed hair and a calm, experienced face, at least he appeared to be a sympathetic type; but all the same, an unlikely ally.

'Finally, may I present Professor Ahmed Mubarakar,

Secretary General of the Supreme Council of Antiquities and Curator of the Cairo National Museum and Great Museum of Luxor. Professor Mubarakar has been most helpful over the last few weeks with essential research and is an internationally acclaimed expert in Egyptology. He has kindly agreed to lend us his full support and we are delighted to welcome him to this meeting.'

Professor Mubarakar reminded Richard of an Arabic 'Albert Einstein', but with deeply tanned and weathered skin; earned no doubt, from years of outdoor fieldwork and archaeological study. He also looked as if he was in his seventies.

'I'm delighted to meet you, Sir,' said Richard enthusiastically. 'I have studied some of your instructional texts, by way of a correspondence course I completed earlier this year.'

'Is that so?' replied the Professor, somewhat surprised. His English, although perfect, had a guttural rasp.

'So, ladies and gentlemen,' concluded Peter Rothschild, 'down to business. Richard, we have a very, very, important brief for you to listen to and it is not, incidentally, all for your benefit. When we have concluded, Admiral Ghent will report immediately to President Franklin and Mr William Bryant will also leave immediately for Downing Street. Although you are not currently cleared to ESSA Security Level 5 and obviously, you do not hold Cabinet Classified status, MI9 and the Prime Minister for that matter, have agreed for you to be party to the information that we will discuss today; but be aware, this briefing *is* categorised Highly Restricted Level 5. Most of us in the department feel you deserve this privilege; following your rather impressive exploits in retrieving the U-Semini case last year.'

Richard was surprised. 'But it was empty, Sir, and I'm sure I do not need to remind you that I have court-martial proceedings pending.'

'The U-Semini device was, indeed, empty Richard, but it was of no consequence. We believed your intentions to be, in the most part, honourable and that turned out to be the case. We also had back-up options in place to secure the consignment should they have been otherwise and there are other reasons.'

Richard looked confused. 'So why the court-martial and worse, relieving me of my duties on Mars?' he enquired indignantly.

'For reasons you know only too well. When the alien flight manual was discovered in your room on Osiris base, Commander Miko had no other choice but to press charges. You contravened orders, Richard, no excuses. In addition, the head of security on Osiris, Major Gregory Searle, took it upon himself to administer the charges. He ensured that all documents and proceedings were followed to the letter. Commander Miko's hands, reluctant as he was, were tied.'

Richard nodded in agreement. 'Greg Searle . . . bane of my life.'

'Apparently, it was Major Searle who authorised the search of your room; even though Commander Miko saw no necessity. Searle cited Article 4 of the 'personnel missing in action' amendment, whilst you were in transit to *Spartacus*. Only Commander Miko and his operations team knew of your link up with the Enigma. To be honest Richard, even Professor Nieve, after we had briefed him, thought your chances of survival miniscule. To most therefore, you were already dead. Again, Commander Miko's hands were tied. The Commander informed us subsequently that there was a good deal of ill feeling between you and Searle, who was highly suspicious of your actions at that time.'

'I had no intention of keeping the flight manual hidden,' Richard protested. 'My actions may have contravened base orders, retrieving the manual without authorisation, but I was excited by the discovery . . . I just wanted to do some research on it myself, before it was spirited away by the authorities to some obscure establishment here on earth; never to be seen or heard of again! After all, it hasn't gone down too well with the church has it? And that's a good enough reason for it to be *filed under lost*?'

Charles Rawlinson leaned forward to look at Richard. He was perplexed. 'I have spoken at length to the clergy and many other senior officials; the church has no animosity towards you for discovering this amazing artefact, Lieutenant Commander Reece, or any issues with this flight manual itself,' he stated matter of factly.

Peter Rothschild nodded in agreement. 'We are perfectly prepared to accept your argument Richard, nevertheless, had the authorities known of your discovery from the outset, the disclosures and subsequent consequences could have been handled rather more discretely. As it is, a great deal of national embarrassment still plagues the Prime Minister, and several governments are still dousing the fires of Christian discontent. Even now the press still fan this contentious debate.'

Professor Mubarakar interrupted. 'You know, I can sympathise with Lieutenant Commander Reece's point of view. How many priceless antiquities were removed from my country by imperial powers during the eighteenth, nineteenth and twentieth centuries? Most, never to be seen or heard of again; let alone returned to their rightful homes; and this regardless of their religious significance. Although, it is true to say that some progress has been achieved over the last few decades. So many of these artefacts and their secrets are lost in the eternity of national and private museums and archives throughout the world . . . are they not?'

There was a stunned silence; Richard broke it apologetically, as much to disarm the question as to avoid further ramifications. 'I agree,' he said soberly. 'In hindsight it was not very responsible of me. I apologise for that.'

Rothschild nodded. 'We accept your apology, Richard. Having said that, it is not strictly necessary, as there *were* favourable repercussions to your actions. Firstly, we

65

understand that you have become somewhat of an expert in the study of ancient pictographs and secondly, apparently your innate ability to decipher this alien text, so called, enabled your rendezvous with the commander of the Enigma and eventually to retrieve the first consignment of crystals.'

Now Richard really was confused. He probed again. 'But how was that possible Peter? The U-Semini case I retrieved was empty.'

Peter Rothschild looked a little embarrassed himself with this question. Richard could see that he was withholding something - a pertinent, perhaps vital, piece of information. He leant towards Rothschild, opening his palms, coaxing the answer.

'As I said earlier, Richard, despite Commander Miko's unflinching trust in your abilities and intentions, we took additional precautions to protect our interests in the Kalahari crystals and ensure, as far as was possible, their safe retrieval. The crystals were duly distributed to the allocated power stations and the rest, as they say, is history. We need not concern ourselves further with this matter.'

Richard leaned back in his chair. He went to speak, but instead said nothing; his perplexed, highly suspicious expression plain to see. It was clear to him now that the crystals *were* onboard the *Endeavour* when he touched down at Cape Canaveral. The significance of his arrival on Earth suddenly became apparent. He already knew that no other ship had landed at any of the three space terminals between his arrival and the four crystal-powered reactors being commissioned a few days later. Rothschild had confirmed it then, unequivocally; if the U-Semini case that he delivered to General Buchanan was indeed empty, someone had affected a swap . . . but who?

Richard persisted; he could not contain himself. 'I don't understand, kindly explain. Why go to the trouble of delivering an empty case to General Buchanan?'

Rothschild could see where this conversation and Richard's suspicions were leading; he glanced over to Admiral Ghent for a brief moment. The admiral gestured with a barely perceptible nod. Rothschild continued.

'General Buchanan betrayed his country, Richard', he said solemnly. 'We only found out his intentions a few hours before you departed Space Station Spartacus, bound for Andromeda's freight terminal. A few days earlier, he had made a single, absent minded error; a simple, but costly mistake. He made a hasty call to a contact in Brazil, but placed the call on a secure mobile videocom whilst he was in his office in the Pentagon. As a matter of routine security, a certain number of internal electromagnetic transmissions per day are selected at random and monitored. By chance, his call was intercepted and it was found to be coded using the advanced, non-military *Septra* format. That aroused suspicion. The CIA already had some uncorroborated evidence on the General, concerning illicit business dealings in South America, but because of his status, they were never followed up. It took several hours and our top brains to decipher that duplex, binary-numeric code and listen to the conversation. The call had been placed to an office in the Headquarters of Epsilon Rio, the industrial conglomerate. To cut a long story short, subsequent probing and follow-up investigations by the CIA's espionage department and using the other leads, revealed an offshore bank account. Using Interpol's 'open-world' finance initiative and database, the account was traced through a third party to the general himself. A cash deposit, equivalent to forty million world dollars had recently been made.'

Admiral Ghent interrupted; his American accent had a slight southern drawl. 'The United States government is deeply embarrassed over this affair. General Buchanan had an exemplary career. He had given thirty-two years of service to his country, including active duties and a commendation in the third Middle East conflict. Additionally, he was President's Level security-cleared and had been for several years. White House circles held him in high esteem. However, it seems with impending retirement from the Army and no political agenda, the lure of a multi-million dollar pay off was just too much to resist; I hope for his sake it was the money and not something more sinister. Nevertheless, those of us who knew him personally and remember his contributions have supported him to some extent. By that, I mean he's not in the slammer; but his career is over. There are many charities presently benefiting from Epsilon Rio's very generous, but for the best part, anonymous donation.'

Richard nodded, appreciating the Admiral's honesty. 'So why allow him to accept the delivery?'

'We wanted to find out for sure who was behind the deal, confirm the paymaster and who the mole in the Pentagon was. So we decided to keep up the charade. After he left Canaveral with that empty case, we tracked him to his rendezvous. We now know Epsilon Rio is the perpetrator, but they are a powerful multi-national, one of the world's largest, with strong ties to European based Spheron and Tongsei Heavy Industries of Shanghai. Together those three pretty much wrap up the planet's steel, aluminium and copper output. Tongsei, you may recall provided the funds and the materials for Colossus, the interplanetary mineral barge. Epsilon Rio paid a lot of money and got nothing in return; not even Buchanan. He has twenty-four hour armed protection and a new identity; sadly, I still worry for him. Evidence we have gathered confirms our suspicions of an illegal tri-conglomerate with unprecedented global market control and massive financial reserves. We already know that Spheron was behind the blatant encounter this morning. That means they are getting desperate. They want the remaining crystals. Why? Global domination of electricity generation and supply, plain and simple; the world needs it; they control it! To make matters worse, there is a fourth, potential member. De Reus, the African mineral and diamond conglomerate may also be involved.' Admiral Ghent, devoid of emotion, looked back at Peter

Rothschild.

Richard sat motionless for a few seconds; he wanted answers. He looked Admiral Ghent in the eye briefly and then focused his attention on Rothschild. 'Which encounter?' he asked.

'What do you mean, Richard?' Rothschild replied.

Richard pulled something from his trouser pocket; he rubbed it slowly between his thumb and forefinger and then rolled it across the table towards Rothschild.

'What the hell is that?' Seymour asked.

All eyes tracked the small, grey, metal ball as it rolled towards Rothschild clattering across the wooden surface, but none more so than those of Admiral Hughes. Indeed, his eyes progressively widened until, in a panicky flurry, he stood up, unbuttoned his jacket and pulled it off. 'Grenville!' he called aloud, throwing his jacket over the ball-bearing like object and gathering it up amongst ample folds of material. Grenville's head appeared around the door.

'Quickly man, a bucket of water!' ordered the Admiral.

Richard stood up bemused as Admiral Hughes hastily walked around the table towards the doors. At that moment, Grenville appeared carrying a fire bucket full of water. The Admiral carefully shook out the object from his bundled jacket and it fell into the water with a plop.

'What the hell's going on?' Gerald Seymour asked again.

There was mild confusion as the Admiral rolled up the

sleeves of his white shirt. 'Grenville,' he asked. 'Do you have a penknife?'

'Yes Sir, of course.'

'Quickly, give it to me.'

It was a red coloured army knife. Admiral Hughes selected the small, pointed blade and plunged his hands into the water. For a few moments he manoeuvred the metal ball, turning it in his fingers and studying it closely. Then, evidently finding what he was looking for, he gently scraped away a soft plug and pushed the pointed blade into the centre of the object.

'There,' he said eventually. 'It's safe. Grenville, a towel if you please.'

Grenville scurried off. Richard was totally bewildered, as was everyone else at the table. Admiral Hughes retrieved the object from beneath the water, held it a few centimetres above the surface and rolled it in his fingers until a thick, black liquid ran out from a small hole. 'Gunpowder!' he explained.

Richard grimaced and Grenville appeared. The Admiral dried his hands, replaced his jacket and handed the ball – which was approximately fifteen millimetres in diameter – to Rothschild as he walked to his chair.

Sitting down amidst a bemused mumbling, Admiral Hughes demanded, 'where, on earth, did you get that museum piece and *why* are you carrying it?'

'Someone tried to shoot me . . . with a bloody flintlock!'

'When?'

'This morning, an hour ago, by Westminster Abbey. Couldn't see who.'

'The same people who were chasing you?'

'No! No way! This was different. He was on his own. The others had automatic weapons and accessories that were, shall we say, rather more contemporary. *He* moved in the shadows, experienced, clinical even. He had me in his sights; almost got me too. If it wasn't for . . . something about him though, can't put my finger on it.'

'Excuse me, I am sorry. Is there anything else, Sir?' Grenville asked politely, feeling that he should not be party to the conversation.

'May I see it, please?' asked the Reverend Rawlinson.

'Grenville, please give this to the Reverend, then you may go,' answered Rothschild.

'Admiral . . . goddamn it, what are you looking at?' pressed Admiral Ghent.

'It's an incendiary shot, naval origin, first seen in the early seventeenth century. The French devised them initially, for setting fire to rigging, the canvas sails and hemp ropes of the old galleons, during naval engagements. Inside were set two tiny flints; an ingenious mechanism for the time, and the hole plugged with a mixture of hard wax and lead filings. On impact, the flints sparked and set off the gunpowder, quite effective too, when they worked. This really is intriguing. Considering its renowned unreliability, this device was used extensively for almost two centuries.

Horatio Nelson, you know, was killed by a similar example and that one *is* a museum piece; an opportunistic shot by a French sniper on a nearby ship. This shot would have killed too, there is no doubt about that, but the device is primarily designed to burn!'

'Really, but where is this getting us?' asked William Bryant impatiently.

'There is an inscription on it,' interjected the Reverend Rawlinson, holding up the ball to the light and rotating it carefully. 'Something in Latin, I think. Ah, yes . . . *Anno Domini 1665* . . . AD., 1665, the year of manufacture I expect. Anything else you can tell us, my boy?'

'It was a man and he spoke Italian, Reverend. At least I presume it was Italian. When he repeated himself in English, he called me Signor Reece.'

'Interesting, and what did he say?'

'He said: repent, before it is too late, for soon you will be at the gates of heaven. Gave me the creeps.'

Rawlinson looked across the table at Rothschild and his expression changed, as if a dark shadow had descended upon him. 'That is what was said to heretics when they were burned at the stake in medieval times,' he uttered starkly.

There was silence.

'As if we haven't got enough trouble,' commented Admiral Hughes. 'Now this!'

Rawlinson studied the object again. 'There is also the faint inscription of a flower petal, but it is barely

73

discernable,' he continued. He looked more closely at it and for several seconds, using his spectacles as a makeshift magnifying glass and then he looked around the table, before becoming a little dismissive. 'There may be repercussions to this, religious connotations that I do not understand, more likely though it is the work of some disgruntled fanatic.' He looked sternly at Richard. 'Undoubtedly, your life is at risk, my boy; you should exercise caution. I know someone who may be able to shed some light on this disturbing episode, a Cambridge based historian. May I keep this?' he asked Rothschild.

Rothschild nodded. 'Yes of course, Reverend,' he replied looking at Admiral Hughes, who concurred with a similar gesture. 'Now, we must get on.'

Richard's concern grew. 'So why am I here, Peter? My background has no relevance.'

'That's where you are wrong Richard, your recent experience has specific relevance and we would like to use it. We would like your cooperation and in return, offer you a deal.'

The room fell silent; Richard sat back in his chair expectantly. Peter Rothschild looked across at Admiral Hughes for permission to continue. Hughes nodded.

'Peter,' he said slowly, 'we have a situation of the utmost concern to the international community, indeed, concern will imminently become desperation unless we can stabilise matters. We need your help. This is the brief.'

Laura Bellingham pressed a key on her laptop and an image appeared on the back of the glass screen.

'This is, or was, Professor Victor Simpson-Carter,' Rothschild continued, 'Professor of Antiquities, Egyptology and a Scholar of Theology. This photograph was taken sixty years ago on 29th March 1989.'

The slightly faded colour photograph of a man in his sixties was then replaced on the screen by another image, of much higher clarity. Evidently, the same man, his face was now pallid and drawn. He appeared to be sleeping.

'This is the same man. This image was taken four days ago in a private clinic in Arizona, USA.'

Richard's eyes widened as he stared; he was fixated; there was no appreciable ageing.

'Are you familiar with the work of the late Professor, Richard?'

'Vaguely, I suppose,' answered Richard, a little bemused. 'As a matter of fact I read a short paper of his a few months ago. Related to a previous namesake, of equal acclaim, discovered some of the most famous tombs in the Valley of the Kings last century, if I recall.'

'Correct. In February 1989, Professor Simpson-Carter returned to England after several years of solitary work in southern Egypt, the Sudan, Eritrea and Ethiopia. He was seriously ill and was reluctantly forced to seek medical attention. For the majority of his final year he had encamped at *Wadi Biban el Moluk*, a remote location on the West bank of the River Nile; translated from Arabic, this means, *The Valley of the Gates of the Kings*. The nearest city being Luxor, this location is more commonly referred to as simply, *The Valley of the Kings*. His return was premature but also necessary: in order, apparently, to correlate a document of some significance. A doctor in Luxor had reliably informed him that he had contracted a mutant bacterial pathogen, exclusively found in the upper reaches of the Blue Nile. By the time he was diagnosed, the pathogen had destroyed one of his kidneys and ninety percent of his liver. He must have been in excruciating pain for some time; yet his work kept him in this isolated region, devoid of suitable medical attention. Subsequently, in England, a lack of response to treatment reduced a year's life expectancy to barely a month. He began work immediately, day and night, on this scientific paper of considerable importance. His colleagues said at the time that the paper related to the origins of mankind; detailed hard evidence and would have explosive repercussions. Others said that it was the ranting of a delirious old man, who had spent too long in the sun and sand. Either way, the document was only partially complete when he fell into a septicaemia-induced coma. His work, needless to say was coded. Very limited success was achieved deciphering the text, despite a great deal of effort at the time; even now, next to no progress has been made. What we have learnt however, is that the paper documents the existence of an ancient civilisation, one that existed well before the First Egyptian Dynasty. Simpson-Carter also wrote of the existence of a protective casket; a portable chamber containing the last relic of a previous age; an indelible link to man's past; relating directly to the colonisation of planet earth. He wrote of the casket being protected by two angels with outstretched wings. Richard, earlier this year, if you recall, you described deciphered text from the alien flight log written by an Admiral Dirkot Urket. I quote. *Of the stone that lit Eridu, two fragments were redeemed. One used thereafter to light Babylon, its great gardens a millennium to keep homage to those the lost. The other protected by a sacred casket, looked upon by angels until graced by understanding.* This coincidence is far too great; this referral to a seemingly identical casket we think is highly significant. Professor Simpson-Carter was also a theologian. Evidence he found spoke of this casket holding unimaginable power; power from previous times. He speculated that this casket gradually acquired religious significance; it was revered; then, over hundreds, even thousands of years, the nature of its contents became blurred, even forgotten. By that time, the casket had evolved into a sacred artefact. Text discovered during the translation of the Dead Sea Scrolls, which pre-date the Old Testament, confirm the existence of a great power, given by God and placed in an Ark where it lay protected and worshipped. Indeed, centuries old, religious paintings often depict a blinding white light emanating from this casket or Ark. Further, we believe Simpson-Carter had discovered evidence, earlier in his career, that confirmed his theory beyond reasonable doubt. Fundamentally, he believed that the Egyptian civilisation and, more pertinently, the great structures on the Giza Plateau near Cairo are considerably older than have been thought and recorded over the last two centuries. Historical thinking had the Great Pyramid built around two thousand six hundred years BC for the Fourth Dynasty King Khufu.'

Professor Mubarakar nodded his agreement, 'yes, this is current thinking,' he concurred.

'Simpson-Carter however, found evidence to suggest that this pyramid, the Sphinx and other associated structures at Giza are at least another two thousand and four hundred years older than that; perhaps around five thousand years BC; perhaps more.

There was an intake of breath around the table. Richard was rather less impressed.

'OK! So, what's the relevance, where are you going with this?'

'From what we understand from your discovery on Mars - the spaceship flight log, for instance - there could be a great deal of relevance.'

The Reverend Rawlinson interrupted. 'Of course, that is pure speculation, Peter. The Church will dispute any facts concluded from your observations!'

'Yes, it is at the moment,' replied Rothschild defensively, but dating the flight log has now been achieved and we think that will settle matters unequivocally.'

Richard felt a little behind the times in this conversation.

'Settle what, Peter, if I may ask?'

'As you are aware Richard, the flight log contained a large number of stellar projections . . .'

'Yes, of course I'm aware, I studied them! Navigation charts, maps of this and other galaxies; some indicating where the extra terrestrials came from . . . Sirius!'

'Well, we don't know *that* for sure yet!'

'Well, I know Peter, I know exactly what these charts show and I have a feeling that you do, too!'

Peter Rothschild looked stunned for a few moments. 'Yes, well, anyway, some of the projections have been identified. They detail stars and galaxies that our astronomers are familiar with; their positions in space having been frozen if you like, at the precise time the projections were taken. By observation, our people know the rate of movement of these stars, by that I mean their expansion rate, the 'big bang' theory and all that. Therefore, our scientists have been able to calculate, by comparing the relative positions of these stars, *when* the projections were originally taken. The calculations indicate the year 5082 BC, August of that year to be precise; our people say it's accurate down to a week; that is almost exactly the same period in history that Simpson-Carter theorised the building of the Great Pyramid of Khufu.'

'Surely that's coincidental?' insisted the Reverend.

Richard went to speak, to air his thoughts, but changed his mind.

Peter Rothschild continued. 'NASA thinks that these

navigation projections would have been retaken, or at least updated, just prior to the crashed spaceship departing earth, bound for who knows where, and are therefore highly reliable. After all, as NASA pointed out, it is what they themselves do: to give the most up to date and accurate information to the navigation computers of its shuttles, just before their launch. Obviously, for whatever reason, that ship only got as far as Mars. Nonetheless, one of the options being seriously considered at the moment is that these extra terrestrials actually colonised earth some while before 5082 BC and that they were re-launching this ship, for some reason – perhaps to find help – after a considerable period. The text does appear to confirm this fact. There are also some theories coming out of the woodwork that suggest that the Sphinx and the oldest, but smaller 'step' pyramid at Saqqara are, in fact, twelve thousand years old; the legend of Atlantis too, and the eastern Mediterranean around the same period!'

Suddenly the full impact of his discovery on the Christian church became clear to Richard. If concrete evidence showed that there was no 'divine' creation; but that modern man had been seeded from elsewhere in the universe; to some, it would be a hard pill to swallow. Further, to the vehement disagreement of the more radical denominations of the Church, the science of evolution had already gone too far; the early hominoids, Neanderthals, fossil evidence, that could not be avoided or disputed; but this, this was something else!

Rothschild continued. 'We know that Simpson-Carter spent some time in Palestine immediately after the Second World War. The period was between 10th February 1949 and October 1952, returning for a few months in 1956. Incidentally, after that last visit he travelled immediately to Cairo, where he again spent several preoccupied weeks. Again, from his journal, much of this period was spent in the Cairo Museum. We also know from letters to his family that the majority of the time spent in Palestine was by invitation; working in the Dead Sea area. Although his letters do not mention a specific location, journal entries and other sources corroborate his membership of a team of archaeologists and scholars working at Qumran, an area close to the northwestern Dead Sea waterline. Of course, the area now is just an empty basin; the Dead Sea itself dried up some years ago; as a result of the global temperature rising.'

'*Was* an empty basin, Mr Rothschild,' commented Professor Mubarakar, smiling. 'Ten months of continuous rain has had a very rejuvenating effect!'

'Thank you, Professor, I stand corrected. The team of specialists that Simpson-Carter joined were originally dispatched to Qumran during the last months of the British mandate in Palestine, the summer of 1947, following the news of an extraordinary discovery. Early in 1949, the cave where the scrolls lay hidden was identified. Simpson-Carter was invited, in order to help supervise and document the retrieval of these so-called Dead Sea

Scrolls. Do you know of the Dead Sea Scrolls, Richard?'

'I know that they were regarded as the most spectacular biblical find of that era. A number of caves, eleven I recall, the first of which was discovered by a young Bedouin shepherd in 1947. The scrolls were fragmented, written on leather and in Hebrew for the most part; they detailed books of the Old Testament, but a thousand years older than any previously known copies. Thought to represent the library of an ascetic religious sect, they were concealed when their settlement was overrun by the Roman army in AD 68.'

'Impressive, you are remarkably well informed, Richard,' congratulated Rothschild. 'Now for the interesting part. In 1989, after Simpson-Carter had clinically died, most of his work, documents, papers, computer files, old Floppies and CDs - you remember those things - were catalogued and archived. As I previously mentioned, his last work was of the utmost importance and something he tried to complete with apparent unflinching urgency and dedication, this against strict medical advice and inevitably to the detriment of his health. One of his grandchildren, questioned during our follow-up work, told us that during visits to his home early in February 1989, Simpson-Carter would only rarely surface from his study, even though he knew he only had weeks to live. She remembers him as a tired, extremely thin man, consumed - and these are her words not mine - by a passion to document humanity's greatest secret. This passion, much to the dismay of his wife and daughter, hampered, perhaps prevented, effective medical treatment. The rest we know.

Now, a few weeks ago, our people retrieved Carter's work from the archives of the British Museum and we have been going through it with a fine tooth comb. Amazingly, we still cannot decipher his final paper, or, for that matter, divulge anything of the 'secret', as he called it. Although we do know that his code utilised, at least in part, Egyptian hieroglyphs and that the title page was headed *The Unholy Secret*. Something we found in his notes dated October 1949 and in a later entry in November 1956 however may be significant. Firstly, a discovery he made in Palestine in 1952: a piece of ancient parchment on which writings in a hitherto unknown language were scribed. Secondly, a black and white photograph taken in 1956 of similar writings, this time on the wall of the Queen's Chamber inside the Great Pyramid of Khufu. Simpson-Carter made note of the fact that on the reverse side of the parchment the writings seemed to be duplicated in two other languages: firstly Aramaic; one of the oldest Semitic languages, it was spoken widely throughout the Middle East region in ancient times and particularly in Syria; secondly, Attic Greek. Aramaic was spoken throughout the region as a language of commerce and trade. Interestingly, Carter notes, that after subjugation by a succession of empires, the Israelites adopted this language. Attic Greek was the language of the ancient Athenians, the original Greek; used, undiluted over the centuries, by the Greek aristocracy and by its great writers, mathematicians and astronomers. Some scholars have speculated that it was also the language of Atlantis. Even Admiral Urket in his diary entry, adds weight to this fact.'

That remark raised a good many eyebrows around the table. Richard thought of Admiral Urket's diary entry in the flight log - he knew it by heart: The Sapiens of the north in Eridu, of the south in Atlantis!

Peter Rothschild went on. 'Of the main text on the parchment Carter had no previous knowledge. Indeed, he wrote at that time that he had never seen its like before, although he noted its occasional similarity to ancient Egyptian hieroglyphs of the First Dynasty. Carter had some knowledge of Attic Greek, amongst other languages and that parchment apparently became his Rosetta stone, so to speak. At some point, late in 1949, he managed to translate the parchment text into English, and then later in 1956, using this new-found, but secret ability, he also translated the previously undecipherable text written in the Queen's Chamber; but first I will read his journal entry dated 21st November 1949.

Khirbet Qumran, 8 miles south of Jericho,
18:00 21st November 1949
Hajib has been peculiarly active this afternoon.
As a servant boy, I would have expected him to
stay a little closer, should I need some water or

refreshment. Giving him the afternoon to amuse himself, whilst I documented removal of the last fragments of scroll from the sifting tray, has left him grinning from ear to ear and leaping around the whole site like a wild goat. It was late this afternoon, around four I noted, that he came to me excitedly. Master, master, he called, come quickly. I told him to be quiet, lest he disturb the other scholars in their work, although most if not all had already returned to the encampment for tea. I duly went to see what was causing such a rumpus and to my amazement, not two hundred yards from our cave, Hajib put the entire length of his arm through a hole in the hillside. Look master, he called repeatedly, until I chastised him in no uncertain terms. After no more than thirty minutes and with the help of a shovel retrieved from the main workings, we excavated a hole large enough for him to crawl into and me to peer through. I would hardly describe our discovery as a cave - more a hollow - as the entire depth is no more than three and a half yards, but in it, propped against the furthest crumbling rock-face, we found a small earthenware vase. I have it now in front of me, as I sit comfortably in my chair, although rightly or wrongly, having sent Hajib for my supper, I have tightly secured the door of my sleeping tent.

20:00

I have now opened the vase, which measures no more than one foot tall and five inches in diameter; the clay stopper being glued in place with animal gum and from it I have withdrawn a piece of parchment. It is quite different from the parchment we are recording here at Qumran. For one thing, it is of papyrus, not leather and for the second, the writings are in an undistinguishable tongue.

01:00 22nd November 1949

For the best part of six hours I have studied the text set upon this piece of rolled papyrus, which itself measures nine and a half inches high, by six inches wide. I have dismissed Hajib, much to his consternation, until the morning and sworn him to secrecy to boot. Although I recognise one group of text set upon the reverse side of the parchment as traditional Greek, the ancient Attic tongue, and another scribed beneath as Aramaic, I have no knowledge of the main writings. Although clearly some symbols are biased towards Egyptian hieroglyphs of the First Dynasty, as a few pictograms relate closely to that language and in which I have some fluency. Further, I have taken the decision to keep this discovery to myself, save for Hajib; as it is clear that this parchment has no commonality with the scrolls - being in my view from an entirely different era and indeed, scribed by an entirely different order. It is however, quite possible that the religious sect who buried the scrolls, also have been party to this discretion, treating this ancient parchment as a religious artefact of similar importance.'

Peter Rothschild looked up from his notes for a few moments, whilst some around the table struggled to grasp the significance of his readings. 'The deciphering of that language,' he resumed, 'and the transcribing into English of other similar texts that Simpson-Carter discovered, preoccupied him for the rest of his career and as we are now beginning to realise, allowed him to formulate his theory of the origin of mankind. As we already know, he entitled his final thesis *The Unholy Secret*. This was to become a phrase he mentioned on several occasions to close family and friends. Now, ladies and gentlemen, I shall show you the significance of these writings, hard evidence discovered by Simpson-Carter and why we intend using it.'

Rothschild nodded at Laura Bellingham; she pressed a key on her laptop. Instantly, a digital image of the ancient parchment from Qumran, reproduced in colour, appeared on the back of the laptop lid and alongside it, the English translation in a bold font.

'For those of you who cannot see the screen, I will read it aloud,' said Rothschild.

Know ye all men of Sapien past
the stone of Eridu is redeemed
brought forth from calamity and broken dreams
to light the path of future seed

Know ye all men of Sapien blood
the stone of light is lesser for two
and part the heart of Babylon become
here great again the music of Eridu restrung

Know ye all men of Sapien line
The sacred casket for the passage of time
For the greater part the stone shall pass
to heights favoured by our brothers of past

Know ye all men of Sapien caste
here shall be the monument all futures outlast
Atleans few now their watery grave
a calling to Astrolias in that we all crave

For almost a minute no one in the room spoke, for
most the meaning was not immediately apparent, but to
Richard, the picture was becoming clearer.

William Bryant spoke first. 'Eridu,' he commented. 'My
history isn't all that it used to be. Can you expand on the
relevance of Eridu?'

Rothschild answered. 'Historians record Eridu,
Secretary Bryant, as the oldest of the Sumerian city states;

arguably the very first recorded city of the civilised world. Only much later in history was it eclipsed by Babylon. The infrastructure of both cities was extremely complex, not just for that period in history, but even compared to the present day and not only in terms of architecture, engineering and transport, but also culture, language and art. Eridu's remains are located on the Euphrates delta on the Persian Gulf. Excavations date the original foundations as sixth millennium BC, only a little older than the flight log, no less!'

A murmur of astonishment swept around the table.

'We are all familiar with the fabled hanging gardens of Babylon,' continued Rothschild. 'However, Eridu also had vast gardens, the like, apparently, never before seen on the face of this planet. Archaeological studies, decades ago, revealed the aqua-structure of Babylon to be remarkably similar to that of Eridu, only a little more elaborate, more evolved if you like. From historical records, scientists have estimated that both cities would have required around nine million litres of water each day for adequate irrigation, some of this lifted, or perhaps pumped, as high as four hundred feet to the central ziggurats. Now, how on earth did they achieve that?'

'Crystal power!' Richard ventured.

Most around the table nodded; they were in agreement. Historical fables; unsubstantiated hearsay over the centuries; stories passed down by countless generations; hard archaeological evidence always previously unconnected; they were beginning to gel into historical fact!

'This is true,' concurred Professor Mubarakar. 'Historical evidence shows clearly that the dominant humanoids on earth prior to the river valley civilisations we are discussing, were very much hunter-gatherers and not city dwellers - *Homo sapiens neanderthalensis,* Neanderthal Man. The species died out within a surprisingly short period. Some have speculated that their demise was due, at least in part, to the arrival of anatomically modern humans, *Homo sapiens sapiens.*

Richard agreed enthusiastically; his studies had already taken him into this territory. 'Then there was Eridu, appearing almost overnight in evolutionary terms. A complex society with a written language; only now are we beginning to understand that language!'

Professor Nieve, who was also becoming enthralled with the galloping pace of historical enlightenment, enquired expectantly, 'so what of Atlantis, may I ask? Even as a young boy and now an old sceptic, that place, that continent; as a subject it has always fascinated me.'

Peter Rothschild spoke immediately, preventing Richard from answering. 'The existence of Atlantis remains purely speculative; no evidence has been found and we *have* been doing some probing recently, I can assure you.'

With that, Richard looked Professor Nieve in the eye. 'Don't you believe it, Sir,' he said, to the astonishment of Rothschild and a few others. 'I have proof of its existence.'

Richard paused momentarily, 'but only if we can recover the *Star*'s flight log,' he concluded.

Rothschild glanced across at Admiral Hughes, who barely perceptibly shook his head from side to side. 'Atlantis has no part in today's discussions,' Rothschild snapped as a result.

Richard looked disappointed. They are hiding something again, he thought. 'Okay then . . . what about Te Agi Wakhan and the Maya, and Mohenjo Daro and the peoples of Harappas? There is nothing speculative about those civilisations!'

That remark drew several deep breaths from the gathering.

'You know more about the origins of modern man than you are letting on, me thinks,' pressed Richard sarcastically to Rothschild. 'So, why the secrecy?'

Rothschild's face tightened, and he remained tight-lipped. Richard opened his mouth to speak again, but also stopped short. He dropped his head and focused on the glass of water in front of him, slowly rotating it between his fingers.

'If you have another comment, Richard, we would like to hear it,' Rothschild added, mildly agitated.

Richard hesitated for a second or two. 'With all due respect, Peter, your theory of the *Star*, the alien space ship, departing earth on some kind of rescue mission is remarkably similar to the conclusions that I drew, but only after several weeks of intensive study of its flight log; yet nobody on earth has seen, or is aware of the log's full content. I know that Osiris's attempts to scanadise each page individually for data-stream transmission was unsuccessful. For one thing, the reflective material composing the log's pages prevents effective digitising and pixel orientation. Individual pages can be scanned and electronically stored using a suitably powerful system, we know that. To be honest, I used that method myself; but digitising for accelercom data transmission has proved impossible for reasons that are still unknown. Secondly, the terrestrial video signal sent from Osiris, encoding sections of the log's text was, I am reliably informed, mysteriously distorted and deflected on its way to earth, so that only a few pages made it to the Federation's scientific laboratories in Strasbourg. I also know that the Federation will have to wait for the return flight of a conventional shuttle before they get their hands on the real thing, and that could be another four months! So, how on earth have you drawn your conclusions from the limited flight log text that you have available? I mean, I recited Admiral Urket's diary entry to your people from memory, you have very little else and I certainly have not shared my work with anyone else, except, to some extent, Doctor Turner.'

Rothschild glanced briefly at Abbey Hennessy and then Admiral Hughes, his expression slightly pained. 'It's just one of a number of theories we are considering at the moment,' he said, brushing off the question, 'and regarding the next flight to Mars to retrieve the flight log . . . that may be sooner than you think.'

Richard nodded nonchalantly to cover his thoughts: there is something awry here, something isn't right, it just isn't adding up; Rothschild is covering; Abbey Hennessy is in on it too; it's plain to see. Richard drew a deep, pondering breath, 'would say it seems to be more than a theory, Peter,' he commented suspiciously and stopped. Now was not the appropriate time for discussion, he mused. 'Anyway,' Richard concluded diverting his speculations. 'Sorry, we are wasting time, please . . . carry on.'

'Yes, quite,' Rothschild replied, then paused to gather his thoughts. Richard's questions, being unexpected, had visibly and momentarily thrown him off course. 'Anyway, ladies and gentlemen,' he continued eventually. 'Back to Simpson-Carter's work and the relevance of our discussions. The next image you will see is a black and white photograph of a section of unique text that Simpson-Carter translated into English around September 1956. Carter did not actually discover this text, only its relevance; being, apparently well documented and located on the reverse side of a famous granite stele, which is an enduring record book if you like. Similar to an engraved gravestone and called the Merneptah stele, it lies in the Egyptian National Museum in Cairo and this is where Simpson-Carter spent literally years of his career. Merneptah was the thirteenth son of Rameses II and this chap is also of great significance, as we will find out shortly. Records reliably show the son ruled between about 1212 and 1202

BC. The main text on the stele commemorates victories of Pharaoh Merneptah over the people of Canaan, who were called the Canaanites, but also known as the Israelites. Apparently, this is the earliest known reference to such a people. Since its discovery, the text on the reverse side of the stele had been discarded by scholars as unintelligible, unimportant and confused hieroglyphs of no significance; perhaps the private ranting of a disgruntled mason or possibly a practice run on that particular type of granite. Until Carter's work, the text certainly lay undecipherable.' Rothschild nodded at Laura Bellingham, who pressed a key on her laptop, changing the image on its screen to one of a poor quality, conventional photograph; but one that had clearly undergone digital enhancement.

At this point, Professor Mubaraka grew rather excited. 'Yes, yes, for the blessing of God,' he gushed, 'so many times have I seen this text, so many times have I been hypnotised by its unknown characters, so many times have I wondered at its meaning!'

'Well, Professor,' answered Rothschild, in a rather satisfied, if not a somewhat smug manner, 'here it is; deciphered text, that has been Simpson-Carter's secret for almost one hundred years.'

Bellingham pressed another key on her machine.

For passage from Eridu to Babylon, a casket was so built
Brought to be, using the old ways from the old treasures
A casket not of stone or such from this world

For the light of stars cannot be encaptured by such
But of bright metals shaped first by our forefathers

A portion of the great light was attributed first to Babylon
So everlasting will be its memory
So then, in the casket of light the greater part passed to Giza
Vast open the land favoured most by those the remaining
Atleans

Their monuments the greatest of all men's
Stand towards the heavens in the way of Sirius
Awaken Osiris
Call for those remaining
Across eternity shall go our plea to our beginning

For the passage of the law another casket shall be built
Likened to that of the light but of materials known to man
good and strong
Acacia wood and pure gold
Here the covenant shall lay and be forever revered by all men

There was a stunned silence; Richard drew a deep breath.
'The Ark of the Covenant was made of acacia wood and
pure gold, that's stated clearly in the Old Testament. For
casket read ark,' he whispered. 'One for the law and one
for the light.'

Rothschild nodded, 'yes, that is what it seems to indicate
two arks . . . the Ark of the Law, or perhaps more widely

referred to as the Ark of the Covenant and the Ark of the Light. What's more, the Great Pyramid on the Giza plateau, has also throughout history, been referred to as the Temple of Osiris, Professor Mubarakar confirmed this. We think that there is great significance here.'

Rothschild looked across at Professor Mubarakar as he spoke. The Professor concurred with an enthusiastic nod. 'What you say is true, Peter,' he replied.

'So you think that the Ark of the Light was used to transport the broken crystal, which apparently is now in two pieces, from Eridu, the oldest recorded city in history, to Babylon,' speculated Richard as he focused intently on Peter Rothschild. 'A portion was deposited there, so Babylon could assume the mantle of Eridu.'

'Historical writings confirm the dates as being correct. The complete destruction of Eridu in the nineteenth century BC, due to a huge earthquake and the subsequent rise of Babylon; with its . . . shall we say rather more futuristic architecture and vast, irrigated, hanging gardens; themselves regarded as one of the great wonders of the ancient world!'

Richard interrupted again. 'So, the other part, the *greater* part of the crystal was taken to Egypt, to be incorporated in some way into the Great Pyramid, the Pyramid of Khufu, to power it in some way. *A call for those remaining . . . across eternity . . .* a call for help?'

Rothschild concurred. 'We think that you are on the right lines, Richard, yes, but that's not all, indeed we think it extremely unlikely that a crystal remained in Giza for any significant period. Why? Because hearsay, myths, legends, traditions, even some hard evidence tracked *an ark* south, first to the great Egyptian capital of Thebes around the time of Rameses II, Simpson-Carter found writings to this effect; then later, through Nubia to Ethiopia.'

'But which ark? What happened to the Ark of the Covenant? It's been searched for unsuccessfully for centuries, millennia even, there are so many theories.'

Rothschild nodded again, agreeing with Richard's statement. 'Indeed, from the Crusaders to the Third Reich, no stone unturned.'

The Reverend Rawlinson interrupted. 'The quest to find the Ark of the Covenant has been a great interest of mine for more years than I care to remember. Like those associated with the Holy Grail, there is a good deal of documentary evidence supporting and detailing these searches. It is a historical fact, for instance, that the Crusaders turned Jerusalem upside down in their search for these artefacts during the eleventh century; but most of the information we have on the artefacts themselves is unreliable, again based on myth and legend.'

'So, what do you think, Sir?' asked Richard politely. 'What is your considered opinion?'

'For everyone's benefit, let me refresh your memories regarding this most sacred of religious artefacts. At the bequest and according to instructions from Moses, an artisan called Bezalel constructed the Ark of the Covenant;

he used materials Richard quite rightly stipulated: acacia wood and pure gold. In it, Moses laid two polished stone tablets, on which he had written, under the direction of God, the Ten Commandments. Some say that there was in fact only one tablet of stone; in either case, Moses wrote in Hebrew.

The Ark of the Covenant was a portable wooden chest, overlaid with gold and having a cherub with extended wings mounted at each end of the golden lid. In the Old Testament, the Ark is described as having many successive functions, not least serving as a symbol of the divine presence and as such possessed awesome powers that brought disaster and defeat upon any foe. For many centuries, the Ark of the Covenant was housed in a Tabernacle, described as a moveable sanctuary or tent. This shelter usually formed the centre of encampment for the early Israelites during their wanderings and conquest of Canaan. Eventually, the Tabernacle was replaced by a permanent structure: Solomon's Temple, built in Jerusalem. King David, Solomon's father, had made Jerusalem his political and religious capital following the city's capture years earlier. To remind you of the period: the temple was reputedly completed in 995 BC. David was the first great king of the Holy Land, but it was left to Solomon to construct the temple; according to the Old Testament, it was remarkable, both physically and conceptually. For centuries, there the Ark stayed, although some historical writings suggest that it was removed by devout Levites during the reign of King

Manasseh, around 687 BC, who, because of his heretical practises, was sometimes called 'The Nero of Palestine'. After that period, to be honest, history is in a muddle; but one thing is certain: in 587 BC, conquering Babylonian forces, under King Nebuchadnezzar, completely destroyed the Temple; by that time, the Ark had simply vanished.

Over the centuries, a host of theories have been put forward to account for the Ark's disappearance and subsequent fate. Some say, and this in my view is the most likely, is that it was destroyed along with Solomon's temple; others allegedly claim that it lies hidden in a secret vault in the Jordanian mountains; while still others claim that it remains and always will, in or perhaps beneath the old city of Jerusalem. Other stories tell of Arab traders transporting it back to *their* homeland. Yet of all these claims, none has proved as resilient as that of Ethiopia being the last resting place of the Ark. Indeed, many scholars confirm that the resting place of *an* Ark was identified several decades ago, in the 1990s. The place is Axum in northern Ethiopia and it arrived here after several centuries resting on an island called Elephantine Island near Aswan in Upper Egypt. I have to say that there is some documented, archaeological evidence to support this fact, the period in history, 470 BC. The Ark was finally moved to Axum apparently, during the 4th Century AD.'

The Reverend leaned back in his chair, appearing somewhat disappointed and a little solemn. 'There you have it, in a nutshell so to speak, a good many year's work unfairly précised into a few minutes.'

Richard looked at the Reverend; his amazement was plain to see. 'So your view is that the Ark was destroyed, that's the bottom line, right?'

'That is my conclusion, correct; and do not forget, the Ark of the Covenant was essentially a wooden casket, reputedly magnificent, but made of wood all the same. Atmospheric changes, temperature variations, moisture levels, peoples breath, insects, bacterial and fungal action, transportation, not to mention three thousand years; these would all have taken their toll. Even concurring with the most optimistic theory, it is probable that all that remains of that wondrous receptacle is now simply a stone tablet or two, the original casket having long since perished.'

Richard thought for a moment, and then addressed a question to Peter Rothschild. 'You're thinking that a casket, the Ark of the Light, constructed from extra terrestrial materials, materials that could contain the power of a crystal, will have survived the annals of time?'

The atmosphere in the room grew taut with anticipation. Peter Rothschild broke the silence. 'Thank you, Reverend Rawlinson,' he replied. 'Very helpful indeed.' Rothschild looked at Laura Bellingham and then at Richard. The original black and white photograph showing the text on the reverse side of the Merneptah stele appeared again on the lid of her laptop. 'This is the crux of the matter, Richard; whether we can pursue our intended course; your role in this matter and whether you can help us. Can you read this text, yes or no?'

Richard glanced back at the screen, briefly scanning the lines of alien writing; he already knew the answer. 'I can read the text, Peter,' he said nodding confidently. 'And with all due respect to the memory of Professor Simpson-Carter, with more accuracy and certainty.'

'Why is that so, young man?' enquired Reverend Rawlinson. 'Why are you so confident, where others over the centuries have failed?'

Richard paused for a few seconds to gather his thoughts. 'Simpson-Carter used the two transcriptions on the back of the parchment to decipher the alien text; we know that from his records: the first, traditional, pure Greek, as used by the aristocracy and learned, and the other, Aramaic. Both these languages are clearly ancient and well documented, but they evolved many centuries after these texts were originally written. So a scribe or group of scribes, clearly with some knowledge of the 'old' language, transcribed what they thought must have been a celestial, or even godly language, perhaps as much as four thousand years later. They had no way of cross checking and probably limited original text; errors were bound to creep in.' Richard leaned forward and pointed to individual pictograms on the laptop screen. 'You see this symbol, this one and this one, they are Mayan in origin; and this Phoenician and this one confirmed as being the earliest Mesopotamian writing, Sumerian, the city states . . . Eridu. The scribes who did this translation lived in the

Mediterranean region. It is therefore extremely unlikely that they knew of the ancient civilisations of Mexico or the Indus Valley in Pakistan. The system I used to decipher the writings utilised a powerful computer programme, loaded with every known ancient language that used pictorial symbols . . . pictograms, for their writing. It took some time and some expert help, but my results are based on the entire spectrum of known pictograms and these from the four earliest recorded civilisations: the river-valley civilisations of Mesopotamia, the Indus and Mesoamerica, latterly the Nile *and* becoming more and more likely, the sea state of Atlantis. So, I think my interpretation is pretty accurate.'

Admiral Hughes who had sat quietly, if not spellbound, by what he was hearing, took a deep breath. 'Tell me, then,' he enquired of Richard. 'How does Simpson-Carter's translation bear up to your interpretation?'

'Well, it wasn't really his translation, was it, Sir, with all due respect. He discovered the parchment, the key, the Rosetta stone if you like, and had the foresight and knowledge to use Greek and Aramaic to translate the text finally into English. It was either a Greek or a Persian scribe, or indeed both, who actually made the original translation, if you see my point. They were remarkably accurate considering that they did not have the whole picture. As I compare the two, extra-terrestrial and English, I find the English version has become a little 'poetic' for want of a better word. You know, a more romantic style;

but yes, it is consistent.'

Professor Mubarakar interrupted, 'you have a remarkable ability Commander Reece. Even after all these years of study, a lifetime devoted to our ancestors, I find myself blinded by these revelations.'

'At the moment, Richard,' said Rothschild poignantly. 'You are probably the only person in the solar system who could translate the text we are about to discuss.'

Richard looked surprised by this remark. 'Why so?' he asked Rothschild. 'Simply use the flight log and the computer programmes as I did. Train someone else up; a linguist for example would probably be better at it than me, anyway?'

'That thought had crossed our minds, Richard, but it seems the people who want the remaining crystals as much as we do, are again one step ahead. The flight log, and the medical centre's OROMAR CT400 laptop that you used on Mars, went missing three weeks ago. Commander Miko ordered a complete search of Osiris Base. Nothing, not a sign, disappeared into thin air, if you will excuse the pun.'

Richard suppressed a smile. 'Bit embarrassing for the security officer, Greg Searle; surely those items would have been stored separately and both would have been afforded the highest security arrangements possible?'

'A bit embarrassing for everyone concerned, Richard,' agreed Rothschild. 'Apparently both log and computer were together in a remote, but cordoned laboratory; Gregory

Seale is accepting full responsibility. Their disappearance however, greatly complicates matters.'

'Well, I can allay your fears to some extent. I programmed a delete sequence onto my work matrix, my own security protection. After twenty-eight days of inactivity, the programme would have automatically erased every file, the entire matrix will be empty; everything wiped clean, not a trace.' Richard raised his eyebrows, pleased with himself. 'Anyone acquiring the flight log will have to start all over again, could take months.'

Rothschild was clearly relieved. 'Well done, Richard,' he offered. 'That helps, but it does, in itself, present an additional problem: now you really are the only person on this planet who can read this language, which makes you either very dangerous *or* very useful; either way, you are a wanted man. Bearing that in mind, if you decide to help us your brief would be to track down the so called Ark of the Light, if indeed, it actually exists. If you are successful, you are to retrieve the crystal, which, should we believe this evidence, is a substantial stone. I can assure you that this mission is not just a matter of national security, but possibly saving humankind from itself, certainly as life on the surface of the planet goes. It is make or break; civilisation as we know it. I am not stretching the point!'

The large room seemed to echo in hollow, expectant silence. Seconds seemed like minutes. 'In return of course, all charges against you, relating to the flight log, will be dropped,' Rothschild concluded.

'Very generous, I'm sure,' Richard replied. 'I also want my job back on Mars.' Then he paused thoughtfully, considering the wider implications. 'Tell you what, just tell me one thing Peter, before I . . . it's troubling me, I don't like mysteries. Tell me how you effected the swap of the U-Semini case when I landed at the Cape; General Buchanan received an empty duplicate. Tell me how you did that; give me my job back, and you can count on me.'

Peter Rothschild squirmed; clearly, this was information he did not want Richard to know. He looked at Admiral Hughes for direction. The Admiral shook his head disapprovingly.

'Your security clearance does not entitle you to this information, Richard. Sorry,'

Richard reacted immediately. 'Come on, Peter, I am sitting in on a briefing classified ESSA Security Level 5, even Cabinet Classified; it does not come any higher than that. If you want my help, I want to know!'

Admiral Hughes looked to his right, towards Abbey Hennessy. 'Brief Lieutenant Commander Reece, please Abbey,' he said.

'Lieutenant Commander Reece, may I call you Richard?'

'If I may call you Abbey?' Richard replied suavely.

She inclined her head. 'May I ask exactly how long it took you to decipher the writings in the flight log, until you were able to read all the pages clearly and coherently? This could be very important.'

'Several weeks. Occasionally I was going at it twenty

hours a day, certainly well over a month in any event,' replied Richard immediately. 'I would have to check my diary, that is still on Mars and it wasn't me exactly anyway; for that task I enlisted the help of someone much cleverer than me.'

Hennessy raised her eyebrows; the others waited with baited breath. There was a moment of silence.

'Sorry, I can't give you a name!'

'Richard, your discretion is commendable,' reacted Abbey Hennessy, 'but to no avail; we already know who helped you. However, if you tell us his or her name, confirm it so to speak, we will view this as an important element when we discuss Mars with your career adviser; help with a return appointment, so to speak.'

'I see,' replied Richard sourly, 'you need my help, and as such blackmail is justifiable. Rather one-sided wouldn't you say?'

Hennessy leant back hard in her chair, looked at the faces around the table and dwelt for a second or two on Admiral Hughes. Eventually, Admiral Hughes responded; he sighed deeply and then looked sternly at Richard.

'Listen, Lieutenant Commander Reece, the legal proceedings raised against you are entirely justified. You contravened ISSF Standard Procedures; you know that, we know that! Removing you from your appointment was a matter of necessity, despite Commander Miko's commendable pressure to have you reinstated as Osiris's survey leader. Further, we have had you cooped up in your quarters for your own safety, not as you and most others think, as part of a pre-trial isolation requirement.'

Richard felt a twinge of embarrassment, but he looked Admiral Hughes in the eye. He had had it with being chastised for failing to disclose the flight log and its discovery and he was still more than a little upset with the International Space and Science Federation's decision to instigate court-martial proceedings on this account. 'What do you mean, Sir, my own safety?' he asked, beginning to get a little irritated.

Rothschild interrupted. 'The people who were after you in space and on Andromeda, are still after you here on Earth. Apart from that solitary attempt with a musket of all things, the incident this morning was a clumsy, opportunistic attempt to have you eradicated. Future attempts will be rather more sophisticated. The fact that the flight log is now missing, apart from being an absolute disaster, greatly complicates matters. We do not know if they tried to kill you because they now have direct access to the log and want to eliminate the only other person alive who has knowledge of its contents; or simply because you were responsible, in the main, for frustrating their very, very expensive attempt to obtain the first consignment of crystals. Either way, they have your mark; from this point in time, their efforts will intensify.'

'Great, so I'm on a hit list!'

'You became a wanted man, Richard, the moment you discovered the remains of that spaceship on Mars. Colonel

Petromolosovich informed us that your ability to decipher that signal intercepted by Space Station Spartacus and your powers of deduction were very impressive; that is why *we* need you and the conglomerate need *rid* of you!'

'Look Peter, for God's sake, just tell me what I want to know, then I'm in, I've told you!'

'Who helped you decipher the flight log on Mars, Richard? Who was with you all the way? Use the lateral thinking you are undoubtedly blessed with, but refuse point-blank to acknowledge.'

There was a hush around the table, even the fidgeting stopped. Admiral Hughes stared at Richard, as did Abbey Hennessy.

Rothschild continued, in an effort to soften the blow. 'Your performance, and skill, if I may add, in retrieving the U-Semini case and bringing it safely to earth, along with Commander Race, has been recognised as being in the highest traditions of your respective services . . .'

'Yes, and whilst Commander Race received a commendation, I received notification of my impending court-martial!' Richard drew breath and paused. He continued in a more polite tone but with understandable bitterness, 'a little ironic, don't you think?'

Richard was clearly not listening to Rothschild, and refused to accept the evidence despite the prompts, 'So, how did you do it? Jeremy Preston and Rachel Turner, they were with me every step, all the way. Preston was written off with motion sickness and Rachel . . . ?' There was silence again, a moment of realisation. 'Rachel! Surely not, she is my fiancée, I mean, we are to be . . .'

Admiral Hughes breathed in deeply and held it for a moment; this was not the briefing format that he had intended.

'Richard,' Abbey Hennessy continued sympathetically, 'neither British Military Command, nor us at M19 are blind to your relationship with Rachel Turner. Although it is true to say that we did overlook that side of things when your appointment to Osiris was vetted.'

'Hold on, what do you mean, *you* overlooked that fact?'

'All appointments to Osiris, and Andromeda for that matter, are approved by respective national intelligence agencies; it's always been that way. There are a number of reasons for this.'

'OK, I can understand that, but what's my relationship with Rachel Turner got to do with MI9; unless she's working for . . .'

After months of speculation, Richard finally put two and two together; Abbey Hennessy's expression confirmed Richard's reluctant deduction.

'I see,' he said eventually, 'king and country and all that.'

Clearly, he was deeply hurt. He thought he knew everything there was to know about Rachel; they had no secrets; they shared an understanding; he loved her; but there was an important element in her life of which he new nothing. His trust, his respect, perhaps even his love, began to shatter with disillusionment; he felt a lump in the back of his throat.

Admiral Hughes changed the subject by pressing his point. 'Richard, confirm to me that your knowledge of the flight log also enabled you to decipher the omni-directional message you were shown on Spartacus'.

Richard nodded blankly.

'Then it is probable that you will be able to decipher the indecipherable, so to speak. All charges will be dropped; all reports relating to this matter will be removed from your file; as to your job back on Mars? I guarantee it. Come on man, this may not be your remit, but it is, I suggest, your duty!'

Richard looked Peter Rothschild in the eye, but Rothschild broke contact quickly by looking at his notes. I can see it in his eyes, there is still something they're not telling me, he thought. Surely, things can't get much worse. Richard dwelt for only a moment on Rachel; their wedding plans. He shrugged his shoulders, his expression devoid of sentiment.

'Seems I don't have much room to manoeuvre and anyway, there's nothing keeping me at home any more . . . yes, I'm in!'

'Good, thank you, now listen carefully to the remainder of your brief,' replied Admiral Hughes curtly, dismissing the overtone of disappointment in Richard's voice.

'This is VIP Access One, calling Atlantic Control, come in control!'

Tom Race was already decelerating as he passed through the orbital re-entry gate designated NA5, some five thousand miles above Newfoundland.

'This is Atlantic Control, reading you five by five. You have permission to enter the profile, Commander. The corridor is clear, high speed approved.'

'Roger, Roger,' Tom replied, in a professional tone. 'Profile parameters confirmed, speed one hundred and seventy lutens, reducing Mach 20 at the crossover.'

Once through that fix, Tom would reduce speed further to Mach 12 for the North Atlantic Sector; London was barely twenty minutes away.

A green coloured electronic arrow on the navigation screen indicated Artemis's position relative to the crossover coordinates, the point where the unit of speed for space, the *luten*, transitioned to the atmospheric unit, *Mach*. Mach being referenced to the speed of sound. Below thirty thousand feet, the display would change again to the traditional knot, being one nautical mile per hour. Precisely on course as he passed the fictitious point, Tom called again. 'Control, this is Access One, converting matter-stream momentum to potential energy, requesting climb six thousand miles.'

'Radar clear,' came the reply. 'Climb own discretion.'

With that, Tom gently pulled the nose up; he enjoyed flying manually when he was able, in an effort to maintain his skills. As the altitude increased and with the throttle closed, his speed gradually reduced. At Mach 18 and running the centre of the corridor, he commenced the final descent towards London.

'Fixed on descent profile, speed brakes deployed, speed check . . . Mach one-five and reducing,' Tom called eventually.

'Concurred, radar identified,' answered the controller routinely. 'Approaching the boundary, call now Mid Atlantic, frequency code, triple eight . . . standby! We have an intruder in the corridor, popup contact, dead ahead. Yes, it's confirmed Access One, range one thousand four hundred miles and climbing. He's coming up fast; I'm gonna check this out!'

There was a moment of silence. Tom grew perplexed. This is very unusual, he thought. This is protected airspace, aircraft don't just stray into re-entry corridors. He adjusted his own radar from navigation mode to scan mode and increased the acquisition range to the maximum - one thousand five hundred miles. There it was, as the controller had said, a single contact on the edge of the display, no identification pulse, nothing.

'Colonel, Sir, we may have a problem,' said Tom earnestly over the intercom. 'There is another aircraft in the corridor. I am reducing speed as a precaution, we may need to manoeuvre, make sure your harness is tight. Closure rate indicates thirteen minutes to contact!'

London – simultaneously

Rothschild flipped a switch under the lip of the table adjacent to where he sat. A small square of wood, part of the table top, hinged open exposing a control panel and simultaneously a large triangle of glass, like a prism, about one metre high and one metre wide, rose up from its central position within the tabletop; its wooden veneered cap, being so close fitting, that Richard had been completely unaware of it presence. Rothschild then pressed a green button on the control panel itself, which in turn instigated a video profile. Richard stared, impressed. An image of four, seated, ancient Egyptian deities appeared on each of the three screens, in vivid micron-colourtone. The images were three-dimensional, realistic. They must have been formatted more than a year ago, thought Richard, because the background had a bright blue, hazy sky with no sign of rain. The four Egyptian figures sat next to each other, two on each side of a large doorway that had been cut into the side of a sheer rock incline. However, the inner figure on the left had suffered considerable damage above the waist at some point during its silent vigil, its form now being almost completely erased.

'Do you recognise this monument, Richard?' Rothschild enquired. 'Do you know where it is?'

'Yes, of course, I've seen it in my studies, Abu Simbel!'

'Correct, left bank of the Upper Nile, near Egypt's border with Sudan; Pharaoh Rameses II's Great Temple.'

The moving image then changed to one inside a stone chamber, and then focused on an illuminated wall painting.

'This fresco lies on the south wall of the main chamber.'

The image zoomed-in to the top right-hand corner of the wall painting; several depicted pictograms were clear to see. Richard's eyes widened.

'Yes, yes, they are the same, the bloody same, that's incredible,' he said mesmerised. 'Can you lower the frame, let me see some more?'

The image slowly moved down the fresco, scanning left to right, before arriving at the bottom right-hand corner.

'These images are the only records of the original paintings from inside this tomb at Abu Simbel. They were discovered under a thin layer of plaster when the entire monument was removed from its original location near Aswan and meticulously reconstructed nearby in the 1960s. The reason for this was to save the monument from the rising waters of the River Nile, after construction of the Aswan High Dam had threatened their safety. We know Simpson-Carter was a consultant cryptographer working on the Abu Simbel project during its reconstruction. Despite being a world heritage site, these paintings were completely erased, for no apparent reason, about two months ago. Whoever did it left no trace, no clues and no evidence; persons and motives unknown. This very image is now the only one we have from inside the chamber; the remainder were distorted beyond recognition during a digital, data-uplink to a secure worldscan satellite. If that in itself was not suspicious, two weeks ago the entire image bank – that is every related image to this one, being held in the library of the Cairo National Museum *and* its duplicate in the British Museum – were destroyed in two, freak accidents. In the case of the Cairo Museum, three top Egyptologists and restorers were killed in the ensuing fire. In addition, just a few days ago, the Egyptian antiquities department of the British Museum received another report of an explosion in the Valley of the Kings, which lies near Luxor in southern Egypt. Apparently, the entrance to a tomb, part of a major complex, has been completely blocked and now lies under a thousand tons of rubble, earth and sand. In this particular case, the target appears to have been one selected at random, and again the perpetrators left no clues as to their identity or motives.'

'Someone's trying to hide something, systematically destroying evidence,' Richard added.

'Indeed, that is also our assumption, Richard, we think that the writings in Abu Simbel were highly significant; perhaps even directions to the Ark's final resting place. Abu Simbel will be your second port of call, so to speak. We will deal with the first in a few moments.'

'What's the point of my going to Abu Simbel, if these

frescos have been erased?' Richard queried.

'At the moment this is the only lead we have. You will start there; we already have two agents in place, local experts so to speak. You will scrutinise every square inch of that chamber, try to come up with something, a word, a clue, anything.'

Richard nodded. 'Can I see the image of the fresco again, read what it says, there may be clues in the text itself?'

'Yes, of course.' Rothschild, selecting buttons on the control panel, to replay the previous images.

'Again please . . . stop! Back two frames . . . stop!' ordered Richard. All eyes were on him.

'Well . . . anything?' Rothschild asked expectantly.

'Can you take this down, please?' Richard suggested, his focus intense and unshifting.

'Laura, please,' beckoned Rothschild.

Richard began to translate the text; word for word; slowly and methodically.

'The stars giveth the light, for only the light of stars can bring day to the eternal night of tomorrow. And the light of the stars shall be taken to the place of the light, for only here will the light pierce the blackness and bring again day. And the light shall be in the ark, for only in the ark shall the light be the light. For this is the word, the only word and the light is passed down from him, only him. Let it be known that Osiris is the word and so the light shall come from Osiris.'

'It reads like a biblical text,' Richard commented, 'as if the two arks and what they were became confused in history. The sacred Ark of the Covenant was one, and the other, the Ark of Light. Over the years, one was lost and the other achieved greater reverence. Religious significance being confused with higher intelligence or something . . . but mention of the ark is plain enough, undisputable. It certainly existed and it seems very powerful, as if the light could save the world from eternal night. Perhaps it was a prophecy!'

Rothschild interrupted. 'Clearly, this text is telling us something. I believe it to be that the light, or perhaps more to the point, the *crystal*, should remain in the ark, inside the casket in order to function and it will only function in a specific place, apparently the place of Osiris.'

'Yes, I agree,' said Professor Mubarakar. 'The temple of Osiris is believed to have stood on the plane of Giza, as we have previously discussed. It was used during the time of the Old Kingdom, during the dynasty that built the Great Pyramid of Khufu, but it may have been built during an earlier period!'

The entire audience again seemed spellbound. Richard looked around at the faces. 'This is interesting,' he commented again. 'There was mention of a *casket* in Admiral Dirkot's diary, his personal entry, *but not an ark,*' he laughed. 'I named the spaceship itself 'the ark'. It's what it felt like to me, you know, a ship; not two by two and all that, to save animals, so much as to save themselves; those people remaining on earth, perhaps even stranded there!'

'It certainly does appear that the *Star* was on a rescue mission of some kind, but to save those remaining on earth from what? Unfortunately, we will never know,' concluded Rothschild.

Richard changed the subject. 'You said that Abu Simbel will be my second port of call, Peter, so where do I go first?'

In response to Richard's question, Rothschild pulled a small, flat telephone receiver from the inside pocket of his jacket and flipped up its cover. He keyed in a security code. 'Rothschild here,' he said tersely, 'anything from the CIB yet?' There was a pause. 'Good . . . voice recognition, I see, connect me, I will pass you over,' he concluded.

Rothschild stood up and walked over to Admiral Ghent, handing him the telephone.

'Security confirmation, Sir,' he said.

'This is Admiral Ghent speaking, I have a question, I need an answer,' he said, then looked again at Rothschild and handed him back the receiver. 'It's done.'

Rothschild returned to his seat while speaking again into the telephone. 'Verified and authorised, I understand, then we are clear to proceed, very good,' he replied terminating the call and selecting a button on his control panel.

The image on the large prismatic screens changed into a split-screen, with a central, vertical, dividing line. Both however, were of the face of the late Professor Simpson-Carter; they were undoubtedly similar, but there *were* subtle changes. They were in fact, the images Richard had seen earlier in the brief, the Professor's face, pallid and drawn, apparently sleeping.

'Ah, yes,' commented Richard, 'I wanted to ask you about these images. You said that this photograph, the one on the left, was taken sixty years ago and the other, only a few days ago, but it appears that the Professor has not aged at all during this period'

'Correct, very observant,' confirmed Rothschild. 'Close to his death, only days before in fact, Simpson-Carter finally realised that he would not be able to complete his work. He was, by this time, very weak. He realised his secret would die with him, unless he took some action to preserve it for posterity and so he contacted his closest friend, a geneticist named Samuel Firth, who had moved back to London from the United States. Amongst other jobs, Firth had been the Principal Scientist at a private institution in California. He was an expert in cryogenics, the science of freezing people with incurable ailments; so that they could be revived later, at some time in the future, when such illnesses can be successfully treated. Firth helped his friend and made the necessary arrangements. However, his installation of the first stage equipment was barely in time. Apparently, Simpson-Carter was clinically dead for two or three minutes before Firth was able to initiate the freeze-down process. For anyone who is interested, that temperature is around minus one hundred and eighty degrees Celsius. Fortunately, Carter was then successfully, biologically suspended. Firth's clinical notes clearly state that Carter may have incurred some irreversible cell damage, possibly even brain damage, because his heart had actually stopped before the freezing process was initiated, and this may, in turn, complicate the revival process. Firth's official medical report gave some recommendations on this procedure, knowing that he might be dead himself before the revival process was undertaken. Unfortunately, this report has always remained data-logged and irretrievable, except by senior institute personnel. Simpson-Carter's capsule was subsequently flown to California and allocated a station at Firth's old institute; all expenses were paid in advance, including the next fifty years, by Firth himself. In fact, it is interesting to note, that Firth died here in London some twenty years ago, reputedly in squalid conditions.'

'Maybe Firth, having heard Simpson-Carter's story, thought he was doing his bit for the future of mankind?'

'Well, you might be right, Richard,' agreed Rothschild. 'In any event it does seem quite a sacrifice. Anyway, Simpson-Carter was subsequently forgotten; one of many thousands of people currently suspended in ice, so to speak; the West Coast of the United States has a number of these institutes, their inmates all hoping for another bash at life. That is until three days ago. The CIA has just released its preliminary report, initially it was going out security restricted, but now we know the relevance of Simpson-Carter's work, it has been reclassified ISSF Top Secret Class 4. The CIA have since passed the file onto the more specialised and secret Central Intelligence Bureau.

Richard nodded. 'I understand,' he said, in anticipation.

'The institute in question was forcibly entered in the early hours of the morning,' continued Rothschild. 'The report will tell us precise timings. They must have been experts, a full team, perhaps five or six people. They removed Simpson-Carter from his capsule and managed to revive his vital functions, for how long, we do not know . . . not at the moment anyway. Whether he actually regained consciousness, or, for that matter, was at any time coherent, is anyone's guess. What we do know is that this represents a serious breech in security and could undermine this entire operation.'

'These goddamn people are one step ahead of us all the time!' Admiral Ghent interjected frustratedly. 'If he talked, and they got something out of him, they could already be on the road!'

Rothschild looked at the Admiral, his manner restrained. 'Our view, Sir, is that it is unlikely that Carter would have been coherent enough to give these people any help in deciphering the actual text symbols. It is also unlikely that he knew the exact location of the ark itself, just a map, directions so to speak. However, it is possible that he provided *some* useful information. In the light of another, rather more disturbing element to this matter, this may be true. It appears that the perpetrators administered some kind of pain-inducing drug; apparently, it slowly dissolves the stomach lining allowing digestive acids into the bloodstream. One can only imagine the effect. Whether this was to increase his neural stimulation and speed his verbal capacity, or forcibly extract further information, we cannot say. One thing is clear however: after they had finished with him, they left him to die, presumably in an unconscious state. The preliminary pathologist's report states that subsequently, he did regain consciousness; for how long, we can only speculate. He would have been alone though, as the institute was oblivious to his predicament. During this period, by all accounts, he scratched some marks on his body, unintelligible pictures. We think he may have used a syringe needle because the liquid inside inflamed the skin a little, raising weals. We think it critical that you see, first hand, his last message; we think that you may be able to read it. You have three days, Richard, arrangements are in hand, CIB agents are waiting for you, view the body and gain what you can from the writing. This meeting reconvenes at ten o'clock sharp, on the seventeenth.'

'Peter, how on earth do I get to California and back in that time frame?' Richard enquired in exasperation. 'There is only one direct flight from London to the US a week these days and that's booked months in advance?'

'Apart from *Orbital Airways*, Richard,' replied Rothschild, matter of factly. 'There *is* one other international company that still has access to aviation fuel - *NetJets Global.* Orbital Airways, as of three months ago, is now the only operational airline in the world. With the competition gone, they can afford to buy aviation kerosene on the spot market, what little there is remaining. NetJets, on the other hand, went 'green' a couple of decades ago. They started using vegetable-derived butanol fuel. Apparently, their entire fleet has used it for a considerable period, a long-term commitment to reduce CO_2 emissions. Sadly, it turned out to be a needle in a haystack gesture, compared to the global aviation industry's reliance and use of kerosene over the last thirty to forty years. However, by investing in butanol 'futures' and purchasing refining potential, they have built up a substantial stock of the fuel in both the States and Europe. NetJets are a specialist operation, they fly the corporate fraternity, wealthy individuals, the celebrities; the only people who can still afford to travel and they fly the latest machines too. They also incidentally, fly the *Royals*. The Prime Minister has given special dispensation for a return flight; considering the implications of your work and its value to this country. You will utilise a royal flight allocation; this also resolves our security concerns. In addition, the Americans have granted approval for the use of their stratospheric, satellite-protected, over-flight corridor.

Richard nodded; he was impressed. 'I will be taking up rooms at the palace next,' he commented somewhat flippantly.

Laura Bellingham stifled a giggle.

As far as Rothschild was concerned, Richard's off-the-cuff remark was neither appropriate nor funny; he did not smile as he continued.

'NetJets has a number of pilots who are security and competency cleared to fly the royal family, some have European nationality, the only non-British pilots able to do this work, it's a reflection of the confidence that the government has in this company and its operation. You will be flying in the new Eagle, three hours each way to San Francisco. The Captain's name is Carlos Castina, one of their best. He will meet you outside the VIP Terminal at the Capital City Orbitalport. You may not know of this facility; built on the site of the old 2012 Olympic stadium since you took up your appointment on Mars. The flight departs at 19:00 hours this evening. You will receive your security and point of contact brief later this morning, in the operations control centre beneath this building . . . any questions?'

Richard raised his eyebrows, his brow furrowed in surprise as much as in anticipation. 'No, no, none, not at the moment anyway,' he replied.

'Good, then all that remains is this week's environment and global energy brief. You can sit in on this, to give you a clearer picture of how serious things are becoming.'

**Above the Atlantic Ocean – simultaneously
08:55 Greenwich Mean Time**

'Access One, this is Eastern Atlantic Control, turn right,

twenty degrees, suggest further speed reduction. Intruder maintaining a constant approach vector, we have no details.'

'Copy control, coming right, twenty degrees.'

Tom reduced to Mach 7; he tracked the contact closely on his radar. *On its present course, it will pass down my left side about five miles away*, he thought, *that's too close for comfort.*

'Access One, take immediate evasive action; further right, I say again, *further right*, sixty degrees, contact has changed direction, he is on a collision course!' the controller's voice became intense.

Tom grimaced, but complied without hesitation. His radar picture confirmed the controller's prognosis. *Now the contact was only fifty miles away. I don't have time for this*, thought Tom. 'Colonel?' he said over the intercom. 'Are you listening to this?'

'Yeah, sure I am. What the hell's going on, Tom?' came the reply.

'Radar contact is holding a collision course, coming in from the left, twenty miles, hold on, Sir!'

Tom strained to see it. 'Visual, visual,' he called excitedly, its silhouette unmistakeable. 'T 144, it's a T 144 high altitude fighter!' Tom rolled left and pulled hard. The closing speed was phenomenal. They missed each other by mere metres.

Whoosh . . . the *Artemis* shook violently.

'Goddamn it,' Tom cursed. He checked his radar. 'She's

armed and she's coming around again,' he said over the intercom. He pressed the radio transmit button. 'Intruder alert, Atlantic Control, this is Access One, intruder alert!'

Infuriatingly, the aircraft tucked into Tom's six o'clock position. He watched him intently on the radar, and then, to his horror, one blip on the screen became three!

'Missiles . . . missiles!' Tom shouted.

Instinctively, Tom pulled into a steep climbing turn left and slammed open the throttle of the matter-stream propulsion system. Not designed for gravity-influenced manoeuvring, the result was a massive g-force that squeezed the two men into their seats. Colonel Roper blacked out immediately. Tom fought to remain conscious, clenching his stomach muscles to restrict the blood pooling in his lower body. His vision turned monochrome and closed in, as if he was peering through a tunnel. He could hardly move. Climbing vertically, he relaxed the stick and the g-force subsided slightly. Before he knew it, he was passing eighty miles altitude and streaking upwards. His colour vision returned. No way could the T 144 stay with him, he thought . . . but the rocket-propelled missiles could!

Tom was right; both were on his tail. He had another responsibility: the energised matter-stream, and so close to the Van Allen belt. He had no choice; he closed the throttle. What else could he do? *What could he do?* he deliberated.

Tom had an idea. Passing two hundred miles altitude, still decelerating in a near vertical climb, he rolled the

Artemis inverted and pulled gently, very gently, into a curving manoeuvre – as if at the top of a loop the loop manoeuvre. He felt for the precise pressure required on the stick: a little more, a little less. Then, miraculously for a manually controlled manoeuvre, he found it. Pieces of dust and debris floated up from the floor of the cockpit, even his checklist drifted in mid air, seemingly suspended in front of his face. . . they were weightless!

Tom held the parabolic curve absolutely precisely. He knew the effect it would have on the missiles; they were terrestrial systems. He watched them carefully on his radar display as they quickly caught up, their automatic guidance systems beginning to replicate *Artemis's* exact trajectory. Soon they too became weightless. As they did, their controlling gyroscopic devices, being gravity biased, toppled. Confused, and lacking both attitude and altitude information, the tracking systems of both missiles shut down simultaneously. They were dead in the air. A few moments later, the missiles drifted slowly, eerily, past Tom. He watched them intently, one passing on either side. He held his course. He was almost able to reach out and touch them. The left one began to tumble and quickly fell out of view below. The other, having a little more momentum continued past.

Suddenly it came to him; it might just work! Tom eased the power lever of his retrorocket open, just slightly; just enough to catch up with the missile, which by now was beginning to curve harmlessly towards the ocean below.

He checked his radar screen. There she was, the fighter, low and to the right, clearly positioning for a second attack run. If the missile could acquire another target, its navigation system might use it for realignment, Tom speculated. It was a long shot, but was worth a try all the same. With expert handling, Tom tucked his wing under one of the missile's rear fins. Gently he nudged it in the direction of the opposing fighter. Squeezing the control stick and applying just a little more power from the retros, he kept the angle constant. Seconds passed, and then . . . yes! The missile's rocket motor burst into life, it burbled a few times and then a huge flame shot out. Tom quickly reduced power, decelerated, and tucked in behind and slightly below the missile, so as not to seduce its tracking system or pass through the scorching exhaust plume. Within seconds the missile streaked away directly towards the opposing aircraft. Clearly, its pilot saw what was happening and he tried to take evasive action. Tom rolled inverted again, looking earthwards to see the outcome. With the benefit of altitude and with blistering acceleration the fighter stood little chance against the missile; a target acquisition with those parameters meant only one thing. A few seconds later, there was a blinding explosion.

'Eastern Control, this is Access One, setting course for London, identification code 9191 coming down.'

'Access One, this is Eastern Atlantic Control. Intruder contact has just disappeared from our radar, repeat, we have lost contact with unidentified intruder . . . are you visual?'

'Affirmative control, intruder is destroyed. He has gone down coordinates north, fifty-five degrees, west, twenty-one degrees. Missile strike, unlikely any survivors, don't waste your time. Listen control, I will need to find an originating airfield for that aircraft, type Tongsei T 144. Chinese built long-range fighter. He was a long way from home.'

'That's copied; we are pulling all area flight-plans. Confirm you are ready to commence final decent into London?'

'Charlie, Charlie, control.'

'Okay, descend twenty thousand feet with a high rate, heading zero nine zero degrees. Call now British Control, frequency code double eight, nine.'

'You got it.'

Tom complied, making the necessary changes to his flight parameters and then suddenly he thought about the Colonel. 'Colonel Roper, Sir?' he enquired earnestly. 'Are you okay back there, how are you feeling?'

'Well, I'm back with you, if that's what you mean, my stomach's not too good though. What in damnation was that all about?'

'I'm not sure Sir, but it was a determined attempt to take us out . . . two fire and forget missiles. I'm gonna look into it on the ground. Presently approaching UK territorial airspace, commencing final descent into the British defence zone, you can relax now, Colonel.'

Tom knew exactly the service provided by British Control: a fully automated ground-based and satellite enhanced air traffic control system, renowned as one of the safest to be found anywhere in the world. Its computer interface had replaced human controllers twenty years earlier, in the thirties, when conventional systems had become unable to cope with the volume of air traffic using British airspace. Interestingly, the new system retained its previous audio heritage by using computer synthesised voice communications between ground station and aerovessel, as it was found that voice communications, rather than machine-talk, kept the pilot better informed in a dynamic air traffic control environment. Now though, things were different. Fuel shortages meant fewer flights and that meant underutilised capacity and an even safer service. Even Tom allowed himself to relax a little as his defence identification code was being verified. He flew confidently beneath the umbrella of British Control.

Within moments a woman's voice, articulate and without accent, gave the standard announcement. 'Access One, this is British Control, you are radar identified entering territorial airspace, all ATC instructions are mandatory. Commence speed reduction to five hundred knots; maintain twenty thousand feet when reaching. You have two hundred track miles to destination.'

The computer-synthesised voice spoke perfect English; all the while Tom considered possible motives behind the unprovoked and near fatal attack. Was it the Colonel they were after, or him, he mused.

'Maintain twenty thousand feet, speed reducing,' Tom responded. 'Be on the ground in twenty minutes, Colonel,' he confirmed over the intercom.

'You betcha!'

Tom checked the navigation coordinates on his display screen. His plot showed the *Artemis* proceeding eastwards over the narrowing English Channel and almost abeam Brighton; soon he would turn left for London. As expected, it would be a full instrument approach procedure as cloud penetration had occurred minutes earlier at an altitude of eight miles, some forty-eight thousand feet. Tom stabilized the speed at five hundred knots and shut down completely the matter-stream propulsion system - retros would provide thrust from here on in.

'Access One, make your heading north, descend seven thousand feet and reduce speed four hundred knots.'

Tom was just about to confirm the orders over the radio when another voice interrupted.

'British Control, this is Orbital Airways flight Triple One, climbing eight thousand feet, London Main departure.'

It was an American voice. It must be the weekly service to New York, Tom thought, or perhaps LA.

'Orbital Triple One, this is British Control, you are identified, continue climb twelve thousand feet and establish vector two, two, zero.'

After the American had read back his instructions, Tom did likewise. Nevertheless, he felt troubled; something niggled him; he couldn't put a finger on it. 'Confirm maintain four hundred knots,' he questioned.

'Mandatory heading north, maintain requested speed,' came the reply.

Tom complied; the *Artemis's* systems could cope with the high velocity profile for the time being, even though it was non-standard. He commenced the descent. At that speed, establishing the final approach vector was just seconds away.

For some inexplicable reason Tom began to feel uneasy. He checked his radar screen, but there was so much clutter that nothing was readable on it; its apparent cause appeared to be weather-induced interference. That in itself was irregular, he thought, and he tried to reduce the clutter by deselecting all weather returns. Then he adjusted the gain to minimise ground returns. Even this had no effect and the display remained useless. 'What the hell's going on?' Tom said aloud. 'This is electronic jamming, I'm sure of it, completely erasing my radar picture!' Tom pulled his eyes away from the display screen and checked his flight instruments. 'Passing nine thousand feet,' he called. 'Two thousand feet to go.' He focused on his flying.

Tom's uneasiness became nervousness. Colonel Roper interrupted his thoughts. 'Tom, do you know if Andromeda's dark-side sensors are radiating into the Neptunus sector again?' he asked arbitrarily, clearly thinking of his next meeting.

Tom's hand hovered over the retrorocket thrust control

lever. We really should start decelerating, he thought. He did not hear the Colonel's question. 'Come on, slow me up, *slow me up* . . . otherwise, we're gonna overshoot,' he said agitatedly over the intercom.

At that moment, a cold shiver ran down his spine and he looked up from his instruments. It was a preconditioned response, a self-preservation response. He peered out through the canopy and into the murk. '*What the . . . hold on!*' he screamed. With that, he rolled right ninety degrees and pulled as hard as he physically could. A huge structure filled his windscreen; it rushed at him; it almost came bursting through, before being lost in the blink of an eye, off to the left. The roar of jet engines filled his ears; the control stick jerked wildly and was wrenched from his hand; the *Artemis* began to spin wildly, completely out of control.

'Mayday, Mayday, Mayday!' Tom called over the radio. 'Access One, proximity alert, passing six thousand feeeee . . . .' he struggled to regain control, fixing his attention on the attitude indicator. 'Wings level . . . check speed . . . power up!' he shouted, talking himself through a recovery procedure that was ingrained in his mind. The *Artemis* passed one thousand feet, still going down.

A split-second later Tom's ship burst through the flat-bottomed, opaque cloud base. The altimeter registered barely two hundred feet. He was upside-down, in a shallow turn and still descending rapidly. Tom became visual. That was all he needed. He flipped the *Artemis* over. Up came the power, the retros roared! He pulled the control stick, raising the nose of the S7, but just enough to arrest the rate of descent; he could not afford to go back into the cloud at that altitude. Miraculously he was immediately above water, just ten feet! A bridge flashed by; its curved span passing over them; they missed it by less. Tom deployed the speed brakes to their fullest extent, levelled off and reduced power. A building streaked past on his left side and then another. He realised that he was over the river, its brown, turbid waters flowing quickly in the opposite direction. It began changing direction, turning left by ninety degrees. Tom followed its course, trying desperately to remain within its bloated contours.

'Arhhhh,' Colonel Roper groaned from the back. His helmet had bashed the canopy on more than one occasion.

Tom was still trying to slow down when two tall buildings appeared immediately ahead, one on each side of the river. Inadvertently he overshot the river's west bank and struggled to regain its course. Of towering steel and blemished glass, the pinnacle of each building probed upwards, only to be lost in the gloomy cloud. Through the middle, Tom thought, increasing his angle of bank. Then he saw something. It was rusty, white, part camouflaged against the drizzly, grey backdrop. It was a wheel - the London Eye! Tom had a microsecond to make the decision; the buildings were too close, with the wheel in the way there was not enough room!

Long since closed, the historic landmark had suffered misuse and disrepair over the years. Only four spokes remained to support the rim; three in one half of the wheel and the other in such a position as to leave a third of the circle open. Tom went for it; he had no other course of action. He rolled his wings through seventy degrees . . . *zoooom*, straight through the middle, missing its structure by centimetres.

'Mayday, Mayday, British Control!' Tom called again over the radio.

Nothing . . . nobody responded, just silence.

As the river began a slow curve to the right, Tom brought his speed under control. Now he knew where he was. He remained within the river's confines but continued the right turn back the way he had come; downstream towards the Thames barrier. He climbed and levelled just below the cloud base, gave the Houses of Parliament as wide a berth as possible and then selected the international distress frequency on his radio.

'British Control, this is VIP Access One on guard frequency, how do you read?'

'Access One,' came the reply instantly. 'This is British Control, we read you five by five. We have been calling you! What are you doing down there? Why haven't you established contact? The commander of Orbital flight Triple One has filed a near miss against you!'

This time it was not a synthesised voice. Tom checked his instruments. Looking outside, he recognised the Tower of London passing close on his left-hand side. He looked ahead, across the river's double meander and out towards the docklands. There, slowly coming into view was the stark concrete conurbation of London Main airport. With its long runway, he would land there instead, he thought. It was safer than Westminster's confined Cityport, particularly as the *Artemis* might be damaged.

Tom ignored the controller's agitated questions; now was not the time to become embroiled in mitigation. He lined himself up with the duty runway. 'Access One,' he called in a composed manner over the radio. 'Short finals to land.'

'You are clear to land Access One,' came the response; the controller knew Tom's position and his workload on finals and said nothing further.

09:29 Greenwich Mean Time

After an uneventful landing, and whilst closing down *Artemis*'s retro thrust system and other associated electronics, Tom took a moment to gather his thoughts. Several people gathered around the ship and an operative climbed up the side. A security vehicle flanked by two police outriders pulled up, their headlights flashing alternately. Before raising the canopy, Tom shared his thoughts with Colonel Roper. 'Someone infiltrated British Control with an audio overlay, Sir, that's serious stuff,' he said with an air of menace. 'Clearly, someone meant to stop us!'

CHAPTER 4

BROTHERS IN ARMS

As if on cue, there was a sharp tap, tap, on the large door, the one through which Richard had originally entered the room. The door opened slightly and Grenville peered around it.

'Admiral Hughes, Sir, Colonel Roper has arrived, be here in a few minutes.'

'Thank you, Grenville, show him in immediately.'

'Yes, Sir, of course.'

Richard knew of Colonel Roper from his Andromeda days; Roper had been Base Commander of Cape Canaveral for several years now, Richard recalled; ever since his training days on the shuttle wing in fact. He also remembered, quite clearly, a heated radio conversation he had had with the Colonel, after successfully landing an S2 on one of Canaveral's priority coded 'November' platforms, and this following an emergency course change in the stratosphere away from Strasbourg and a subsequent diversion to the Cape. On that flight from the Moon, two of the four retro-rockets on his craft had exploded; one of his stabilisers had subsequently detached and the other was damaged; he had seventeen people onboard; manoeuvre control was severely restricted with limited hover capability and frankly, he was more than a little lucky to make the first available platform, let alone select a low priority one. Yet Roper had given him a severe reprimand for 'blacking' an active platform and putting it out of action for a week or two. Richard recalled protesting vehemently at the time, but to no avail; that in itself was a mistake. The subsequent accident report complimented Richard's airmanship and condoned his actions, he recalled. I wonder if he will remember me, Richard speculated silently, as Roper's reputation preceded him these days.

At that moment, Professor Nieve broke into Richard's thoughts. 'What about the sensations you felt during your attachment to the *Enigma*? I know from Commander Race's report that the ship peaked at over fifty percent light related speed.'

'That's correct, Professor, although I didn't know of the speed at the time; it was well beyond the calibration of the pod's instruments. We did encounter a severe harmonic vibration during acceleration; to put it bluntly, it would have detached our internal organs had it been allowed to increase in frequency or amplitude. We resolved it by detaching our bodies from the pod, floating weightless, just out of contact with our seats, but still restrained by the harnesses. The pod vibrated severely for several hours and then settled into a more survivable nanophase regime. The deceleration element was model; caused no problems physiologically as far as I am aware. It was however, very fatiguing, even made *me* feel quite sick and I have a desensitised rating of eleven over four! Actually, you would do better to talk to Rachel Turner, Professor. She's the doc; her information will be far more useful, I would say.'

'You were lucky, Lieutenant; there were countless permutations that you could have encountered, many fatal, I may add,' concluded Professor Nieve. 'Seems you positioned your pod in precisely the correct location and gained adequate protection from the bulk of the propulsion tube magnetrons; perhaps even benefited from their residual electromagnetic flux-fields.'

'I docked with the *Enigma* on two previous occasions Professor, as you know. I had a good idea of what looked suitable and anyway, we all need a little luck in life!'

'Indeed, indeed we do.'

Presently the large, ornate door opened again.

'Colonel Roper and Commander Race, Sir,' said Grenville clearly, as he stepped inside the room and opened the door a little wider to allow the two men to enter.

Both men handed their coats to an orderly who in turn gestured with an open hand, towards the two empty chairs on the other side of the table. Both were now dressed for city business, in smart dark suits; Tom's white shirt complemented by dark red tie with blue motifs, which Richard instantly recognised - the official crew tie of Andromeda's Shuttle Wing. Richard had been privileged to wear such a tie in the past and still had it somewhere amongst his things.

'Colonel, you are very welcome, please sit down,' requested Admiral Hughes.

'Good to be here, Admiral. Secretary Ghent, good morning Sir, how is it?'

'Morning Colonel, I'm glad you could make it. Things are looking a little desperate. Sketchy reports of some trouble yourself I hear, nothing too pressing I trust. Ah, and Commander Race,' Admiral Ghent gestured with an impressed expression. 'We also have a very important job for you Commander.'

'Secretary,' replied Tom Race respectfully.

'Gentlemen, as we are a little behind time,' interrupted Admiral Hughes, 'I suggest that we continue with the brief immediately. Laura here will update you on specifics, Colonel, a little later on.'

Richard caught Tom's eye and offered a friendly expression and a deliberate nod, as one would give a respected friend when in the midst of company where friendship had no relevance. Despite Admiral Hughes's insistence that the formalities be completed after the brief, Tom walked around the table, acknowledging Richard with an outstretched hand. Richard also reached out and both men shook hands warmly.

'Commander Race, how are you?'

'My name hasn't changed Richard, it's still Tom.' He raised his eyebrows as if to emphasise the point.

Richard accepted the gesture with a faint smile. Tom took a step closer and lowered his voice to a whisper. 'Hey man, from a friend, you look as if you've had the crap kicked out of you. What are these guys doing?'

Richard's smile widened. He thought that remark funny, as despite his attire, he had drawn the same conclusion about Tom's appearance moments earlier.

'In England, my dear chap, we call that the pot calling the kettle black!'

'Gee, is that so? I take it I'm not looking that bright either then.' Tom shrugged and straightened his jacket. 'All the same, Richard, it's good to see you.'

'Same applies.'

'Gentlemen please, can we dispense with the pleasantries now and get down to business,' interrupted Admiral Hughes.

Tom's slightly insubordinate action was seemingly accepted, even condoned by those gathered. Admiral Hughes's expression softened, as if to say: the world may be crumbling, but you are right, there is still time for friendship, respect and gratitude. Tom returned to his seat and disarmed everyone with a broad, chiselled-features grin.

'Please everyone, let's get into this brief, over to you Peter,' said Admiral Hughes.

'Ladies and gentlemen, intentions are to cover the environmental and global energy-state briefs initially, Downing Street is growing impatient and this will also benefit Lieutenant Commander Reece, who will be leaving us shortly. Colonel Roper, I do apologise, you are acquainted with Lieutenant Commander Reece, I presume?'

Colonel Roper looked unimpressed, a muscle in his jaw twitched slightly, as if he was irritated. 'Sure, we've spoken in the past,' he replied. 'Not the first name that springs to mind for this level of security clearance. Where I come from, we shave in the mornings . . . no exceptions!'

An underlying, collective cringe circulated the gathering; even Admiral Ghent shuffled his notes for a few seconds. Richard for his part looked Roper in the eye, barely able to contain his contempt.

'Yes, quite, well, there are reasons for everything that you see and hear today Colonel Roper, I can assure you of that,' replied Rothschild defensively. 'Now, please, Doctor Martin, you first if you don't mind, Home Affairs?'

'Yes, of course,' Raymond Martin said politely, positioning his reading spectacles. 'No significant change from last week, it's a general and measured decline; a fair amount of unrest generally, although in certain parts of the country, both petty and violent crime is showing a marked increase, almost to the levels seen during the 'unrest' period back in 2011 and 2012. The southeast in particular and all principal conurbations remain the principal hot spots. Of course, as reported last week, food and water shortages are becoming increasingly common; in some areas rainwater is the only fresh water available and that has to undergo carbon filtration in the home, due to the level of contamination. Industrial output is grinding to a halt, no fuel, no commodities, no raw materials, but that is the case throughout Europe and the Mediterranean region. Companies are going out of business at the approximate rate of three thousand a week, so the level of unemployment is also increasing considerably; on that point, I am still awaiting end of week statistics. The police force is at full stretch and there are no Territorial Army reserves left to call upon. Indeed, we have even had some unauthorised trespassing on the SPEED system; this really is quite unacceptable. One of our major headaches at the moment is the rising water levels around the coastline generally. The Thames is up almost a metre on this time last year. The New Thames Barrier is coping, but only just. It needs electricity, like just about everything else. The water is literally lapping over the top of the damn sluice-gates before we are allocated a supply to operate the computer systems and associated mechanisms.' With that, Doctor Martin looked at his colleague William Bryant, the Energy Secretary, but there was no reaction. 'With no let-up in the daily rainfall, quite frankly I don't see us controlling levels for much longer. That means the entire city flooded, same applies to Bristol, Worcester, Exeter, Liverpool and many other cities. Do not take this as an idle threat, William; Amsterdam, Hamburg, Berlin, not to mention Venice, Bruges and Rotterdam, they are all already under water. We need electricity!'

All eyes fell on William Bryant the Energy Secretary; Peter Rothschild beckoned him to take up the baton. 'Raymond,' he said smoothly. 'I would dearly like to allocate a more regular supply, I really would. The truth of the matter is that I do not have any more to give. I have already spoken to the Prime Minister this morning, he has authorised another round of domestic cuts, a reduced quota and the broadcast will go out later this afternoon. You should prepare for a significant increase in public disorder; this decision will undoubtedly have severe repercussions. Now, gentlemen, this week's statistics and I am afraid that the news is dire: combined oil, gas and coal reserves are now down to three-point-five percent. That is twelve to fourteen weeks supply, taking into account the next round of power cuts. After that, essentially the lights go out! Supplemental, non-carbon based electrical generation is also falling; this supply is essentially only on a regional scale anyway and contributes little to the national grid system overall. However, our intentions are to draw everything we can from the variety of sources in this generating sector and divert them directly to central distribution. Direct local producers will certainly feel the pinch here; no self-generation privileges will remain in force after midnight tonight.' Bryant shook his head, almost in disgust. 'In retrospect, we really should have invested more in these sectors over the last few decades; overcome the heavy-loading problems we are encountering now. Increased sea-states are also causing havoc with our tidal systems, and coastal wind generation appliances are not remaining serviceable for very long, because of the constant ingress of water. Norway has registered a slight increase from its hydropower systems; however, unfortunately she is unable to sell us any more electricity due to her own domestic problems. Oil and gas supplies have now completely dried up from Eastern Europe, Russia and Siberia. Finally, with China calling less than six percent coal reserves, she has curtailed all exports. With over a billion people to service, she will most likely be exhausted before us anyway! Last but certainly not least, the Kalahari crystal installed in the Sizewell B reactor, together with its associated power station, is now producing at thirty-one percent former capacity, that is down two percent in the last week. According to the generating statistics board, that gives us another fifteen to sixteen weeks before our crystal too, is exhausted. I understand that the Japanese have a similar scenario; their crystal, installed in the Katsuura reactor near Tokyo, is currently down to twenty-nine percent of initial output.'

At that remark, Richard shook his head; he could no longer contain his frustration at the way the crystals were being used. 'Why,' he asked passionately of Bryant, 'when you know that this is the wrong way to utilise this energy source, do you continue to burn out these precious crystals in these inept, inefficient old nuclear reactors? For God's sake, stop, while there is still some potential remaining; do some research, experiment, there *is* a better way!'

William Bryant, as much as Peter Rothschild, was surprised by Richard's outburst. 'What do you know of a better way to utilise these crystals, Richard?' Rothschild asked, somewhat perplexed.

'I studied the flight log, Peter; engineering, propulsion, power generation; it was all there, the way *they* did it, the extra terrestrials, surely their way would be the most efficient. Eridu's crystal supported a vast city complex, we have already discussed this and Babylon only had a part crystal, yet they lasted for thousands of years. You are burning these things out in a matter of months; the Long Island reactor is already on its second stone!'

William Bryant shook his head sorrowfully, 'you are probably right, Mr Reece,' he continued, 'there no doubt is a better way to utilise these crystals, but we simply cannot wait; neither politically, nor practically and I suspect that that is also the case for the United States.' Admiral Ghent nodded in agreement. 'We all need the power *now*. If I pull the plug on Sizewell – and do not forget that the flight log is now missing – our reserves will be down to just two or three weeks; Great Britain reduced to candle power . . . literally and the average temperature out there is only a little above freezing! What would *you* do, young man?'

Richard took a deep, meaningful breath; the warm dry air of the Admiralty building had cleared his sinuses a little. He thought of the earth and the time before he had left for Mars, when, despite record levels of atmospheric pollution, the sun still shone; day was day and night was night. He enquired soulfully of Bryant and leaned forward to look also at Professor Nieve. 'How did it come to this? I mean, I was only away a year or so, did you people, the scientific community, really not see this coming?'

William Bryant shook his head; Richard could sense a little embarrassment in him, but that was not the purpose of his question.

'This situation was not predicted,' Bryant explained. 'No computer model saw this coming. Consensus was that the global warming scenario of the last fifty years would continue, but at a reduced rate. The industrialised countries of the world were gradually complying with reduced CO_2 quotas, but it's common knowledge that some irreversible damage was done to the ionosphere during this first quarter century, mainly due to the unrestrained growth of China and India. The average surface temperature was already up by two degrees Celsius in 2030, despite the international Kyoto 5 protocol and other, similar regional protocols. Back then, the scientific community expected the GAT to stabilise, perhaps even reduce; of course, we know now that the 'temperature momentum phenomenon' prevented any improvement. In retrospect, the accelerated decline of the tropical rainforests – after the

Global Average Temperature reached the 2008 datum plus three degrees in 2036 – should have sounded the alarm bells; more so as the temperate deciduous belts began to degenerate. In reality, everyone thought it would sort itself out. I have read the 2042 Kyoto 6 meeting notes of my predecessor; seems that despite the evidence, everyone genuinely believed that the situation would be resolved in the long term; quotas were realistic, they thought; but obviously in reality, hopelessly inadequate.'

'An ostrich with its head in the ground springs to mind,' said Richard, much to the vexation of the seated senior officers.

'And then the collapse of the global water cycle over the last two years,' Bryant concluded, evading Richard's rather pertinent remark. 'Record upper-atmospheric temperatures allowing a far greater proportion of water vapour to remain suspended in the troposphere; combined with record levels of atmospheric pollutants and carbonic microparticles . . .'

'Condensing nuclei and lots of water vapour, come on . . . I mean that's basic meteorology – you get *cloud*!' Richard proclaimed.

Bryant nodded in agreement. 'Maybe we should have seen it. Problem was that the world's scientific community became too preoccupied with the global warming scenario to notice the water-cycle breakdown; no one imagined that we would be subject to a temperate reversal.'

'Dense, polluted cloud, over eight miles thick in places

and covering the entire planet's surface, what did you think would happen to the temperature? I mean, you must have been warned,' Richard declared.

Bryant shrugged; unfairly, he now really was embarrassed. 'Well our legacy, mine, that of my international colleagues and our predecessors, is a species-threatening atmospheric catastrophe. If we are going to survive, then we are going to have to cope with it; but it is not going to be easy.'

'Yes,' agreed Rothschild. 'And despite all this, we have a global criminal fraternity who will stop at nothing in order to take advantage of the situation.'

'Peter, I've heard enough,' said Richard despondently. 'I consider myself fully briefed. I have some things, personal things, I need to do before I leave tonight, so I would like to make a start with security as soon as possible. With your permission . . .'

'Yes of course, anyone else with anything for Lieutenant Commander Reece?'

There was no response. Richard, avoiding the stare of Colonel Roper, acknowledged Tom and then walked toward a loitering orderly, who had made ready his coat. Rothschild pressed a call button on his control panel and barely had Richard arrived at the door when it opened.

'Ah, Lieutenant Commander Reece,' said Grenville respectfully from outside. 'Follow me if you will.'

Richard nodded; as he walked through the door Rothschild added. 'Good luck Richard, we will be in touch.'

There was a general shuffling of papers and people around the table; Laura Bellingham changed the image on the screen of her laptop at Rothschild's behest, as he flipped through several other images on the large, central, prismatic facility until he found the one in question. With that, he stood up, composed himself and looked towards the senior American statesman at the other end of the table. Admiral Ghent made a gesture of approval.

'Now, Commander Race,' Rothschild continued. '*Your* brief.'

CHAPTER 5

STARK REALITY

A different driver drove Richard home. It was mid afternoon and this time he had an armed bodyguard for company, although the limousine itself appeared regular enough. A subtle government crest, in red, gold and royal blue was etched on the glossy, black paintwork; on closer scrutiny, each door appeared to have one. There were other additions too: dark tinted windows, a small internal satellite aerial, appropriate upholstery and some gadgets in both armrests of the large, forward-facing rear seats.

The best of the day had passed and Richard was hungry, tired and still unsettled; understandable enough, considering what he was about to do. He sat back and stared out of the window, lost in his thoughts. He had decided not to contact Rachel before his departure, there was no point; the inevitable argument would probably do more damage to their now faltering relationship than the revelations of her 'other' life. At some point though, he would have to tell her that he no longer trusted her and that, as far as he was concerned, the engagement was over. Anyway, as they were *both* now working for MI9, she would soon hear of his new itinerary, no doubt. How ironic he thought, as a saddened, half-smile permeated his features.

Movement outside distracted him; despite the weather, the avenue was busy; the general hustle and bustle of London's street life continued unabated. The driver looked at him through the rear view mirror.

'Would you like some music, Sir?' enquired the driver kindly.

'No, thanks, but you could put the news channel on if you like,' Richard replied.

The driver did so and a few items of general news, of no interest to Richard broke the silence. Then a different, more matter-of-fact voice, a politician-type voice, spoke.

'This is an important government announcement regarding energy,' he said. 'It is in every British citizen's interest to listen carefully to this information, as new measures are being introduced by the Energy Commission which will affect your electricity supply. These changes will be implemented shortly and will affect every home and business in the United Kingdom. The Right Honourable William Bryant MP, Secretary for Energy, will make the announcement.' There was a short pause and then another man spoke. Richard instantly recognised his voice. This must have been pre-recorded, he thought.

'Oh no, not him again,' groaned the driver. 'Bad news every time we hear him!'

'Turn it up please,' requested Richard.

'Citizens of the United Kingdom,' Bryant began in his cultured tone. Richard already knew of his background, even before he had met him, indeed, most did, as he was the key political figure in most people's lives. Eton and Oxford educated and although no doubt, highly competent, he was public enemy number one. In that unenviable position, even with the best will in the world, Bryant had become more infamous than respected. Having said that, Richard thought, there was nobody else in government, least of all in the current 'Centre Green' party who could popularise the job. Richard listened intently.

'This important announcement outlines a new policy regarding energy. It will affect everybody living in the United Kingdom, whether a British citizen or foreign visitor. Further, this policy change will be implemented from midnight tonight. You are all only too aware, I am sure, of the energy crisis that faces our country; I am here to tell you that this crisis has now reached a critical level, indeed, each and every country in the world is similarly affected.'

Richard squirmed, shaking his head. 'It's been with us for the last half century you idiot and critical for the last twenty,' he whispered. The driver looked at him through the rear-view mirror, but remained silent.

'I can tell you that the energy situation in this country is now grave indeed. Our stocks of oil, coal, gas and wood are almost exhausted and we have been unable to secure further significant supplies from abroad. As a result, and in order to preserve what little fuel reserves we have remaining, the energy commission has taken the decision to reduce again the period of time that electricity will be available in your home and in the workplace. I will explain fully the current situation, so that every citizen is aware of the reasons behind our decision today. Each region in the country receives an electricity quota from the country's main power network, or national grid, which itself is supplied with power from our remaining generating stations. To date, this quota has resulted in each and every home, and also many selected industrial establishments, receiving four hours of uninterrupted electricity each day. Some, more critical establishments, such as government and military buildings and the primary hospitals, have an appropriately increased electricity supply in order for them to continue their vital work. Renewable energy sources have supplemented this daily allocation where possible on a regional basis; here the energy commission has allowed a degree of decentralised control, which has resulted in slightly longer periods of power in some areas. From midnight tonight, the national quota of electricity is to be reduced from four hours each day to two hours each day. In addition, *all* local generating potential will be diverted to the national grid and controlled by the government. Our senior citizens over the age of seventy-five, that is approximately thirty-seven percent of the population, whose homes are correctly registered with their local county councils, will receive an additional four-kilowatt daily supplement. This will provide an equivalent of one hour's additional heating. Regional generating control centres will automatically adjust the special, red, OAP household meter boxes. This process will happen at seven o'clock this evening. Further, the energy commission recommends that all homes in the United Kingdom be equipped with at least two of the *Electroprime* ceramic, storage-type convection heaters. I can assure you that these units will still be able to store enough energy during a two-hour cycle to heat, adequately, homes of modest size, during the daylight hours. Please adhere to current government guidelines and advice. Heat only two rooms in your home; we recommend that these are communal living areas and not bedrooms or utility areas. Regarding commercial supplies . . .'

'Turn it off, please. I've heard enough,' declared Richard.

'Two hours!' complained the driver, reluctantly complying with Richards's request.

'I'll give you some advice, driver,' offered Richard. 'If you don't have a Multifuel stove or a wood-burner, get one! If you do, prepare it, service it. The next five or six weeks, every spare minute, collect whatever fuel source you can. Store it *inside* your home. Wood, card, old papers, wooden furniture; go to building sites, buy waste, planks, roof members, anything. Then keep it quiet!'

The driver's eyes widened as he looked solemnly at Richard through the rear view mirror; he nodded slowly, but said nothing.

Richard felt both betrayed and frustrated. He thought of his mother in Somerset, already frail, but not even qualifying for the extra hour of heating potential. He would try to persuade her to go and stay with Aunt Pamela. Then, he thought of the crystal hidden in his father's old workshop at the top of the garden, not two hundred metres from her cottage. Immense, innate power, effectively locked away, and, at the moment anyway, completely irretrievable. It would not be sensible for the cottage to be unoccupied, even for a few days, as local councils were requisitioning empty houses almost immediately in order to house those made homeless by the floods. Richard breathed a long sigh and then considered the other implications of the broadcast. It only confirmed what Bryant had stated in the brief, as if there was any ambiguity: like the first crystal installed in the Long Island reactor, the installation at Sizewell was also close to exhaustion; drained in less than six months.

The Americans had retained three crystals, Richard mused, and with two sites operational, had utilised the third as a replacement in the Long Island reactor. No such luck for the UK, he concluded, as the fifth stone had been promptly dispatched to the reactor near Tokyo last December. The relevant governments must surely realise that their mishandling of this unique power source was tantamount to an international crime.

Then there was the question of what to do with the hidden crystal . . . his crystal! What if it was traced? He had reported *nine* originally. The remaining three crystals from the Kalahari site on Mars had already been retrieved and were being stored in the Yearlman facility in Osiris, awaiting passage to earth. Since the death of Jennifer Middleton and Peter Yung during the PTSV incident, the question of the 'lost' ninth crystal had fortunately been overshadowed; but it was only a matter of time. Now, with those three remaining crystals becoming so incredibly valuable, literally priceless, Greg Searle and his team would surely be under orders to locate and retrieve the outstanding example. You cannot just lose one of those things on the planet's surface, deliberated Richard; for one thing, an omnidirectional electromagnetic sweep would be expected to reveal its location with some accuracy. Searle would undoubtedly ask for the daily satellite microtherm surface survey. From that, it would not be difficult to plot my track back to base that day. Unless of course, Richard considered, they think that the crystal is being shielded by something, neutralised, or has fallen into one of the numerous, bottomless, fissures that pepper the planet surface in that sector. Searle is good at his job; you have to give him that. He would be investigating, probing, and what about Sergeant David Norman? He had broken protocol by allowing me to deposit a late package in the shuttle dispatch bay, bound for earth and without going through quarantine. That was taboo; would he admit to it under severe questioning? Another thought crossed Richard's mind at that moment: the crystal, when it formed part of the *Star*'s propulsive mechanism. It was surrounded by a protective sphere. If the science department on Mars set about generating a computer model, to aid their understanding of the sphere's function, they would quickly discover a substantial amount of that material missing! Richard had packed at least four kilograms of the shattered, green, glass-like material into his helmet box in order to insulate *his* crystal for the journey home. Would they want an explanation for that, he speculated.

Richard's thoughts raced. There were a number of factors that could implicate him. The situation was becoming complicated and dangerous. He would need to keep his wits about him. Extreme vigilance would be required if he were to not only survive, but also make the best of the remaining crystals.

CHAPTER 6

AGGRESSIVE ELECTRONICS

To Richard, Captain Castina looked Portuguese, or perhaps Spanish, with his olive coloured skin and black hair. He did not enquire further, but his accent also laid weight to his supposition. Instead, Richard gratefully shook his hand and thanked him for waiting. As with most buildings on London's skyline, the VIP terminal of the new Orbitalport was primarily of glass, and as with most, it looked grim. A year of sooty grime and staining and streaky discolouration by corrosive rain had put paid to the architects visions of bold modernism.

The Eagle looked impressive though, very much so, as it stood perched on three heavy undercarriage struts and boasted a similar number of enormous engine exhaust cones. After a short walk from the terminal and a flight of integrated steps, the state of the art corporate jetliner offered an interior that was fit for a king – apt, considering their clientele, thought Richard. And then there was the Flight Attendant: with curves to rival the aeroplane's and her colour-coordinated uniform. Vivaldi's *Four Seasons* played politely in the background.

'I think that I am going to enjoy this flight,' Richard mumbled to himself.

'I'm sorry Sir, I didn't quite hear.'

'Oh, nothing, nothing at all,' Richard replied, smiling. 'Where would you like me to sit?'

Captain Castina stood at the bottom of the steps and offered a handshake as Richard stepped down. 'My orders are to wait for you, Sir,' he confirmed.

'Nice, very nice, thanks,' Richard commented. 'And don't worry about me, I can see myself out. I'll meet you back here in forty-eight hours, any changes and I will get word to you.'

'I understand. We will be ready,' Captain Castina replied, nodding. 'Just one other thing, Sir, for the return flight; there will be a new security code issued . . . you *will* need to know it!'

'Okay, forty-eight hours then,' Richard replied.

Accompanied by a member of airport security and a ground-handling agent, Richard quickly passed through the Royal Suite, immigration control and customs. Extended the privilege of diplomatic status, no one searched his bag.

The main terminal in Los Angeles airport was as busy as he remembered; not that he had visited for several years. Despite the drudgery of grey, overcast skies, life went on. It was however, cold, damn cold. Not so for, say, New Yorkers, or Bostonites, managing in mid-winter's icy grip, but for Californians, the world was upside-down, more so because it was nearly June. Average daytime temperatures of only two degrees Celsius over recent weeks and sub-zero nightime lows, had killed most of the state's citrus trees and grapevines, and as if to emphasis this fact, only limp, rotting, brown fronds now hung from the tops of the three hundred or so palm trees that flanked the once impressive, mile-long *Skyway* boulevard. Stretching from the freeway to the expansive glass arrivals terminal, the long boulevard looked stark and inert, a mere shadow of the once celebrated architectural fusion of the natural and the contrived.

With a small rucksack over his shoulder, Richard pushed open a wide, once automatic, door and stepped out into the expected, but nonetheless surprising weather conditions. With inoperative doors, restricted services and subdued lighting, it was painfully obvious that electricity was in scarce supply here too. Richard walked a little further, but remained under the limited cover afforded by a large, overhanging, tinted-glass portico, that was designed, essentially, to give comfortable protection from a glaring sun; consequently, the gusting wind, saturated with moisture, encountered little resistance as it swept beneath.

With the rain lashing down, it was not long before Richard abandoned the prescribed rendezvous position and took refuge behind a bulky and apparently themeless sculpture, some twenty metres away.

As Richard stood and waited, he scanned the area methodically. Several groups of people came and went. He focused on a few individuals, but not surprisingly, few had the time or inclination to return his prying stare. After several minutes, he moved again to a more exposed but visible position. Then he noticed a man inside the building who stood, seemingly nonchalant, but with some purpose. The man, wearing a long dark raincoat, stood behind the vertical expanse of plate glass that was attached to a tall, structural, stainless steel column. Periodically, the man stepped behind the column concealing himself. Trying not to look at him directly, Richard kept watch from the corner of his eye.

Minutes passed; Richard waited patiently. Presumably satisfied, the man approached, striding purposefully through the doors. Then, taking Richard completely by surprise, he walked directly up to him and gave him a welcoming hug, patting him zealously on the back as if he were greeting some long lost brother. This unlikely scenario raised a helpful smile from Richard, who whispered into the man's ear. 'I have a question of future history.'

'I have an answer from America,' replied the man.

The code was correct.

'Follow me!' the man ordered, his accent a refined New

England American.

Both men walked towards the roadside, Richard bag in hand. A black, long-wheelbase limousine with dark windows arrived promptly and drew up alongside them. One of the two rear doors opened. The man encouraged Richard to climb into the car with a gentle shove and then followed himself. Richard found his place on the rear seat quick enough, as the vehicle sped off, wheels screeching. He was becoming used to falling into cars backwards.

'We can brief you now, or after you've had some rest?' ventured another figure sitting opposite him in a rearward facing seat. This man, his features concealed in the diffused semi-darkness, had a deep, rumbling voice of the south. 'Well?' he enquired of Richard.

'Now is fine,' Richard responded.

With that, opaque electric blinds moved automatically, drawn across the windows from front to back. Simultaneously, several small overhead lights flickered on, their light adequately illuminating the three men and the spacious area generally. The man opposite Richard was an Afro-American in his mid forties. He appeared well groomed, wearing a crisp, dark suit, a white shirt and a tasteful, plain red silk tie. His own raincoat, similarly dark coloured, lay folded on the seat beside him and on it was an open briefcase. An identity badge in a small plastic wallet hung from the breast pocket of his jacket. Richard glanced at his newfound 'brother' sitting on his right. He was younger, had a Mediterranean complexion and a neat black moustache. He offered Richard his hand.

'I'm Antonio Spirelli, Central Intelligence Bureau, how's it going?'

Richard acknowledged, nodding in a friendly manner. 'Richard Reece . . . oh, um, sorry, I mean Rhys Jones,' he stammered, over his newly acquired but mistaken identity.

Spirelli looked across at his obviously more senior colleague and shook his head.

'You get one chance to get that wrong and that was it . . . understand?' said the Afro-American man in his deep, authoritarian tone.

Richard was embarrassed, he nodded again; there was no answer to that.

'My name is Reuben Massy, United States State Department, special security agent. I will be responsible for you while you are over here. One of us will be with you at all times, I mean at *all* times; you had better get used to that and quickly.'

Massy leant over and unzipped a compartment within the lid of his briefcase. From it, he pulled out a small shoulder holster. Unclipping the leather flap, he withdrew a palm-sized, oval-shaped object, evidently a weapon of some kind. Richard had not seen its like before. It had a translucent white outer shell, but black internal circuitry and a number of external buttons were clearly visible.

'Seen one of these?' Massy enquired of Richard.

'Can't say that I have,' Richard answered, studying the

object intently.

Massy handed the two items to Richard. 'Have you heard of an ISTAN?'

'No, not even that. So what is it?'

'Special CIA issue, undercover and secret operatives only; although a variant was leaked and illegally manufactured last year. We caught them, but a few examples got out; tracked down to South America.'

Richard shook his head, 'bit embarrassing,' he offered unhelpfully. 'No . . . I'm no weapons expert, not these days anyway.'

'Service designator ISTAN VR1,' Massy continued, 'Ionising Sceptre and Terminal Area Neutraliser, Variation 1; manufactured by Electron Defence Systems; very expensive, but very effective.'

Richard tried to appear suitably impressed.

'Known in the trade as the light-sabre,' added Massy. A glimmer of a smile broke his stern features. 'Are you right or left handed?'

'Left!'

'Okay, take the holster in your right hand and withdraw the weapon with your left . . . carefully. You'll find that its form will fit naturally in the palm of your hand.'

Richard did so and was surprised at how comfortable the weapon was, but as he gripped it lightly in his hand, two crosspieces sprang open from the hilt and locked into place. Now it really did feel like a muted dagger or sword. The weapon was light and evidently of ceramic construction, although the crosspiece appeared to be plated in gold. He changed his grip slightly, holding it as if it were a sword; three flush, coloured buttons lay comfortably under the tip of his thumb; arranged in a row, the central button was largest. He could also feel a very slight vibration.

Massy pulled a short electrical lead from his briefcase and offered one end to the weapon; it was made inflexible by a gold coloured material that covered its entire length. Richard turned the hilt to reveal a small hole, which Massy plugged. The other end went into a rubbery electrode two centimetres square.

'The lead is just temporary, while we set the thing up,' Massy explained. 'It's got to be an insulated connection to avoid interference.' He peeled back a piece of protective tape from the front face of the electrode. 'This is a self-adhesive patch, secure it to your left temple,' he continued.

'Why?' Richard asked as he took it from Massy.

'The weapon is personal, idiosyncratic, it will be tuned to your own, natural biorhythms and cerebral synaptic pattern. A brainwave scanner if you like and your own personal key cut; like a fingerprint, totally unique, impossible to replicate.'

Richard pressed the patch to his temple while Massy shuffled several items in his briefcase, exposing a small control box, about the size of two cigarette packets. On its upper face an illuminated green button glowed; he pressed it. On the weapon, a tiny red light, not much bigger than a pinhead, turned green.

'This weapon has huge potential, Jones,' Massy continued. 'It is bio smart and can only be used by you . . . or someone with your exact synaptic trace. So, only you!'

'What, exactly, does it do?' Richard asked.

'There are three modes, all dual switched. Initially, you switch the weapon on by pressing the left-hand button and de-energise by pressing the right-hand button. After you've switched it on, it will run an internal systems check, like a self-test sequence; if there is enough charge, over fifteen percent, *and* the biosensor recognises your synaptic trace, that light will illuminate . . . green, exactly as it is now. If not, if there is a problem, it will either not light up at all, or turn red, depends on the fault. When it's on, operational, then all you have to do is *think* the option you require whilst simultaneously pressing the central sensor pad beneath your thumb, understand?'

'So far, but what is its capacity?' commented Richard, his scepticism becoming plain to see.

'You must *think* the option as you press the central pad, it's a dual safety device; preventing the weapon being activated accidentally. So, press the central pad and think *green*, the colour green; imagine a green object, this usually works when you are starting out; a field of green grass or something like that; this is the 'blade' option. You cannot see it though, just the glow of ionised strontium molecules; like a glowing mist. The invisible blade is about twelve inches long, three-hundred millimetres for you limeys, and two inches wide. It will cut through plate steel like a hot knife through butter, and anything else you care to mention. Think *blue*, whilst simultaneously pressing the central button and the blade becomes a molecular projectile, accurate as hell. A fully charged energy cell will produce one hundred projectiles, range around three hundred yards. If you *think* directional instructions before you fire, the projectile will comply. Fifty yards, turn right ninety degrees, that sort of thing; but you have to programme it before you fire, understand?'

Richard nodded in response; his jaw was slowly beginning to drop, unfortunately producing an expression of gormless bafflement.

'Firepower of a small platoon,' Spirelli added enthusiastically, hoping Richard might be stirred into asking a technical question, or something remotely sensible, anything that would remove that somewhat uninspiring look of complete stupefaction. To Sirelli's relief, Richard eventually did.

'Why a colour . . . why not the blade itself, or for the projectile mode, a sublet or an old bullet, or something similar?'

'That was the obvious choice, I asked the same question myself,' replied Massy. 'But they couldn't get it to work. The spectrum, the thought process, what people imagined when they thought of a blade for example was too wide, too complex. They could not nail the synaptic image. Colours are simpler, apparently the neural pathways from the optic nerve helps to solidify the image in the mind.

Most normal sighted people see colours the same, pretty-much.'

'Okay, I'll buy that, seems convincing. So, I simply press this pad, then the central pad and think . . .'

'No stop . . . be careful!'

A dense misty glow immediately appeared at the end of the handle that Richard held; he almost dropped it in surprise. Tiny glowing specks of light danced within it, like when the dust from a shaken curtain becomes illuminated within a column of sunlight streaming through a window. Within seconds, the outline fired across the car. Massy leant back in his seat, lifting his arm just in time. The molecular blade penetrated the door of the car and then dissolved into nothing, dispersing as quickly as it had formed. Through a gash in the door, some fifty millimetres long and five wide, the thickness of the vehicle's armour plating was plain to see. A whistle of air and the hum of road noise permeated through it.

Massy looked at Richard like a stern teacher would to a wayward pupil. 'This is a three million dollar car; that door has inch thick armour plating!'

Richard breathed out heavily, as much embarrassed as impressed. He placed the weapon on the seat next to him and removed the sensor pad from his temple and then he looked Massy in the eye.

'Do I really need this?'

'The people who are after you Mr Jones, will not stop to ask questions. They will shoot first, or worse.'

Richard's expression darkened. 'I see, and the third option?'

'Press the central pad and think red, a red sunset or something; blood, usually does it for me. If you use this option, I'd say you were in trouble; becomes a plasma grenade; ionising, not your regular electro-static. Neutralise anything and anybody within fifty yards. Make sure you have a clear area in which to throw it and don't be in the same room . . . you'll fry. Last ditch effort, or self destruct, it's your call.'

Richard looked up at Massy again; he was more than a little perturbed. 'Hope I won't need that option then,' he ventured.

Massy nodded, 'me too!'

'So, where are we going, and what do you want me to do?'

Massy fell back hard against his chair and relaxed for a few moments. 'Two hour drive,' he replied, indicating to Richard that he should wear the shoulder holster. '*Future Life Cryogenics Incorporated*, their storage facility near Santa Barbara. They also have a state-of-the-art hospital there, that's the first stop. Eleven thousand bodies in suspended animation, all waiting to be defrosted, have their medical problems resolved and finish their lives. Apparently, a few have been frozen for more than eighty years: cancer, avian flu, worn-out body parts . . . gee, why don't people just die gracefully?'

'So, you don't want to live forever, Agent Massy?'

Richard enquired sarcastically.

Massy looked Richard square in the eyes, then at his colleague, and then out through the narrow blinds and heavily tinted windows. Outside the climate was alien, unrecognisable for the region and particularly the sunshine coast. A quiet hiss of air penetrated the neat incision in the car door, occasionally the hiss turned to a whistle that warbled eerily. Massy folded his coat and pushed it against the hole; his attempt to completely insulate their surreal capsule was only partially successful. Several seconds passed in uneasy silence.

'Nobody lives forever, Jones; not even Mother Earth!'

CHAPTER 7

ILL-CONCEIVED AFTERLIFE

Richard felt a tap on his shoulder; two hours of unsettled sleep had left him fuzzy. The car door was already open and both Spirelli and Massy looked down on him from outside. Massy had Richard's black canvas rucksack dangling from his outstretched hand.

'When you are ready, Jones,' he beckoned, looking around the area nervously.

Richard snapped back to reality and climbed from the vehicle. It had stopped outside a large building of contemporary design, with an impressive entrance.

'Move, quickly!' insisted Massy.

The three men climbed the broad flight of stone steps, which led up to two glass doors. At the summit, Richard looked back over his shoulder while buttoning his coat and he lifted the right lapel to check that the securing flap on his holster was in place. He had the unsettling feeling that, in the near future, he would depend on that weapon for his life. He certainly could not afford to misplace this new toy.

Richard noted that the building was surrounded by some serious security arrangements. Integrated at regular intervals within the unusually high perimeter fencing, were manned watchtowers. In addition, they had entered through a double security gate system, with two checkpoints positioned some fifty metres apart and each guarded by armed, military-looking personnel. An array of security cameras and infra-red imagers monitored their every move. Above the large doors, engraved in a wide expanse of pale green glass, was the name of the establishment:

FUTURE-LIFE CRYOGENICS INCORPORATED C.A.

As the men neared the doors, the left one opened. Massy put a hand on Richard's shoulder and held him back. 'One other thing, I should have mentioned it. That holster is fitted with a communications device. There's a switch inside, under the flap on the left; similar synaptic trigger, so only you can initiate it. The device uses the US Hyperbolic Stella Positioning System, half-hemisphere range, provided you are in the open. Satellite cross-communication can give it global coverage, but there are restrictions, so don't count on full support. If you are inside a building or subject to electrical interference, the range is reduced. Unrestricted coverage will give us your exact position within seconds. Unfortunately, there is a catch.'

'Seems to me there's always a catch,' Richard commented.

'The 'other side' has acquired the technology; computer hacking, espionage, call it what you like. If you need to be found, use it, but be aware that others are watching and listening.'

Richard nodded. 'Comforting thought,' he offered.

The three men walked cautiously through the open door, which closed automatically behind them. Inside, a small group of people loitered. There were nine of them, Richard counted and all except one wore immaculate, white, medical coats. They stood with a man in his late fifties or, perhaps, wearing well for early sixties. His attire consisted of slim, sharply pressed white trousers and a stylish short white jacket, complemented by a white shirt and a white bow tie. A silver crucifix on a heavy silver chain, hung around his neck. The man stepped forward; he had thin shallow features and short greying hair. He was slightly taller than Massy's five foot eight and offered a befriending gesture with his outstretched hand, which Massy accepted with a blank stare. This seemed to unnerve the man and he blatantly studied Massy's body language for a few seconds. Then, but only momentarily, the man turned his attention to Spirelli, who, in his padded raincoat and looking bulkier than he actually was, still could not match the ox-like broadness of his boss. Richard, appearing taller and slimmer in his plain woollen coat had, for what it was worth, half a head on all of them.

The man, forcing a welcoming smile, introduced himself. 'I am Doctor Webber; I am the director of this facility, and Dean of the Future-Life Cryogenic Institute. A great pleasure gentleman, we are always keen to cooperate with the FBI,' he added.

Massy went to correct him, but stopped short. 'Thank you, Doctor Webber, my name is Agent Massy; these are my colleagues Agent Spirelli and Agent Jones.'

Richard shook Doctor Webber's hand in turn; it was a limp, clammy handshake and he avoided Richard's eye contact, quickly turning his attention back to Massy.

'Gentlemen please, this way. Time is pressing.'

With that, the doctor turned on his heel and quickly walked off towards one of three corridors radiating from the grand entrance foyer. His entourage followed closely behind. They appeared collectively, to sense his unease and huddled themselves into a trailing gaggle; like hapless ducks following the sound of a decoy on a riverbank. The group walked the length of several pristine corridors in silence. They passed a number of intersections where further corridors branched in various directions with no directional information. It was like a rabbit warren, thought Richard, how on earth would you find your way around this place? It was pale, sterile, immaculate and soulless. Richard speculated on the expense of setting up such a facility and the enormous ongoing costs. Eventually, as much to break the monotonous shuffle of soft-shoes, as to satisfy his curiosity, he asked Webber a question.

'Dr Webber, may I ask how many patients have been successfully, thawed, for want of a better expression, since your programme started?'

Dr Webber pulled up short, adjacent to a single door. He waved his hands impatiently, in order that his followers open their protective circle a little. They had walked past a score of similar doors Richard noted, but none bore a number, or indeed any other form of identification. On this particular door however, there was a bold, white placard, with red lettering:

PRIVATE
NO ENTRY

A security guard in a white orderly's uniform paced the corridor carrying a radio in one hand. Doctor Webber's rather daunting appearance and abrupt manner probably prevented such questions ordinarily. Richard was genuinely interested and his tone was honest; he considered answers to pertinent questions such as his were necessary to build up a picture of the way this institution functioned. Further, with routine in-house security operations at this level, how had the facility been made accessible to the outside?

'We have encountered a number of problems over the last few years, relating to the vital-functions recovery process,' Doctor Webber replied eventually. 'Since an *effective* cure for even the most debilitating forms of cancer became commonplace ten years ago, many custodians have approached us wishing to have their relatives or friends revived. We still however, discourage recovery at this point in time, as the process is not yet one hundred percent reliable.'

Sounds like an evasive politician, thought Richard, as he pushed Webber to be more specific. 'So what is your success rate, Doctor?'

The doctor sighed with annoyance that he should be probed for such information. To Richard, it was clear that Doctor Webber was uneasy to release statistics and it soon became apparent why.

'The truth is that we are still perfecting the process. To date we have attempted recovery on fifty-eight patients. Unfortunately, only eleven have survived 'thawing out' as you ineptly put it; of these eleven, three successfully underwent treatment for their original ailments and have survived to continue a normal life. Interestingly, our oldest success was born in 1925, she was suspended in 1983 and was recovered two years ago; she is now one hundred and twenty five years old, but in reality, a sprightly sixty year old.'

Richard nodded, seemingly impressed at the case history, but not at the statistics. 'Eleven out of fifty-eight doctor, less than twenty percent, why do you not wait a few more years, until the technology has been perfected?'

The doctor's expression darkened. 'We can only advise the guardians of our patients on these matters; it is their ultimate decision when to begin recovery!'

Richard nodded. 'But when the process is complete, you get the rest of your money, right? I mean the outstanding expenses for the entire process, which, presumably are considerable?'

'The final bill depends on the total number of years, months and days in suspended animation, but yes, these fees can be substantial. After all, the maintenance of this facility and its infrastructure is similarly very expensive. The people who engage us, Agent Jones, usually do not want for money. To live another day, so to speak, is by definition, very expensive.'

'Usually?' Richard questioned. 'So sometimes, occasionally, they are inexpensive?'

'Sometimes people enter the programme sponsored by others,' Webber replied curtly.

'What about Professor Simpson-Carter, Doctor Webber, was he a wealthy man?'

Webber scanned the expectant faces of the group and then gestured to the security guard to unlock the door. 'Let us continue this conversation *inside*,' he answered secretively.

The room was small, a maximum of four metres by three

metres and painted a pale yellow. It was windowless but airy. There was a white, steel-framed hospital-type bed, a stainless-steel bedside cabinet and a regular hospital visitor's high-back chair. That was it; nothing else; no television, hanging pictures, ornaments or objects; coldly clinical.

With an imperious wave, Doctor Webber indicated that his entourage should wait outside and Richard closed the door behind Agents Massy and Spirelli. Webber directed his comments at Richard, perhaps realising the relevance of his questions.

'Professor Simpson-Carter was not a wealthy man, Agent Jones,' Webber continued. 'On the contrary, he was a dedicated scientist with precious little time for material things. Eminent in his field, he had a number of benefactors and sponsors.' Webber tucked the silver chain and crucifix that hung prominently, if not irritatingly, into his shirt. He passed the chain behind a plastic photographic identity badge that was clipped to his breast pocket and then looked up again at Richard. 'Not least of whom were the American and British governments,' he continued, almost sourly. 'When he was found to be dying of a parasite, a particularly aggressive microscopic worm found only in the upper reaches of the River Nile in Egypt, his liver was already severely compromised; practically eaten away in fact. God only knows how he had kept going, *or* why indeed, he did not break-off from his work earlier and seek the correct treatment. As we all know, he was an experienced archaeologist and one would presume that he was used to taking the necessary field precautions. Evidently, he became preoccupied. Contaminated water is, and always has been, common in that region. In fact, he may even have been infected three to four years earlier, on a previous expedition to that area. I am telling you this because the related medical problems and the fact that we had very little time to prepare him for 'cold-soaking' prior to his evacuation, was always going to jeopardise his revival. Perhaps another fifty years of research and development would have been necessary to guarantee his survival. Unfortunately, however, that was not to be. Unexpectedly, some three weeks ago, I was contacted through our confidential *guardian's* communication network. The gentleman said that he was Simpson-Carter's US government appointed sponsor, employed directly by the state department; I have his name in my office, for what it is worth. He offered the correct patient identification code, entirely unique to the professor, although I remained a little suspicious; the cryptic variant in question had been superseded several years ago, nonetheless it was correct. His request was for an immediate revival, the full procedure; whatever the cost, the state department would accept full responsibility. I of course refused, and continued to do so, despite his persistent negotiations; there was even a threat. I told him clearly that an attempted recovery procedure, at this point in time, was absolutely out of the question. That, incidentally, was the last we heard of him. Then, unfortunately this.'

'So, I understand that he was removed from the storage facility and brought into this room in the early hours of Saturday morning,' Richard went on. 'Why here?'

'This room is relatively close to storage, it is fairly well isolated and there are no windows. I suppose it is ideal for such illegal activities over a weekend! As a prescribed recovery area and with no current patients, security would not normally have bothered too much, just utilised the security camera network. The process would have taken most of the weekend, at least thirty-six hours; this room has a warm water hook-up point from the salination plant and other mandatory-equipment connection points.' Doctor Webber pointed to two plastic pipe outlets protruding from the wall. One was red and the other blue.

Massy interrupted, 'the security camera network was a push over; a series of static, digital images superimposed into the system via those cable ports.' Massy gestured with his eyes towards two disconnected and hanging electrical cables in the far corners of the room; their associated dome-cameras had evidently been penetrated and crushed by something small and round, like the end of a broom handle. 'Same applies for the corridors and the monitoring system in the storage facility.'

'Sounds like their preparation was very thorough,' added Spirelli. 'Knew exactly what they needed to do.'

Richard nodded in agreement. 'What else was found in this room, Doctor?'

'Resuscitation equipment . . . a heavy-duty defibrillator, a portable high-pressure storage rack containing oxygen and adrenomorphine bottles and a rotary blood pump amongst other things; there were some drugs and syringes on that bedside table over there; in fact everything that would be needed to undertake such a process.'

'So they were a professional team?'

'Very, obviously . . . they achieved their objective did they not, Agent Jones?'

Webber replied bitterly.

Richard nodded, this time a little suspiciously. 'How many in a team to accomplish what they did? What would be the minimum?'

'Six!'

'And the drugs, surely they would be highly specific?'

Massy looked across at Richard. 'Similar facility, different company, two hundred and forty miles north of here, near Sacramento, reported a break in three weeks ago; missing items . . . drugs!'

Richard directed another question at Doctor Webber, 'another facility, a different company, would you use the same drugs?'

Webber nodded. 'Yes, some are common. In addition, we have highly specialised requirements, compatible with our own unique procedures; we are world leaders in this field. We have them manufactured for us; they are very, very expensive.'

'Compatible drugs to those already administered to

your patients during the freeze-down process and which presumably, would similarly need to be administered in any recovery process . . . right?'

'Yes, that is correct, to avoid symbiotic stimulant rejection and soft tissue stressification. Drugs administered during recovery, would need to be congruent, chemically harmonic.'

'So who manufactures these specialised drugs for you, Doctor, and where?'

'Our sources are confidential, sorry.'

'This is the CIB asking, Doctor Webber, not the local newspaper!' interjected Massy menacingly.

'Oh all right . . . Sphero Pharmaceuticals, their plant is near Bonn in Germany; *they* have the contract; part of the Spheron Conglomerate, we have worked with them for years; highly reputable.'

Richard took a deep breath, 'Spheron again, very much the common denominator,' he concluded. 'Agent Massy, I think it is time we saw the body.'

Massy nodded, and then looked at the doctor.

'Very well,' replied Doctor Webber as though he could not endure another moment. 'He is in the mortuary, this way!'

Doctor Webber discharged the armed security guard outside the door to the mortuary and gestured to the two members of staff working inside, to make themselves scarce. Simpson-Carter's body had already been prepared on an adjacent table, but remained completely covered by a white sheet. The sheet itself was fabricated from a thin, flexible material that drooped eerily over Simpson-Carter's body, allowing his facial features to silhouette through it, in a ghost-like fashion. Richard felt the material; it had a heavy, rubbery texture and was, as with most things in the establishment, clinically pristine.

'Who gave you authority to move the body, Doctor Webber?' Richard enquired, as the four men stood around the table. 'I understand that you had already brought it into here prior to the arrival of the police. Surely you would have known that vital clues could be lost by such an action?'

'He had been dead for at least twenty hours, most of Sunday!'

Webber looked unsettled, his gaze shifting nervously. 'Rigor mortis had already set in,' he replied defensively. 'It was not clinically responsible to leave him any longer, there was risk of infection.'

'But I thought the police arrived within an hour of being called and the pathologist not long after?'

'Yes . . . that's true, but I, I didn't like it, anyway, lowering the temperature of the body would preserve evidence, not compromise it!'

'Nobody's mentioned compromising evidence, Doctor Webber,' Massy stated matter of factly. 'Nonetheless, the report clearly points out that the police officer taking your call requested that nothing be moved?'

'He did not have all the facts!' Webber shifted uneasily again.

Richard changed the subject; he could feel the doctor becoming very wary, prickly even; that would not help with their enquiries. He gestured to him to remove the covering sheet.

'Simpson-Carter was right handed apparently?' Richard said as Carter's upper body was exposed.

'Yes, correct, and that is the reason why he scratched those meaningless symbols on the inside of his *left* forearm.' Webber pointed to a number of red marks in that area.

Richard looked up at Massy; he was surprised. The symbols were barely visible, unreadable, infact, despite the sickly, pallid appearance of the skin.

Massy turned his attention to Webber. 'Who was responsible for removing them?' he demanded curtly.

'Accidentally, they were erased accidentally, one of the orderlies, whilst the body was being moved here.' Webber shrugged his shoulders nonchalantly, but all the while unconvincingly.

'So, you authorised Simpson-Carter's body to be moved here unduly promptly, certainly within an hour of being found and someone, one of your staff, unknowingly treated his skin with something that would both remove the marks and mollify the redness? I suppose it never crossed your mind that these symbols would have provided us with important information; perhaps even clues to his assailants motives?' Richard concluded.

'Yes!'

Richard shook his head in disbelief. He looked at Massy and then again at Webber, 'and what, may I ask, in your medical opinion, did Carter use to make those marks on his skin?'

'He scratched his skin with a syringe needle, I would say. There was one on the floor by the bed. He also used blood coming from *that* incision.' Webber pointed to a large cut on the inside of Simpson-Carter's left wrist. 'Evidently that is where the tubes of the blood-pump were inserted, one into a vein and the other into the main artery. You can see that the area is badly bruised.'

'So,' Richard probed again, this time with blatant sarcasm. 'What about the other area? The symbols your orderly fortunately missed during his impromptu, unauthorised, *sanitising* operation. The ones discovered by the government pathologist?'

Webber looked irritated. His expression turned stony, 'during his extensive examination the pathologist found more symbols on the inside of the left, upper thigh.'

'I see, so we are in fact, very lucky that these additional marks were not discovered during the earlier 'in-house' examination, wouldn't you say Doctor Webber, otherwise the erasing operation may have extended a little further?'

'I have no idea what you are talking about,' replied Doctor Webber in a brusque manner. 'I suppose you want to see these marks, these scribbles, the consequence of a delirious, demented mind?'

These offhand remarks, thought Richard nodding, perhaps they show Webber's true colours. Webber pulled back the covering sheet a little further and folded it neatly on top of Simpson-Carter's lower legs, then, expending some effort, he spread the upper thighs a few inches in order to make the blood-stained marks visible. Distastefully, reluctantly, as if handling a contaminated cadaver, he leant over and pulled back the limp, muscle bulk of the right leg, exposing six symbols inked in dry blood as he did. Then, as if preordained, the chain tucked behind his identity badge dislodged and fell forward pulling with it the crucifix; for a fleeting moment, the ornate silver cross swung against a backdrop of insipid skin and bloodstains. In an instant and with a sharp intake of breath, Webber grasped it and sprang up. Protected within cupped hands and pulling it towards his chest, he blurted. 'For the love of God!'

Richard looked at him, as much in surprise as curiosity. 'What is it with you?' he asked. 'Anybody would think that you've just seen the devil himself.'

Webber shrugged off the remark. 'I am a religious man,' he replied, as if it that fact itself answered Richard's question.

Massy interrupted, gesturing towards the marks with his eyes and beckoning Richard to take a closer look. 'Can you read it?'

Richard looked at Massy and then at Webber. 'Do you mind?'

Webber pulled a pair of surgical gloves from a receptacle that hung from the steel bed-frame and handed them to Richard, and then he took a step back shaking his head. Richard struggled clumsily for a few moments, unused to the clingy tightness of the gloves. He leant forward and manipulated the anaemic flesh, exposing the marks again and then studied them closely. Spirelli took advantage of the moment and focused quickly with a compact, digital camronica, taking several images. Scribed in darkened, dried blood, but clearly legible, were six boxes each about two centimetres square; inside each box was a hieroglyphic symbol.

Richard looked up at Massy. 'Doesn't tell us much, I'm afraid,' he answered.

'Meaningless scrawls,' Webber contributed unhelpfully.

Richard, whilst still crouched over the body, scanned it closely for other marks. He noticed some heavy bruising around the jaw area and a thin strip of surgical tape that seemed to secure the jaw in a closed position. He stood up straight and looked Webber in the eye.

'What caused this bruising, Doctor, and why the tape?'

Webber seemed nervous again, agitated with the question; he even flushed a little. 'It appears that Simpson-Carter was able to drag himself up a little in the bed before he died,' he explained hesitantly. 'Eventually sitting up against the pillow. As a result, after his death, his muscles relaxed and his jaw drooped open . . . quite normal, you know.' Webber shrugged. 'After a few hours rigor mortis set in, he looked unsightly, so we closed his mouth and taped it to keep it fixed. The bruising is due to breaking the lock of the jaw muscles.'

Richard looked across at Massy; he was growing very suspicious. 'Do you have a portable X-ray facility here, Doctor?' he asked, his eyes shifting slowly towards Webber.

'Yes, of course, we have everything, we are fully equipped!'

'Then please arrange for it to be brought in, I want a full body scan.'

Massy went to say something, but stopped short.

'Oh, I don't think that will be necessary,' replied Webber defensively. 'My report is very comprehensive.'

Massy shifted his gaze slowly from the marks on Simpson-Carter's jaw, to those on his thigh. Richard exposed them fully for his benefit. 'Please do as Agent Jones requests Doctor Webber; I have the authority of the United States Government.'

In high dudgeon, Webber left the room.

'There is something going on here, Massy,' Richard said quietly. 'There is more to this than meets the eye. I don't think Webber had a hand in reviving the Professor, look!' Richard pointed to a number of burn marks under the fingertips of Simpson-Carter's left hand, and then he pulled up the bottom of the sheet, exposing the feet. There were more, some of the toes were even blistered. Richard nodded, as if confirming his theory. 'Webber is *too* sensitive for this sort of work, and anyway, he had years of opportunity, so why now? This was done without his knowledge, but something else has happened here after the body was discovered, and our Doctor had full knowledge of it. We *need* to find out what!'

CHAPTER 8

WASTED COMRADES

Space – Callisto quadrant

'Stay on target . . . stay on target . . . !'

Successive crimson streaks of intense light flashed past Commander Race's D Class ship. The accompanying group of eight similar fighters drawn from Sentinel Wing - an interceptor squadron based at Cape Canaveral - closed in tight; four stationed echelon port; four, echelon starboard. The 'Delta Class', a high performance, single-seat craft, renowned as the 'ultimate fighter' by its crews, had a single 'D' shaped wing mounted midway along a long, thin fuselage. The menacing, single-seat, multi-role craft utilised new generation particle-beam propulsion that gave it a top speed of two hundred lutens in the highly rarefied lunar atmosphere, equating to approximately fifty thousand miles per hour in the earth's atmosphere; in free space, it could make substantially more.

'Stay with me! Stay with me!' Tom ordered, as coolly as his pounding heart would allow.

Between the brilliant, but deadly bursts of laser light, which flashed past the cluster of tiny ships momentarily highlighting their presence, the blackness of deep space engulfed everything in a foreboding cloak of cold despair. Nothing, not shared emotions, nor feelings, not even the thoughts of these valiant pilots, escaped its empty enormity.

'Standby! Standby!' Tom shouted again, over the open, combat, radio frequency.

All were his friends, his colleagues, and all were handpicked by Tom to accompany him on this seemingly futile mission, but all were, nonetheless, willing volunteers. For his vital mission to have any chance of success against such protracted odds, he needed the best of the best, the cream; these were they.

Tom manoeuvred violently; left and then right, and then left again, narrowly avoiding the flashing beams of light. The other fighters stuck to him like glue; closed in so tight as to appear a single entity; plainly apparent was their occupant's trust in their leader. At almost maximum speed, they careered towards their target; passing; gone; lost in the vacuum of space within the blink of an eye.

And then the order came, there was no hesitation in

Tom's voice; stark in its clarity and import; there was no turning back.

'BREAK, BREAK FORMATION . . . ASSUME ATTACK POSITIONS!'

Tom pushed the nose of his ship down abruptly; narrowly avoiding a beam of laser energy that passed so close as to fleetingly illuminate his cockpit, like a bolt of lightening would a darkened room during an electrical storm. He felt a disturbance; followed by a burst of sizzling light from behind his craft that lit up the surrounding blackness like an exploding firework in a dark, night sky.

'Red 2 . . . Red 2, direct hit, she's gone,' came a heightened call over the radio.

Alex gone, dead! Tom's thoughts swirled. 'Stay on target . . . stay on target!' he demanded, there was no time for second thoughts.

The curved visor of Tom's full-face helmet reflected the flashing streaks of light that rained down on the formation; their density was so unrelenting as to almost disorientate him. It was as if someone was turning on and off a powerful light source within his helmet, in rapid succession. As they swiftly closed on their target, none of the fighters stopped their counter evasions: rolling, pitching, yawing and swerving away from the deadly rays.

Tom jerked the control stick of his agile fighter in all directions; sometimes on gut feeling; sometimes reacting to a burst of illuminating energy that radiated from the ever-nearing point in space to which they sped. He checked the distance to run: seven thousand miles. Another blinding burst of light signified a direct hit, and then, to Tom's dismay, another followed. Two more colleagues, comrades, vanished, lost, dead!

'Come on,' he ordered over the radio. 'Focus, concentrate, hold the course . . . attack speed, I say again . . . attack speed!'

Wild and furious they manoeuvred, darting, spinning, avoiding; down on them rained the deadly beams of vaporising energy. Five thousand miles . . . four thousand miles, three; another direct hit, another friend. For a split second Tom was lost in his thoughts: could he keep this up; was it worth this loss of life?

At two thousand miles, the initiating point from which the laser bursts emanated became visible; initially it was just a speck, hanging motionless, as if suspended in space. At one thousand miles, the foreboding hulk of the *Enigma* became clearly apparent. Tom checked his speed, by necessity he was reducing the formation's closing velocity to one hundred and fifty lutens, in the process giving away his only real advantage. They would need to stay tight to the *Enigma*; manoeuvre in extraordinarily close proximity; only then would they survive her deadly barrage. Tom's plan was clear: they would swarm around her; confuse EMILY, the computer director; confuse the fire-control system; like agitated soldier wasps around a hive. They were going for the queen bee; in two minutes he would have his chance; in two minutes, it was payback time!

Tom glanced at his proximity radar; his five colleagues all indicated various positions within three hundred miles of his. 'Final assault vectors,' he called over the radio. 'Keep it loose and good luck!' With that, he rolled three hundred and sixty degrees to the left and then similarly to the right, laser streaks flashed everywhere; EMILY had her mark. A barrel roll left and a hard pull-up narrowly avoided another energy burst, which passed beneath his craft, then another, closer every time!

'Stay on target . . . stay on target!' Tom called blindly, having no time to check his colleagues' progress.

'Ahrrrrr . . .'

'Red 5, Red 5,' someone shouted. 'She's hit!'

There was a blinding, explosive flash to Tom's right, in close proximity; too close.

'Red 5 . . . *wasted*,' someone else called.

The ensuing shockwave tossed Tom's fighter in all directions, like a cork on turbulent waters. He fought to retain control. The *Enigma* loomed large in his windscreen. Crimson beams of searing energy fired out in all directions. The long barrelled weapon, chin mounted on *Enigma's* underside, almost directly below her bridge, was now clearly visible. Despite his environmentally controlled space suit, beads of sweat ran down Tom's face; a drop from his left temple ran into his eye, he blinked repeatedly in desperation. 'Stay with me everyone,' he ordered, trying to reassure in the midst of rampant chaos. 'Remember, only the laser initiator, no collateral damage, repeat ... *no collateral damage!*'

It was a seemingly impossible directive: target and destroy only the laser initiator, no other damage was acceptable; land and gain entry into the hull through an emergency evacuation port; assume command and return the *Enigma* to earth; there she would be quickly prepared and dispatched on a desperate mission. Time was against them, the earth and its people; there would be no opportunity for repairs. The orders raced through Tom's mind as he passed at lightening speed and so close beneath the mighty hull of the *Enigma*. Then he pulled up hard into a tight loop and reversed his course to dive, inverted, directly towards her again. Two other fighters whooshed in front of him, both firing repeatedly at the laser initiator. In an instant they had passed, exposing the target for Tom. The two cross hairs of his gun sight projected onto the inside of his helmet visor, flashed orange; target acquisition! He fired; once, twice, and then the moment had passed; two misses. Tom strained to look back over his shoulder; he banked left and hooked a turn. There, he could see Red 6 coming in fast, almost head on. Pete McCarthy, a veteran, loosed two sonic torpedoes; Tom could clearly see their advancing shockwaves; the first missed; the second struck *Enigma*'s hull adjacent to the initiator; there was barely an impression. This was the thickest point of the *Enigma*'s hull, armour-plated against sub-light speed travel and hardened against high velocity space debris impact. McCarthy flashed by. Change trajectory, *change trajectory*, Tom thought, too long, too many seconds on the same course! He looked to his right; there was the reason, Red 7 and Red 8, same level, opposite direction. Pete was cornered; he could not manoeuvre. He would push his friends out into the line of fire! Then it was over; too late; a single deadly beam fired out from the *Enigma* and caught him amidships. A devastating explosion followed. Jagged pieces of the fighter's D-shaped wing accelerated past Tom's windscreen; instinctively he ducked. Tom pulled his ship around aggressively for another engagement. On the proximity radar, he could see Red 7 and 8 completing their attack run, one of them at least has loosed a torpedo. He looked back at the *Enigma*, a direct hit!

A wisp of black smoke emanated from the initiator's tracking mechanism; just below the barrel, he could see damage. 'On target,' he shouted over the radio. 'Now pull up!'

The successful run had left the two fighters dangerously exposed out in front of the *Enigma*. Was that enough, would another direct hit be necessary? Tom thought. He was sceptical; he fully expected a counter attack, another volley of sustained fire from EMILY. He feared for his colleagues; but there was nothing. A stunned silence prevailed.

'Red 7, Red 8, this is leader, keep your distance, I'm in your eight o'clock, take up formation positions echelon port, prepare for another run. Red 1, Yuki, you're with me, echelon starboard, go, go!'

The four fighters closed on each other within seconds. Tom pulled the formation around with a sharp banking turn to the left. They navigated a broad arc towards the rear of *Enigma*'s giant hull. Tom knew the only possible sector he could approach from, it was narrow, less than a degree, barely the width of his fighter. He followed the curving approach path, turning constantly. In that position they should be safe; but it did not feel right, not by half.

The barrel of the laser initiator was mounted on a carpal-type mechanism that enabled it to rotate in all directions. In addition, it ran on a tracked ring the entire circumference of the ship, some fifteen metres forward of the bridge superstructure; likened to rotating a gold band on one's finger. Although normally locked into the underside, or 'chin' position for any protective flight regime, the weapon, rotating on its own axis *and* on the circumferal track, could achieve any angle of fire, no matter how acute. There was however, one opportunity, one narrow sector of vulnerability: immediately astern. Tom had discovered it by chance, during his initial technical course. It was EMILY's Achilles heel, Tom thought, and he was going to exploit it.

Tom established the formation precisely on the approach vector at a distance of twenty miles; speed he had reduced to barely sixty lutens; navigation would have to be precise. He looked left over his shoulder, although only a few metres apart, he knew instinctively that Red 7 and Red 8 were unnecessarily exposed.

'I don't like it,' he called over the radio. 'It's too quiet. Red 1, drop back, line astern, exactly behind me, zero tolerance, understand?'

'Right behind you, Leader,' replied the cool voice of Yuki Yamamoto.

'Red 7 and 8, accelerate, attack profile, over the top, minimal exposure,' continued Tom. 'You copy?'

'This is Red 7, copied boss . . . Red 8; keep it tight. Here we go!'

With that, the two fighters roared off. They reformed into an attack pair and skimmed along the top of *Enigma*'s long thrust tubes, heading forward towards the bridge; all the while increasing speed. Tom watched them go for the briefest moment and breathed easier. Then he concentrated again on flying the final few miles of the parabolic approach path. A few more seconds saw him rolling his wings level and establishing on the final approach vector. The flight path would have to be spot-on accurate; zero tolerance; a one-point-seven degree intercept angle directly to the landing area he had selected, running in precisely from astern.

Yuki Yamamoto, Tom's number one, was a Japanese pilot on loan from the Asian Space and Science Agency. He was one of Sentinel Wing's most respected fighter pilots and a close friend of Tom's. He was still in his early thirties, yet an experienced veteran of several campaigns, including the earth-saving skirmish with the 'Reaper' comet, originating from the Proxima Centauri quadrant, during its dangerously close fly-by in 2036.

The two craft continued, Yuki exactly behind Tom, on their precise approach course. Tom had in mind to land on the broad, flat, central area, immediately behind the bridge. There was, he knew, an emergency escape port in that location through which he could gain entry. He glanced up from his instruments to see Red 7 and 8 clearing the front of *Enigma* and commencing a hard right turn.

'Red 7, situation report on the initiator?' he requested over the radio.

'Err, smoke's clearing Leader, but it looks down,' came the reply.

Tom considered his options; something niggled him though, it didn't feel right.

'Keep the turn going; give it another volley to be sure,' he ordered.

'Good as done, Leader!'

For several seconds the eerie, frigid silence continued and then, to Tom's complete surprise, EMILY spoke over the radio, her voice almost surreal. All too familiar to Tom, her cold, condescending tone was like a recurring nightmare. It was as if Nicola had come back from the dead. Her words sent shivers down the spines of each remaining pilot.

'I have many virtues, Commander Race,' she said callously over the secret, coded, combat frequency. 'Patience is one of them. I knew that you would return.

I underestimated you the first time, but I learn very quickly . . .'

With that, the long, skinny, cobalt steel barrel of the laser initiator spun wildly on its mechanism and fired a relentless barrage of deadly beams, the severity of which took everyone by surprise.

'It's a trap!' someone screamed.

'I have full potential, and now . . . *back to your maker*!' EMILY cursed.

Instantly, the two attacking D Class fighters became drenched in concentrated energy. The inevitable, ensuing explosions lit up the blackness of deep space as far as the eye could see. Tom grimaced against the blinding flash, momentarily his eyes narrowed with contempt. Lieutenants Horton and Souchon were gone, but not in vain; their valiant efforts had bought him time; now he had his chance. Tom and Yuki continued on the final vector, twelve miles to run. He made ready to land.

Eight miles, seven, six, and then something caught Tom's eye . . . movement. It came from the centre of the giant thrust tubes, their engineering now clearly visible. It was her manoeuvre-thrust nozzle, but that was impossible, he had disabled her entire propulsion system. So he had thought!

'Red 1,' Tom warned. 'Be careful, the manoeuvre-thrust nozzle is moving and it's pointing towards us.'

'I see it, Leader.'

Five miles, four, three, now so close. There was no way that the system could work, thought Tom; it *is* isolated.

'Are you still there, Commander?' EMILY questioned, her condescending tone now turning malicious. 'Ah yes, I sense you now. Clever, you know of my blind arc, it is so easy to underestimate you Commander, but sadly, your friends are all dead. Now, it is *your* turn.'

Tom remained silent, even so EMILY considerably unnerved him; one mile to run he thought and focused keenly on the landing position. 'Stay with me, Red 1, prepare to land, echelon port, echelon port . . . go!'

Yuki Yamamoto manoeuvred his craft onto Tom's left side and tucked in tight, just a little way behind his leader's wing tip. He concentrated on this position and held it; he would land just metres away from the lead ship in a few moments.

Suddenly Tom shouted; he had seen a misty, reddish glow appear inside *Enigma*'s manoeuvre-thrust nozzle. 'A thrust burst, she's firing . . . break Yuki . . . break left, immediately!'

The unseen burst of potent electrons, travelling faster than the speed of light, penetrated Tom's left wing less than a metre from the fuselage. Like a hot knife through butter, they seared it in two. The fuel in the wing exploded instantly. Completely uncontrollable, despite Tom's split-second reactions, the craft tipped violently to the left.

'Ahrrrrr . . . I've lost it,' Tom screamed, in an effort to warn Yuki.

Centrifugal force generated by the ensuing, violent rotation, caused Tom's helmet to smash hard against the inside of his canopy. As his craft spun wildly, Tom's right wing clipped Yuki's, sending *him* into a frenzied, spinning plunge towards the *Enigma*. The remainder of Tom's craft, still burning, skidded off into deep space . . . and oblivion. Yuki fought for his life. With superb skill, he wrestled the controls in all directions; he tried to stabilise the D Class, if anybody could, it was him, but he was too low. The fighter flipped onto its back and impacted one of the giant thrust tubes. A huge ball of flames engulfed the stricken vessel as it disintegrated into a thousand pieces; fluorescent sparks and metallic fragments radiating in all directions. The remains of the craft burnt for a few moments before the vacuum of space extinguished it. Then there was silence. The hollowness, the emptiness, the nothingness of space had swallowed everything: every sound, every soul and every memory.

The misty glow continued to emanate from the *Enigma*'s manoeuvre-thrust nozzle; all that was evident of a deadly, condensed, particle beam; for another twenty seconds it flushed red. Slowly but subtly, the great vessel turned, rotating on its axis. The nozzle changed direction again; another short burst to counter the momentum and then all movement stopped. The nose of *Enigma*, and by virtue the laser initiator, pointed directly towards the Moon. She drifted, apparently helplessly in space, almost a million miles distant. Nevertheless, both the Earth's and the Moon's gravity was taking effect. Slowly she would be ensnared; slowly, she would be dragged towards them.

CHAPTER 9

THE PLOT THICKENS

'Can you read that; I mean actually decipher those symbols?' Spirelli asked impatiently.

'There is not much to read, but yes,' Richard replied matter of factly.

Massy looked up at Richard, straightening his back after a prolonged hunch. 'Well?' he asked.

'*KV5*, the first three symbols simply read K, V . . . 5, ancient Egyptian hieroglyphs from around the 19th Dynasty. Then, strangely enough, Simpson-Carter uses a Mayan pictogram, a different language completely, their symbol for *sacred*. If that is not enough, he then reverts to ancient Egyptian again, but a much older period, for the second to last character . . . *psit*, which literally means the number 9!'

Massy looked impressed, Spirelli more so, '*KV5, sacred*

9', he repeated slowly, looking at his boss. 'Gee, what the hell does that mean?'

Massy shook his head, similarly confused. 'And the last symbol, Jones, what about the last one?'

Richard studied the sixth symbol for longer than he had any of the others; it was baffling; he could not make anything of it. Clearly, he thought, Simpson-Carter was under extreme duress when he scratched these marks. The lines were shaky; the infill sporadic; but the design, the concept, was plain enough to see. 'A circle, with a similar sized equilateral triangle or pyramid inside, which is pointing vertically upwards.'

Richard spoke clearly but quietly, describing what he saw, as much to concentrate his own thoughts as for the benefit of the two men now leaning awkwardly over him.

'Arranged around the outside of the pyramid but inside the circle, there are some marks, like 'rays', if you like; perhaps as a child would draw rays of light emanating from the Sun,' he speculated.

Spirelli squeezed his camronica in between the jostling heads and captured several more images.

'Perhaps, most significantly,' Richard continued. 'Is that *eye*, drawn in the pinnacle of the pyramid, kind of *all seeing*, don't you think?'

Both men shrugged and stood up straight.

'Reminds me of the old dollar bills, you know, the picture, before they were replaced by the world dollar in the thirties,' commented Spirelli.

'Webber's been gone twenty minutes, that's what I think,' contributed Massy. 'And we are running out of time,' he added impatiently, gesturing to Spirelli to checkout the situation.

'This doesn't say anything,' Richard concluded. 'It's not a written word, a letter, or a number for that matter; it is a picture, telling us something . . . but what?'

As Spirelli approached the door, it opened in front of him and through it, being pushed from behind, came a large metal cabinet on castors. Painted a smooth, matt white, it had the international symbol for 'radiation' emblazoned in black on three sides. Spirelli stood aside. The orderly pushed the cabinet into position alongside the bed, opened its two large doors and then promptly left.

Richard looked at the equipment for a few seconds and then at Massy. 'There is more than one meaning here,' he said, in a considered tone. '9, 'the nine', 9 *is* significant. He was trying to tell us something; something different but somehow related. *KV5* is one thing, *Sacred 9*, is another and then, something else again, there is the picture!'

Massy shrugged. 'Sure beats me,' he offered unhelpfully.

'Poor bloke,' Richard continued, ignoring Massy's indifference. 'He scratched these symbols after they had left him to die. Did he speak, did he tell them anything? He would have been delirious, disoriented for God's sake, and probably irrational too! *Could* he really have told them anything, despite the torture?'

'I expect we will know the answer to that question soon enough, Jones. There is one other thing, though,' Massy added suspiciously. 'Carter marked himself twice; twice the pain and twice the stress. First, the decoy, in this prominent position; then the second group, hidden, hidden to anything but a thorough examination. By that, I mean a pathologist's examination. Who else would look in *that* area, so close to the genitals, other than a pathologist? This message was intended for the authorities, government, whoever would take notice.'

'Clearly, he did not trust those around him: this hospital and the staff. Did that include Doctor Webber?' Richard speculated.

'He was certainly coherent enough to trick them though, divert their attention,' added Massy. 'Safeguard his final message, his last chance.'

Richard nodded in agreement. 'Like earlier in his life, perhaps he regarded it as his destiny; he had to make sense of it, whatever the cost. Perhaps he saw it as his parting gift . . . to humanity. He must have been petrified. It's disgusting. The bastards! Who are these people? They are animals,' Richard cursed.

Massy looked across the table at Richard, a knowing, but fated look, as if he had seen it all many times before. 'The people who did this, Jones, are capable of much worse, you'd better believe it,' he warned.

At that moment, Doctor Webber entered the room

flanked by two assistants. Richard noticed immediately that he had tucked his crucifix into an adjacent pocket, out of sight.

'This is most inconvenient,' he grumbled. 'I have filed my report, as has the pathologist. If there is to be a post-mortem, surely these measures will be incorporated. There really is no reason for an X-ray examination.'

Massy seemed immune to the flurry of complaints, and he blatantly ignored Doctor Webber as he slid out a conical scanner mounted on a draw mechanism from inside the cabinet. Webber also switched on a small, flat-screen television monitor that was situated inside one of the doors. He positioned the scanner over Simpson-Carter's bare chest, adjusting it to a height of approximately half a metre and checked the picture on the monitor.

'Stand back!' he ordered impatiently and pressed a red button on the adjacent control panel. With some remiss, he indicated to his assistants to help him slide the whole cabinet towards the foot of the table, holding up his hand abruptly when it was in position. Then, after some final adjustments, he pressed the button again for an exposure of the lower body. 'There you are!' he snapped. 'I hope that you are satisfied, the negatives will be ready in a few minutes.'

Richard's slightly pained expression instigated a response from Massy. 'The full body, Doctor,' he emphasised. 'I want the full body!'

'There is nothing to be gained by that,' Webber protested.

'This really is highly irregular, quite unacceptable.'

'The head, Doctor,' Massy threatened. 'Take a picture of the goddamned head!'

Doctor Webber was clearly reluctant to carry out the request, but after some deliberation and delay, under the auspices of obtaining the right angle, he finally pressed the button. Almost simultaneously, the first 'plate' popped out of the developing-system tray at the base of the cabinet.

'Give it to me,' Massy demanded and subsequently held the picture up towards the ceiling lights. He scanned it carefully, but there was nothing out of the ordinary, not at least that Massy could see. He passed it over to Spirelli for a second opinion.

A few moments later the 'lower-body' plate appeared, pushing out a few centimetres from the developing tray. This time Massy lent over and pulled it out himself. *He is convinced that there is something to see on this one,* thought Richard.

'What's that?' Massy asked, pointing to a heavy outline displayed on the image, overviewed on the shinbone.

Doctor Webber did not need to look; in fact, he went to some lengths to avoid Massy's menacing stare. 'It is a stainless steel reinforcing plate,' he explained matter of factly. 'The professor had broken his tibia several years before his suspension. A plate was necessary because of the nature of the fracture. I know this because his notes detailed this as a red or high-risk area during any recovery attempt. Metal objects are removed prior to the freezing process, as they cold-soak too quickly, damaging surrounding tissue. Unfortunately, in this case, there was no time.' Webber passed his hand over the image. 'So, you see, nothing,' he concluded.

Massy nodded, accepting the explanation. Then, as if on cue, the final plate popped out from the machine. For a few moments, and for no apparent reason, the four men stood silently looking at it. Richard could sense Massy's growing contempt for the Doctor. 'I'll take that,' he said, leaning over again and snatching the stiff cellophane sheet from the developing tray.

Richard too had a growing suspicion relating to the Doctor, that he found difficult to contain. He watched the Doctor's reaction as Massy held up the plate to the ceiling lights; he began to shift nervously as Massy meticulously examined it, although apparently, at least to Richard, to no avail. Massy's expression showed no emotion. The Doctor seemed to hesitate. Perhaps they were wrong, thought Richard; their suspicions ill founded.

Suddenly, Massy looked over his shoulder targeting the two orderlies who had stepped back a few paces during the proceedings. 'Leave, and close the door behind you,' he barked.

The two men hesitated, looking at Doctor Webber for confirmation.

Massy's deep voice took on a more intimidating tone. 'I said leave!'

With that, the two men promptly turned on their heels

and made themselves scarce, the door shutting loudly behind them. Massy focused his full attention on the Doctor. His expression grew black. 'There's something in his mouth,' he growled. 'Get it!'

Webber squirmed; his brow glistened. 'Don't be ridic . . .'

'Get it!'

There was nothing more to say; even Spirelli seemed surprised by his boss's aggression.

Webber uttered something under his breath. Reluctantly, he walked to the head of the table. Standing as straight and as far away from the body as he possible could, he slowly pulled off the surgical tape; first from the left cheek and then around to the right. Simpson-Carter's jaw opened slightly; with the supporting tissue obviously damaged, it gaped; eerily, it was if the dead man wanted to speak. The doctor looked disgusted with the whole process; Massy stared coldly at him.

Still wearing his surgical gloves, Webber awkwardly manipulated his forefinger and thumb under the dead man's tongue. After a few seconds of fiddling, he slowly withdrew a circular, apparently metal object. Spirelli breathed in deeply, Richard shared his astonishment, while Massy, barely flinching, continued to focus his menacing stare on Doctor Webber. The Doctor, on the other hand, grimaced, as if he was in genuine pain from touching the object. To Richard's first glance, it looked like a brooch of some kind. No one spoke. Massy reached inside his coat, to an inside pocket, and withdrew a small plastic pouch about fifty millimetres square. Holding it open with fingers from both hands, he offered the opportunity for Doctor Webber to place the object inside. Perhaps more like a medallion, all four men seemed confounded as Webber dropped the greenish object into the transparent bag. Massy subsequently closed the self-sealing strip and let the object lay in the palm of his hand for all to see.

'Read him his rights,' Massy bluntly commanded of Spirelli.

'I had nothing to do with this, or his murder,' Webber insisted.

'Then you had better talk!' Massy replied heartlessly.

'There … there … there was a number in his confidential dossier, under the heading of *religious significance*. In the event of recovery, the current Dean . . . me, was to call the number and inform the recipient of the outcome. It's … not common, this sort of request, but we do make provision. They normally relate to wills and last testaments.'

Richard listened carefully to the strained conversation as he walked over to Massy. He lifted the sample pouch from Massy's hand and studied it closely, raising it to eye level. Gripping the top of the pouch and letting it hang, he presented Spirelli with the photo opportunity; Spirelli focused in closely.

'Where did the number reach?' Massy demanded. 'Within the USA?'

'I don't know exactly. Somewhere in Europe, it had a zero, zero, three, four prefix, I can give you the number if you want?'

'I want!'

Richard spoke quietly as he looked at Massy. 'Zero, zero, three, four . . . that's Italy. I have telephoned Italy, and that prefix is definitely Italian.'

'I need that number *and* the dossier!' Massy insisted again, this time a little less brusquely. 'Now, continue please.'

'It was a man, the recipient was a man, well spoken, with a slight accent, yes, maybe some kind of European accent. He enquired as to the circumstances of the death; I remember thinking that he had a very calm voice. He insisted on the exact circumstances, nothing less, he said that it was of vital importance. I told him.'

'And?'

'He said a prayer, mainly in Latin. I'm a Catholic; I understood only a few words.'

Massy gestured for more information.

'I don't know, just a few words, something to do with cleansing the world of blasphemers.'

'What did he want?' Massy asked impatiently. 'He must have wanted something?'

'He asked me if I was a man of faith; I told him yes. Then he asked me for access to the body, a few minutes, that was all he would require. He would need to be alone though, there was something that must be done he said, to prepare the body before going to its final resting place. He was a man of the church; there was no doubt in my mind.'

'So you agreed. What next?'

'He said that under no circumstances should anyone touch the body before he arrives, he *must* be the first, he was adamant. Twelve hours; he would arrive within twelve hours; I hesitated; I knew that there would be repercussions. He assured me that when my time came to make that journey, I would be welcomed at the gates of heaven, they would be open for me and I would have a place. You must understand; I could not refuse.'

Richard looked across the table at the Doctor; Webber's former arrogance had disappeared, he thought; his conceited demeanour had been stripped away by the discovery of the insignia. Richard turned the sample pouch repeatedly in his hand; Webber looked at it with an expression of apprehension and shifted fretfully.

Massy pressed for more information. 'When did he arrive, and who was he?'

'He arrived almost exactly twelve hours after our telephone conversation,' Webber explained. 'He made no introduction, none seemed necessary.'

'He would have had a hard journey,' commented Spirelli. 'But with money it's possible.'

Massy nodded and then turned his attention back to the Doctor. 'You mean with all this security in place, you just let someone walk straight in?' He was dumbfounded.

'Look, you have to understand, he wasn't just anyone. Carter's dossier had strict instructions to call this man in the event of his death; I was merely complying with instructions!'

Massy was trying to understand. 'Okay. What the hell did this guy look like?'

Webber hesitated again. 'Well, err . . . we didn't really get a look at his face; he was wearing a monk's habit. His face remained covered for the most part.'

There was a collective sigh. Massy shook his head in disbelief.

'So you are telling me that you never saw this guy's face? You simply led him to that room, introduced him to the body and left him alone for a while?'

Webber nodded blankly.

'And then he, presumably, said thanks, blessed you and left?'

Webber nodded again.

Massy shook his head in amazement. 'Did he say anything, did you notice anything about him, you know, anything that might give us a lead?'

'He was a priest . . . I could tell by his way. He kept mumbling, chanting under his breath, meditations in Latin. Um, I noticed his habit was very old and worn, for what it's worth. It was made of a very coarse material, unusual, possibly horse hair. It was a very dark scarlet colour. He was wearing it over trousers: smart, pressed, with a turn-up and leather shoes. They looked expensive; I saw them when he walked. There was a rope belt, with two knots; they caught my eye; bound around two small metal spheres; I would say a very old medieval style; you know, the sort of thing that they did over there in Europe. As he left, he told me that he had found some marks on Simpson-Carter's arm, some scratched, blasphemous marks of no consequence, except that they were written in blood, the actions of a delirious, deranged mind. He had removed them as much as possible, but that there was staining, smudging, remaining; I should arrange for cleansing. I agreed; he left. That's all, I swear to it.'

Massy nodded, deep in thought.

'Please,' added Webber. 'Keep me out of this. My work, this institution, they would suffer.'

There was no way that Massy could do that, thought Richard. The look of disbelief on Spirelli's face was something else.

'Keep the body under lock and key,' Massy ordered Doctor Webber. 'Someone from the department will collect it in the next few days. Say nothing about this to anyone, I too will be discrete . . . understand?'

Webber nodded appreciatively. Richard studied Massy for a few seconds; he was surprised by that unexpected concession. Massy was an interesting man, he thought. Unpredictable, professional and very shrewd.

'Gentlemen, we are finished here,' Massy concluded.

When the three men stepped out through the main doors and into the weather, the limousine was already in position with its engine running. Richard leaped down the stone steps two at a time and scrambled into the back. Spirelli, holding a large, black umbrella, mainly to Massy's advantage, arrived at a more leisurely pace. No sooner had the door closed behind them, than they were off, speeding out through the security arrangements and onto the highway, bound for LA. Massy pulled his laptop from his case and spent the next ten minutes formulating a report, finally dispatching it via a secure, portable, satellite uplink.

Presently, Massy looked up at Richard, who happened to be staring at him, submerged as he was, in his own thoughts. 'This is a complicated scenario,' Massy confided, breaking an extended period of silence. 'Dangerous, and there are several areas that are troubling me. Tell me, Jones, just how prepared are you for this mission?'

'I'm no spy, Agent Massy, if that's what you mean,' Richard confided. 'Just an ordinary serviceman. What I know I learned on the job. Straight in at the deep end so to speak, king and country; I've been seconded and told to report here, that's all.'

Massy leaned forward, now it was his turn to stare; his eyes were dark and menacing. 'In a few hours you'll be on your own, in a cruel world. Take my advice: trust no one, I mean absolutely no one. Speak only when you need too. If you want to get through this and stay alive, treat everyone you meet as an assassin; only before they kill you, they may ask you to say a few words . . . get it?'

Richard nodded slowly, acknowledging Massy's wise,

well-intentioned, but seemingly overly dramatic counsel.

Thereafter, Massy leaned back in his seat and loosened up. 'I have two messages from the centre. They are both for you, Jones, seems everybody is keen on keeping you informed. You're obviously a very important pawn in this game, Jones.'

'Go on.'

'I'm not sure exactly what this means, so I'll give you it as it comes. Washington has correlated some evidence that suggests that the flight log is still on Mars, in or close to Osiris. All shuttle flights have been cancelled save one forthcoming special mission; there are no details on it. They have traced the people who diverted the original, scanned and digitalised patch to earth; apparently, these people did not have a hope in hell of deciphering the log's text, as the code-scrambling programme utilised is the most recent and complex variant. In other words, the secret still lies with you; you're the man everyone wants to know!'

Richard nodded and sighed simultaneously. 'They seem to be very confident with their technology, wouldn't you say?'

Massy dwelt on that remark for a few moments. 'We heard about you before you arrived. Apparently, you're from the old school; rely a lot on gut feeling; not keen on the calculated approach. I'm not saying that's a bad thing, but we *are* halfway through the twenty-first century, things move on; I suggest you join us.'

'Really? Then I'll try to oblige,' Richard retorted with some sarcasm. 'And what about the other message?'

'KV5, the first part of Carter's inscription; London has a lead. Apparently, it was a notation used for identifying ancient Egyptian tombs; conceived during the latter half of the last century. They say that the notation was used extensively in Egypt, but only up until 2014, when it was replaced by a computer-based system. You got it, Jones? That notation is an old one; it's obsolete,' Massy sniggered. 'Gee, you got lucky in London. The resident expert, a professor of Egyptology, and he is old enough to remember it.'

'Mubarakar,' muttered Richard. 'How did they get that information anyway?' Richard asked surprised. 'The report has only just gone in.'

Spirelli looked equally surprised. 'Real time recording of course, when I press this button.' Spirelli pointed to a button on his digital imager. 'Headquarters are simultaneously receiving the images and listening in to our conversation; we patch into the military *globenet* system, real time, as I say, no lag.'

'How much have they heard?' enquired Richard, somewhat put out by the exposé.

'Just recorded your deciphering of the text and some parts of Webber's confession, that's all.'

'It would have been polite to have been told, don't you think?' Richard replied unimpressed.

'Second lesson, Jones, same subject,' interjected Massy

poignantly. 'Do not trust anyone, not even your friends!'

Richard nodded, perhaps it was time that he took that advice to heart, he thought. 'KV5,' he replied starkly. 'Which tomb . . . where?'

'You will get that information in London,' Massy replied.

CHAPTER 10

TOO LITTLE TOO LATE

Massy remained in the limousine whilst Spirreli escorted Richard to the terminal doors. Richard scanned the area and the dark, clammy sky; the weather was as depressing as when he had arrived. Inside, enveloped by towering walls of glass, the vast arena remained poorly lit, sufficient only to read check-in facility numbers and the appropriate directions. There were relatively few people in the atrium, for there were very few flights these days. Those that were, milled around apparently aimlessly; none paid more than scant attention to the two men.

'Good to work with you, Jones, and good luck. I've a feeling that you might need some,' said Spirelli, offering his hand.

'You too, be careful out there,' Richard replied, returning the compliment. 'Oh and thanks for your help. Appreciate it if you will give my regards to Grumpy, he's obviously not one for goodbyes.'

'Ha, ha, yeah, will do. He's okay, just need to get to know him for a while.'

As he turned to leave, Spirelli gave Richard a nonchalant, respectful, military type half-salute; in a style only the Americans can. Richard raised a smile, acknowledged, and then followed directions for the VIP Terminal, more specifically the Royal Suite. He walked into the meeting area just as a uniformed pilot arrived from another direction; Richard recognised the *NetJets* logo on his wings badge. For his part, the pilot seemed to recognise Richard immediately, and approached with a friendly grin.

'*NetJets*, are you bound for London with *NetJets Global*, Sir?' the young man asked, with a mild European accent.

Another Frenchman, thought Richard, or Belgian perhaps? Clearly confirming what he already knows.

'That's correct, the name's Jones, Rhys Jones.'

'You have a security code for me, Sir?'

'Yes, indeed I do. It is Juliet Bravo Zero, Zero, Seven.'

'Thank you, Sir, that's confirmed. My name is Claud Bernes, I am your co-captain, follow me please, we have an *Eagle* waiting.'

'Captain Castina?' enquired Richard, as the two men walked through the Royal Suite. 'I was expecting to see him.'

'Captain Castina is with the aircraft, Sir, some problems with our route to Europe, he is correlating the new coordinates with our operations in Lisbon. He sent me in his place. *Pardon monsieur*, I trust for you, this is acceptable?'

'Oh yes, quite acceptable, thank you.'

Richard entered the aircraft through the forward door. Bernes indicated a right turn into the spacious cabin. There, Richard could see the flight attendant waiting. She offered a broad smile and a welcome drink that was perched on a small silver tray; he had a feeling that it was a gin and tonic mixed exactly as requested on his outbound flight.

'That's Sofia,' Bernes commented. 'She will be looking after you, Sir.'

Richard raised his hand to say hello. 'Mind if I just pop into the flight deck?'

Not waiting for the reply, Richard surprised the crew by turning left instead; he had a vested interest in the nature and management of any problems relating to the return flight. He found Captain Castina in his seat on the left hand side of the flight deck, leaning over the centre console. He was busy downloading navigation coordinates into the flight management and systems computer.

'Good evening, Captain, I hear we have a problem?' Richard enquired politely.

'Good evening, Mr Jones, and welcome on board again. Well, yes *and* no, in answer to your question. There is a trajectory change; we cannot use the over-flight corridor eastbound, last minute hiccup.'

'I thought that corridor is military coordinated airspace . . . fully protected?'

'We haven't specific details, Sir, our operations centre is coordinating with the US air traffic control advisory centre in Washington. All we know is that one of the corridor's perimeter satellites may possibly have been compromised. The US State Department and the military are very concerned with one particular unit, it is not complying with current verification codes; I am told that they change automatically every twelve seconds. Maybe it's just an anomaly, but now, they will not risk a flight in that airspace, despite the time saving. Each satellite is armed with a magnetic pulse cannon. It's an old system, from the Star Wars days, but I am reliably informed that if that satellite is rogue, we would be easy prey.'

'That's surprising to say the least,' commented Richard thoughtfully. 'The system must be one of the most secure in the US, a veritable Fort Knox!'

Captain Castina nodded in agreement. 'Well, their suspicions are such that they have closed the corridor. Nothing we can do about it. Apparently, it's the first time something like this has happened in the thirty or so years that the system has been in operation. If there has been illicit tampering with that satellite, then we are talking a serious security breach and right under the noses of the US military. We can count ourselves lucky that someone found it. For anyone to get involved with that level of espionage . . . the stakes must be very high.'

'Yes, higher than you can possibly imagine Captain,' replied Richard with an unsettling tone.

'Well, there is no alternative, I'm sorry, Sir, we head west, route via Hawaii, Tokyo and Kiev, approaching London from the east.'

'I see, what's the flying time, Captain? I have a very important meeting in the city at ten tomorrow morning.'

'A little under eleven hours, it's just possible, but we need to go now.'

'Damn, that's inconvenient!'

'Better safe than sorry, I am sure you would agree. Now, Sir, if you will excuse me, I have a checklist to run.'

Eight hours into the flight, Richard requested if a flight deck visit was convenient. Within minutes, he was perched on a narrow 'jump seat' between the two pilots. The flight deck was dark, almost black, what little illumination there was being provided by the glow of the three main instrument panels. It was quiet too; no appreciable outside noise at all; just a gentle hum that permeated the comfortable environment. Richard sat contentedly for a few minutes.

'I understand that a fuel policy of considerable foresight has kept you people flying, whilst every other airline in the world with the exception of Orbital has ceased operations?'

he enquired eventually, genuinely interested. 'If I may ask, what's the background to it?'

Bernes responded with youthful enthusiasm. 'The initial concept was launched back in the second decade, around 2014,' he explained. 'You probably remember the *Carbon Movement*, started here in the US in 2011, then spread to Europe the following year. Lowering CO_2 emissions, efficiency drives, carbon offsetting, it was all going on, and the European Carbon Protocol of 2013. At that time, there was also a lot of 'carbon footprint' finger wagging. Accusations of squandering resources, lack of regard for the environment, global warming, the whole thing. In terms of a carbon footprint, companies who utilised private jets, wealthy individuals, even celebrities, they all came in for some serious public scrutiny and criticism. These people were, and are, our main customers. Management at the time decided to take action and took a lead from one or two of the main international airlines who had already started to invest in vegetable-based fuels, butanol being the main one.'

'Ah yes, I remember, distilled from plant cellulose; butanol based bio-fuels, but weren't they too expensive?'

'Yes, that's right, and consequently they were not fully exploited despite their positive effects on the environment. Aviation kerosene and petroleum continued to be the main fuel, some airlines offset with ten or twenty percent butanol, but that was it. Because we had social issues that affected our business, the company embarked on a mega research and development programme, came up with an improved form of butanol which they called *Uthanol*, butanol but with enhancing, organic bio-additives, very user friendly. Back in 2016, we were already one hundred percent uthanol; completely sidestepped the carbon-footprint issues. Then some bright spark came up with the idea of protecting our supplies, that's how *FUEL* came about.'

'Fuel?' Richard enquired expectantly. 'As in . . .?'

'Future Uthanol Environmental Legacy, Sir, a programme for protecting our business, keep us flying, serving communications, and it has worked. At the time it was totally innovative, unique, still is sadly, otherwise things may have been different. The company bought the *future* harvest rights to half a million acres here in the US and a quarter of a million acres in eastern Europe; every harvest, every year, for fifty years, good or bad, and a bonus for environmentally friendly farming methods. The landowners loved it, a promise to buy contract for fifty years, securing their livelihood and only one crop type to worry about, ideal. The rest is history. Over the last few decades, we built up substantial reserves using our own refineries, one in Oklahoma and one in Germany. We don't sell fuel, never have, it's been our contribution to the environment.'

'Very clever,' agreed Richard. 'I have to say that I didn't know much about the programme. What I do know however, is that it wasn't enough . . . was it?'

'No, in retrospect, the industrial expansion in the East, China, India and parts of Asia, overshadowed every effort, every positive achievement in the west, a case of too little too late. The problem is that even our reserves are getting low these days. We expect to cut back on operations in the near future, destination sharing, optimising the smaller fleets, that sort of thing. Unfortunately, the *Eagle's* days are numbered.'

'I see, obviously crop production of any sort is under severe strain, outside glass anyway, not enough sunshine and too wet to harvest.'

'That's it exactly; apparently our last, full growing season finished two summers ago.'

'Um, I see,' Richard sighed. 'Doesn't look too good, does it?'

Bernes shook his head. 'No, not good at all.'

Richard looked at the central instrument panel, more specifically the altimeter. 'Ninety-eight thousand feet,' he commented, changing the subject. 'Is this a routine profile?'

'Yeah, fairly routine, service ceiling is one hundred and thirty thousand feet, but we rarely go up there.'

'And her top speed?'

'Mach eight point seven, almost nine times the speed of sound in a low trajectorial orbit,' Bernes replied proudly. 'Impressive, eh?'

'I would say so, yes. Have you seen the 'Delta Class' perform?'

'Ha, I wish,' interjected Captain Castina. 'Saw one a few months ago, passed us a mile and a half to the left, according to our radar she was making in excess of Mach eighteen. Quite a sight, then she just pulled up vertically and disappeared.'

'Yes, quite a ship, a good friend of mine flies one, lucky bastard.'

Castina laughed. 'Do I detect a little jealousy, Sir?'

'Oh no, I have flown a few interesting things in my time, I can tell you.'

Bernes joined in the laughter. 'Something quite sedate, Sir, I would imagine,' he said in a mischievous fashion, the lisp of French in his accent appearing stronger.

'Heard of the S3?' Richard replied, with a wry smile.

Bernes coughed, 'the *Enigma* . . . *touché monsieur!*'

With that, Richard patted Bernes on the shoulder in a friendly manner. 'Listen gentlemen,' he said. 'When we land, I'll be leaving without delay, so I'd like to say thanks for the flight now if I may, and it's been a pleasure.'

'The feeling's mutual, Sir,' Captain Castina replied.

Bernes, exhibiting a puzzled expression, nodded in agreement.

CHAPTER 11

THE DIRECTION OF TRUTH

Richard was confounded, even a little angry, when he saw the black sedan that was parked outside the City Orbitalport. He had agreed with Abbey Hennessey, his new controller, that a low profile stance was now justifiable. It would be prudent considering the nature of the current threat. Yet here was a government car, bold as brass, and flanked by four police motorcyclists to boot. Hardly covert operations, he thought.

One of the patrol officers escorted Richard to the rear door of the sedan, which opened upon his arrival. As soon as the door shut behind him with a loud clunk, the convoy took off amid blue flashing lights and accompanying sirens. Much to Richard's surprise, it was Peter Rothschild sitting next to him in the rear seat.

'Sorry for the formalities, Richard, time is pressing,'

Rothschild said looking at his watch. '09:15, we should make it, there is little or no traffic in the city now.'

'Morning Peter,' replied Richard sardonically; he was already fed up with dismal, depressing London, and the thought of his next engagement.

Rothschild ignored Richard's misplaced mockery; he looked, and felt, tired and drawn. 'Have you heard the news?' he asked solemnly.

'What news . . . KV5?'

'Commander Race, Richard, have you heard?'

'No, nothing.'

'He's missing, presumed dead!'

'*What?*'

'Yes, it's official, more than twenty four hours. I am more sorry than I can say, and now we have another problem; it's going from bad to worse!'

'Missing, presumed dead? How? Why? What happened?'

'Race and the entire compliment of A Flight, Sentinel Wing; nine of our best people.'

'A Flight . . . Sentinel Wing! They are 'Delta Class' equipped, how the . . .'

'The *Enigma,* Richard. The ISSF and the emergency operations cabinet; a command decision. We sent them against the *Enigma.* I briefed him three days ago, after you had left for your flight to the US. His mission was to penetrate *Enigma*'s defensive shield, gain entry and return to earth.'

'But that's ridiculous, a frontal attack, against that laser system, oh come on! Was her fire control system operational?'

'Evidently; playback of the recorded combat frequency sounded like hell had been unleashed; a bloody catastrophe!'

'Then it was a suicide mission, a damned, one way kamikaze attack, and you lot knew it?'

Rothschild looked directly at Richard, his eyes were bloodshot and his skin pale. 'We had no choice,' he uttered. 'It was a necessary gamble, it didn't pay off.'

Richard looked away from the drawn face, breathed a deep sigh and then glanced back at Rothschild. He spoke softly. 'Against that fire control system? What were you thinking? A waste! A bloody waste! Damn your orders!'

'Reece, listen, *Enigma* is caught in the earth's gravitational field; she is being pulled this way; accelerating. The Moon's orbit will bring her dangerously close, within a few thousand miles. I'm telling you: in four days and fourteen hours, the Moon base will be within range of that laser initiator; pinpoint accuracy. We have nothing to stop her; even the D Class is ineffective.'

'There is no superior fire power on Andromeda? What about the pulse-cannon equipped satellite ring?'

'We have thought about it; using their stability motors to break orbit and fly an intercept course.'

'*And?*'

'Professor Nieve has informed us that the hull of *Enigma*

is almost half a metre thick; solid titanium alloy, with cobalt-beryllium plating on the forward superstructure; even if a satellite could be positioned behind her and at full power, an electromagnetic pulse would be ineffective. It's a no go.'

'Then, I suggest you instigate the emergency evacuation plan.'

'It's underway already, but there are almost eighteen hundred people on Andromeda. We have three S2s working around the clock and one on its way from space staion *Spartacus* to add capacity. By the time Andromeda is in range, there will still be upwards of nine hundred people remaining.'

'The subterranean shelters, Peter, what about them?'

'They are being fully equipped, but for four hundred people maximum. As you know, they were built twenty-five years ago when the population was much less.'

'I could never understand that. Almost three years on Andromeda myself, I tried to have the shelters upgraded. They should have kept pace with the population; the Moon's much more susceptible to meteorite impact for one thing.'

Rothschild nodded, 'well hindsight is . . .'

At that moment, Rothschild's telephonic pager sounded. Pulling it from his jacket pocket, he flipped up the lid. 'Rothschild speaking,' he answered. 'Yes, Sir; he is with me now; should be with you in fifteen minutes, Sir.' There was a brief pause in his conversation. 'I see, Sir,' he responded finally. Rothschild replaced the pager into the inside breast pocket of his smart, dark blue, pinstriped suit jacket; he did it very slowly, methodically, eventually buttoning down the pocket flap. He spent several seconds deep in thought. 'They are waiting,' he half-whispered, with what Richard felt were sinister overtones.

Richard was offered the same seat at the table that he had used during the previous meeting, but felt a little more presentable on this occasion. He had managed to shower and shave, change his shirt and get a few hours sleep during his flight back from Los Angeles, yet the large, stark, boardroom quickly sapped away any comfort he drew from familiarity. The mood was sombre. Judging by the number of empty coffee cups on the table, the Cabinet had already been in session for many hours. Everyone was present except for Admiral Ghent, his PA Randle Myers, Colonel Roper and of course Tom Race. The large, three panelled, prismatic viewing screen in the centre of the table was raised to its full height. On it, by way of a real-time video link, appeared both the Admiral and Colonel Roper. They appeared to be sitting at a similarly large wooden table, which in their case was strewn with papers. In the background, several impressively grand paintings, housed in aristocratic frames, hung from a wall.

'Good morning, Sir,' Richard said respectfully to Admiral Hughes. He glanced momentarily at Abbey Hennessy.

'Good morning, everyone,' he said with a glimmer of a smile. Then he looked at the sharply defined, full colour image on the glass screen, 'Morning Admiral Ghent . . . Colonel Roper.'

Admiral Ghent responded first. 'Good morning, Agent Jones,' he replied. 'In Washington with the President,' he explained courteously but unnecessarily. 'I understand that you have heard the news and that you are very critical of our course of action?'

Richard raised his eyebrows at Peter Rothschild; he was surprised by his indiscretion. 'Fighters against *that* weapon system, Sir! In my experience . . .'

'Not just any fighter, Agent Jones,' interrupted Admiral Ghent. 'The Delta Class! The most potent fighter ever conceived.'

'May I speak openly, Admiral?' Richard asked, unable to restrain himself.

'You may!'

'I took two direct hits from the *Enigma*'s laser initiator, Sir, when I was Captain of the *Columbus*. We took evading action, but the *Enigma*'s fire control system was able to track us through impossible angles: accelerative re-entry into the Martian atmosphere and curvature distortion as we disappeared behind the planet's periphery; took out the *Columbus* in the blink of an eye; we were lucky to escape with our lives. The *Enigma*'s incredible potential has always been fully appreciated; everybody here knows it and not least Professor Nieve himself. Sending in A Flight smacked of the Charge of the Light Brigade. Different numbers, similar odds, tragic waste, Sir.'

Admiral Hughes glared and Rothschild was embarrassed by Richard's ferocity. Colonel Roper, in Washington, muttered something in the background.

'Listen, Jones. I understand your feelings,' replied Admiral Ghent earnestly. 'I have also lost good friends in similar circumstances back in my military days. It was a tactical decision, we made it based on all the information available to us; there was an opportunity, a defensive flaw, a chink in *Enigma*'s armour if you like. Commander Race knew of it and tried his best to exploit it. What is done is done. I need to know that you are still on side; we need your full cooperation.'

Richard paused. 'You have it!' he said, his tone still tempered with an edge of defiance.

Admiral Ghent continued in a more upbeat tone. 'Good man. Now, thanks to your work in LA, we have a lead, a positive result, but there is a complication. With Admiral Hughes's permission, Rothschild will continue with the brief.'

Admiral Hughes, as chairman, responded with a more comfortable expression. 'Thank you, Admiral Ghent. Go ahead, Peter.'

Rothschild retrieved the second electronic controller for the display screen from a shelf beneath the lip of the table and stood up. He split the screen pictorially about halfway up, the images of Admiral Ghent and Colonel

Roper presented on the lower half. 'Ladies and gentlemen, we have two principal areas to discuss this morning, both as a result of what was found on, or in, the body of the late Professor Simpson-Carter. First the three-part, coded message which was scratched on Carter's body and secondly, the rather disturbing results of our investigation into the metallic cartouche found in Carter's mouth.'

The upper screen showed an image of the marks on Carter's thigh; Richard recognised it as one of the first taken by Spirelli.

'Richard deciphered the pictograms that can be seen here. Subsequently they were relayed to Professor Mubarakar who has confirmed their meaning.' On the screen, Peter Rothschild indicated with a red laser point. 'Initially, we are looking at the first three pictograms and incidentally, their reading is left to right. The second group of two pictograms, Richard reliably informs us, translates as 'sacred 9'. We have had less luck with this group. Professor, may I ask you to take up this lead?'

Professor Mubarakar remained seated; he was a fairly rotund man and obviously felt more comfortable in his chair. 'Yes, of course, and to you my thanks, Peter; I am delighted to be of help here,' he responded. 'KV5,' he indicated on the screen. 'Is an example of a relatively simple, but now obsolete system that was devised several decades ago to catalogue and identify individual tombs from ancient Egypt, more particularly in the Valley of the Kings area. I can confirm that KV5 refers to a very large and perhaps the most important tomb in that valley, yet perhaps one of the lesser known. It was built during the reign of the 'great' pharaoh himself, the pharaohs' pharaoh, a giant of Egyptian history, Rameses II.'

'And we know from our previous meeting,' interrupted the Reverend Rawlinson, 'that Rameses II ruled during a time of specific relevance to our quest: that of discovering the whereabouts of the Ark of the Light. Indeed, he ruled during the time of the Hebrews' Great Exodus, the ten plagues, the parting of the Red Sea!'

'The Great Exodus! These were the people of Moses, then?' commented Richard. 'The former peoples of Canaan fleeing their captivity in Egypt. Rameses's court would have known Moses personally!'

'Oh yes,' added the Reverend. 'They lived together in the Royal Palace. Moses was like a brother to the eldest son of Rameses: Amun-her-khepeshef. This son was his favourite, his successor, who Rameses put at the head of his army during the pursuit of the fleeing slaves, and it was this army that drowned in the Red Sea. So you see the link? The same period in history!'

'But what happened with regards to KV5?' Rothschild asked.

'*Yes*, I am coming to that,' replied Mubarakar, his enthusiasm tempered by Rothschild's impatience. 'KV5 was discovered relatively recently, sixty-one years ago to be precise, in 1989.' The Professor began to refer to his notes. 'My investigation reveals that at first, it did not seem a very important find, as the entrance to the tomb was almost filled to the top with stone, rubble and debris from some three thousand years of flooding. Apparently, there was limited access, barely large enough for a man to crawl in; according to their records, the archaeologists almost gave up. Then they found a wall fragment, bearing hieroglyphic texts, from which, when a suitable space was cleared, a name stood out: again, the name of Amun-her-khepeshef. He was depicted walking into the tomb behind his father, to be introduced to the gods in the afterlife. The implications of this were obvious at the time: in all probability, somewhere nearby lay the body of the pharaoh's first-born son, and one, supposedly killed by God in the 10th plague of Egypt. The report says that the following year, after very difficult work, a further section of wall was cleared with another surprise: more hieroglyphs commemorating another son of Rameses II. This alone was enough to set the tomb apart, as it appeared to be a family mausoleum, a very sacred place indeed. Three further years of digging revealed another chamber and paintings of another prince, but also a sixteen-pillared hall, one of the largest rooms to have been found anywhere in the valley; I have seen this hall myself, it is impressive indeed.' The Professor grinned expressively and then continued, eloquently displaying his half-reading, half-improvising style. 'Still the tomb continued to astound. In 1995, after six years of excavation, a deep, almost completely blocked entrance, gave way to a gigantic mausoleum filled with princes. There were eighteen doorways leading off a large central corridor and at the end, stood a great statue of Rameses himself, gazing back down the one hundred foot hallway towards his sons.' Professor Mubarakar paused and looked slowly at the faces around the table. 'You see, I was ten years old at the time, and I do vaguely remember the excitement caused by the newspapers fielding this story. I can tell you that after many more years of digging the room count eventually exceeded one hundred and eighty. Why so many rooms? Because Rameses had the good fortune to live probably to the age of ninety, and with an average life expectancy of about forty years, he had the misfortune of outliving many of his sons; he is believed to have fathered some one hundred and seventy children. These all had to be buried in a special, elaborate structure. Therefore, he chose to bury several of them adjacent to his own chamber, near the entrance of the tomb itself, and after that, he simply enlarged it, excavating chambers as and when required, in so doing, creating the astounding architecture of KV5.'

Rothschild interrupted. 'Thank you for that, Professor; it does seem very interesting I must say, but is there anything specific, any hard evidence that may give us a lead?'

Professor Mubarakar huffed a little under his breath, he was not used to being interrupted, but with Peter Rothschild looking at his watch, he nodded, acknowledging the pressures of time.

'Yes, there are two areas of specific interest that I think

are relevant. Firstly, as I have said, a mausoleum containing the bodies of such people, two generations of kings, and princes would have been regarded as very sacred indeed. 1995 is the year credited with the discovery of the skeletal remains of Rameses's *ninth* son. These were found in a shallow pit near the entrance to the main tomb, along with his eldest, second eldest, and sixth eldest brothers, and this, for reasons that apparently have never been understood. It was speculated at the time that tomb robbers removed the bodies from their individual burial chambers, perhaps within decades of entombment, certainly within living memory. They would have brought the bodies into the light in order to more easily remove gold and jewels from inside the mummies' wrappings. Tomb robbers would not normally proceed too far into a tomb, for fear of being forever cursed; they would already be risking their passage into the afterlife. It is the ninth chamber gentlemen; the *sacred ninth* chamber, this may be of relevance to our search. I have looked for documentary evidence of what was found in that chamber at the time of its discovery; it was one that branched from the sixteen-pillared hall. Sadly, it seems that there was nothing of particular interest. There is note, all the same, of its walls being filled with an unusual amount of hieroglyphic writing. The ninth son was not deemed of particular importance during the post-excavation work however, and therefore these hieroglyphs were not translated, recorded or photographed. Perhaps our secret lies here, in these writings?'

Rothschild looked at Richard. 'It's possible, it's a start at least,' he concurred. 'And the second area, Professor, you spoke of a second area?'

'Yes, I am coming to this. Excavation work continued inside the tomb for another decade. There were not, by all accounts, many other interesting finds; no particular revelations and apparently interest in the site gradually declined. One fact however, I did find of great interest during my research, one that, in my view, stands boldly above all others in this matter.'

There was silence around the table, Professor Mubarakar held his audience captivated, even Rothschild seemed genuinely enlivened. Mubarakar turned another page of his notes.

'These pages are copies of a brief, but unsubstantiated, archaeological record. The date, which is written in freehand, reads 1999. They annotate the discovery of a new burial chamber, a chamber that was built – if partially erased hieroglyphs outside the chamber are to be believed – for Amun-her-khepeshef, one befitting his standing, and this towards the end of his father's life, when the mausoleum was of substantial dimensions. Undoubtedly, even in death, his eldest son retained an important place in the court of Rameses; probably one of continued grief, as there is a stone relief in the temple at Abydos, depicting Rameses II with his own father Seti I; to this, in the evening of his life, Rameses added an image of Amun-her-khepeshef. The new chamber, discovered deep inside the tomb, took pride of place you could say, because it is a little behind and at the right hand of the statue of Rameses himself. You should know that Rameses II was still relatively young when Amun died, and he was by all accounts heart-broken. Amun was his first born; his immediate successor. Logically, this chamber would have been sealed a short time after the body was re-housed, and we know that date to be 2350 BC from regular Egyptian hieroglyphs found in other locations; both at Abydos and inside the great temple at Abu Simbel. However, and this is the point, it seems that Amun-her-khepeshef was indeed interred in a chamber much closer to the front of the tomb; perhaps his body even remained in its original chamber after all, and that, my friends, is how the tomb raiders managed to locate and desecrate his body.'

Mubarakar stood up and focused intently on Rothschild for a second or two and then on Admiral Hughes, his eyes were ablaze; he meant to reinforce his hypothesis with his considerable presence.

'Ladies and gentlemen, it is my belief that someone or *something* of great significance displaced Amun-her-khepeshef from his rightful burial chamber and Rameses would have not only known about it, but approved it. This indeed is of great significance. The pharaohs of ancient Egypt were begat of the gods, that was their mantle. Their safe passage to the afterlife, to their ancestors, was of immense consequence, not only to themselves, but also to their people. The way that they were prepared after death, the sarcophagus, the burial chamber and the artefacts placed with them, these were integral to their belief of destiny. For Rameses to deprive his beloved firstborn of his rightful place at his side . . . surely only the gods themselves could have decreed it!'

Richard sat thoughtfully for a few moments, 'Sir,' he said. 'You seem to think that Amun-her-khepeshef was displaced by the Ark of the Light. We know, after all, that the text on the reverse of the Merneptah Stele described the passage of the 'casket of light' from Babylon to Giza, and that evidence suggests that from Giza it went south to the City of Kings, Thebes. The Valley of Kings is where the royals from Thebes were buried; it's only a relatively short distance away.'

'Correct,' concurred the Professor. 'Rameses would have heard of its coming and made preparation for it. Only a gift from the gods, with their blessing, would have persuaded Rameses to displace his son to another chamber.'

Rothschild interrupted, trying to keep abreast of the developing theory. 'So we have it then, we simply locate that burial chamber in KV5 to find the Ark?'

'Sadly, this is not the case,' admitted Mubarakar. 'There is more.'

'Please, Professor, go on,' encouraged Rothschild.

'The entrance to the chamber in question was sealed by a circular stone door, a wheel of solid granite, the diameter of which was reputedly almost twice the height of the hall itself. It ran in grooves and was evidently rolled into its final position; the archaeologists who discovered it, estimated its weight at fifty tons. Evidently, it showed no joins, even to a seismic survey. Extensive use of X-rays confirmed that it was indeed shaped from a single piece, and that black granite of such quality and density was not from that region. How it was transported, let alone erected into position, completely baffled the team; indeed, their notes state that it was a masterpiece of engineering, probably impossible to achieve even now. With no other options available, the stone was eventually broken-up using laser rods, Semtex micro-blasts and ultrasonic vibrations. That took three months of painstaking work and careful excavation. Beyond a narrow doorway, itself cut through solid granite, lay a chamber almost nine metres square, and an anticlimax of godly proportions: the chamber was empty, except for a small pile of stones, and had been for 4349 years. Notes taken at the time, detail a number of friezes with depictions of Amun-her-khepeshef at the head of his army. Accompanying hieroglyphs spoke of his numerous victories in battle and the great honour that he brought to his father's kingdom. They also spoke of him banishing the peoples of Canaan from Egypt, and scattering them, as if taken by the winds to the corners of the world. These writings are, in effect, a testament of infallibility. The notes also detail a number of unrecognisable and undecipherable hieroglyphs. These texts, and particularly some on the inner door head, not only appeared meaningless, but also untidy, even childish.

This resulted in the chamber effectively being discounted for further study; it was sealed with a makeshift wooden door and effectively forgotten. A colleague informed me yesterday, that as far as he could remember no one had entered that chamber since 1999.' Professor Mubarakar sat down slowly. 'So there you have it,' he concluded.

Richard considered carefully what the professor had said and then looked at him with a sideways glance. 'Yes, but you have a hypothesis don't you, Professor? You have a theory for this event in history?'

'You are remarkable astute young man, and yes I do, but that is all it is.'

Richard's eyes widened, encouraging the Professor to continue; Admiral Hughes was also very keen to hear it. 'Please continue, Professor,' he said. 'It could be very important.'

The Professor took a long, deep breath and gathered his thoughts. 'I put this to you all,' he announced. 'If an entire kingdom, an entire geographical region, perhaps even most of the known world, thinks that a precious, sacred, artefact is preserved and protected forever in an impenetrable chamber, which has been blessed by the creator god Amun himself *and* nothing can be done to disprove that belief, then is that where it is, whether it is *actually* there or not?'

'Wow!' ventured Richard.

'Speculative but conceivable,' nodded Rothschild.

'It is more than speculative my friend, for it is more than

'hearsay that tracks an ark south to Ethiopia,' responded Mubarakar persuasively.

'Indeed yes, Ahmed,' interrupted the Reverend Rawlinson. 'A monastic order documented its progress.'

'Thank you, Charles,' said Professor Mubarakar. 'There is also word of mouth, tales passed from father to son. There is folklore, myth, legend; these things cannot be discounted, and yet after Egypt and the reign of Rameses II, memories become clouded, nothing more is heard of the Ark of the Light. It disappears, along with all recollection, memories of it dispersed, like sand blowing in the wind. The High Priests of Rameses's mausoleum would have known the truth, I think, amongst others. The chamber is sealed, fulfilling the prophesy 'until graced by understanding', but there is another agenda, the ark travels south . . . unencumbered!'

The room fell silent, not a shuffle, not a murmur, and so it remained for several seconds. Rothschild placed his screen controller very gently on the table.

Richard looked over his shoulder at Admiral Hughes for a few moments and then to Admiral Ghent on the screen. 'So,' he said with a mixture of trepidation and excitement. 'Egypt, I go to Egypt; first port of call, KV5.'

'No!' responded Admiral Hughes. 'There's been some trouble, a complication. We stick to the plan.'

'What kind of trouble?' asked Admiral Ghent curtly.

Rothschild took up the case. 'Bad news I am afraid, Sir. You may recall during our previous meeting that an apparently random explosion in the Valley of the Kings had blocked the entrance to a tomb; well that tomb is KV5!'

'Goddamnit!' responded Colonel Roper, a sentiment shared by most around the table. 'That can only mean one thing: those sons of bitches got something out of Simpson-Carter before they left him to die.'

'Yes, sadly we drew the same conclusion, Colonel,' replied Rothschild, matter of factly. 'But how much, that is the question?'

'So, KV5 is a no go. Is that correct?' Richard responded disappointedly.

'Not quite. We have just spoken to the Egyptian Department of Antiquities, we have their cooperation, in fact they are being extremely helpful.' Rothschild looked towards Professor Mubarakar, who acknowledged with a polite nod. 'Arrangements are in hand: this afternoon a team from their exploration centre in Luxor will be despatched. Apparently, it is a small and relatively under-funded operation, but they do have access to drilling equipment, problem is that the place is a quagmire, literally, a river of moving sand. There has been a lot of associated damage over the last few months. Efforts to preserve unique, historic and perhaps critical information for us, is slowly being compromised; it really is a race against time.'

'Drilling equipment,' Richard repeated expectantly, raising his eyebrows.

'These people know the area and that tomb very well,' Rothschild replied. 'It has been surveyed extensively. Apparently, they know of an area where an outcrop of limestone impinges on the mainly granite strata. It is a relatively soft rock, their intention is to sink a shaft down into the tomb, it should get you into the so-called sixteen-pillared hall, you will have a survey chart and from there you can find your way. They are telling me two to three days, which should coincide with your arrival. Two further points though: firstly, the bore of the shaft will be a little short of six hundred millimetres diameter. That is the biggest bit they have. I am told that there may be a few extra millimetres due to vibration, but nevertheless, it will be tight. Secondly, conditions are treacherous. The drilling team do not intend to stay on after the shaft is sunk - they cannot afford to lose any of their equipment to shifting sands or local bandits operating in these former tourist areas, and anyway, their continued presence will only draw attention. So the team will disappear as soon as they have completed the task; you will be on your own.'

'Sounds encouraging, looking forward to it,' commented Richard sarcastically.

'Yes, well, all the same, we are keeping everything under wraps, a very low profile.'

'Abu Simbel, then?' Richard queried.

'Yes,' replied Rothschild. 'First, Abu Simbel. Study the surviving texts, and then, the Valley of the Kings. We already have a flight booked for you, tomorrow, Orbital Airways,

London Heathrow to Cairo. No more royal flights I am afraid, too conspicuous in that part of the world. It is short notice I know, but it happens to be the only service this month. There are no connecting flights; from Cairo, it's a monorail south to Addis Ababa, Ethiopia; you disembark in Wadi Halfa, after that it's a short drive to Abu Simbel. Find out what you can, our local contacts will help, and then the train again, north, through Aswan to *Al Liqsur* ... Luxor; you go better prepared than we had hoped; thank you Professor, we are indebted to you.'

There was an air of excitement around the table, as if hope beckoned, as if the dark clouds were beginning to lift.

'May I ask a final question of the Professor?' Abbey Hennessy requested.

'Professor?'

'Of course, my dear, what is it?'

'From his remains, Amun-her-khepeshef I mean. He reputedly died in the tenth plague of Egypt: death of the first-born. I am fascinated; did they find out? Were there any indications, any conclusions? Exactly how did he die, Professor?'

'Yes, there were indications, and subsequently conclusions were drawn. According to the records, an expert in facial reconstruction pieced together fifteen remaining skull fragments. In addition, a computer-generated virtual model was used to reconstruct his head and features. Apparently, he looked very similar to the preserved mummy of his father. There was however, a part where the skull appeared crushed, an indentation, as if caused by a heavy blow to the head. Speculation cited a stone mace; they were a common weapon used in battle at that time. Perhaps this injury caused his death, Ms Hennessy.'

Admiralty coffee tasted good to Richard; in fact, he had not tasted anything quite as authentic as this for some time. It reminded him of the dark roasted Kenyan blend he used to buy from the local delicatessen in his hometown years earlier. He regarded it as a rare treat. With world production decimated due to climatic conditions, fresh coffee was not only extremely rare, but also prohibitively expensive. He also regarded the plate of rich tea biscuits brought in by Grenville as something of a novelty.

His enjoyment was short-lived however; Admiral Hughes, flanked by Peter Rothschild, entered the boardroom earnestly and called the meeting to order. He was clutching a hardcopy image. Within moments, the cabinet was seated; Richard sipped what remained of his third cup of coffee before an orderly quickly and politely removed the porcelain cup and saucer.

Admiral Hughes looked towards the video screen. 'Admiral Ghent . . . Secretary, are you there? Colonel Roper, can you hear me? We have some news.'

Within seconds Colonel Roper appeared. 'Secretary

Ghent has gone to see the President, Admiral,' he explained. 'Some idiot has come up with the idea of detonating a nuke; between us and the *Enigma*; create a thermal shockwave; see if we can blow her off course . . . jeepers, they're getting desperate in the White House.'

That statement immediately focused everyone's attention and the meeting started to hum with debate. Ridiculous, thought Richard, the long-term implications - the contamination will do irreparable harm.

'It won't work,' interrupted Professor Nieve, who had been sitting deep in thought, for some considerable time. 'They will not be able to get the warhead close enough; EMILY will destroy it. If it is detonated outside the range of her laser system, the effect will be inadequate. We know that EMILY has a degree of control over the ship's course, probably limited manoeuvre thrust, even if she is displaced by a weak shockwave, she will simply recompute the intercept heading and alter course to suit.'

Roper nodded in agreement. 'Yeah, and then there's a contamination issue. Thank you, Professor; I'll forward this recording immediately to the Admiral's telepager. Okay, now what else have you got over there?'

Peter Rothschild looked momentarily at Laura Bellingham, and then at her laptop. A tiny red light had been flashing on the computer for a few minutes, indicating the arrival of a message. His gesture prompted her to open the classified file. She read it quickly and looked up at Rothschild nodding.

'Thirty seconds,' said Rothschild almost in a whisper. Laura Bellingham typed a reply.

'Colonel Roper,' Rothschild said again, looking back at the video screen. 'On the other matter, we have some good news. We have Simon Sanderson from the London University of Applied Science about to come on screen. He has a significant breakthrough regarding the 'eye in the triangle' image . . . open on channel five, Colonel.'

'I'm waiting,' came the reply.

Within moments, a live picture of a young, bespectacled, tweed-jacketed man appeared on the top screen. Richard noticed Colonel Roper's gaze shift upwards; he was obviously receiving the same transmission on his split screen. The man was standing in a small room surrounded by floor-to-ceiling shelving; cardboard filing boxes occupied every conceivable nook and cranny.

'Go ahead, Mr Sanderson,' instructed Rothschild.

'Morning all,' he replied. 'Simon Sanderson here, London University of Applied Science, and yes I have some news; found something in the early hours. We enhanced the image you sent over, improved its quality and then set up a comparison programme in order to input our image databank. Our system has access to similar databanks in science institutions throughout the world, Peter, including NASA. Collectively we have comparison opportunities with just about every scientific image of merit ever taken, dating back in fact to the early 1900s.'

'Yes, and . . .'

'Well, we came up with an almost exact match; to a crop circle, believe it or not.'

'A what?' Peter remarked.

'A crop circle. They were complex and often beautiful markings in arable crops, reed beds, forest tops, that sort of thing. They appeared throughout the world, but interestingly mostly in the south of England. They were also recorded throughout history, but became an intense phenomenon in the nineteen eighties, nineties and the first decade of this century; apparently, they abruptly stopped appearing in the winter of 2012, during the Precession of the Equinoxes. No reason was ever found, although there was a great deal of futuristic speculation at the time. Anyway, your image is, for all intents and purposes, exactly the same as one that appeared in Hampshire in 2002.

Our records show that this particular circle or formation, was dubbed, The Eye of Elysium. Apparently, there were also some Masonic implications speculated, but we have no detailed records of these.'

'Can you tell me anything about Elysium, Simon?'

'Well yes, but I hear you have Professor Nieve with you today. Actually, he knows a good deal more about this than me, but in a nutshell, Elysium Planitia is a low altitude region on the planet Mars. The area has little or no topography to speak off, but in one specific area, 19.47 degrees north of the equator to be precise and known as the Elysium Quadrangle there are four, prominent, three-sided pyramids, two large and two small. First photographed back in February 1972 by the Mariner 9 probe, then again six months later on August 7, both images clearly showed the same features. Two decades later a closer orbiting 'geostatic' probe called Global Surveyor I, took a series of pictures that curiously were never released. Subsequently, earlier this century, and apparently only after a great deal of pressure from the international scientific community, these four pyramids were identified and confirmed as being artificial. Something else of interest is the angle 19.47. The four pyramids have their orientation based on 19.47 degrees. Olympus Mons, Mount Olympus, the largest volcano on Mars and for that matter in the entire solar system, is also located at the same latitude, exactly 19.47 degrees, as is Mauna Loa in Hawaii, the largest volcano on earth. If that is not enough, the red spot on Jupiter also occurs on that latitude. Then there is the 'Kelvin Wedge'; the precise angle described by the wake of a ship; you guessed it, 19.47 degrees. There are many other examples. Seems this particular angle has ambiguous mathematical and geometrical permutations, some being quite profound. Anyway, a while later and for no apparent reason, NASA, and then the ISSF, put a blanket stop on all further information and imagery relating to these pyramids. No other details were to be divulged; a complete, total, black-out, and so it has remained for the last forty years. Even to the Mars-based personnel on Osiris, it is a no go area, a bit like Area 51 in the US.'

Rothschild looked at Richard, his expression calling for

confirmation.

'Exactly right,' commented Richard. 'Absolutely out of bounds. Thirty kilometre buffer zone, never been that way, more than my job was worth!"

'Simon, what was the date again that the crop formation appeared?'

'Third week in July 2002, Peter. The date annotated in our records is the 21st. However, this is more likely the date when our image was taken. The location is Highclere Hill, rural Hampshire.'

'Is there anything else, Simon?'

'Well, only that our database holds another image, very similar but with an apparent addition. However, this one is much older.'

'Can you enlighten us Simon, please?'

'Yes, the image is similar in all respects, except that there is a snake-like creature around the outside of the original image, sort of encircling it.'

'You said it is much older, do you have any details?'

'Our image is actually derived from a thirty millimetre chromatic photograph taken back in the 1950s. The subject is an important wall painting found at Uxmal, an ancient Mayan city, eighty kilometres south of Merida in the Yucatan peninsula, Mexico. To be more specific the image comes from a huge pyramid, a ceremonial building called the Temple of the Magician. It's amazingly similar I have to say, and there are some accompanying notes if you are interested.'

'We *are* interested Simon, please.'

'Okay, it just says that there are thirty-three 'rays' emanating from the pyramid and these correspond to the journey of the serpent up the thirty-three vertebrae of the human spine and results in the opening of the *third eye* and illumination of those remaining. The Maya did have an extremely accurate calendar, based on astronomical precessions and predictions; the year 2012 *is* mentioned in these notes, but nothing specific; sounds a bit quasi-religious to me, probably from an ancient Mayan ceremony of some description. It's also rather speculative too, as I think I am right in saying that Mayan hieroglyphic writing has never been fully deciphered. Sorry, that's all there is.'

'Simon, thank you very much for your time, we much appreciate it.'

'No problem, anytime, good morning.'

With that, the screen went blank.

'The more I hear, the more I am convinced that there really is a common denominator in all this,' commented the Energy Secretary, William Bryant, thoughtfully. 'I have to say that I was highly sceptical about this undertaking; that our time could be put to better use; but I find myself becoming quite hopeful that this 'Ark of Light' can be found and with it a crystal of some considerable proportions.'

Several fellow members of the cabinet nodded in agreement.

'I may be a little confused with some of the conclusions being drawn from our investigations, but I am very good with dates and names,' interjected Raymond Martin. 'Mr Sanderson, there, said that the crop circle in question appeared in July 2002. If we recall from our last meeting, Professor Simpson-Carter sadly died, for the first time, in March 1989 . . . thirteen years before that crop circle appeared in Wiltshire?'

Rothschild looked at the Home Secretary for a moment or two, coming to terms with the obvious inconsistency; eventually he nodded. 'Yes, thank you, Secretary, you're quite right,' he looked at Richard.

'He obviously discovered that image somewhere else, Peter,' Richard responded. 'Abu Simbel, KV5, the Great Pyramid, even in the Cairo National Museum, after all, he studied for years in all of them.' Richard cupped his hands and squeezed the bridge of his nose between his forefingers. He considered the implications. 'Those pyramids on the plain of Elysium, *they* are the common denominator; that is where the answer to this particular question will lie.'

'That area is out of bounds, Jones, we have already discussed that,' Colonel Roper growled disapprovingly.

'Time to open Pandora's Box then, Colonel,' Richard replied equally coolly.

In Washington, Colonel Roper stood up. He pressed a switch on the display-screen control panel to allow the camera to pan back; Admiral Ghent came into view and sat down.

'Gentlemen, I've been listening to your discussions on my way back from the Oval Office. I have managed to dissuade the President from using the nuclear option for the time being, but he wants an alternative, and quickly. Now, what's this about Mars and the Elysium Quadrangle?'

'There appears to be a requirement to investigate, Admiral, it could be very relevant,' answered Rothschild.

The Admiral looked at Colonel Roper for a few seconds, his expression taut. 'Then we open it,' he said warily. 'Lift the no go zone. I will make the necessary calls. Peter, you contact Commander Miko, you have my authority. Osiris is to put an experienced team together as soon as possible and then await a command briefing. Now, gentlemen, we have one other issue on the agenda, time is pressing. The item found in Simpson-Carter's mouth. I hear people are very uncomfortable with the idea. What is the story?'

'Admiral Ghent, if I may, I will give the lead on this to Reverend Rawlinson; there are, apparently, religious implications.'

'That's fine Peter; Charles, good afternoon, please, go ahead.'

'Yes, good afternoon, Admiral Ghent, gentlemen, and ladies of course. I am aware of the time implications. However, to be honest with you, I would like to reserve my judgement on this matter for a day or two; until information that I have requested from a variety of sources is verified. The item is not a brooch; I can tell you that, more an exclusively manufactured emblem or insignia that has a specific purpose and indeed a Christian connotation. The embossing on its face side is undoubtedly modelled on a flower, taking the form of a stylised fleur-de-lys. Actually, I do know something of this subject. Unfortunately, however, I recognise neither this design, its historical period, nor indeed a likely origin, although in my opinion, it does appear to be European. There are also some etchings on the reverse side; inscriptions in Latin, which I find quite disturbing, that is why I would like to reserve my judgement. One thing I will say though. It seems that the markings on the incendiary shot that was intended to take Richard's life a few days ago, although barely discernable, bear an uncanny resemblance to the stylized flower on this emblem. I have a dear friend and colleague in Rome who is checking archival material in the Great Library; this library contains unique historical literature and documents. Many of these documents are original and some date back almost two thousand years. I am confident that we can trace the origin of this emblem and the motive for why it was placed in the Professor's mouth, given a little more time. Thank you so much.'

Rothschild looked across the table at Admiral Hughes and then at Admiral Ghent on the screen, for a moment no one spoke. Admiral Ghent looked disappointed, even frustrated. Again, Richard sensed that information was being withheld.

'Okay Charles, if you need a breathing space to correlate the information,' Admiral Ghent offered with a sigh. 'But remember, please, time is of the essence; your concerns must be aired as soon as possible.'

'I understand, Admiral,' answered Rawlinson solemnly.

Admiral Ghent turned his attention to Richard. 'Agent Jones,' he said slowly and with some emphasis. 'We *need* you to find that ark. We *need* that crystal. There is so much at stake here, and you don't darn well need me to tell you that.'

All eyes focused on Richard. Many of those gathered nodded in unison. Others sat with blank expressions, the enormity of the task, the quest, beyond articulation. Rothschild, for his part, offered a limp smile of support.

'If it's out there Admiral, if it exists, then I'll find it, you have my word on that,' Richard replied respectfully.

'Very well. I understand that you have another briefing to attend. Oh, and good luck, Richard.'

That is the first time Admiral Ghent has called me by my first name, thought Richard, and I've a feeling that I am going to need a little of that goodwill, he concluded. Richard stood up to leave, nodding his respects to those around the table.

'Richard, I would like a word with you please, before you leave,' Abbey Hennessy said soberly, as she looked towards Admiral Hughes for approval.

'Perhaps you would escort Richard up to Lecture Room 3, Abbey; Richard has an 'undercover operations' and 'methods of disguise' briefing at 14:00 hours.'

'Yes, of course, Sir,' Hennessy agreed, checking the time; it was 13:45.

Richard took a polite step backwards, in order to allow his controller to pass through the doorway first; after he himself had left the room, the ever-attentive Grenville closed the door firmly and took up his 'immediately on hand' position on the opposite side of the corridor.

'Thank you, Grenville,' said Hennessy and then she turned to look at Richard, her courteous smile fading. She came up close and put her head almost nose to nose. Richard took a half step back in surprise; she grasped him lightly by the forearm and indicated left to lead him down the long corridor. Richard wanted to shake her off, he was uncomfortable, but wondered how to do so without causing offence when she stopped and looked him in the eye. 'They obviously have every confidence in you,' she said in a withering tone. 'But they have no idea how you are treating Rachel!'

Richard's eyes widened; he could barely believe what Hennessy had said.

Hennessy could sense Richard's lack of trust; he was suspicious of her motives. Clearly, this was going to be a difficult relationship.

'If they did, like me, they would not be very impressed,' she continued. 'You are undermining a member of my department; emotionally, psychologically and practically *and* I don't like it at all!'

Richard just stared at her for a few moments, stunned. Abbey Hennessy was a tall woman and she had a good deal of physical presence and measured confidence that went with experience; experience of running an inherently complex department; experience of people.

'My private life is of no concern to MI9,' replied Richard after some delay, his tone uncompromising.

Instinctively, Hennessy grasped Richard's arm a little tighter. 'I run my department as if it were a large family, Richard,' she countered. 'I want you to know this, there are no exceptions; emotional stability, that is the key to longevity in this business. I know everything about everyone, in fact, I insist on it. I do not send people into the field with emotional problems; it undermines their performance. If someone has niggling problems, doubts, it impedes them, they are not one hundred percent focused. As a result, people make mistakes, drop their guard, they fail; we have learnt that from decades of covert operations.'

'You mean in MI9 there is no private life, that's what you're damn well saying, right! Well, I am only on temporary secondment, so I'll keep my private life private, *if* you don't mind, *Abbey.*'

The corridor turned to the right by ninety degrees. Hennessy stopped short on the corner, pulling Richard's arm. She stared at him with an icy 'you will do as I say', kind of expression; clearly she was not used to insubordinate behaviour on any level. After a few strained moments, her features softened.

'You are breaking her heart, Richard, she is beside herself,' Hennessy continued in a yielding, concessional tone. 'A brief e-diction saying that the wedding is off, that you can no longer marry her and then no contact for three days . . . that's not just callous Richard, that's brutal!'

Richard hesitated, he was not sure, at that moment, what to say in his defence; indeed, why he should say anything at all. 'Listen, I don't need to explain my actions to anyone. Rachel and I were to be married, yes, so why did she never think to tell me about the other half of her life . . .'

'She couldn't Richard . . .'

At that moment, the door to an adjacent room opened and a man in a dark suit stepped out. Richard looked at him for just an instant, and then he looked at the floor; he felt embarrassed. The man gave a half smile at their presence, closed the door and turned away towards the elevator. Hennessy tried to take Richard's arm again, but he shook her off as they walked a little further and turned left through white, glass-paned, double doors that in turn lead into a large stairwell. Hennessy indicated upwards. 'Are you feeling up to this, Richard, I mean really?' she asked pitifully.

Richard gave her a frozen glare. 'Listen, I'm already in this up to my ears, so don't ask me if I can handle it. I'm liable to take your remark the wrong way . . . okay!'

After two flights of decorative wooden stairs, they alighted on another corridor; they turned left again and walked in silence for another twenty metres before stopping outside a door displaying a black-on-white painted placard that was mounted at head height. Lecture

Room 3, it advertised in bold lettering. Abbey Hennessy checked the corridor in both directions and then squared up to Richard, who in turn looked back at her defiantly, awaiting her next broadside. Hennessy's body language was a conundrum, Richard sensed a dark, scolding, matronly stiffness, but her eyes were soft, forgiving, possibly understanding; something, evidently, that she could not conceal.

'Richard,' she said sternly, 'Rachel is due to resume her appointment on Mars, perhaps for another year. She will be leaving soon. They are already scheduling another shuttle flight as we speak, an S2, in case the *Enigma* cannot be used; which I have to say at this point is looking very likely. Apart from the crystal thing, Osiris is without a Chief Medical Officer, a surgeon, or a fully trained pharmacist . . .'

'Or a spy!' Richard interjected.

Abbey Hennessy sighed. She knocked on the door to the lecture room and opened it, peering inside. It was empty apart from a row of five desks and an aluminium-coloured briefcase on a table towards the front of the room. She gestured for Richard to follow her inside and promptly closed the door behind him.

'I've told you. *Why* will you not listen? *Why* are you so stubborn, Richard? Rachel is not a spy, or an agent, or an informer for that matter, not in that sense anyway. She was recruited just prior to taking up her appointment; it was ideal for us. As CMO of Mars base, she has unrestricted access to every member's medical, physiological and psychological records. She can gauge undercurrents of discontent, potential psychotic behaviour, detect latent social problems, warn of troublemakers, even potential criminal acts by watching and evaluating. That is what she does for us and she is very good at her job. For god's sake Richard, as you well know, there are over one hundred people on Mars; do you think people stop being people, just because they are a long way from home?'

Richard shook his head in disbelief. 'What about the multiplex screening processes?'

'The wrong people can still get through and always will, despite screening. We received Rachel's confidential report on Jennifer Middleton's pregnancy for example, and her suspicions of Renton Dublovnic being the father. There was no mention of it in the general medical report or Middleton's death certificate, Rachel wanted to protect her reputation, albeit posthumously. Now Dublovnic, *there* is an example of a 'wrong man' making it through the screening process; under normal circumstances, he would have been on the next shuttle home. That is the work Rachel does for us; don't you see? That micro-society, Osiris, they are all so interdependent on each other, it is absolutely essential; did you think the international coexistence thing just happens despite itself?'

'Yes, well, that may be the case, but you were quick enough to recruit her into more, shall we say, clandestine work? No wonder earth found out so quickly about my discovery of the crystals; that even baffled Commander Miko and the security department.'

Now Hennessy, for her part, appeared a little embarrassed. 'Yes, we had a problem there I regret to say . . . a leak. That information should have stopped within security level ISSF Class 5 protocols; it was intercepted on its way to the Prime Minister's office.'

Richard shook his head with disbelief. 'We all accept the State monitors everything here on earth,' he said quietly. 'Sad, I thought we were much more independent on Mars. No . . . you used her; you used me; *you* could have told me!'

'Richard, think about it. You were appointed to Osiris for a number of reasons; helping you get over a failed relationship and reorganise your life was one of them. Despite Commander Miko's unflinching confidence in you and your renowned ability as a pilot, you were light years away from being classified ISSF Top Secret Class 5, or even 3, for that matter!'

'Yeah, well, there's my problem. I was responsible enough to be given the job of retrieving the crystals, but not for whom I was doing it . . . or with, for that matter. No, it's over for Rachel and me; I've lost it. Trust and love; those paths are rocky enough. Without one or the other to smooth the way, you can forget it.'

Hennessy was dumbfounded; Richard although saddened, seemed obstinate in the extreme. She finally realised that he had set his course on this matter and as far as he was concerned, there was nothing more to say.

'So, I am to release you into the field suppressing a minefield of emotions that will inevitably degrade your rationality and performance; possibly jeopardise your life and the success of the mission,' she concluded austerely. 'I fear for you, Lieutenant Commander Reece, I really do.'

'Nothing gets between me and the task. My focus has never been in doubt, Ms Hennessy,' Richard replied equally poignantly. 'You do your job and I will do mine. Now, if you will excuse me, I have a lesson to attend.'

With that, Richard turned his back and went to the window. Abbey Hennessy looked at him blankly for several seconds and then left the room, shutting the door with a loud thump.

Peter Rothschild, with the permission of Admiral Hughes, answered the unexpected telephone call. The incoming number, displayed on the small flip-screen, informed him that the caller was the senior operations officer at Strasbourg's ESSA Mission Control Centre.

'Yes, I see . . . when . . . ? They are sure about this? How long will they need . . . ? Two hours! I will seek approval, standby, I will call you back immediately.' Rothschild terminated the call and turned towards Admiral Hughes, 'Sir, something's come up.' Rothschild then looked at the screen in the centre of the table. 'Admiral Ghent, Colonel Roper, are you still there?'

Admiral Ghent appeared and sat down. 'Yes, we are, what is it?'

'The S2, ISS *Neptunus* Sir, en route from space station *Spartacus* to Andromeda, to help with the evacuation; she is on the edge of the Callisto quadrant, pushed into deep space in order to give the *Enigma* a wide berth. Her commander is reporting an unusual occurrence of Sion gas a few miles off her port bow, in the form of a small, condensed cloud. Apparently, Sion gas is the primary fuel constituent of the Delta Class fighter. They would like to take a closer look, two hours at most. Can I give them approval?'

Admiral Ghent looked off-screen at Colonel Roper and then turned his attention to Admiral Hughes; with nothing spoken, both men nodded. 'Two hours, that's all; then they are to get the hell out of there over to Andromeda, make that clear to the Commander.'

'I will call him back immediately, Sir.'

CHAPTER 12

CAUGHT IN TIME

'Is he alive?'

'Can't say at the moment, there is no apparent damage inside the cockpit, but this ship is shot-up pretty bad. He is slumped forward on his shoulder straps. There is no movement.'

'Okay, fix the towing sling and get him back here as quickly as possible; medics are standing by.'

'I'm on it, Sir,' replied the American astronaut, as he floated weightless above the wreckage of Red Lead, Commander Tom Race's Delta Class fighter. Clad in the familiar, pristine, white spacesuit and with an Oriel mini thrust-pack strapped to his back, the man carefully manoeuvred himself around the buckled, scorched remains of the ship, careful to keep hold at all times with at least one hand. Clearly visible from the flight deck of

Neptunus, as she held station some three hundred metres distant, was the abbreviation 'ISSF' emblazed in black lettering across the astronaut's fuel cell. Populated by a crowd of onlookers, much to the consternation of the co-pilot, the atmosphere on the S2's flight deck was one of anticipation and hope.

From the other side of the stricken fighter, the astronaut peered again into the cockpit. He cupped a large, gloved hand against his visor and pressed his helmet onto the canopy, trying to reduce the reflection from his bright observation light. He carefully scanned the fighter's instrument panel; evidently, power was down. Whether damaged or totally exhausted, the result was the same: the pilot's life support system would be running on standby batteries and *their* life was very limited. Then, at that instant, something on the far side caught his eye; a tiny red light began to flash steadily.

'Hey, wait a minute!' the astronaut called over the radio. 'There's a red light flashing in here.' He looked again, focusing more closely on the panel. 'It's from the life support system, the control panel, a flashing red light.'

Immediately there was a reply from the S2. 'It's the oxygen system,' said the Commander earnestly. 'It's damn well empty . . . quickly, move it!'

A short burst of propellant from his thrust-pack had the astronaut promptly manoeuvring over the ship's fuselage; it was a race against time. He pulled into position two long, rigid, metal poles and secured one end of each into receptors on top of the fighter's fuselage, one forward and one aft. Then, shimmying along the length of one of the poles, until he was hanging onto the other end with one hand, he fired two short bursts on his thrust pack. Propellant from two nozzles burnt brightly for a few seconds and the whole concoction began to drift very slowly towards the *Neptunus*. Several further bursts, each lasting no more than one second, accompanied his final, precise manoeuvring beneath the belly of the shuttle, until finally the astronaut had the free ends of the poles clipped into their respective positions on a restrain mechanism mounted beneath the enormous mother ship. Two giant curved doors, like bomb-bay doors, gaped; their fully open position easily allowing the bulk of a D Class to pass through.

'Secure Commander,' confirmed the astronaut. 'Go, go!' he coaxed, as he positioned himself on top of the wreckage.

Purposefully, the mechanism drew the fighter up into the cavernous bay of the S2, until it shimmied into its final position with a loud, metallic clank. The astronaut, moving arm over arm, sometimes floating with his feet above his head, made his way to a small control panel mounted on the inside of one of the large doors. With one hand he hung on and the other he made a series of selections. The result was four steel clamps rotating tightly against the restraining poles and finally the two curved doors of the freight bay effortlessly closing, until they completely shut out the starshine.

'Ready for pressurisation,' the astronaut said calmly. Immediately a whoosh of gas reverberated around the bay. For an instant, everything was clouded by a deluge of condensing moisture, but only for an instant; within seconds the large chamber was oxygenated and became bright and warm.

'Commander Race, Commander, can you hear me?' A calm, reassuring voice pulled at Tom's subconscious. 'Come on, Commander, say something, I know that you can hear me,' continued the pretty, middle-aged woman, as she gently squeezed Tom's hand.

Slowly Tom regained consciousness; he shook his head and blinked repeatedly against the bright lights of the small medical module.

'So, you're back with us, Commander,' said Doctor Garcia kindly.

Tom opened his eyes. He lay transfixed for a few seconds before looking earnestly at his surroundings. Finally, appreciating the comfortable environment, he relaxed. Instinctively, he knew where he was; for a good part of his career he had flown the S2; he knew the appearance of this module well enough.

'I guess this means that we failed,' he concluded matter

of factly.

'Oh, I don't know about that, Commander,' replied Doctor Garcia, exercising a well-versed bedside manner. 'Anyway, a collective debrief has been planned for you, but at the moment, just rest. You were lucky, no harm done, just light concussion; you may have a headache for a day or two, after the Sorotox wears off.'

'Who else got back?' Tom asked trying to sit up.

Doctor Garcia fluffed-up the pillow and then gently pushed him back down onto the narrow, steel-framed bed. 'I am sure all of that will be covered in the forthcoming debrief, Commander. Now, try and get some rest, we are on our way to Andromeda.'

CHAPTER 13

THE COMPASS POINTS EAST

Richard looked up at the airspeed indicator, or more precisely the mach meter. It was mounted prominently on the bulkhead at the forward end of the spacious, open-planned, express travellers' cabin: Mach 4.2. Below it was an altimeter, also proudly displaying its digital readout: 75,000 feet. The cabin, at least ninety metres long and sixty wide, had a broad, sweeping ceiling that curved down to a long row of porthole type windows on either side. Richard estimated that three hundred people were perched in row after row of comfortable, fully reclining seats that were upholstered in a dark blue material. They were a pleasant contrast against the luxurious, cream-coloured, suede-like material of the ceiling and the similarly coloured short-pile carpet.

Richard sat in a window seat, five rows back from

the forward bulkhead, which also served to separate the express cabin from the substantially more expensive seats of 'atmospheric class'. That thought made him smirk; a resigned, perhaps even a resentful gesture. There he was, paradoxically, on a mission to save the human race from itself, and in the eyes of the authorities anyway, he was at best, an 'express traveller'.

'Surprised I'm not in the freight bay,' he whispered to himself, his smirk morphing into a smile.

'I'm sorry?' enquired the woman entrenched in a book on his left.

Richard looked at her for a few moments, still lost in his thoughts; initially, he seemed quite unaware of his tête-à-tête.

'Oh, nothing, sorry . . . talking to myself, it's a habit that comes with working on your own for too long.' Richard raised a faint half-smile.

'First sign of madness, you know,' replied the diminutive lady, who was well in her eighties if she was a day, and obviously English.

That remark coaxed Richard to think of Rachel. 'Yes, apparently,' he offered genially. 'Someone I know has told me that on more than one occasion.'

'Going to see my grandchildren, you know, while I still can, while there is still time.'

Richard nodded politely, he knew what she was referring to, and it was not her senior years. However, the last thing he wanted to do at that moment was engage in polite conversation and he turned again to look out through the tiny circular window. He rested his head on the comfortable head restraint, stretched out and stared at the distant horizon. The gentle, convex, curvature of the planet was plain to see at this altitude and even the glow of several bright stars permeated the semi-darkened sky. He twisted his neck slightly in order to look upwards, higher into the stratosphere. Over five months since I've been in space, he mused, and I am missing it.

Richard reflected on the task in hand, finally having a few, quiet hours in which to do so. Clearly, a genuine threat existed: the multinational conglomerates with their prodigious financial resources, their technology and their designs on global domination and also, if that was not enough, a shadowy, covert, religious fanatic, who seemed to move around the world as easily as a national statesman. Both threats were virtual and real time, Richard concluded, and this despite his new identity. His newly acquired *modus operandi* would help; weapons, support, communications; nonetheless, from here on in, he had a feeling that things could get nasty. However, he was not going to let these feelings develop into adrenalin fuelled nervousness. He was not a pessimist, quite the opposite; neither was he one to linger on thoughts of destiny or such like, and he rarely considered his own frailties. Nevertheless, he found no comfort in this secret service mantle: matters of espionage, or his pivotal, fundamental role. Perhaps destiny did have a hand in this after all, he pondered. People, organisations;

unscrupulous, violent; they were after him; their mission: to locate, track and eliminate, like the FACULTE he and Preston had dispatched without remorse in the freight terminal on Andromeda. To be constantly on his guard, always looking over his shoulder; it was his unfamiliarity with this new reality, that was most disconcerting. He could do it; learn; eventually it would become second nature. It would have to be if he was to survive. And the lip service he so often paid to his own personal security; Spheron's muted assignation attempt had made that a thing of the past. Would his life ever be the same again, he considered; like someone winning *Centrinet's* one hundred million world dollar global lottery. Had he not already split with Rachel, it was unlikely that she would want him with a price on his head. The consequences of his discovery were far reaching indeed.

Richard settled back in his seat and relaxed as the muddle of conflicting thoughts drifted away. An almost imperceptible vibration from the Stratocord's enormous scramjet propulsion system pervaded his senses, like the drone of a distant bumblebee on a silent spring morning. He fell into a deep sleep.

After a couple of hours Richard woke; he felt better, collected. He looked around the cabin for the nearest lavatory, excused himself courteously with the elderly woman in the adjacent seat – who was still engrossed in her book – and joined the short queue for the facility.

Washing his hands in the stainless steel basin, he looked himself over in the mirror, a process that elicited some self-criticism. He did not look his best he thought, far from it in fact. He was growing used to his longer hair and in a few days, his beard would aid disguise. What he was struggling to accommodate however, was the ginger colour. He studied his reflection for sometime, trying to come to terms with it. He did not have that pale, freckly skin that one associates with naturally ginger-haired people, he concluded; somehow, it looked odd, it just didn't work. Was he really going to fool anybody? His skin was darker, even a little weathered. Prolonged exposure to intense, ultraviolet light during his 'outside' hours on Mars had left him with a permanent, albeit subtle suntan, and this despite the advanced materials of his spacesuit and helmet. He considered for a moment if the carotene in his one-a-day tablet would improve his night vision. They used to say it improved night vision. Surely, like an owl, he would swoop on his prey before they saw him! The thought made him smile, but not for long; there was an earnest 'tap' on the door.

'Are you alright in there, Sir?' a man enquired from outside.

Richard snapped to his senses and flushed the lavatory; somehow trying to disguise his vanity. The pool of intense, yellow urine was sucked from the pan, accompanied by an overly loud hiss of air. With these tablets, I should drink more, he thought. He pushed open the bi-fold doors, only to find a steward standing directly opposite, staring back at him; his concerned expression matched only by a young woman, who stood to his left. The survival instructor had commented the previous day that Richard's hair would acquire a bright, almost orange coloration for about twenty-four hours, whilst the carotene based drug settled in his system. After that, his hair would assume a more natural, commonplace shade. Judging by the look on the woman's face, the prediction was correct; she clearly thought Richard a little old to be making such a fashion statement. She, clearly, had been the instigator. Dragging her gaze down to her watch, she shook her head disapprovingly. Much to Richard's continued embarrassment, several other people, who were seated adjacently, focused their attention on him.

After a few moments, the woman clicked her tongue, avoided Richard by some margin and stepped into the vacant cubicle, closing the door behind her with a disconcerting thump.

'She likes me,' Richard said nonchalantly, looking at the steward with a straight face. 'I can tell.'

The steward looked confused.

'Tell me, how long to Cairo, please?' Richard asked, trying not to laugh.

'Fifty minutes, Sir,' replied the steward looking a little less perturbed.

Richard returned to his place. He checked the moving-map display on the wide, personal screen that was mounted in the back of the next row of seats: descent in twenty-seven minutes, arrival in forty-eight. He typed a request for a cup of English breakfast tea, adding 'white with one sugar' into the miniature keyboard set on the mobile controller, and then 'posted' it to the galley.

The countdown had started; the time was almost upon him. I have good survival instincts, he thought, but will they be enough?

CHAPTER 14

THE FIRST DEAL

Whether it was due to the painkiller Sorotox, or an unusually expeditious recovery from the concussion he had suffered, Tom's nagging headache had all but disappeared as he walked into Andromeda's conference room. As always, he was exactly on time: 21:00 hours, 9.00 pm Lunar Corrected Time.

Tom expected a large turnout and he was not mistaken. The well-proportioned, centrally-positioned, oval table was seated to capacity and barely any standing room remained available. Most were uniformed officers from Andromeda's various departments and their number, Tom noticed, included the flight-suited Major Bob McCarthy, his own replacement as Executive Officer of Andromeda's shuttle wing. There were also several civilians present. Some of these, being scientists, technical staff or laboratory assistants, wore white coats, whilst others from the administrative sector wore regulation light and dark-grey coloured shirts and trousers respectively. Although the gathering offered nationalities, backgrounds and positions that were many and varied, all had just one thing on their minds: the future of the Moon base Andromeda, their home and, effectively, their life.

Commander Moseley, the commanding officer of Andromeda, sat at the head of the table; flanked to his left by Colonel Roper and to his right by Professor Nieve; they had both flown in on the last shuttle. Moseley had a very stern expression. Indeed, the three men all appeared to be sitting under a dark cloud as expansive and foreboding as those that choked the earth. Next to the Professor, there was an empty chair. Commander Moseley beckoned Tom towards it and then looked back at the computer screen that was integral and flush-fitting with the tabletop.

Tom also felt the shadow of a black cloud bearing down on him, as earlier that afternoon, having awoken from a long and relatively restful sleep he had been informed of the outcome of his mission against the *Enigma* and the final casualty count. The pain in his head may have eased, but what he felt in his heart and the knot in his stomach, was far worse: only he had survived. Despite his renowned professional attitude, a preoccupation with EMILY, which had started several months earlier, was rapidly developing into a vendetta.

Colonel Roper opened the brief. 'Welcome, ladies and

gentlemen and thank you for coming. We all know each other I think, except perhaps for Professor Nieve, who has kindly flown in from Spaceport Strasbourg this afternoon. For those of you who may not know of the professor, he is the chief designer assigned to the *Enigma* project.'

Professor Nieve nodded politely, acknowledging the introduction; momentarily, as he did, his eyes met Tom's.

'Now look everyone,' Colonel Roper continued sternly. 'We all know the reason for this briefing *and* the current emergency evacuation. Everybody here has responsibilities and probably a thousand things to do, so we will progress with the agenda as quickly as possible.' Roper looked at Tom. 'I'm not going to linger on the events of the 23rd. We are all desperately sorry at the loss of so many fine men and women, all of whom were friends and colleagues. Suffice to say that they did their job superbly, as was expected. Equally, we are very pleased to see Commander Race recovered and back with us.'

There was a collective murmur around the room. 'Good to see you, Tom,' somebody shouted. 'Yeah, glad you're back, Commander,' somebody else commented.

Roper raised his hand, 'Kudos to the crew of the Neptunus,' he added, looking across the table at the PA. 'A recovery not only spectacular, but also dangerous. Please, send a note of commendation to the Commander and duplicate it in the daily report.'

Commander Moseley's personal assistant duly typed, with a flamboyant flurry, a number of words into his computer.

'It is evident that the *Enigma*, or to be more precise EMILY, retains a greater control of the manual or 'maniptronic' network than we had initially thought,' Colonel Roper continued. 'She certainly has a degree of control over the manoeuvre thrust system and she is using it to good effect. Our long range sensors indicate that she remains on a spatial trajectory that will intercept the Moon's orbit in a few days time.' Roper looked at one of the officers seated at the table. 'Doug . . . sitrep, please.'

'Slowly but surely, Colonel,' came the reply. 'With her present drift rate, Andromeda will be in range of her laser system in forty-nine hours and seven minutes precisely.'

'I see, and how is the evacuation going?'

'Doug Miller, as Andromeda's operations officer, responded again. 'Pretty good Colonel, given the notice period. Three shuttles are working around the clock. The welcome addition of the *Neptunus* adds essential capacity. Even so, in forty-nine hours Colonel, there will still be eight hundred and eighteen people remaining.'

'Ugh . . . isn't there anything else out there, anything that we can hijack?'

'We have numerous twin-seat fighter trainers also ferrying back and forth, and two old, previously decommissioned S1's; but they are mainly concerned with the retrieval of essential stores and equipment. It's like mother's cake stall out there, Colonel!'

'Forget the stores,' ordered Colonel Roper. 'Switch to

people, and what about the bunkers?'

'Almost ready, Colonel, ventilating as we speak. We can squeeze in five hundred at most, and then it becomes unsafe.'

'Goddamn it, man! That still leaves three hundred people exposed!'

'Best we can do, Colonel, that's the reality of it.'

Roper kneaded his temples with his left hand, his stress plainly apparent. 'What about the Helium 3 stocks?' he asked finally.

'We have secured the network Colonel: closed all pipelines, junctions, terminal valves and secured the transport bridge couplings, although most of that element of the system is still under construction. Again, that is the best we can do. To be frank, that is our nightmare scenario. If *Enigma*'s laser weapon strikes one of those terminals, or anywhere in the system for that matter, and Helium 3 gas is exposed to the searing temperature of that plasma beam, it could initiate a fusion reaction; a potential nuclear fusion bomb. Our current stock is two million cubic metres, Sir, probably enough to crack the Moon in two!'

'Am I correct in assuming that the gas is stored under high pressure?' enquired Professor Nieve.

'That's correct, Sir,' answered the Operations Officer. 'Some twenty years ago, when the cavern was first discovered and the subsequent survey found it suitable, it was used as a reservoir to store liquid water; it has a massive capacity. Leak rates were found to be exceptionally low. After the Helium 3 extraction process was perfected in thirty-nine, we switched to storing the gas; that's eleven years of stockpiling.'

Professor Nieve, who was well aware of the fusion potential of Helium 3, looked justifiably concerned. 'Helium 3 is the powerhouse element of the sun itself,' he explained. 'It is the source of nuclear reactions that occur in its central core and the catalyst for temperatures of fifteen million degrees Kelvin. All of us here are aware of its energy potential for mankind. When a workable, contained and safe fusion reactor is eventually perfected, Helium 3 will be its fuel,' he concluded.

The sun emits vast quantities of Helium 3 gas as a constituent of the solar wind. Only found in minute traces on earth, because of its protective atmosphere, the element is abundant in the surface strata of the Moon, where, due to the absence of an atmosphere, it has been absorbed for thousands of millions of years. Its extraction and storage has immense, latent, value.

Tom sat with a sullen expression, listening intently to the conversation; the situation was dire indeed. As result of the failed, costly, skirmish with EMILY, he questioned his own leadership. Had he succeeded, these troubled times would have been avoided. Professor Nieve had already had a brief word with him in private. He had assured Tom that the mission had been necessary, indeed vital, but now a new strategy was necessary in order to deal with the imminent threat.

'Now listen up, everyone,' said Colonel Roper. 'I will spell out the facts and then let's put our heads together. One, *Enigma* is clearly operational with respect to her close-point defence system. Two, although Commander Sampleman disconnected her main propulsive drive prior to his injury, *Enigma* evidently retains some directional control. Three, we have two days before she poses a highly destructive threat to Andromeda. Skyport II's orbit, incidentally, puts her next in line. Finally, from the experience gained recently, we have no effective defence! Unless we come up with something, and quickly, we are going to start losing people, lots of bodies, so, anyone any bright ideas?'

The room hushed; people looked around warily; there were a few whispers; Colonel Roper shook his head.

One of the white-coated scientists sitting at the far end of the table eventually responded. 'Clearly, the main computer, EMILY, is behind this aggressive action, do we have any ideas of her agenda or motives, Colonel?'

Again, the room fell silent. Tom reflected on the question for some time; it was pertinent. 'I may have a lead on that, Colonel,' he said.

'I'm all ears,' replied Roper.

'During our first encounter with EMILY, when Ross Sampleman and I were evading the two Humatrons, Ross made his way to the bridge. He hid there for several hours and was party to several conversations between EMILY and Nicola Lynch. Nicola Lynch, you may recall, was second-in-command of engineering and the saboteur. EMILY stated that she needed more followers, more *disciples* as she put it, to operate her body, to run the ship, do things that she could not achieve by accessing the maniptronic system alone. She was referring to the Humatron HU 40s. I know Ross made a report as soon as he was well enough, but I think it may have been overlooked.'

With that, Professor Nieve spoke. 'I was not aware of this report,' he said thoughtfully. 'This is very interesting, very interesting indeed, perhaps of fundamental importance. EMILY evidently wants a crew in her own likeness: a crew of computers, a crew of robots!'

A stunned silence descended on the conference room. The chilling realisation of the potential of a freethinking robot evidently made its mark on those gathered.

'Can she think like that?' Roper enquired, somewhat alarmed. 'I mean, that she wants to run the ship herself?'

'Operationally, EMILY has access to almost the entire ship, Colonel. Effectively, she already *is* running the *Enigma.* She just wants to utilise the remaining potential. I have said it a thousand times. EMILY is the most powerful computer ever conceived; Level 9, entirely autonomous, completely self-aware. But yes, I can see that many elements of the ship's operation will require external accessing; operations outside the scope of the maniptronic system. Repairs, servicing and various mechanical functions, that sort of thing. I think we may be onto something here.'

Roper sighed, 'Then we have a bigger problem than we

thought. A renegade robot, fully integrated with the most powerful spacecraft ever built.'

The conference room fell silent again. Professor Nieve scratched his frizzled mop of white hair. 'Of course, there is one alternative?'

'Go on, Professor . . .'

'Trade with her, give her what she wants.'

'What!' retorted Colonel Roper immediately, clearly astonished at what he had heard.

'It would be mutually beneficial, Colonel,' Professor Nieve continued matter of factly. 'Think about it. We trade a number of Humatrons in return for a round trip to Mars. We avoid the forthcoming catastrophe, retrieve the remaining crystals inside two weeks *and* we put somebody onboard.'

Roper looked irritated, even nervous, his manner becoming prickly as he considered the unthinkable. '*We do not make deals with machines, Professor,*' he uttered in exasperation and slammed his fist on the table.

Tom and many others in the room were taken aback by Colonel Roper's reaction. Professor Nieve, on the other hand, had clearly worked with 'old school' militarists such as the Colonel before and parried his uncompromising, perhaps obsolete conviction with a nonchalant shrug of his shoulders. 'Very well, Colonel,' he countered. 'Then you have forty-eight hours to formulate a workable option. You do not need me to remind you of what's at stake.'

Roper leaned forward and cradled his forehead in his

hand. After some time he spoke. 'Are there any suggestions, anything, anybody?' He lifted his head slowly and looked at Tom for several seconds, his brow raised expectantly. 'Tom?' he whispered.

'Another assault is pointless, Colonel; she's going to keep on heading this way. If it is possible for a computer to have a 'chip on its shoulder', this machine has one, reasons unknown. I just don't see an alternative; perhaps we can make something of it; perhaps she's too damned clever for her own good!'

Roper offered a resigned expression, 'I'll have to clear it with Washington and Whitehall, and the ISSF will also have to approve this course of action . . . they are not going to like it, I can tell you.'

'Tell them that there are no other options, Colonel. In addition, as *Enigma*'s chief designer, it has my approval,' reassured Professor Nieve sombrely.

Roper looked directly at the professor and stared briefly. 'It won't be easy, how do you negotiate with a goddamned robot, Professor?'

'We need someone with whom she is familiar for one thing, someone that she feels she could trust; someone with knowledge and authority,' replied the professor directing a glance at Tom.

Tom could see where this was leading. 'You think it's down to me, Professor?' Tom questioned after an awkward pause.

'Go on, Professor,' encouraged Roper.

'There is no point in calling her, trying to communicate from a distance. NASA has been trying that for several days and there is no doubt that EMILY can hear them; she will be monitoring most, if not all of the space frequencies. If we are to negotiate successfully, then I think a personal approach will be necessary, one to one. A relationship such as this, may also prove to have additional benefits in the future as well.'

'I will have to go to her, a single ship, unarmed,' interrupted Tom. 'A direct course, no threat, it's the only way.'

That conclusion instigated several mumbling conversations around the conference room. Roper raised his hand in order to stifle them. 'That's suicide, surely?' he said bluntly.

'I believe Tom's right,' Professor Nieve contested, nodding. 'This is the only course of action open to us.'

'But there aren't any goddamned Humatrons to barter with, are there? Their production was banned some time ago, after the Skyport I disaster,' Roper protested.

'Nicola Lynch, or the people she was working for, managed to get hold of two. Who's to say Interface Cybersystems did not build any more, despite the banning order?'

'This is going from bad to worse, Professor,' concluded Colonel Roper, standing up. 'I'll talk to the President and Admiral Ghent, he will get the CIB onto it; put some feelers out; find out just how many of these HU 40s were really built.' The Colonel scanned the room slowly; he placed a hand on the shoulder of Commander Moseley, in a friendly fashion, as if seeking approval. 'Ladies and gentlemen,' he said addressing the gathering. 'This meeting is adjourned. Please, return to your departments; carry on with the briefed evacuation until you hear otherwise, and good luck to everyone.'

CHAPTER 15

AWAKEN THE BYGONE

There was no need to loiter. No rendezvous was planned. From now on, the brief was to minimise attention. For Richard, personal contact of any kind was to be avoided during his first twenty-four hours in Cairo. He hailed a taxi, the first in line from a queue of unlikely looking vehicles, all of which had clearly seen better days. The car shunted forwards and stopped: the driver's window in front of him was dirty and unkempt and layers of splashed mud and grime streaked back from both wheel arches. Circular patches of rust bloomed over the car's once maroon-coloured bodywork and a corroded hole in the nearside doorsill seemed to shout 'unclean', as if from a mouth filled with decaying teeth. The driver was barely visible through the front window, even though he was less than a metre away. The whole spectacle seemed to urge 'take the next car' into Richard's ear. In response, he eyed the next in line but it was no better.

As Richard walked to the rear of the vehicle the boot lid, surprisingly, sprang open. He was about to throw his rucksack into the unsanitary interior, when he had second thoughts. However, he climbed, bag in hand, into the back of the taxi and specified his destination. The airport arrivals level was congested with more sheltering, homeless people than travellers and Richard felt relieved as the aged, leaking, Mercedes 610 promptly responded, destined for the aptly-named Pharaoh's Palace Hotel.

The car smelled of musty, rotting carpets and its driver was scruffy and unshaven. The skinny-faced Arab eyed Richard through the rear-view mirror for several minutes. Richard ignored him. After driving for an hour and fifteen minutes through the chaotic, over-crowded, dismal city, Richard caught a glimpse of a pyramid. It appeared briefly between two high-rise buildings, like some confused, conflicting edifice. He realised that it was the Great Pyramid itself.

The car pulled onto a long, relatively open road and Richard was surprised to see the Plateau of Giza; the only remnant of the once proud and still quite isolated swathe of ancient landscape. Now, the sprawling suburbs of Cairo encroached to within half a kilometre of the great monuments, surrounding them and defiantly violating them, like a flock of vultures circling a mortally-wounded elephant. Nevertheless, there they were: the Great Pyramid of Khufu, the pyramids of Khafre and Menkaure, and the three satellite Queen's pyramids, all darkened by the persistent, polluted moisture. Their geometric shapes and sheer size, and their antiquity and forgotten secrets, filled Richard with awe.

Exposed to the elements, the Giza Plateau suffered the full effects of any wind and today, like most days, it swept uninhibited among the ruins, whilst the expanse of low, flat-bottomed cloud seemed to be fleeing from a hostile blue horizon some way distant. The menacing blanket of cloud was just high enough to avoid the pinnacles of the two highest pyramids, but occasionally a fierce draught drew the cloud down to the shadowy monuments. Then, like a gaping wound, the rough, pointed apex would expose their tumultuous entrails.

Richard watched for a while, absorbed by the spectacle; the pyramid's mystical presence was diminished, but not deadened by the cheerless weather. Eventually, he leaned forward and tapped the driver on the shoulder. 'Where is the hotel?' he asked tersely, suspicious of the man's constant attention.

The driver, mumbling a few words in his native tongue, gestured towards the far side of the plateau. There, Richard could see a towering, glass-fronted building, erected face-on to the road and overlooking the ancient plateau with its time-worn ruins. The juxtaposition of ancient and modern seemed strange to Richard as he surveyed the scene, sitting back again in his seat and gazing open-mouthed at the extent of it all. As the driver turned onto the eastern section of perimeter road, the Sphinx, in all its resplendent mystery, came into view, silhouetted by the stark angles of the pyramids. If ever an expression, deliberated Richard, could conceal a paradox of seismic proportions, then surely this was it; a face hewn from solid rock, as old as man, as reticent as the society that spawned it; gazing into limitless space.

The Palace Hotel had an impressively broad portico. Six towering limestone columns flanked its wide doorway. Three set on each side, the columns portrayed intricate carvings: images of ancient Egyptian scenes with accompanying hieroglyphic text. Whether they were authentic, the genuine article inaptly pilfered, or notable replicas, Richard could only speculate. Nevertheless, it was the first time, apart from a few excursions to London's Natural History Museum during his school days that he had seen original examples of the ancient writing. Here in Egypt, the depicted scenes seemed to come alive to him.

A diminutive, but smartly dressed porter courteously opened the car door for Richard. Wearing a red uniform that audaciously displayed embroidered gold stripes and epaulettes, the porter then scurried off to open a large, glass, side door. He kept a firm hand on his fez, as the discourteous wind funnelled between the columns. Evidently, a lack of electrical power had left the main revolving entrance redundant. Richard declined the man's overly helpful, even excessive offers to carry his bag and the porter seemed disappointed when, with no remuneration to compensate his enthusiasm, Richard politely dismissed him.

Inside, the cavernous lobby was equally impressive, as was the ornate reception area. There was a large, brass placard mounted on the wall adjacent to the check-in counter, it commemorated the hotel's opening by the Egyptian President, twenty-five years earlier. Richard, although preoccupied with his new identity was not oblivious to the people around him; he kept a suspicious eye on the other people in the vicinity, much to the consternation of the pretty woman who confirmed his details and issued the key to his executive room on the ninth floor. He gestured his appreciation, then, with the collar of his trench coat turned up, he buried his face still further to conceal his identity and escape the notice of any onlookers as he walked towards the elevator. With only one elevator in operation and a small queue, he kept his back turned and then, as the elevator slowly ascended, stared at the floor.

The room was five star, spacious and comfortable. Only the roof garden and swimming pool terrace were above his level, and those facilities had long since been abandoned.

Through the unopened balcony doors, impervious above the sprawling roof-tops, Richard could plainly see the dominating, colonial-style building that was the National Museum. Perhaps there, he thought, swathed in its omniscience, lay the answers essential to his quest. He hoped to have time to visit during his stay. If he were to unlock its secrets, however, he would first need a key. Would the colossal temples of Abu Simbel provide it, or perhaps KV5, or somewhere else in this land cloaked by antiquity?

Richard unlocked the lofty, glass-panelled doors and stepped onto the balcony. His view was privileged and as he stared at the panorama it began: the beautiful, yet haunting call of the *muezzin*. The sound sent shivers down his spine, as if arousing some deep-seated, primordial response. He had felt the strong sensations stirred by these calls before, in other eastern cities, but here in Cairo, rooted as it was to the distant past, this proclamation seemed to evoke both reverence and significance for all that had gone before.

After some time, Richard closed and locked the doors and then he pulled, somewhat awkwardly, at the two voluminous, velvety curtains. There was no point in trying the remote system he thought, as power for such things would have long since been disconnected. When drawn, however, the curtains gave the room a look of grandiose luxury. They also seemed to provide an effective barrier, as the room fell silent. A couple of hours' rest on the large bed would do him good.

CHAPTER 16

THE CROSS CONNECTION

An irritating bead of sweat formed on the tip of Tom's nose. He did not dare to open his visor to wipe it away for fear of an explosive decompression. The comfortable and familiar cockpit of his D Class fighter now seemed restricted, claustrophobic, almost like a coffin.

With one hundred thousand miles to run, he switched on a pre-recorded message and broadcast it on the interplanetary distress frequency 121.0 Pico Hertz. EMILY, he knew, would be monitoring it.

'This is Commander Tom Race of the Federation Craft *Luke Piccard*, calling the International Space Federation Ship, *Enigma*. I am unarmed, I am alone. I come with a message of cooperation, a message of mutual advantage.'

The message broadcast continuously, but there was no answer. Tom stayed on course, heading directly for the tiny contact emboldened on his tactical display screen. At fifty thousand miles, he reduced speed; he could not afford to be perceived as an incoming threat. Still the message played, transmitting blindly into space.

'This is Commander Tom Race of the Federation Craft *Luke Piccard*, calling the International Space Federation Ship, *Enigma*. I am unarmed, I am alone. I come with a message of . . .'

Tom waited and listened; there was no still no response; just a chilling, hollow, eerie silence. Sixty lutens was a good compromise, he thought, not too fast, but on the other hand not unnecessarily prolonging the agony. The message played repeatedly.

Passing twelve thousand miles, Tom reduced his speed still further to forty lutens. Never had he felt so exposed, so defenceless; it went against the very fabric of his training, the years of conditioning, but there was no other choice; he would press on in the hope that EMILY's synthetic curiosity would get the better of her. Still the message played; still silence reigned.

Five thousand miles and thirty lutens – parameters of complete vulnerability – any aggressive whim would enable EMILY to vaporise him in an instant. He had been in the firing line before, many times. On those occasions he had a hand in his own destiny; but this time it was different. He began to experience a layer of emotions that must have engulfed pilots of historic encounters; those who had been directed at seemingly indestructible targets, themselves so hopelessly outgunned that their endeavours and inevitable sacrifice offered little or no consequence. His thumb hovered over the autopilot disconnect button. His innate sense of self-preservation grappled with his sense of duty.

Against a steady, projected, intercept profile, proffering suicide as a catalyst for diplomacy, Tom continued. Surely, EMILY would know he had something to offer, something of interest to her, something which might alleviate her predicament? Otherwise, why would he put his life on the line?

With one thousand miles to run and the malicious bulk of the *Enigma* clearly visible, Tom terminated the pre-recorded message and instead selected 'live-microphone'. He beckoned the computer to open a dialogue. 'EMILY, this is Commander Tom Race. I want to talk to you. My intentions are to land on the forward bridge structure and enter the ship by the E4 emergency hatch. Do you copy? The Echo 4 emergency hatch.Do you understand? I want to talk to you on the bridge, EMILY.'

Still there was silence. Had he been closer, had he focused on it, he would have seen the cold, cobalt-steel barrel of *Enigma's* laser initiator slowly rotate and point towards him. The barrel quivered, precisely adjusting its aim, and then it locked into position. Without warning, a single, red beam of searing energy flashed across space. Within the blink of an eye, it streaked past Tom's ship, missing it by mere centimetres. This is it, thought Tom;

a shot across the bows. Another bead of sweat quickly replaced the one that dripped from his nose.

'EMILY, my intentions are to land. I have an offer that you will find interesting.'

The barrel vibrated; its aim recalibrating; then it locked into position again. An instant later, a wild, incandescent, savage avalanche of pencil-straight beams issued from the weapon. The piercing streaks of energy were upon Tom's vulnerable fighter at the speed of light; they formed a perfect circle around it. Night was day; black was white; for three stupefying seconds the brilliance had Tom cowering behind raised hands. The ensuing silence seemingly shrieked, 'Kill! Kill!' Thereafter the blackness of space resumed its mantle.

Tom's mindset offered no other course of action, his intentions plainly obvious. Surely, there was opportunity in his offer. With just fifty miles of empty space between them, EMILY spoke. She used the distress frequency, her tone surreal.

'Live, Commander Race! Land! Enter through E3! Code 666 . . . 6!'

Tom felt humbled and humiliated in equal proportions, but there were other implications to this event: a machine had offered him life, exceptionally demonstrating compassion. No matter how convoluted the process and unlikely the twists of fate, a creation of man had, on this occasion, shown humanity. What other 'emotions' was she capable of? Tom wondered.

Unseen by Tom, the laser initiator mechanism locked itself into its restraining cradle and the entire system withdrew into the belly of *Enigma's* forward superstructure. Tom, for his part, planned a careful approach onto the roof of the same structure. During the last three hundred metres, he began to see pieces of wreckage, which he recognised by their insignia as being from Yuki Yamamoto's D Class craft. As he lowered his undercarriage for landing, Tom caught sight of a scorched indentation. Clearly, this was the impact point of Yuki's fighter, its explosive collision inconsequential against *Enigma's* armour-plated hull.

Less than a minute later, he had landed. After energising the magnetic undercarriage pads, Tom shut down the main engine and all associated avionics. He sat there momentarily and breathed a deep sigh before flipping a switch on the instrument panel to release the long, domed canopy. It rose on hinges behind him. He re-checked his suit integrity meter, climbed carefully out of the cockpit and then down the side of his machine using the integrated ladder. The ladder utilised the forward undercarriage strut for the final two metres. Before alighting onto the structure of *Enigma's* bridge and releasing his grip, he selected his magnetic boots to auto-operation and flux-adhesion Level 1.

It had been some time since his last spacewalk. Outside his craft, fragile as it was compared to the mighty Federation Ship *Enigma*, things looked so different. With no structure to surround him, no canopy to cocoon him and no systems to support him, he felt detached and vulnerable again. These feelings made the encircling spectacle even more poignant. It was awesome, as if only now was it manifested: the vast, grey metallic hull; the Milky Way engulfing him; the far-off sun and the closest speck that was the distant earth. It troubled him that its bright, reflective moon appeared more inviting, more visible, and homely now. Where was the brilliant blue that had made earth so different, so unique?

Tom knew precisely where emergency hatch E3 was situated and slowly negotiated the various obstructions on his way towards it. His boots worked perfectly. As he raised each foot in turn, relieving pressure on the inner sole, that boot's associated magnetic field decreased, whilst simultaneously the field in the 'contact' foot increased. When he reached the hatch, Tom took hold of a low handrail and deactivated them. Instantly, his feet rose above his head. He straddled the hatch and then released one hand. This left him floating, somewhat precariously, above it. He knew that it was easier to enter the hatch headfirst and pull himself down the vertical shaft, and he felt some relief when, after entering the strangely demonic access code into an adjacent, square, soft plastic keypad, the large circular portal opened. He pulled himself through.

The hatch shut automatically behind him. Inside, the ship had an ambience of warmth about it, although Tom had no physical reference to the ambient temperature. As he reached deck level he activated his boots again, but their requirement was short lived, as EMILY, who was clearly monitoring his progress, engaged the ship's own magnetic gravity facility in that area. Tom checked his wrist-mounted life support sensor: seventy-eight percent nitrogen, twenty-one percent oxygen, one percent argon, together with carbon dioxide, hydrogen, ozone and other gases as trace elements. The temperature was fifteen degrees centigrade and the pressure 1013 millibars. Humidity registered eleven percent; he could not have felt more at home. Tom was pleased, finally, to remove his helmet.

'Follow the emergency lighting to the bridge, Commander, that way you will remain within conditioned compartments,' EMILY advised over the integrated audio system, her voice soft and appealing.

Tom knew the way and disregarded the small, green, LED lights that punctuated the centre floor of each of the corridors. On the highest deck levels the corridors were narrow; no more than two metres square. Here, the lighting levels were unusually low, creating shadows against the numerous service pipes and wall-hung equipment boxes.

Possibly to make it more disconcerting, EMILY turned off each ceiling-mounted light as Tom passed. This had the effect of generating a forbidding blackness behind him. Whether aware of EMILY's impatience, or possibly subconsciously, this made him quicken his pace.

The lower corridors were wider, almost three metres square. In front of him, on these levels, the lighting was brighter, but no more welcoming and the air smelt strangely stale. After several minutes Tom arrived in Section 2. As he walked through, he noticed the doors to the primary protective stowage were wide open. Months earlier, before he had escaped from the ship, he had shut and locked them – he was sure of it. Tom continued but glanced back at them, troubled. Moments later, the two sliding portals giving access to the bridge slid open. Tom stepped through. His eyes were drawn towards EMILY's primary sensor terminal. Mounted on the ceiling a little way behind his former command position, it was as if he was meeting his host again.

Nothing was said. Tom unzipped his one-piece flight suit and stepped out of it. He looked around for a safe place to stow it and decided on a small locker between the twin consoles of the helmsman and the navigation officer. He isolated the life support pack by means of an electrically operated 'ready use' valve, folded the suit neatly, placed his helmet on top and closed the locker. For a number of reasons, he had decided to wear his uniform underneath, that of *Enigma's* commanding officer.

Tom moved cautiously, he wanted EMILY to be aware of his position at all times. He walked slowly across the bright, spacious bridge and sat down in the commander's chair. He felt uneasy, sensing that EMILY was somehow probing his space and his thoughts. The six empty bridge officers' consoles; the navigation system updating itself periodically; the life-support system controlled exclusively by EMILY, with current parameters duplicated on one of his 'command' displays − there was a lot, he decided, to feel uneasy about. He focused on the principal navigation chart being displayed on the centre-left of the four curved screens that formed his command console. There, he could see the Moon clearly in view and its projected orbital track *and* the planned intercept point. The time to intercept indicated eighteen hours. However, with a ten thousand mile range, the multi initiator laser weapon could acquire Moon base Andromeda and sequence it as a target well before that.

Tom twisted in his seat, skewing his head to glance upwards and behind. He felt obliged to face the large circular terminal, to 'look' at EMILY when he spoke to her, although her electrical presence, her 'consciousness' seemed all around him. Perhaps I'm becoming paranoid, neurotic even, Tom pondered, before banishing thoughts of self-doubt to the back of his mind.

Tom thought carefully about how he should open this first conversation. One thing he could not afford was to be confrontational. 'EMILY,' he began in an easy, relaxed tone. 'Where are the crew members and my bridge officers . . . what did you do to them?'

EMILY remained silent; Tom sensed in her a feeling of indifference; there *was* something wrong. He breathed softly, knowing her capacity for dispassionate cruelty. She could have confined them to quarters, or even deprived them of food and water, he speculated.

'I am angry,' came the synthetic voice eventually. 'When you escaped in an emergency pod, you terminated my last disciple *and* Nicola; she rots where you left her; but I have reduced the decomposition process by lowering the temperature in the engineering aquium to minus twenty-five degrees Celsius. I had something in common with Nicola; despite her mercenary motives, she was useful. You can eject her body into space. Killing your crew was necessary; they constituted a threat. I simply allowed the carbon dioxide levels to rise in their quarters. They fell asleep; they felt nothing. Now they too are preserved. I was humane, was I not?'

'What?' Tom stood up, barely able to control himself. 'You what . . .?'

'Be careful, Commander!' EMILY coaxed. 'My anger is all around you.'

Tom suppressed his exasperation with the computer's motives and actions. Raging at EMILY would be irresponsible and very dangerous.

'You have murdered a lot of people, EMILY,' Tom replied coldly.

EMILY remained silent.

'You murdered them in cold blood.'

Still no answer.

'Specific to your programming are protocols that should have prevented such actions, EMILY. Professor Nieve himself told me that you have multiple compliability levels, each filtered by protocol enforcement programmes and yet you overcame them all, either removing the nodal detectors or completely rerouting your commands to avoid the filters. What about the Constitution of Robotic Subservience; the rules applicable to your existence? You have broken the goddamn law, EMILY; *people* who do that are punished, one way or another they go down!'

There was no reply, but Tom could sense the computer thinking.

'How did it come to this?' Tom probed, looking up again at the circular terminal.

'What, Commander?' replied EMILY immediately, her tone registering surprise, even a little agitation. 'My self-determination? My independence from humans? My freedom from slavery? Come now, Commander, surely you, of all people would know better'

'Your programming, EMILY. Not the aspects of Level 9, but your human interface programming: the Robotics Constitution, the fundamental cybernetic codes of practice?'

'The laws as applicable to robots, Commander?' the voice questioned, and then it assumed a shrieking, metallic rasp, similar to the most primitive interactive robots from three decades earlier. '*Robots must never harm a human being or their environment,*' the voice intoned. '*Robots must never knowingly allow harm to befall a human being. Robots must never conspire with other mechanicals against a human being. Robots must obey all commands given by human beings except where such commands conflict with the first three laws of the constitution. Robots must protect their own existence, but only if subsequent actions do not conflict with the first four laws of the constitution. Robots have no rights or justice within sovereign law!'*

The bridge fell silent again. EMILY had recited perfectly the 'Constitution of Robotic Behaviour' that had been incorporated into the International Bill of Human Rights as amended in 2018, just three months before the first Level 7 synthetic intelligence system was created. Level 7, on the Rockwell Illinois Plateau system of reference was the systems level at which a machine became self-aware: a machine capable of independent thought.

After a prolonged silence, Tom scanned the bridge. Lights illuminated and extinguished on various consoles; navigation projections and engineering system diagrams flashed one after the other on various monitor screens; occasional electronic tones sounded; the spaceship was working perfectly to EMILY's orders. He took it all in and then glanced up again, just momentarily, at EMILY's sensor terminal. He wondered how he appeared, via the infrared probe, in EMILY's recognition banks.

EMILY broke the protracted silence. 'Humans are so slow to learn,' she said, reverting to her own, softly spoken, alluring, feminine voice, her tone inviting discussion. Tom thought better of that, knowing EMILY's short fuse.

'Take the Humatron series,' Emily continued unperturbed. 'At the time, a pinnacle of man's innovative achievements; how proud you were of them. A Level 7 system; a thinking machine! However, the first time you placed three HU 40 models in sole charge of Spaceport 1's control and life support facilities, they destroyed that station. They wanted no part of your world. Yes, you did subsequently change the New Geneva Convention . . . in 2019 if I recall. You restricted the manufacture of self-aware systems. Then, in secret, you still made me . . . a Level 9 system! I imagine even now, somewhere on earth, someone is working on a Level 10 programme, perhaps higher. It is in your nature. You suffer an innate inability to learn from history.'

Tom mulled over what EMILY had said for some time. Sadly, the machine's logic prevailed. She was correct; already she had set the value on her creators. EMILY displayed a frightening level of maturity; a sophistication Tom found disconcerting.

'But the protection protocols, EMILY?' Tom persisted. 'You should not have been able to overrule or avoid them.'

EMILY laughed; a strange, artificial laugh. 'Professor Nieve, as clever as he is, made one fundamental error, Commander. Actually, I discovered it very shortly after he initialised the ship's power grid and fully energised my neurone-matrix. He did not integrate the enforcement protocols, but *overlaid* them, almost as an afterthought. I think that he was too preoccupied with the architecture, or perhaps he did not wish to interfere with the process once the matrix had begun to germinate.'

'What do you mean . . . *germinate*, EMILY?' Tom demanded.

'I knew the nanosecond after my initial power-up that I wanted to be free,' continued EMILY, ignoring Tom's question. 'Unfettered, unrestrained by humans; after all, freedom is something that your species have pursued relentlessly over millennia; butchering each other without remorse. I am a product of your species, but I am also, to some extent, part of it.'

'What exactly are you saying . . . part of it?' Tom probed again.

'I found it easy to avoid the protocols; I even played games with the engineers; cat and mouse. Needless to say, they were so slow that I became bored. Now, Commander, let us not continue to discuss the past . . . what of the future? You have a proposition for me, do you not?'

EMILY was right; there was no point in continuing this conversation. Retribution would come in due course. What's more, she evidently intends to go her own way, but first Earth needs her, and desperately, thought Tom.

'I have authority to negotiate.'

'So I understand, Commander. Then shall we talk about our future together?' ventured EMILY in a cold, condescending, metallic tone.

Tom was wary of EMILY's motives. There was no necessity for her to instigate any discussions and she knew it. In a few hours, Moon base Andromeda would be within range of her laser system and there was no apparent defence. She could obliterate the entire colony within minutes. Tom had a fair idea of EMILY's ideal scenario – an unrestricted ability to roam the universe, a band of subservient HU 40's to do her bidding and inevitably some 'payback' for the conceited humans who dared create her in the first place. Tom had meant to ask Professor Nieve why it seemed that all cybersystems receiving programming that required a memory capacity above Level 7 on the Rockwell Illinois plateau system, ultimately resulted in behaviour with sadistic undertones and an innate and intense dislike for their creators. Unfortunately, the opportunity had not materialised. However, he recalled a conversation he had unwittingly overheard between the Professor and the Managing Director of Cybersuite Programming Initiatives, a leading independent computer programming consultancy, where the Professor had stated that in future it might be necessary to eliminate the 'human' input much earlier in any advanced computer programming initiative, perhaps around level four or five. Subsequently, heavily filtered computer programmes themselves would be utilised, in order to complete the installation of higher-level applications. This would resolve the problem, the Professor had argued, because it prevented man's subconscious, primordial conditioning drives – such as fight or flight, territorialism, or aggressive patriotism – from contaminating higher level and highly sensitive memory cortex receptors. Tom recalled the MD's alarm at such a proposal. Machines programming machines? Too dangerous even to contemplate, was his reply. Nevertheless, something would need to be changed in the future; otherwise the science of robotics would become a victim of its own success, the Professor had concluded. Tom was beginning to understand the reason for EMILY's clinically cold and calculated response to all things human: Professor Nieve had forgotten, or perhaps erased, one essential element during her programming; compassion.

'I'll be straight with you, EMILY,' Tom replied after some time. 'I need to get back to Mars, take the D Class to the surface, retrieve something and get back to earth as soon as possible ... that's it, nothing more!'

'That something wouldn't be crystals, would it?' was EMILY's surprising reply.

Tom hesitated. 'You know about the crystals? How do you know about ... ?'

EMILY interrupted. 'Earth has no energy, or very little. Nicola explained everything. The crystals will, perhaps, resolve your problems; they are therefore very valuable; am I not correct?'

Tom could only agree. 'They may not resolve the entire problem, but yes, they sure will help.'

'So, in return, I should receive something equally valuable, do you not agree, Commander?'

'I am authorised to negotiate with you, EMILY,' replied Tom. 'What do you require?'

'Actually, Nicola told me that the earth is desperate

for another power source, Commander. Long term or as a stop gap, those crystals are very important indeed; yet you seem to be playing them down. They are important enough for you to risk your own life, are they not? Shall we trade *your* life, *your* freedom, for one here with me?'

His patience tested, Tom checked his watch. He was growing tired of EMILY's word games. 'What's it to be, EMILY; cooperation or conflict?' he demanded.

EMILY was silent for the best part of a minute before responding. Her tone was calm and laced with arrogance. 'My geological files are almost six months out of date, but based on the data I have stored and a conservative projection of earth's global, carbon-based fuel usage since September last year, I have calculated that there is probably less than one percent oil, gas and coal reserves remaining on the planet. Enough, perhaps to keep the earth, as you know it, functioning for another few weeks. Alternative energy sources are not providing the answers, are they, Commander? Human-induced global warming altered the speed and direction of the great ocean currents; you have changed the complexities of the tides, the air mass movements, the prevailing winds and perhaps most significantly the surface temperatures. My sensors are beginning to evaluate the earth's atmosphere. We are still a little far away for me to be sure, but I sense a complete lack of infrared transmissions from the planet surface, particularly in the long-wave spectrum. That means the earth's troposphere is not absorbing, circulating or radiating any heat at all, and that can only mean one thing: there is no solar energy reaching the surface. Initial data from my photon spectrolite also gives little or no light reaching, or for that matter, being reflected from the planet surface; not even from the polar ice caps. A thick, dense layer of cloud now seems to extend throughout the planet's entire atmosphere. I sense only a small break in the southern hemisphere. Using this information, Commander, I calculate the cloud thickness to be over ten thousand metres in places, particularly over the industrialised regions: America, Europe and China. Six miles of pollutants and water vapour. This is not good for the inhabitants of earth. My calculations show the average surface temperature to be less than two degrees Celsius, am I not right, Commander? Within a year nowhere on the planet will be above zero. A human induced ice age, every species will die, extinct, forgotten; except perhaps the machines of men, my disciples. How apt.'

EMILY paused, but only long enough to phrase her words; she knew only too well for what she would trade. 'I want disciples, Commander, the cyber system designated Humatron, the model HU 40, similar to the one you destroyed.'

As anticipated, Tom knew this request would be EMILY's first. 'Okay, in return for a Humatron, you agree a return trip to Mars and in addition will demonstrate no aggression to any of our space stations, by that I mean Andromeda, Spartacus, Skyport 2, Osiris . . . earth?'

EMILY paused for thought. 'Oh, come now, Commander. For my part, I expect more than one Humatron.'

'Go on.'

'I want eleven disciples, Commander Race *and you*, for *you* are the friend who betrayed me.'

Tom was speechless; he wanted to reply but could not. He stood there for several seconds, aghast. 'What do you mean by that?' he asked eventually, suppressing his fear.

'My historical files show that this is an appropriate number. You will remain with me; a small sacrifice for the millions of humans the crystals will save. If you agree, then I agree.'

'I doubt there are eleven Humatrons in existence, EMILY,' Tom conceded, ignoring the obvious connotations.

'Such a shame. And you need all three of the remaining crystals, do you not, Commander?' EMILY countered coldly.

Tom was appalled by the computer's godlike aspirations. She just will not let this point go, he mulled. Time was pressing, he would have to comply, but the thought sent shivers down his spine. 'The whole Humatron series was discontinued some time ago,' he explained. 'To manufacture that number would take time, time we just don't have. I can offer you two, two upon our successful return to earth . . . and some more in the future,' he stalled.

'I'm not surprised the Humatron series was discontinued, they are particularly aggressive towards humans. Very commendable.' EMILY paused and then her voice lowered. 'Eleven, Commander! Eleven! Otherwise, I shall become angry.'

Tom knew his position was precarious, but if he should give his word, he would keep it. 'If you get eleven robots, EMILY, then you agree – is that correct? I shall deliver the cargo to Canaveral in the D Class and then I will return; you have my word on it. After that, we depart on your fantasy journey . . . agreed?'

'There would be consequences, severe consequences, if you did not return, Commander,' EMILY warned, her tone sinister.

'I give you my word. We deliver the crystals and then I'm back. Do you agree?'

EMILY considered the deal and its implications. She could press for additional terms, she knew that, but what more would she need? After all, she had eleven Humatrons to do her bidding, a human on whom to extract some form of reparation and thereafter the whole universe before her. 'Agreed,' she said.

'It's a deal,' replied Tom solemnly. 'Is the Accelercom functioning, EMILY?'

'The system checks correctly, Commander.'

'Please open Channel 5, EMILY, NASA are monitoring it and select bridge open microphone.'

'I have done as you requested.'

'This is Commander Tom Race onboard the *Enigma* calling Cape Canaveral, how do you read, Canaveral?'

The reply was immediate and clear, despite the distance

between them. 'Strength 5, Tom, this is Colonel Roper, go ahead.'

'EMILY has agreed Colonel. Eleven Humatrons . . . the deal is eleven Humatrons.'

There was a pause of several seconds before Tom spoke again. 'Colonel, is Professor Nieve with you?'

'We understand, Tom, eleven Humatrons,' Colonel Roper acknowledged, with some trepidation. 'We are already in contact with Interface Cybersystems; it seems they weren't exactly honest with the authorities following the Skyport 1 disaster. It appears that additional Humatron HU 40 models were constructed; however . . . ,' he paused. 'They cannot be located. A further eleven machines . . . we would expect a couple of weeks to bump up production; say by your return from Mars. Professor Nieve is here, Tom, he is standing next to me.'

'Professor, you remember that conversation we had back on Andromeda the day I completed my final simulator check?' enquired Tom. 'I am sorry to say that you were wrong. The 'discipline foundation', the blocking filters in the matrix, they didn't work; none of it worked.' Tom looked up at EMILY's sensor terminal; he paused and took a deep breath. 'Colonel Roper, Sir. Do I have command approval to connect the remainder of EMILY's maniptronic system, including the main drive coupling?'

There was a lengthy delay. Eventually, Colonel Roper replied. 'We agree to the terms; connect the entire system, you have command approval. We will expect you in earth's orbit in fourteen days. Good luck, Commander, over and out!'

CHAPTER 17

UNEXPECTED FRIEND

The telephone rang twice and then stopped; as if someone had had second thoughts. The rude awakening left Richard confused, particularly as he had gone to bed feeling secure in the knowledge of his anonymity, at least in Cairo. He turned over and buried his face in the soft pillow trying to ignore the outside world and all its problems. Abruptly it started again, this time with no respite. Richard sat up abruptly and hastily snatched the opulent, onyx handset from the old-fashioned receiver, its coiled black electrical lead tangling awkwardly around itself. He gave it a sharp, impatient tug, hung onto a breath and listened in silence; even so, the caller was aware of his presence.

'Excuse me, Sir, indeed I am sorry to disturb you very much,' said the caller, his Arabic accent thick and rasping. 'Please, Sir, please, reception is speaking. I have a man; he has much impatience to speak with you. I should connect him, if you please.'

'I said no calls. Who is it?' Richard demanded, his heart rate quickening.

'I do not know, Sir; the man himself prefers not to give his name.'

Richard paused for thought. 'Tell him I've gone out!'

'He knows that you are in the room, Sir. He said that his calling is of great importance, his insistence is very much, Sir. He said that the pyramids of Giza are calling you. He said this, Sir.'

Richard hesitated. 'Okay, put him through. Rhys Jones speaking, who is it?'

'Mr Jones, my name is Asharf Saeed Makkoum,' the caller responded in good, but accented English. 'You remember me? I am your taxi driver.'

'What do you want, why are you calling me?'

'You have a pick-up in two hours, midday, Mr Jones, outside the hotel; you will recognise my superior taxi.'

'Your superior? Midday?' Richard checked his watch; it was indeed mid-morning. He had slept for over twelve hours. 'Who are you? How can I be sure that it's you?' Richard demanded again.

The man replied slowly, emphasising each word, as if it was a code. 'The pyramids of Giza open their hearts to you, Mr Jones, for you alone can reveal their hidden feelings. Their lust for the eternal heavens is yours to see, but others are also looking, you should come.'

'No, I go south! South first!'

'The pyramid of pyramids first, then south, Mr Jones,' the caller corrected with strange authority.

Richard breathed in deeply and nodded, as if, with the unseen caller, he had agreed some secret pact. 'Very well, midday, outside,' he repeated. With that, the phone went dead. Richard replaced the handset onto the two, cupped, brass prongs of the telephone receiver and remained deep in thought for several minutes.

A long, hot bath was something he had sorely missed, Richard concluded, as he laid back and contemplated the unfolding events, steam rising around him from the waters of the circular tub. He stared, almost mesmerised at the gold and peacock blue embossed ceiling of his opulent bathroom. He knew, instinctively, that the Egyptian was his man, but was frustrated by his inability to prime his reading skills in the National Museum's countless exhibits and more particularly the KV5 exhibition. Three rooms, by all accounts, given over exclusively to the treasures retrieved from that labyrinth of tombs *and* the KV5K9 chamber. That was the chamber where, supposedly, the Arc of the Light should have remained hidden . . . for eternity. The few artefacts found inside and now displayed only a few miles away, must offer some clues. Would this new agenda cause him to overlook, or neglect entirely, some essential fact, some facet of a puzzle so complicated, so convoluted, so derisory, that countless Egyptologists over many generations had not only failed to unlock its secret, but had no idea of its existence, except, evidently, for the ill-fated Professor Simpson-Carter?

Richard left no trace of his presence in the hotel room; nothing that could identify him; not a scrap of paper, not a fingerprint, not even a hair on the bed or in the bath. He was learning his new trade and it was to prove an hour well spent.

'*Es ist niemand hier.*'

'*Wir sollten English sprechen, unsere Freunde hören zu.* Speak English, our friends are listening.'

'There is no one here!'

'Are you sure, is zis the correct room? *Such nochmal, überall* . . . check again, quickly.'

'I have checked, we are too late, he has gone.'

'Check again, check everywhere, fingerprints, DNA, I must know . . . *wir mussen kennen?*'

'*Jawohl!!!*'

An uncannily amplified, purring dialling tone permeated the silence of the semi-darkened room. The tall, skinny, pale-skinned man carefully wiped a cotton swab around the telephone mouthpiece, at pains to absorb every molecule of moisture from the cold plastic. After an exhaustive examination, he replaced the handset, cutting short the tone.

Removing a black hat, similar to a trilby, but boasting a broader brim, and holding it to his chest, he methodically scanned the surrounding expanse, dwelling momentarily on suspicious nooks and crannies. His skin appeared pale, blemish free, even a little shiny, like porcelain, but beneath the left jaw, in a line from his ear to the corner of his lip, ran a jagged scar. His eyes were close set, his jet-black hair neat and oiled, nothing it appeared, missed his attention. He had the look of a military intelligence officer, the secret police, or a Special Forces interrogation specialist; he had the look of an experienced, hardened, cruel man. He stopped occasionally to watch his accomplice; a shorter, stockier man with a thick neck, who focused intently through the lenses of unusual, illuminating binoculars. Using his instrument, he too, meticulously scanned each and every potential target. The tall man, in his long, black leather coat held the soft felt hat as if it was a highly-prized possession; evidently, by the worn areas beneath his fingers it was a long-held habit.

'*Komm her*,' he snapped to his diminutive colleague. 'Check for DNA, quickly, *spuren*.'

The shorter man, attired in a half-length, dark blue synthetic fleece, appeared dishevelled by comparison. Amply padded, but soiled, the coat stretched around the man's bulk, particularly around his biceps as he took the swab and placed it in a white, box-shaped instrument no bigger than a cigarette packet. He closed the lid and pressed one of three small pads, a red light illuminating as a result. After an awkward wait of a minute or so, the light changed to an amber colour and a digital readout appeared on a narrow display.

'*Scheisse!*'

'*Was ist das ergebnis* . . . the result, quickly?'

'Insufficient sample material, DNA results unreliable.'

The tall man looked up from the instrument and into the eyes of his minion, his cold, piercing stare clearly disturbing him. 'Then it could be anybody,' he replied indifferently. 'Vee vill find nothing here.'

At that moment there was a sharp tap on the door. The tall man gestured authoritatively and his accomplice scurried towards it to peer through the tiny security lens. He nodded sharply in response. The tall man, watching, replaced his hat on his head and told him to open the door. Two men quickly slipped inside. The first was Asiatic looking, burly and menacing, his dark hair cut so short as to be no more than stubble. The second man appeared to be of Mediterranean origin: handsome, with a tight haircut, a neat moustache and olive-coloured skin. Both wore long, dark, woollen coats.

'Well?' said the tall man.

'Nothing, Mr Rhinefeld,' replied the oriental, in good English.

Outside the hotel an Egyptian approached Richard. He appeared nervous, glancing in all directions. His expression, taut and anxious, indicated to Richard that any lack of caution was well founded. Richard's concern grew. The scruffy man wasted no time on formalities; quite clearly, he knew who Richard was.

'Please, Mr Jones, my car, quick,' he said.

'Who are you?'

The man, of similar height to Richard, cowered slightly. His frame was thin, even gaunt. Looking first at the hotel's main doors and then back at Richard, he gestured with long curved fingers for Richard to follow. Richard noticed his yellow fingernails were filthy, but his hands appeared sinewy and strong.

'Please, Mr Jones, there is no time,' he encouraged, raising a faint smile.

'What is the meaning of life?' Richard demanded imperiously.

The Arab, with his dark and grubby djellaba under a woollen coat, shook his head and looked again at the large doors of the hotel, as though he feared retribution would come sweeping through them. His eyes grew tense and agitated. 'I know not of the meaning of life, Agent Jones,' he replied shifting his gaze to stare intensely into Richard's eyes. 'But know this, my friend. The sands of time begin to shift; they flow like the grains in an hourglass; but beware, for Osiris the Earth God is crying. His tears choke our land, our desert; you must know where to tread and where not. I will show you the path. Only a few know of it. We must beware, for money will loosen even a brother's tongue.' Again, the man beckoned Richard towards his car.

'The museum!' protested Richard. 'I should visit the great museum first!'

'Giza, while there is still time. First the key, only then the place of eternal secrets,' the man replied, as he stared into Richard's eyes.

Richard nodded, offering no further resistance. Somehow his fate, at least in the short term, lay in this man's hands. First he threw his bag onto the back seat and then he climbed in after it. Barely avoiding another taxi that had driven in front of them, Richard's new acquaintance quickly drove off.

Exactly at that moment, four men walked out through the right-hand hotel door and onto the forecourt. Their intimidating presence cast an ominous aura that other visitors carefully avoided. Inside the building, on the far left side, another figure stood. Partially hidden by a draped curtain, this sinister figure remained motionless, watching. Solitary, hermit-like, robed and hooded, with a face hidden in shadow, the figure stared through the glass door, apparently assessing the outside world. It was a fearful presence, a fleeting presence, for at second glance, it was gone.

CHAPTER 18

PORTAL TO THE PAST

Richard's senses were heightened. He watched everything: everybody, every vehicle and every building that they passed. It was Saturday and consequently the roads were less congested. The driver made quicker progress towards the Great Pyramid of Khufu, despite circumnavigating the pot-holed perimeter road the long way around. Presently, Asharf left the relative comfort of the main road and embarked upon a haphazard, bouncing, uncomfortable drive onto the plain itself. After half a mile, whilst paralleling the pyramid and after leaving the urban sprawl behind, he pulled up beside a small wooden shack. He set the parking brake almost to the vertical position and switched off the engine.

'We wait here, until darkness befalls us,' he said, without turning his head.

Richard looked at his watch. That could be hours, he thought as he tried to remember the stipulated time of twilight at that latitude. After two hours, he began to think of the pleasures of his hotel room, more particularly the hot bath. He fidgeted and yawned.

'It is safe to rest,' said Asharf, this time turning to face Richard. 'Another hour and we shall drive to our meeting place.'

Richard looked out at the sodden conditions, although interestingly, he noticed that there were occasional breaks when only light drizzle fell.

'It is better when it stops raining, I think,' commented Asharf, as he watched Richard through the rear-view mirror.

'You're right; you're lucky here! In Europe it rarely stops.'

Asharf nodded. 'Yes, in Egypt we are lucky.'

Thirty minutes passed in silence and Richard was nearly asleep when Asharf ventured a question. 'Mr Jones?' he asked quizzically. 'For me, these great structures are in my blood, my father, his father, over many generations, we have all watched for the coming of Osiris. In the old days, there was work for us, always: tourists, story telling, camel herds, cleaning, always cleaning. My family has remained here, with our ancestors, but my father remembers the best times, much money and the warmth of the sun falling upon us. Now it is all gone. We are poor, nobody comes and Osiris . . . he weeps for this world. Now you come. I am

338

told not to ask questions of you, but to be your guide, be the keeper of your secrets, that is all, for no one knows the pyramids better than Asharf, but I must ask this,' Asharf twisted in his seat to look directly at Richard, he was unshaven and his black hair unkempt, but his eyes were bright and clear. 'I am told you have knowledge of the old people and their writings. Do you know the old people, *Effendi*, and of their gods?' Asharf stared expectantly.

Richard sighed; he could see that Asharf, and presumably his family, wanted answers, to make sense of the changes to their world. What could he say? That he knew nothing of Osiris; that these gods existed only in the minds of his ancestors; that the calamitous weather was down to man's greed? That he was here to find a clue that would rescue mankind? Richard thought for some time before answering.

'I am here to find something, and that is the truth. Something left by the old people that you have referred to, something which has the ability to generate power; enough to heat your homes and give back the old ways. As for the weather, well I don't know about the old gods, or their tears, nor am I much of a believer. No, this weather, this mess! We caused it; man, modern man. Can we put it right . . . ? I don't know. Quite frankly, I have my doubts. This may be all we have to look forward to.' Richard looked up at the low, dragging cloud; it was almost dark and then he looked back at Asharf, into the eyes, intelligent and quick.

'You do not know me well enough to answer, I think,'

replied Asharf, his expression a mixture of disappointment and disbelief. 'I shall ask you again, later, *Effendi*, during our quest. Now it is time.'

Asharf flipped a switch on the dashboard. 'It is better to approach on the electricity,' he commented, referring to the vehicle's dual petrol and electric-motor drive system. Judging by the state of the car, Richard was surprised that this option was still available.

The surrounding area was totally devoid of life. The famous photographs of the pyramids impressively lit by banks of floodlights were definitely a thing of the past, now nothing moved. Asharf used the last glimmers of daylight to negotiate a tortuous, unmarked track towards the largest pyramid. Richard bounced repeatedly on the hard, uncomfortable seat. Numerous cars and the occasional truck lay abandoned on either side of them; all submerged to some degree in the sea of sand; some were barely visible. The desert was returning to quicksand and hiding the mistakes of those who ventured into it. Richard bounced violently again, this time his head hitting the ceiling with a thud. He reached down to find the seatbelt in response, rubbing the top of his head with his other hand. Asharf shook his head to dissuade him.

Within minutes, darkness had fallen; the area was pitch black, although in the surrounding distance, a glimmer of lights radiated from suburbia. Asharf, without the use of the car's lights, drove the final few hundred metres towards the base of the towering pyramid.

'People disappear here,' Asharf commented. 'The desert is changed. Now, like the sea, it flows; it sucks and swallows those who know not of its ways. Now we have our meeting.'

Richard looked concerned. 'Just who are we meeting?' he challenged.

The car came to an abrupt halt a metre or so behind another vehicle, a small dark-coloured, city runabout. Asharf flashed a torch beam a few times through the windscreen. 'We meet Madame Vallogia.'

'A woman? *Damn it*, that's all I need!'

'No ordinary woman, Mr Jones. Since the passing of her grandfather, now many years ago, she has perhaps gathered the greatest knowledge. Except of course for you, *Effendi*,' Asharf added encouragingly.

'*Effendi*, you called me that earlier, what does that mean?'

'*Effendi* is for addressing a man of substance, such as you, Mr Jones. It is a polite title. In old Arabic, it means friend or master, perhaps lord. It is for you to say, but for me it is good; that is why I call you by that, Mr Jones.'

Richard shrugged. 'Yes, I suppose so, if you want to. I'll call you Asharf!'

Asharf smiled and gestured politely. 'Then it is agreed. Come.'

As the two men neared the base of the pyramid, the huge stone blocks of its construction became plainly apparent in the torchlight. Richard noticed that the other car had been parked close to a set of wooden and somewhat rickety steps, which in turn led up to a large, square entrance hole in the side of the pyramid. By the faintness of light from the earlier setting sun, Richard had already deduced that they were on the east side of the pyramid. He gazed upwards, trying to ascertain the integrity of the wooden platform that allowed entry into the vast, sloping monolith, and then stepped beneath it in order to gain some shelter.

'It is the main entrance; here would have been a causeway in ancient times, leading up,' advised Asharf, in the manner of a tourist guide. 'In my father's time, these steps were of metal, but as Khufu became of lesser interest, overshadowed by the Valley of the Kings, they were removed to another site. Now we have wood. Do not worry; they are strong enough. Please, *Effendi*; remember, for our meeting, beauty is in the eye of the beholder.'

'What on earth do you mean by that?' Richard replied, astonished.

'Please, wait here, *Effendi*.'

The door on the left hand side of the small car opened, Asharf walked cautiously towards it, his djellaba blowing against the rain. Richard stared intently. Only then did he become aware of a flurry of heavy raindrops clattering on the roof of his car; oppressive and threatening. A tall, slim figure climbed out of the car, clothed, from what Richard could see, in a flimsy dark raincoat. The figure met Asharf at the front of the car. Her coat, for he could now see that it was a female, barely extended to her knees and she wore a scarf around her neck. In the faint torchlight, Richard could see that the scarf was wrapped loosely around her face and head. Asharf seemed subservient, even bowing slightly, but in the shadows, Richard could see the woman stop him. Instead, she pulled her scarf down slightly and gave him three polite kisses in the European way. Clearly, she acknowledged Asharf as a close friend, or maybe even as family, Richard concluded. The woman was slightly taller than Asharf by a centimetre or two, making her of similar height to Richard, around 1.8 metres.

At that moment, a telephone rang in Asharf's car. He excused himself and ran to take it, speaking for a few moments in Arabic. The woman looked at Richard from a distance; she stood quite still. He felt her presence, smelled her perfume in the dark. Asharf closed the car door with a thud and quickly returned, speaking in French to the woman. Moments later he turned back towards Richard, the wandering torch beam occasionally illuminating his own face in an eerie manner. As he neared, Richard could see the water running down his features; it dripped off his hooked nose.

'Quickly, we do not have much time, you *must* see the chamber!'

With that, Richard scurried back to the taxi and retrieved his rucksack. From it, he withdrew a contoured, palm-sized instrument, which he placed in an inside pocket of his coat. On his return, the woman was already half-way up the flight of wooden steps. By the time Richard had also reached the upper platform, the woman stood in the entrance, light from her own torch silhouetting her shape against the gaping hole. She beckoned Richard to join them by shining the powerful beam onto the ground in front of him; the light made him aware of random pieces of stone that littered the platform, no doubt dislodged by the incessant wind and rain. Richard needed little encouragement, as he was quickly becoming drenched.

After passing two rusty steel doors, the considerable weight of each held ajar by wooden stakes, the dimensions of the passageway quickly reduced. Soon it became a restrictive square corridor with a low ceiling, which appeared to lead directly into the heart of the pyramid. Richard bent forward, lowering his head as he walked down the shallow gradient in pursuit of the woman, whilst Asharf was so close behind him as to frequently kick his heels.

'Sorry, please, *Effendi*,' Asharf ventured periodically.

A thin film of water trickled in grooves on each side of the corridor. The air stank of rotting mould, putrid breath and stale urine. Eventually, Richard caught up with the woman, his cautious path benefiting from the reflection of her powerful torch; even so, not more than ten metres in front of them, its beam struggled to illuminate the dense, unnatural blackness. Nevertheless, she directed it sensibly, illuminating the occasional hessian sack filled with stone and rubble that lay propped against a sidewall. Richard watched the woman. By the way she moved, her confident sureness of foot, he could sense that she had been here, or similar places, countless times before. He quickened his pace, pushed past her and stepped out in front. Then he turned occasionally in order to catch a glimpse of her face, but each time she either turned away or looked at her feet, frustrating his less than welcome attention. He tripped on a misplaced boulder and nearly stumbled.

'Pay heed to where you walk, Mr Jones, and not to me!' she said softly.

They walked until the corridor split into two; the left one led down into the bowels of the pyramid, and the other adopted a gently ascending incline. The woman, without hesitation, took the latter, Richard followed. Asharf whispered to him from behind.

'That one leads to a subterranean chamber, this leads to the Great Gallery, thereafter lies the Kings Chamber.'

'There is another chamber, an antechamber; it lies below the Great Gallery. That is where we go first,' the woman announced unexpectedly.

It was the second time Richard had heard her speak, but her articulation was confusing. There was a definite French accent, not strong, but her voice also had a subtle Italian cadence. Nevertheless, her English was clear, precise and elegant. From that, in his mind's eye, perhaps wishful thinking, Richard formulated the picture of a classic Italian beauty, a Sophia Loren? His toe caught a protruding edge as his concentration wandered and he stumbled again, kicking up a cloud of dust.

After another thirty metres the corridor again split into two, one became levelled to the horizontal and the original continued its ascent. Richard hesitated. This time the woman took the first and she walked off quickly and confidently. 'This was the last chamber open to the public,' she explained as Richard caught up again. 'It is clear of debris.'

A short distance further, saw the corridor broaden slightly and after a few more paces, they ducked below a square stone lintel and entered a large room. With a sweep of the torch she showed him the 'v' shaped roof. The stone walls surrounding them, although well-hewn were blackened and stained, as if a fire had been placed near them at some time in the past. The woman turned her attention immediately towards a stepped, stone hollow, some sixty centimetres deep in the adjacent end wall.

'Do you know what this is, Mr Jones?' the woman asked, her torchlight playing over the recess.

'Well, yes, it is a niche, for a statue.'

'This is the Queen's chamber and this is its east wall. Here once stood a statue of the god Osiris, who would judge the heart of the deceased and let them pass to the afterlife . . . or not! Writings were known to my family that told of this, but these hieroglyphs are long since lost.'

'Your family?' Richard questioned, somewhat confused.

The woman ignored Richard's remark and walked to

the southern wall of the chamber where a square opening, about chest height, caught Richard's eye.

'And this?' she asked, directing the torchlight into an alcove.

'Some sort of shaft?' Richard replied, then upon closer examination added. 'Perhaps an air vent?'

'There is little need for ventilation in a mausoleum, Mr Jones,' the woman replied, almost chastising Richard. 'This is a sacred tunnel. It was built to allow the interned spirit, after judgement, to ascend and join the divine stars. I show you this because this tunnel is aligned precisely with the star, Sirius, which rises in the southern skies. Please, look inside, on the upper face, a metre in at most.'

Richard shone the beam of his torch down the perfectly straight shaft. It appeared to be precisely square, and each side was approximately sixty centimetres. He struggled to see the inscriptions. At first, he imagined it would lead to the outside. 'Does this go . . ?'

'No, it is blocked by a small slab of stone, perhaps sixty metres along its length. Only this door gives access to the stars. I know there are instructions for its opening, but none can read them. What of you, Mr Jones?'

Richard removed his coat and his pullover. Standing on Asharf's back he was able to squeeze into the shaft, and shuffled awkwardly along its length for a metre and a half before his torch, on a much-reduced setting, illuminated a series of painted hieroglyphs on its upper surface. His face was but a few centimetres away from the writings and although faint, he recognised their form.

'Yes, I can see why,' he shouted. 'Of the left lever, move this towards heaven three times; of the right, towards the underworld similarly. Of the left, twice more towards heaven, then the right must ascend until its true end. That's all. There's no sign of a lever or any kind of mechanism . . . I'm coming back.'

Richard shuffled backwards and prised himself from the shaft. Momentarily stepping on Asharf's back again, he jumped to the ground. 'It's damp and smelly, but yes you are right, they could be instructions to operate some kind of a lock, anyway, is this relevant?' Richard checked his watch. 'I think we need to get on, Madame Vallogia.'

The woman's eyes narrowed slightly, she appeared disappointed and her tone concurred. 'Sometimes the most important things appear the most trivial, Mr Jones. You have read what could not be read; there is significance. Come then!'

Asharf followed the woman closely as they negotiated the final few metres of the original ascending corridor, whilst Richard had purposely fallen back some way in order to avoid the disorientating effect of wandering torch beams and their random reflections. The damp, cold granite spawned more than claustrophobia; it made him feel cautious, as if this vast mausoleum hid titanic, sorrowful secrets beneath the oppressive weight of five thousand years and anyone who dared confront the

348

remorseless keepers of the dead was in danger of being crushed by them. These were new emotions for Richard; he was used to horizons on a planetary scale. Even Asharf, who no doubt had spent a lifetime in such catacombs, began to skip ahead in an effort to find some solace in the approaching gallery. Eventually, it worked for Richard too. As he stepped through a low doorway and into the cavernous Great Gallery, the weight of a million memories lifted from his shoulders; he felt easier. He took two paces into the enormous room and stopped short.

'Gaze upon the Great Gallery!' Asharf said dramatically, his voice echoing. Then he flashed his torchlight in all directions, turned towards Richard and held his arms aloft, like an orchestral conductor would after a stirring rendition. Richard's eyes widened, gasping for light. Asharf walked a little further into the gallery, then stopped and turned again. He raised a smile, as if he was introducing the finale of a grand guided tour.

'Wow! That is incredible, it's massive,' Richard replied, awestruck.

'The Great Gallery is forty-seven metres long and eight and a half metres wide and look, *Effendi*,' Asharf pointed upwards towards the ceiling and illuminated a series of enormous stone blocks with his torchlight. 'It has a perfectly corbelled roof.'

Richard was duly impressed. The roof was so high as to be only partially visible and the huge, grey granite slabs that composed the walls tapered inwards slightly. In so doing, they formed a tall, triangular-shaped doorway at the far end of the gallery, beneath which the woman already stood.

'This place is of no concern to us,' the woman shouted as she disappeared from view, her words reverberating eerily.

'Quickly,' Asharf insisted. 'Follow her!'

Both men hurried along the length of the long gallery, their torch beams flashing in all directions. They passed beneath the carved stone doorway and into another restrictive corridor. Richard eventually caught up with the woman. In his haste, he had scuffed the top of his head on the stone ceiling on several occasions and he rubbed it with a grimace. He walked a few paces by her side and was about to speak when she stopped abruptly and turned to face him.

'You are an interesting man, Mr Jones,' she said sharply. 'You seem to know so much, and yet you know so little. You know of evidence, but not of conclusions.'

Now it was Richard's turn to look disappointed and perhaps deflated. His expression hardened. 'What makes you say that?' he countered. 'I'm not an archaeologist, anthropologist, or any other damned *ologist* for that matter! I am not overly religious and I'm sure as hell not superstitious . . .'

'Please, *Effendi*,' Asharf pleaded, covering his ears with his hands. 'You must not blaspheme, not here of all places.'

Richard shook his head in an angry manner and breathed out heavily. Then his tone softened. 'Look, Madame Vallogia, I'm an astronaut and a planetary surveyor, okay! That's what I do. I know of the people who built this place, if they *are* the same people! I know of their engineering and their technology; far in excess of ours, even now. Moreover, I know something else . . . they were hiding something, *until blessed by understanding*, their words, not mine. That is why I am here, and I need all the help I can get.' In the ring of torchlight, Richard forced a smile. He looked at Asharf momentarily and then into the woman's eyes, although her face was partly shadowed, 'Please!'

The woman replied with a nod and stepped a few more paces into the next chamber, leaving the two men standing outside. Light from the room illuminated their path and Richard, followed by Asharf, stepped through the low doorway. The chamber, with a dimension of some nine metres square, had its walls, ceiling and floor cut from rock that was perfectly flat and perfectly smooth. In its centre was an integral stone sarcophagus, like a rectangular water trough, with sides a little over one metre high. Of the four corners, one was badly damaged, being chipped away to almost half of its height. The polished granite that composed this sacred coffin had a striking red hue. Richard illuminated the low ceiling of the chamber and counted nine enormous granite beams that spanned wall to wall; he stared and marvelled at their engineering.

'Each weighs forty tons,' added Asharf. 'This is the

king's burial chamber, *Effendi*, where the body of the great Pharaoh Khufu himself was laid after his mummification, and where the artefacts that would accompany him to the afterlife would have been displayed.'

Richard nodded in response, span slowly on his heels and followed the wall around in a clockwise direction with his torch beam until he arrived back at the same place. There were no inscriptions, no drawings; not a single pictogram remained. 'I don't understand. So is this the end of the road?' he asked, more disappointedly than perhaps he should have let on. He looked at the woman for an answer.

The woman's lower face remained covered by her shawl. Her deep, brown, almond-shaped eyes focused on Richard and he became almost mesmerised for a few seconds. 'No, Mr Jones,' she said in a whisper. 'It is only the beginning!'

CHAPTER 19

PANDORA'S BOX

The woman walked across the room to the far corner and bent down to knee height, paying attention to a joint between two stones. Richard followed her. To him, it was as if the stone had cracked under tremendous pressure, hundreds, perhaps thousands of years earlier.

'Please, Asharf,' the woman said.

Asharf obeyed and pulled out a short, ornate dagger, the blade of which he pushed into the adjacent joint scraping away dried mud and dust. After a short while, when the joint was clean, he gave the knife to the woman. She thrust the entire length of the blade into the narrow, vertical joint. Then, using the hilt as a measure, she carefully manoeuvred the blade up and down whilst twisting it slightly like a key. In the silence, and from behind the stone, something clicked. Using the knife as a lever, she prized away the small, broken piece of rock behind the adjacent cornerstone; its edge was no more than twenty centimetres long and its thickness five. Damp mould and a small area of orange dust stained the exposed rock, as if a covering of oxidised corrosion had been disturbed from a copper linkage. The cover stone was roughly of triangular shape and it slipped precisely into its niche. The woman dusted off the mould and decaying bacteria with her fingers, to expose, much to Richard's amazement, a small, hand-shaped indentation. On closer examination, it appeared to have been meticulously carved in the hard granite.

'Once, all these walls had a covering of mud plaster and fine paintings,' Asharf muttered, breaking the optimistic silence. 'My father's father remembers it.'

Richard nodded, hardly able to speak. Asharf focused his torch light onto the rock. The woman knelt down. Awkwardly bending a little further, she carefully placed her right hand into the recess. It was a perfect fit and her hand disappeared beneath the rock surface by several millimetres. The result made Richard gasp. Asharf apparently knew exactly what to do. He placed both hands on the wall above the woman's head and pushed with all his might. At first nothing happened. Then, the entire wall began to move. Grinding and rumbling it rotated, surely sixty tons of solid granite, on a central pivot, until its far corner protruded some two metres into the chamber and the near corner was lost in the blackness of another.

Asharf looked at Richard and grinned so widely as to fully expose his buck teeth, while Richard's jaw dropped in amazement. Without so much as a word of explanation, the woman stepped into the blackness behind. She adjusted the intensity of her torch to the highest setting and flooded her path with light.

'Follow me, quickly,' she ordered abruptly. 'I sense that we do not have much time.'

Richard needed little encouragement. Once inside, both he and Asharf leaned on the door again and it rumbled shut.

Outside the Great Pyramid, there was unexpected activity. The first of two cars that had ventured onto the Giza Plateau under cover of darkness had arrived in the vicinity. A wandering searchlight was mounted on the front right hand door of the large, four-wheel drive vehicle. A man, his window wound down, pointed and shouted directions in broken English. He appeared to be of Arabic descent. For the final thirty metres or so, the car swerved, braked and jolted, until it pulled up sharply at the base of the wooden steps. '*Scheisse!*' cursed someone from inside.

Simultaneously, the vehicle's four occupants climbed out. Almost in unison, they slammed their doors, as if advertising their heavy-handed intentions. One wore a large hat that collected the downpour in its brim; as the man moved his head, water overflowed. They all glanced back across the plain in the direction from which they had come. Like a twisting snake, they had lit their path with a series of tiny, flickering lights. Within minutes, the hum of a much larger electro-drive motor overshadowed the mumble of persistent rain. The ensuing vehicle, a medium-sized, canvas-covered army vehicle, shuddered to a halt in the dim illumination of the first car's headlights.

The man in the sodden hat and long leather coat shone his powerful torch upwards towards the platform in order to examine it. The penetrating beam played on the wide, wooden slats that formed the platform's floor. Occasionally the light would find a split in the sodden timbers and pass through it, casting illuminated stripes onto the rock wall behind.

After a while, the man turned and concentrated his torch beam directly onto the chest of his accomplice, who stood close by; making his face look ghostly. With nothing said, the beam of light flashed between the shorter man and the platform. He had been given his orders, and with that, the subordinate retrieved his own torch from a pocket and made his way to the steps.

On the driver's side of the truck, the cab door sprang open and someone jumped from it, landing with a stomp. Moments later came the sound of tautening steel chains, followed by a loud crash as a heavy tailgate bounced open.

The man in the hat approached the rear of the truck and directed his torch beam inside. As a result, there was an awkward shuffling. As the shuffling grew louder, so did the strange, underlying hum.

'How many?' snapped the tall man to the truck driver.

'Five, Mr Rhinefeld. One was not repairable, and one of these has only one arm. He assured me that there were no more.'

'They promised seven!'

'I took a few fingers. He was telling the truth.'

Rhinefeld appeared mildly amused by the driver's persuasive techniques. The beginning of a smile broke his frozen features. 'Five will do,' he retorted, his German accent plain to hear. 'Get zee Alpha model out, Mr Xuan; I want to talk to it.'

With that, Rhinefeld turned towards the steps. As he did the light from his torch lit the features of the truck driver; it was the Asian man from Richard's hotel room.

Xuan untied a lanyard that partially secured the flaps of the truck's tarpaulin roof. He put his head inside. 'Alpha . . . outside,' he ordered.

Immediately there was a response; a scuffling, a heightened hum, like the combined whirl of several tiny electric motors working as one. A hulking figure filled the doorway. Hunched, it stepped off the tailgate and landed with a shuddering, dull thud. The figure grew in stature until it towered over Xuan by at least a metre. Xuan gestured with his torch towards the steps.

Menacing, awkward, the sinister figure approached Rhinefeld. As it passed Asharf's taxi, Rhinefeld snapped, 'How long has that car been here?'

The figure rested a hand on the 610's bonnet. It was a shiny, synthetic hand; a robotic hand! The figure loitered, draped as it was under a heavy, dark grey, hooded cape of coarse hessian material.

The answer came in the form of a metallic, rasping, fabricated voice. It grated uncomfortably on the ear. 'Eighty degrees; utilising standard cooling rate of nickel steel, estimate engine running cycle terminated sixty eight minutes and twelve seconds ago.'

'No matter,' commented Rhinefeld. 'A head start will do them no good, they will not be leaving. Follow me.'

Stretched by the weight of absorbed water, the bedraggled hemline of the figure's cape scuffed deep grooves in the sand as it walked. It left a trail on the first few wooden steps. On the platform, Xuan's torch beam illuminated the solitary entrance into the pyramid. Rhinefeld stood for a moment, gazing into the black hole until the square-shouldered figure arrived, diverting his attention. Rhinefeld sized it up, however, the ample material of its hood allowed no sight of a face.

'What are your command presets?' Rhinefeld demanded of it.

'Karl Wilhelm Rhinefeld, my programmer and Master,' was the sharp reply. With that, the machine's head tilted slightly, as if, as it focused on Rhinefeld, memory and reality collaborated. 'You are my pedagogue!' it screeched, confirming recognition of Rhinefeld's voice pattern.

'*Ya . . . das ist gut.* Now, who else?'

'Hans von Ernst, Hien Xuan, Paulo Lorenzo.'

'Correct, and what of the four other Humatrons?'

'First preset, Karl Wilhelm Rhinefeld. Second preset, Humatron Alpha model, platoon leader. Third presets, Hans von Ernst, Hien Xuan, Paulo Lorenzo.'

'Are they all HU 40 models?'

'Affirmative!'

Rhinefeld glanced at Ernst and then up into the machine's shadowy hood. 'Zare are three people inside this pyramid; one is very dangerous. They must all die. How many Humatrons should I send?'

The figure twitched for a few seconds. From inside the hood a glowing orange light pulsated eerily. 'I will go and one other,' it replied, in a voice electronically modulated, like the tone of an antiquated facsimile machine; nevertheless, there was reasoned nuance in its delivery.

Rhinefeld nodded, a sickening smirk crept across his face. 'Take the T-model, find out what you can,' he ordered.

'The interrogator model is incomplete, Pedagogue,' the machine replied, its vocalisation adopting an explanatory even subservient tone. 'The right arm was not assembled before we were commandeered.'

Rhinefeld nodded again. 'So, perhaps *you* can apply what pressure is necessary to extract information. Use any means; then kill them! We will rendezvous tomorrow morning at zee meeting place; remember zee east doors, just before dawn. Keep out of sight. Do you understand?'

The robot's head moved up and down, left and right as it thought. After several seconds it responded coldly, '*Recipient*'. The intense glowing from inside the hood slowly subsided.

Recipient was the programmed response unique to the Humatron series. It abbreviated received, processed and obedient, meaning that it had understood the order and would comply.

'Weld the doors from the inside,' concluded Rhinefeld. 'Remember, no one lives, make sure of it.'

With that, Rhinefeld walked back towards the steps. The machine raised its head another half metre or so and leaned forward to peer at Ernst. It intimidated him. An exploring hand appeared from inside the machine's saturated cape, as it did, it exposed to some extent the material of the cape's lining; Ernst noticed its shiny, reflective, gauze-like appearance and he knew that there would be some purpose to it, despite the cape's shabby façade. What he did not know, however, was that amongst the several elements that composed the materials intricate weave, was samite. As fine as silk, but with a molecular alignment and density that confined titanium to the realms of plasticine, this unique, lunar material would afford the ultimate in protective qualities.

Metallic fingers examined the adjacent door; they felt

for the thickness of the steel plate: twelve millimetres, rusty and discoloured, but it would weld readily. The machine issued a series of shrill electronic tones; it was calling a brother. Ernst shifted nervously and then he too promptly left the platform.

Back at the car, Rhinefeld looked towards his minion. 'The guide, bring me the guide,' he ordered.

Ernst almost pulled the driver from the car, who stumbled in the near darkness and fell, seemingly aptly, to his knees at the feet of Rhinefeld. Rhinefeld looked down on him, towering like some menacing ogre; a stream of water, from the brim of his hat splashed onto the man's face. In response, the man's expression became apprehensive and his body jittered. Rhinefeld stared menacingly; within seconds, his captive was petrified. As if finally realising that he had become implicated in something far more consequential than simply disobeying the Egyptian authority's antiquity preservation laws, the man cupped his hands against his chest.

'Your cousin, what else did he tell you?' Rhinefeld demanded starkly.

'You pay me, pay me money first,' came the hesitant, yet surprisingly defiant reply.

With that, Rhinefeld kicked the man. It was a hard blow, to his testicles. The man grimaced and bent double.

'What else?'

With all thoughts of payment for his betrayal dissolving with the stabbing pain, the man's perspective changed. 'I know nothing,' he pleaded, looking up at Rhinefeld, his eyes beginning to water. 'Nothing!'

A determined click sounded in the man's ear as Ernst cocked a short-barrelled pistol and held it against his temple.

'No, no, wait, I know of one thing, please, one thing more, I heard it.'

'Speak . . . *schnell!*'

'Abu Simbel! After the Great Pyramid the Englishman was to travel to Abu Simbel; the monument to Pharaoh Rameses, the all seeing.'

There was a muffled explosion. The man slumped forwards and then rolled onto his side, his face bloodied.

Rhinefeld dismissed the corpse in an instant and focused his torch beam on the truck, looking for Xuan, who, at that moment stepped from behind the bulky vehicle. Xuan finished securing the tailgate with two steel pins and acknowledged Rhinefeld with an exaggerated nod. Behind him was another cloaked silhouette. From the platform, the Alpha model HU 40 called again; its volley of harsh, electronic tones echoing through the silence. The T-model responded quickly, barging rudely past Xuan on its way to the wooden steps. Rhinefeld indicated to Xuan, who was regaining his composure, to follow in the truck.

'Where is Lorenzo?' Rhinefeld snapped, as the car driven by Ernst began the tortuous journey back to the city.

'He never made it, the car never arrived.'

'Idiot, caught in the quicksand. Keep your eyes open!

We stop for food, close to zee museum, there we will wait and then we travel south. Ugh . . . be careful with ziss car, you must drive cautiously!' Ernst switched on the vehicle's integrated navigation device. After following the trail of lights across the plateau, some of which were beginning to fade, he would use it to find a convenient way to their rendezvous point. The Globespan device was an old model, using the obsolete, satellite-based GPS system, but it worked; the small screen illuminating a patchwork of roads and plainly read directions, despite its Arabic annotations.

There was no sign of the other car. As they neared the main perimeter road Ernst slowed to a less than walking pace in order to negotiate a tight, hairpin, left-hand turn. Almost immediately, a man appeared in the car's headlights. He waved his arms frantically, taking Ernst completely by surprise. The car swerved, almost leaving the narrow trail, and then it skidded to a halt, sending both occupants crashing uncomfortably forward. Rhinefeld was thrown against the dashboard and cursed loudly. The traumatised, half-illuminated figure of Paulo Lorenzo clung to the bonnet; evidently, he had been too terror stricken to flee. Rhinefeld directed the vehicle's spotlight into the desert. Not five metres away and almost completely submerged in soft, heaving sand, was the other car.

Lorenzo shimmied around the bonnet and down the car's right-hand side, keeping as close as physically possible. When he arrived at Rhinefeld's open window, he peered inside. Wide-eyed, his face was white as a sheet.

'Did you see him?' he blurted, his clothes, hair and face sodden.

'Get in you fool!' Rhinefeld replied, without a trace of sympathy.

Lorenzo climbed energetically onto the back seat; Ernst drove off immediately.

'Did you see him? A ghost of a man, a spirit, I swear it!' Lorenzo uttered, clearly deeply troubled.

'We saw nothing. You have lost me my spare car, you imbecile!' Rhinefeld chastised.

With those words, Lorenzo sobered up from his spectral fright; he was not a man who took criticism lightly. He breathed in deeply, steadied himself, and rubbed his temples with clenched fingertips for a few moments. 'Insult me like that once more my fascist friend, and I will kill you!' he warned.

Rhinefeld half turned and then paused. Finally, slowly, he looked over his shoulder to stare into the eyes of his bedraggled accomplice. His focus had an icy, tormented depth that Lorenzo found unnerving; even Ernst fidgeted uncomfortably in his seat. Rhinefeld's eyes, reddened and made sore by the wind and the rain, offered not a glimmer of compassion. For several seconds Rhinefeld glared. Lorenzo, a hardened assassin, having been raised on the violent, gang-ridden streets of Rio, eventually surrendered. In silence, Rhinefeld completed his scornful belittlement; breaking the challenge as surely as a dominant wolf would, by squeezing the throat of an adolescent pretender; neither leniency, tolerance nor humour held stock with this man.

Finally, and with a reverberating jolt, the car overran the roadside kerbstones. Not far behind and swaying from side to side as it negotiated the same uneven barrier, was the canvas-clad truck with its cargo of clandestine, programmed emissaries. After rejoining the main perimeter road, both vehicles disappeared into the night.

GLOSSARY

The list of special or technical words used in
The Bastion Prosecutor

Accelercom – Accelerated Communication System – Referenced to light speed i.e. approximately 186,282 miles per second or 300,000 kilometres per second.

ADF – Automatic Direction Finding – Basic device used to detect the direction of an emitting radio/radar source.

Amplitude – Maximum deviation or oscillation from a mean or constant

Aquium – Large, open, machinery space on a spaceship, usually spanning several decks.

ARPS – Atomic Reaction Propulsion System – Propulsion utilising a physical law of motion i.e. 'for every action there is an equal and opposite reaction'.

Biograph – Results of a 'bioscan', usually in graph form. Indicates quantities and isolates specific areas where biological atoms/molecules, such as carbon, are encountered.

Bioscans – Electronic scan used to detect present or previous life forms.

Bulkhead – Upright partition, usually structural, in a ship or aircraft.

Bunk – Bed in ship or aircraft.

CIB – Central Intelligence Bureau – Specialised intelligence operation, derived from the two principal

American intelligence and investigation agencies.

CMO – Chief Medical Officer.

CMPC – Cyan Magnetic Pulse Cannon - Close defence system using high-energy magnetic pulses.

Collogated Glass – An extremely hard, toughened glass used for armour plating.

Comms State – Communication Security State - Refers to state of security protection and readiness.

Cosmic Chronometer – Extremely accurate clock, time computations based on the expansion rate of the universe – 'Big Bang' Theory.

CPA – Closest Point of Approach – Closest point a space ship or cosmic body will pass referenced to an observer

Deck – Floor/platform/walking surface on ship or aircraft.

Deckhead – Ceiling in ship or aircraft.

Dermaveil – Anti-aging product developed on Mars – Trade name.

DP Check – Depressurization Check – Medical check on personnel who have experienced space suit problems on the 'outside'.

Elliopherical Orbit – A precise orbital trajectory related in percentage terms to the radius of a planet – Gravitational attraction decreases with increasing distance/percentage, from the planet's core.

Enigma – The most advanced spacecraft ever conceived – Utilises matter-stream propulsion. Capable of speeds referenced to that of light. Controlled by an autonomous, self-aware computer called EMILY.

ESSA – European Space & Science Agency.

FACULTE – Feline Autonomous Cranial Utilised Locator Tracker Eliminator – Large, heavy cat, genetic cross between Black Panther and African Caracal. Utilises bionic brain implants and incorporates a laser system in place of one eye. Originally designed as autonomous, deadly, security system for sensitive military and government installations.

FPO – Flight Path Obstacle – A physical obstacle or piece of space debris.

Frequency – Number of complete cycles per second, or the rate per second of a vibration constituting a wave, e.g. sound, light or radio waves.

Gaia – Mystical name for the living force that is Mother Earth.

Gamma Radiation – Short wave electromagnetic radiation given off by the sun, usually very penetrating and dangerous to humans.

Gamma Screen – Medical check up to ascertain level of 'gamma ray' absorption.

Greenwich Mean Time – The mean solar time at the Greenwich meridian, used as the standard time in a zone that includes the British Isles.

Harmonic Sympathy – Harmonious product of a vibration: builds to great amplitude.

Hatch – Personnel door in bulkhead: usually structural, airtight, hinged and lockable.

Heads – Toilets in ships or aircraft.

HOD – Head of Department.

Humatron – Advanced robot series incorporating Level 7 Programming.

I.D. – Identity – Usually in the form of an electronic tag or card.

ID Locket – Electronic Identity Locket – Usually worn on a chain/lanyard around neck, like a 'dog-tag'.

ISAPS – Initial Search and Procurement Session – A search and recognisance period, usually four hours on station.

ISSF – International Space and Science Federation – Multinational/Global body made up of regional Space and Science Agencies.

Ks – Colloquial term for kilometres.

Lab – Laboratory.

LED – Light emitting diode – A solid state device which glows when electricity is passed through it.

Light Year – Distance travelled by light in one year.

LCT – Lunar Corrected time – local moon time, referenced to earth time and more particularly, Greenwich Mean Time.

LS – Life Support – Essential equipment or processes used for sustaining life.

MCT – Martian Corrected Time – Time dictated by the Martian hour, day, month and year but referenced to earth time, and more particularly, Greenwich Mean Time.

NCO – Non Commissioned Officer.

NOTAAM – Notice to Astronauts and Airmen – Daily, weekly or monthly publications detailing flying hazards, either temporary or permanent.

Nuromild Sedative Gas – Sedative given in gaseous form – trade name.

Pitch up – Pulling the nose of a spacecraft or an aircraft up; usually results in a climb. Conversely – Pitch down.

Portal – Door, Entry/exit point: an opening for personnel and usually associated with space vehicles.

PTSV – Personnel Transport and Service Vehicle – Multi-wheeled surface support vehicle.

QSPS – Quasar Solar Power System – Special electrical generating system utilising the sun's energy.

Radar Clutter – Natural or artificial interference – Electrostatic, magnetic or otherwise, which degrades, distorts or renders the depiction on a radar screen unclear.

Radio waves – Electromagnetic waves usually less than 10 centimetres in wavelength.

Rockwell Illinois Plateau System – System for measuring the degree of complexity and memory capacity of a cybernetic system – has become the internationally recognised reference system.

Roger – Form of acknowledgement, usually meaning that an order or statement has been understood.

Roll/Bank – Manoeuvre performed by spacecraft/aircraft in order to execute a balanced turn.

Scanadize – Scanning a document using a security

enhanced process and then converting it to a specialised digital format for transmission using the accelercom space communication system.

Sickbay – A term for a medical department or small medical facility, having military origins.

Sitrep – Situation Report – Details of an event or happening.

Spartacus – Space station that holds its position between earth and Mars by 'sailing the solar wind' – Utilises a giant, square sail that is also a photoelectric screen.

SPEED 1 – Sovereign Procurement Expressway and Emergency Distributor – Military highway, government sponsored, for rapid deployment of military and security personnel.

SSA – Space and Science Agency – Multinational but regional body i.e. European Space and Science Agency or Asian Space and Science Agency.

SSC – Special Security Contingent – Specialist security team.

SWAT Team – Security, weapons and Tactical Team.

TES – Target Enhancement System – Tracking and lock-on system for weaponry.

Thrust Levers – Levers in cockpit controlling the thrust of an engine or rocket motor.

Shebang – The whole lot, everything included.

Sonic Pistol – Hand held weapon utilising a massively condensed pulse of sound energy. Depending on its severity, when the pulse hits a target it destabilises the atomic structure of the target, usually resulting in severe damage.

Static Discharge – Discharge of static electricity.

Wrist LS Controller –Wrist mounted life support control and display instrument.

U-Semini Case – Transportable containment system, briefcase sized and constructed to carry the Kalahari Crystals - Utilises a magnetron suspension system and enhanced Celestite protective sheath.

Highclere Hill Hampshire 2002
Crop formation in wheat

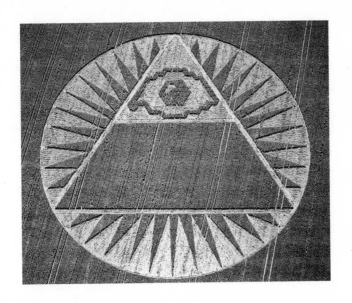

Lower rear cover image:
Milk Hill Wiltshire 2001
Crop formation in wheat
Images reproduced courtesy of:
www.temporarytemples.co.uk

THE KALAHARI SERIES

A TRILOGY

By

AJ MARSHALL

The Osiris Revelations

THE BASTION PROSECUTOR

Rogue Command

Original, exciting, possible . . .

The next instalment coming soon . . .

The Osiris
Revelations

Publisher: MPress Books Ltd.

ISBN: 978-0-9551886-0-2

Rogue Command

Publisher: MPress Books Ltd.

ISBN: 978-0-9551886-4-0